LAB RAT ONE

Touchstone: Part Two

April to mid-July

by Andrea K Höst

Lab Rat One
© 2011 Andrea K Höst. All rights reserved.
ISBN: 978-0-9808789-8-1
E-Book ISBN: 978-0-9870564-1-2
www.andreakhost.com
Cover Art: Simon Dominic

In the previous volume

During her month alone on the abandoned planet of Muina, Cassandra Devlin found food, shelter, and mystery: glowing ruins, moonlight condensing to intoxicating mist, and hills which moaned of sorrow and loss. When the psychic soldiers known as Setari stumble across her on a lightning visit to their dangerous home world, she is more than ready to be rescued.

Taken to storm-wracked Tare, Cass is processed as a stray, a refugee of a disaster which tore gates between multiple worlds. Despite the wonders of Taren nanotech computers, Cass struggles with a new language, aching homesickness, and the question of what kind of place she can make for herself on a planet where no-one has even heard of Earth.

When the Tarens discover that Cass has the ability to enhance psychic talents, she is sent to work with the Setari, and learns more about their never-ending battle to keep Tare clear of monstrous creatures known as Ionoth. The strict military life led by the Setari is more than a little different for an Australian schoolgirl, but among them she still finds kindness and some measure of worth, offset by an increasing loss of privacy.

A near-disaster leads to an investigation into Cass' time on Muina, and an expedition is formed to search for answers to the phenomena she observed. The secrets of the planet's past are critical to the battle to hold back the Ionoth, and the Tarens have long been prevented from hunting among their home world's ruins by inexplicable deaths.

The sentry-creatures known as Ddura prove to be key to both death and safety, and when Cass identifies the Tarens to the planet's defences, it is a watershed moment. Cass believes that unlocking Muina will free her to concentrate on finding a way back to Earth, but an offer from a different faction of ex-Muinans to return her home leads her to reject the idea of abandoning the Tarens who first rescued her. Whatever the future, she has chosen to stay and help.

APRIL

Tuesday, April 1

Fool

April Fool's Day. Totally appropriate for the idiot who turned down a chance to go home to Earth because she thinks she should play hero. Fortunately, all my contribution to the hero-ing business involves is standing where I'm put, ready to be hauled about by the people whose job it is to save the planet, or the galaxy, or however much of the universe is supposedly at risk. And what I've really signed up for is more labrattery, to figure out what 'touchstone' means.

I missed having a diary yesterday, and considered switching to an electronic version, but I'd have to use Taren script. Being able to write in English, to have a book filled with the things no-one here can understand: I think I need it even more now I've decided to stay. This new diary comes all the way from Kolar, and has thick, white-brown paper, and a picture of endless waving grassland on the cover.

Starting fresh like this made me feel like I should write down some missed-it-by-a-few-months New Year's Resolutions, but everything I've thought up so far is something I don't really have any choice about. I can't choose not to be on second level monitoring, and I don't want to resolve to not get injured, or save the universe, or anything completely out of my control. But the least I can do is try to:

- Make more than a half-assed effort at training.
- Find a way to be Cass instead of Caszandra.
- Remember that even kittens might be evil.

Some of those will probably fall into the too-hard basket as well, but it's something to go on with.

After my meeting with the Nuran, I emailed Mara and asked if I should send her dress to laundry, but she said to just bring it down to her rooms the next morning and we could go on into the city. I was pleased, because I'd been expecting my security to be tightened, not relaxed. The invitation did make me remember "psychological aspects", but I think I'll go nuts if I don't take most things at face value, if I waste my time trying to decide if people like me or have been ordered to entertain me. I have to accept that it's probably both, and move on. Part of my strategy for coping with staying.

Besides, I was very interested in seeing Mara's apartment, which turned out to have the same layout as mine, just with a mildly cluttered and lived-in air. I liked the public space decoration: all the walls looked like gauzy curtains that shifted as if the wind was blowing them. Not what I was expecting for a world where hardly anyone has or wants windows.

"Lohn's just getting ready," Mara said, when I handed over the bag and dress. "Maze's description of your expression when he gave this to you has made me regret not going along to watch."

"Was wondering just exactly what wanted me to do with Nuran," I admitted.

"We're going to have to get you some clothes without unfortunate messages written on them. Sit down."

She took the dress off into her bedroom, and I sat down and was gazing about interestedly when the bathroom door opened and Lohn came out.

"Mar, did I leave my–" He stopped and we looked at each other for what couldn't have been more than a couple of seconds, but felt a good deal longer, and then he turned and went into the bedroom and I thought about how fit and good-looking the Setari are. Lohn's got an incredible body, and has the added advantage of being fun and easy to get along with. Of course, he and Mara are so obviously a couple that I've never spent much time thinking about him in terms of being an attractive male creature, but I gave the question some serious consideration just then.

"Sorry about that," he said, coming out a minute later with Mara, this time with clothes on. Very pink in the face.

"Now you don't get to tease me about dress," I said, trying not to laugh or display any recollection of thoughts about attractive male creatures.

Mara, once she saw that I wasn't going to act like a twelve year-old about seeing a hot naked guy, smiled and said: "I don't think he's capable of that. He's been thinking up silly questions to ask you all morning."

"Is going to be very disappointed then." But I knew he'd ask anyway. I don't mind Lohn's teasing. He's never mean. "Can we really go out into city? Was worried I end up confined to quarters."

"For the moment the rule is that anywhere outside of the core Setari areas you must have at least two people escorting you, and one of them must have Combat Sight." Mara led the way out of her apartment. "If we take seriously the idea of the Nurans having a reason to kill you, then you're a good deal safer anywhere with us than alone in your rooms. Fortunately you were already in a suppression room, but we don't have any real idea of the limits of the Nurans' abilities or whether they'd be able to locate you through the suppression."

"Maze said he didn't have any threat sense from your Nuran," Lohn added. "But called him 'beyond formidable', which is Maze-speak for 'I don't think I could take him'. Still, this idea that they might decide to eliminate you rather than, ah, rescue you is just speculation. For one thing, it doesn't match what little we know of the Nurans' philosophies. And if your talent set really is that rare, it doesn't seem likely that they'll give up on the rescuing option."

I wondered if the Setari would be sent to try and rescue me back, but didn't ask, only hoped it didn't come to that. I sure as hell don't want to play Helen in a space-aged Trojan War.

It was a great day out. We went to a Tairo match, had lunch, shopped a little, and toured some of the more scenic bits of the city. There was a wonderful flower garden, and we spent some time on this amazing game, where the aim is to get from one side of a room to the other, except the room is full of constantly moving platforms going in every direction, and a 'Levitation field' slows your fall if you miss jumping from one to the next. That impressed me immensely, for all that I spend my days with flying psychic space ninjas. I let myself enjoy it all. Lohn and Mara are great together, and they treat me like a younger sister. It was easy to forget they'd probably been assigned to me for the day.

I kept thinking about my decision to stay, about how immediate my refusal to go with the Nuran was. It wasn't just a fit of heroic self-sacrifice. I mean, I'm miserable a lot of the time, and I'll never stop missing my family, or real music, or all the things I liked to read and do which just aren't here. But now that I'm getting better at speaking the language I'm having fun more often, even when First Squad aren't going out of their way to entertain me. Enough to make me wonder if going home to be just another noob at university would be a little bland.

I think in part I've caught Mum's I-want-to-know-what-happens-next disease. And, seriously, visiting other planets, cruising around exploring lost alien civilisations. Working with psychic space ninjas. It's far from dull. I want to help the Setari win. To fix the problem, and stop monsters getting out and killing people. And play more amazing games, and see more planets. I guess, in a stressed, periodically lonely and uncertain of the future way, I'm happy here.

At the least I was in quite a cheerful mood when Zan came swimming with me today, and only briefly wondered if it was her turn on the Baby-sit Devlin Roster. She seemed tired and less Zen than usual. And I think she was curious about the Nuran, since she made a few oblique references to him without outright asking questions. I'm not sure how secret he's supposed to be, but since Zan's one of 'my' captains, I figured it wouldn't hurt to explain what had happened.

We had lunch afterwards, and I told her about April Fool's Day and hoaxes I'd thought funny, and then about that *War of the Worlds* radio play, where all these people thought Martians really were invading. Then our schedules for the next month were updated, and I'm being posted back to Muina, along with Twelfth, Fourth and First Squad.

When I asked, Zan said she didn't know how she felt about the trip; Muina was a nearly mythical thing in a way and the idea of being able to go there, to touch the past which was so central to her present, was something she wasn't sure she was equal to. That's the most open speech she's ever given me, and it left me pleased but also worried about her.

Twelfth are going to be boring themselves with guard duty at Pandora, and First and Fourth are forming an expeditionary squad with a small team of greysuits to start investigating the biggest of the big cities. This is a lot more dangerous than guarding Pandora, since the Ddura don't seem to sweep places without patterned roofs nearly as frequently. And I'm assigned to Fourth Squad, so a lot of enjoying looking at Ruuel in my future – not sure whether that's a good or bad thing. And Zan might get in a bit of enjoying looking at Maze, heh.

Zan is still the only person here who pronounces my name the right way. Of course, I've never tried to correct the initial misspelling, but I like Zan for paying attention when I first talked to her.

Wednesday, April 2

Moving base

The Nuran is the main reason I'm being sent back to Muina. Not only in the hopes it will make it harder for him to find me, but because KOTIS figures Fourth Squad dragging me around interesting Muinan buildings is the best way to go about finding out what a touchstone is. They're hoping for more security clearance, and I naturally want nothing to happen. Still, on the scale of things I've had to do as part of my career as an experimental animal, exploring lost civilisations rates far higher than blood tests and brain scans.

I'm already itching to be outside, out of Tare's endless box cities, though I'm going to miss Ghost. I did think semi-seriously about smuggling her along in my backpack, but, meh, I don't need another lecture and they might want to capture her again. So far as I can tell, after she escaped she hasn't been sighted by anyone but me. I'm happy to keep it that way.

I'm in 'my' pod again, comfortably surrounded by First Squad. Alay's on the mission, although she's still walking with a pretty pronounced limp. She'll be on limited duty until she can move about properly.

Ruuel is in the opposite corner from me, in the pod Taarel used last time. The pods all face forward, so all I can really see is a bit of arm and a leg right now, but that's probably all to the good. I'm currently in one of my wish-I-didn't-like-him moods. Mainly because of a dream I had last night, where I kept following him around until he gave me this irritated, long-suffering glance and I woke up feeling absolutely mortified.

I guess that counts more as a nightmare than a dream, and I can put it down to a pre-Setari era show I started watching in preparation for working with Fourth Squad called *Super Sight Six*. Psychic detectives! The main character is a nightmare-ridden Place Sight talent, who is recruited by this hilariously 'New Age Guru' Sight Sight talent. There's a good-looking but temperamental Combat Sight talent, who I bet is going to turn out to be the love interest; a Gate Sight talent constantly distracted by distant, undiscovered gates into near-space; a Symbol Sight talent who loves puzzles; and a Path Sight talent who prowls about restlessly, then bounds off on the track of something. These are the Taren stereotypes of what the various Sights are like, but I'm particularly finding the Place Sight talent's story useful, because it helps me understand both Ruuel and Halla far better. The feelings, even the thoughts of living creatures leave the strongest impressions for Place Sight, and that can be as wonderful as seeing 'patterns of joy' as a musician plays, or as horrible as a brush against someone's arm bringing a flood of hidden hate or lust or resentment. It's considered rude to touch Place Sight talents, and if you do, whatever you're feeling strongly at that point is likely to be very clear to them. Fortunately the visual component isn't as clear-cut, and the touch component usually needs direct contact, meaning the gloves shield most of it. And back when Ruuel and I had our handholding marathon, it hadn't occurred to me to lust after him.

Unfortunately Sight Sight *is* very visual, and whether through Place or Sight, he is no doubt completely clear on the fact that the enhancing stray thinks he's hot. And who knows what Tsur Selkie has seen watching mission reports?

Cringe factor 9.

Architectural Fail

The Setari squads on this mission are all very upbeat. They like this assignment. Even those who simply consider Muina a part of the past hope that by being able to properly explore it they might find records and explanations and solutions. They so rarely get to do anything except fight an unwinnable war.

I'd wanted to talk to Zan during the flight, but she and Ruuel and Maze went off to be captainly at each other. Still, I had a nice chat with Mori Eyse from Fourth, and Dess Charn and Sora Nels from Twelfth, about our various assignments on Muina. Since I mainly knew Twelfth Squad from the grim race of the Pillar retrieval, I'd been curious to know if they were as temperamental as Lenton, and whether they seemed to resent Zan as much as he does. But they were unexpectedly normal – overly serious as almost all of the Setari are, but polite and with hints of personality behind the rigid professionalism. Very few of the Setari are willing to be 'off-duty' around me, but Twelfth unbent enough to ask questions and have non-controversial conversations.

Pandora looks horrible: a big white blot on the landscape. The main building is up to its third story and still growing, though most of it hasn't had the interiors finished. No sign of balconies, though there's more windows than I feared. There's a bunch of smaller outbuildings which are in use, though – amazingly quick construction. Sora was telling me that they don't dig the foundations, that the buildings send down roots (like teeth, given what they look like) and that fittings like pipes and ducts grow themselves, all based on an immensely detailed scale model. Around the construction site are tents and vehicles and people and dirt trampled to mush, and the beginnings of paths spreading like white filigree.

"How many people are here now?" I asked, as we took one of the floating sleds across to what had become a place I barely even recognised.

"Over two hundred and fifty." I'd asked Mori, but it was Ruuel who answered – since I'm assigned to them, it means I travel with Fourth Squad rather than First, who were on a different sled.

"For now this is Muina's capital," Ferus added. "I was very disappointed that the meaning of the name wasn't included in the announcements."

"Meaning of name is gift," I said. "Or giver of gifts or something like. Been a while since I read Greco-Roman myths."

"Do you know all the different beliefs of your world?" Mori asked.

"Not even close. Earth has hundreds of different languages and cultures. Greco-Roman stuff comes from over six thousand Tare years ago – it's not an active mythology." At least, I'd be really shocked if anyone was actively worshipping Zeus and Hera and all them.

We only spent an hour at Pandora, watching more supplies and people being unloaded from the *Litara* and waiting for the *Diodel* to arrive. The *Diodel's* a smaller ship than the *Litara*, and has been off surveying, and is going to be our base during the mission. It 'beds' (pods) thirty and the crew, in addition to First and Fourth Squads, are a bluesuit called Onara who commands five greensuits, a pinksuit, a medic called Learad with an assistant called Vale, and eight greysuits who are the research team – mainly archaeologist sorts. The head greysuit is a woman called Rel Duffen, who doesn't seem keen on either the Setari or me, but at least isn't overtly hostile.

The pods are in long lines down the centre of the ship rather than grouped in rooms. I'm between the two squads, with Zee in front of me and Sonn behind. And Ruuel one behind her. While I was waiting for the ship to take off I sent Zan an email which said: "On Earth, if someone seemed unhappy but not like they wanted talk about it, I'd send them a message which said *hugs*. If you get any free time, I recommend going to watch the otters." I attached a very badly drawn map, and was glad when she sent me a reply: "Thank you."

I don't want to prod Zan too hard. I'm starting to accept how unlikely second level monitoring makes it for anyone to talk about anything sensitive with me. And how I've got Buckley's chance of being taken off second level monitoring any time this century.

Today's going to be a long day. We're heading to the largest of the old cities, which is several time zones away from Pandora, and the sun will set in our new location well into what would be sleep shift for the squads who started out from Tare this morning. They think the city was once called Nurioth. Guess the Nurans named their moon after it.

Once we were underway the ship captain, Tsel Onara, gave us a to-the-point rundown of what we would be doing that day. Over the last few days the *Diodel* has been making an air survey of Nurioth, mapping it and looking for a place which was both central and clear enough to set down. They'd located a patch where there were no buildings beneath the trees, so first up the Setari (and me) are going to go down and 'weed' a clearing. They want a very big area, as level as possible, with a large perimeter so they could see anything approaching the ship.

After that, the Setari are going to tour the immediate surrounds and clear out any threats. Depending on what the Setari's threat assessment is, the greysuits may or may not be permitted to enter the nearest building, guarded by a mix of greensuits and Setari. Everyone is to be back at the ship before the sun starts to go down.

Archaeology is a slow business, so I don't see how a team of eight can do anything more than a basic review. They're really just checking to see what the conditions are like here, and whether useful things like writing might be better preserved. We're flying over the city now and it's seriously huge.

Thursday, April 3

Demolition

We levitated down into the park, both Setari squads together, and me tucked under Par Auron's arm. It was a gorgeous park. Tremendously overgrown and neglected of course, but the whitestone paths were still in place, and the leaves were just starting to turn red and yellow, gem-like against black wood. Once the *Diodel* had stopped hovering overhead and zoomed off to circle the city, birds began to peep and chirp cautiously. We'd come down in a relatively clear section in the very centre, and in one direction was an avenue of trees – the strength of the whitestone had kept all but a few trees to the outside of the path. The spot where we'd set down had a barely visible round shape – either a filled-in pond or a border of a garden – and the plants underfoot were fine and feathery.

"Mark two," Maze said. "Distant."

'Mark two' is a bit like saying 'ten o'clock'. When a squad enters a space, they count the direct left of the gate as mark 1, and continue around to nine for a semi-circle, or sixteen if the gate is central rather than on one side of the space. Since there'd been no gate involved here, they'd set a direction for mark one before leaving the ship.

"Structure at mark five," Ruuel added. "Beyond that is out of range. Sweep?"

Maze nodded. "Take ten to sixteen." First Squad enhanced before heading out, leaving me to trail along with Fourth Squad in a big semi-circle through the half of the park in the opposite direction to the big avenue. I think that half must have been more cropland than park, since there was barely a trace of paving and I saw occasional patches of some kind of grain plant, struggling in the shade of the trees.

Just like with Pandora, the place was seething with life, except some of that life was Ionoth. I guess the memories of monsters are just another predator to deer and pippins, and the miniature pigs, and some things very like chipmunks which I hadn't seen at Pandora. Birds in every direction, especially a really annoying plump and hysterical type which stayed hidden in the grass until you were right on it and then shot up into the sky shrieking its head off. I was busy being guilt-ridden that we were about to level the entire area, and kept thinking of that old song – I've no idea who it's by – that goes "They paved paradise and put up a parking lot". It's not like we don't clear-fell on Earth, but having been fed environmental awareness since grade one, I couldn't help feeling responsible all the same. It overwhelms me at times: accidental or not, I changed a world. Worlds.

First Squad took care of whatever was at mark two with a minimum of fuss, and it wasn't until we were at the mark thirteen that Fourth Squad found anything of interest, pausing.

"Underground," Ruuel said. "Hold here, off surface. Sonn, with me. Stay unenhanced."

That was an odd one. Auron and Ferus levitated those staying behind while Ruuel and Sonn walked to a patch of leaves which seemed totally unthreatening until these huge greyish tentacles whipped up out of holes and tried to grab them. Ruuel cut one in two, dancing back out of the spurt of blackish blood, and then lifted himself and Sonn into the air so she could blast the tentacles with bolts of lightning. Trap-door octopus. Other than that, there was only an encounter with a handful of toothy monkey things, nothing that made Fourth Squad even break a sweat.

It was a big park and too overgrown to walk through quickly, so it was over half an hour later when we met back up at the central circle. Then the stronger Telekinesis talents – Maze, Zee and Ferus (whose first name is Glade, which I thought very ironic) – had a logistics discussion before enhancing and pulling trees from the area I thought had been fields, stacking them to form walls dividing the park into a half with trees and a half without.

You don't just pick up a tree; they're too firmly rooted. Instead they quiver, and rattle from an invisible wind, raining leaves and bugs, then burst upwards in showers of dirt. We kept a respectful distance after the first one, and Lohn and Sonn followed along behind looking alert as scores of critters ran in every direction. Ruuel took everyone else on a little hunting trip after something which had strayed within his detection range, and I trailed along at Maze's elbow, trying not to fall in the holes, and thinking over how much Jules would love to be in my place.

"What are you trying not to laugh at?" Lohn asked me, when we were about a third through the field half of the park.

"Setari have great future landscape gardeners. Get Maze add nice water feature."

Maze heard that, and shot me an amused look over his shoulder, but kept concentrating on uprooting trees.

"Not our usual style of mission, true," Lohn said, surveying the destruction all around, but then giving the telekinetics a narrower glance. "More difficult, in some ways. We're not really designed for sustained output."

That also got a look from Maze, but then he nodded and said over the interface: "This is sufficient clearance. Meet back at the centre point."

We turned and walked back, Maze, Zee and Ferus occasionally filling in the larger holes left behind, or tossing boulders over at the stacked rows of trees. They looked extremely tired, and I was starting to feel that way myself. Enhancing people never feels like effort, until I abruptly fall asleep afterwards. We sat down on the rim of the central circle and waited for the *Diodel* to show up and kick up a lot of dirt and fallen leaves in our faces and make us really want the shower we were all looking forward to anyway. There's six to share between the Setari and the greysuits, and I wasn't at all inclined to object when Zee took me along for first shot at them, and then to eat and straight to bed. Even though it wasn't yet sunset, it had still been a long day for everyone, and I felt sorry for whichever of the Setari had to sit up during the sleep shift, since someone with Combat Sight has to be on watch at all times.

It's still night out. I woke ridiculously early, well before everyone except the people who were on duty, but that's given me a chance to catch up writing this. I think it will be dawn soon. I'm sitting in the common room area, which has a window giving me a lovely view of darkness. It was a little eerie walking past everyone's pods, the covers all closed and opaque. They have good sound-proofing and I couldn't hear breathing, though there was a hint of someone snoring.

Setari Summer Camp, day one.

Very expensive guards

It was starting to grow brighter outside when I finished writing about yesterday, so I turned out the lights in the common room (faintly chuffed that I could do something like turn the lights out – I still haven't fully recovered from my early days in medical purgatory when I didn't have access rights to do anything). The window wasn't facing fully in the direction of the rising sun, but I still had a great view down a slight slope to a flat area with a large number of buildings, and then a steep rise up a hill and some very impressive buildings on top of it. It's all very overgrown, but beautiful in the dawn, the whitestone gradually picked out in pink light. It must have been a very grand city once.

It was still only half-light outside when I had an uneasy sense of being watched and turned my head to find Ruuel standing looking at me. I've no idea how long he'd been there.

"Is watching the dawn a custom of your home?" he asked, coming over to where I was sitting on a window seat arrangement before one of the long viewing windows: my favourite spot on the ship.

"Think I've seen more Muinan dawns than Earth's." I turned back to the window, since that was the easiest way to deal with how good he was looking just then. "Generally stay up a lot later on Earth, so don't get up as early. Is better when you can hear the birds."

He didn't say anything, so I risked a quick glance at him. Ruuel has a way of gazing off at things – maybe using Sights, maybe just thinking – wearing this distant, contemplative expression which makes me want to stare at him in turn. I hastily looked back outside, and said: "More sensible roofs here."

"Sensible?"

"The trees are what Earth calls deciduous – they're losing their leaves in Autumn – so chances good it snows in this area. Flat roofs like those at Pandora must have needed a lot of clearing in Winter. These almost all seem to be sloped." Though I guess, since they were built out of whitestone, the weight of snow on the roof mightn't be a big problem. "Couldn't work out what they did for heating and cooking, either. Nothing that looked like a chimney or smoke vent in those houses. Only found a couple of kilns or ovens and those were separate from the other buildings. Could find very little information on Tare about what daily life was like on Muina."

"We have lost almost all that we were." He didn't sound particularly upset, but it made me wonder just how much the Nuran had gotten under his skin, saying that Tarens don't even know what

Setari means. And almost as if he knew what I was thinking, he added: "If we are to believe the one calling himself Inisar, we are not to be trusted with the past."

"Nurans as human as Tarens or people from Earth. Chances are just as fallible and ready do stupid things."

"An observation almost equal to Tare mostly treating you as civilised people should."

That made me turn around, but he was already walking away. And of course after that I spent the *entire* day thinking about him and being stupidly aware of everything he did, which was annoying. Being assigned to Fourth Squad is giving me way too many opportunities to look at Kaoren Ruuel, and my resolution to just sit back and enjoy the scenery isn't all that easy to keep.

Otherwise it was an uneventful day for me. First Squad, minus Alay, roamed about killing Ionoth and mapping the immediate area, while Fourth Squad escorted the greysuits about as they uncovered and looked over a small pavilion in the park, and then moved on to the buildings nearest to the ship. The greysuits switch constantly between eager excitement, nervous glances at all that sky without ceiling, and avoiding creepy-crawlies. All of us were slathered in a very effective insect repellant, but every so often someone would turn over a rock and try not to shriek.

I stayed with Fourth Squad, watching Ruuel not reacting to the way the leader of the greysuits, Islen Duffen, made it clear she wasn't interested in hearing the observations of Setari Sight talents. I guess it's true they don't have any formal archaeological or historical training, but Place Sight is a powerful tool, even factoring in the amount of time it's been since anything except animals and Ionoth were here to leave traces of self behind.

If Ruuel cared, he didn't show it. Ferus thought it was funny, and Auron doesn't seem to let much get under his skin. Halla and Eyse were briefly annoyed, then decided to look on the light side. Sonn was fuming, but Ruuel sent her to do a patrol of the outside of the building with Halla, and she'd cooled off by the time she came back. I did school work, and read books, and thought about the enormity of cataloguing an entire city. Even the initial recording of sites, while looking for any kind of writing, will take months. The entire planet will take centuries. Archaeologist is definitely going to be a booming career choice – KOTIS didn't have any on staff until Pandora was founded and Islen Duffen is a brand new recruit, who will ultimately be coordinating an ever-increasing horde of minions if the reclamation of Muina goes to plan.

Fortunately, once the immediate area is a little clearer, fewer Setari will be devoted to babysitting. And, no matter what Islen Duffen's opinion of the value of their observations, Fourth Squad's more likely to be able to detect and analyse strange Muinan installations than any of the greysuits.

And Ruuel has some vestige of a sense of humour and I'm liking him more than ever. Damn.

Friday, April 4

Chipping away at the whitestone mountain

Today was First Squad's turn to baby-sit greysuits, while Fourth Squad continued the wider area patrol. Our survey site was chosen because the buildings in this part of the city are large and suggest importance, and the Setari are systematically going to each one, doing a circuit of the exterior, and then looking inside. The greysuits aren't very keen on the Setari going inside, so they're only allowed to do more than look from the door if they're dealing with Ionoth.

I guess there were bones everywhere, but it was only when we went into some rooms which had been partially closed off that it was really brought home to me that this must have been one of the places where everyone abruptly dropped dead. Where, most likely, the Ddura had killed everyone. It was a lot harder to think of it as a big, lonely energy-dog after seeing so many grey and dusty skeletons lying where the people who lived here had fallen.

Yesterday First Squad were thoroughly tired by afternoon, and this time Fourth Squad were starting to look worn by lunchtime. They didn't do that much fighting compared to clearing the spaces, but wandering around constantly combat alert, and using Place Sight when they thought it appropriate, gets pretty draining after hour upon hour. Setari missions are usually two to three Earth hours, not all-day assignments. They stayed typical Fourth Squad, practically talking in abbreviations while on duty, but I think part of the strain was the place itself, by the history and the deaths of more than memory monsters. When we finished our second patrol loop they were more subdued than businesslike.

Fortunately they're growing a little less formal back on ship, and I ended up sharing a dinner table with Lohn and Mara, Mori Eyse, and the two junior-most greysuits, Katha and Dase, who were very interested in Earth's early civilisations. We moved to the common room afterwards and I tried not to feel too pressured when my attempts to dredge up memories of archaeological expeditions and discoveries on Earth attracted a larger and larger audience. I talked about Macchu Piccu and the discovery of Tutankamen's tomb and even Islen Duffen was interested, though she acted tremendously disapproving and asked lots of Devil's Advocate-type questions. It's so strange to be the only person who knows any of this stuff, and to have my rambling memories treated as important. I wish I'd paid a lot more attention in all my classes.

No-one stayed up too late, though, which was good for me since I had been walking all over the city as well. It's a little hard to tell how much I'm effected by enhancing, but I know I am now, though I wasn't dropping with exhaustion today the way I had been after all that tree-uprooting. Time to go to sleep now, and to try not to think too much about Ruuel asleep two pods over.

Saturday, April 5

Dase

It took me half the day to figure out that Dase (Dase Canlan, one of the junior archaeologists) was trying to flirt with me. Flirt seriously, I mean, not the teasing-flirting that Nils from Second Squad seems to do almost unconsciously. Dase and Katha had asked Islen Duffen if they could explain to me some of what they were doing and rather to my surprise she agreed, so I had some lessons on 'field archaeology'. I do wonder where Taren archaeologists usually do their archaeology – there can't be that much left of the early days of Tare's settlement that doesn't have mega-buildings sitting on it.

Before I twigged, I was just enjoying having some people to chat to who were willing to be not 'on duty' every second of the day. It was only when we went in for lunch that Dase switched more to asking about my family and how I felt about the things I was doing on Tare that it filtered through to me that he was smiling at me a lot. He wasn't pushy or sitting too close or anything; it was just that kind of vibe.

Looking back, it's funny how disconcerted I felt. It's not as if I've never dated. And Dase isn't some damp mouth-breather. Not so fantastically fit as any of the Setari, unsurprisingly, but with this cute, flopping-into-his-eyes fringe. Twenty-two or three, possibly, which still seems too adult to me, but I guess isn't so much older than me. He'd probably score a 7 on the Orlando Bloom-meter, and is a pretty nice guy. A bit earnest.

It's not easy to decide how to react to a guy when you know people are watching. But the main hurdle was that Orlando Bloom would score about a 7 on my Kaoren Ruuel-meter. And Ruuel was sitting at the next table. Fortunately facing the opposite direction, though I held no hope that he wasn't sparing a fraction of his attention to the "psychological aspects". I am part of the Setari's duties.

I dealt with Dase by asking Katha a lot of questions, always keeping the conversation group-focused, acting completely oblivious to any kind of undertone. Hell, for all I know he was just being friendly and I was reading way too much into everything. But I did spend the rest of the day trying to work out how I would feel if I wasn't so fixated on Ruuel.

That wasn't easy, and I had an annoying internal argument about whether or not I should try and get to know Dase better, because it was silly to push a perfectly nice guy away in favour of a one-sided crush. But that's how it is. The thing with Ruuel will either fade or it won't, but right now there's only one person I want flirting with me.

For all that the mind boggles at the idea of Ruuel flirting.

Sunday, April 6

Umbrella of the Apocalypse

Ruuel woke me up just on dawn with an override and a typically curt text message: "Aft lock."

Not sure if it was an emergency, I released my pod's lid, making my nanosuit grow back its feet and gloves as quickly as I could manage. I did bring a bag of normal clothes along, but it's simpler to wear the suit to bed precisely because of mornings like this one, though I guess I mainly wear it because I would have felt embarrassed slopping around in pyjamas while everyone else was in uniform.

Mara was with Ruuel and one of the greensuits, standing on the small ramp down to the trampled dirt outside. Ruuel touched my arm and then turned to gaze into the half-light.

"Possibly just a false alarm," Mara said, squeezing my shoulder in apologetic greeting. "Combat Sight is giving me nothing specific, but I can't escape the sense that something's there."

Mara's turn for the late watch. She'd woken Ruuel, who in turn had woken me because he was no more certain. I looked out at the hazy shapes of the stacked trees and the endless stretch of whitestone buildings. The air was sharply crisp, with a fragment of breeze rattling leaves. Otherwise, nothing.

"No birds," I noted. That early, bird-calls should have been just starting up, but it was like the city was holding its breath.

Ruuel glanced back at me, then nodded at Mara. "Something is coming. It's still in near-space." He set off a full alert alarm and headed back into the ship.

"Go quickly and grab something to eat," Mara told me, after a rather wry look at Ruuel's back. "There's only one thing any of us are likely to be able to sense while it's still in near-space. This isn't going to be easy."

A massive. That's what Ruuel said, as he brought all the Setari and the greensuits and Tsel Onara into a channel and gave them one of his terse briefings.

"We'll retreat," Tsel Onara said immediately.

"No time," Maze said. "If we can feel it, it's right on the verge of emerging. The *Diodel* isn't manoeuvrable enough to avoid an attack during take-off, even if we could manage that immediately."

I'd run, not to get something to eat, but to go to the toilet and to wash my face. Maze ordered both squads outside even as Mara said: "It's emerging. Mark seven, almost on top of us."

Eight squads. That's what I was remembering as I ran back to the aft lock. The last time they'd fought a massive they'd needed eight squads, and Maze's wife had died. We didn't even have any of the big hitter squads, and for all I knew how much more powerful I made the Setari, I still felt bug-small when I reached the ramp and felt what was above us.

Not with psychic senses. Felt in the way you do when there's something really big moving, like when the *Litara* is flying overhead. The thing was standing beside the park, not directly over us, and was bigger than the *Litara*. It had to be one of the weirdest things I've ever seen – a black and bulky central section low to the ground, but with two twisty 'sub-bodies' raised far higher up on either side by scads of long spindly legs which reminded me of the collapsed spokes of an umbrella. I watched one of these reach with a lazily deceptive speed and pluck something from the ground below. It was too far to see just what it was, but the massive moved it over to the central body and dropped it on top.

"We'll draw it away from the *Diodel* first," Maze said. "Spel, Gainer, Eyse, Halla, remain with the ship on alert for accompaniment."

"First assessment is that it will be resistant to elementals," Ruuel said calmly, and gave me one of the molasses food bars which were standard mission fare. He had a handful of them, was passing them out.

Maze grimaced, but didn't seem particularly surprised, setting the enhancement rotation as he touched my arm. "We'll go over the top," he said. "Don't underestimate the reach of those arms."

Eight people. Instead of eight squads, they were going to try and fight the thing with eight people. But still, even though they were looking super-serious, they weren't acting like they thought it was impossible, so when Auron hitched me into his side all I did was hook my arm obediently across his shoulders.

We went very high very quick, the cold air making my eyes stream. There was a crunching noise below, and I realised it was one of the buildings the massive's main body was resting on. Even whitestone couldn't stand up to the weight of it. After one brief glance where I saw that the top of it looked like a massive Venus flytrap, I didn't look down again.

"Higher – we're in reach," Ruuel said, and we shot up abruptly even as some of the umbrella spokes came toward us. Maze set the tip of one, a horrid fingery arrangement, shrivelling and burning and Ruuel said: "Sonn," which prompted her to drop a ball of lightning down into the mouth, and then we were on the far side.

"The large building at mark nine," Maze ordered, and we dropped down to the roof of a long, single-story building, moving way too fast for my comfort. The fact that I have to be carried instead of levitated makes whizzing about scary.

"Swoops at twelve mark," Ruuel said. "Fast approach."

"Your targets Kettara, Senez." Maze re-enhanced, starting the cycle over. "How much reaction to that lightning?"

Ruuel's eyes were fully open as he gazed back at the massive. "No more than pain."

It was moving toward us, surprising me by being a lot quicker and less awkward than something that big and weird should surely be. Off in the direction Mara and Lohn had gone was the white flash of Lohn's Light wall, and a gargling wail before some heavy things crashed and skidded in the street below.

"Focus debris damage on the join points between the centre body and the outliers," Ruuel continued. "Then debris and elementals on the outliers. They are its weapons."

"Right side first," Maze said, wasting no time in pulling a boulder out of the ground below and hurling it at the massive. It fell short: we were too far away. Even Ferus, who has the strongest Telekinesis of the two squads, couldn't quite reach.

"Haul above," Maze ordered, and he, Zee and Ferus gathered everything loose and heavy from the immediate area – trees and rocks and chunks of broken whitestone – and zipped upwards.

"Retreat back four streets," Ruuel ordered, because the massive was uncomfortably no longer too far away. Auron lifted me, Mara, Lohn and Sonn backward to the roof of a two-story building up the hill, landing just as the others began hurling things downward with maximum strength.

The massive didn't like that. It made a low, deep noise and stopped moving as its right segment was almost completely severed. As the three telekinetics dipped back to the ground to gather more missiles, the massive's two outer segments lowered all their spindly umbrella arm-legs until they were about the same height as the main body. The right segment didn't seem like it was going to drop dead or stop moving just because it was no longer fully joined, although both of the segments had pulled down completely into defensive bunches.

The tiny constellation of the Setari rose again, moving to attack the other segment, which seemed to be tilting so that it faced in my group's direction.

"Scatter!"

I gasped, wrenched by abrupt and rapid movement. Ruuel had stepped behind me, slid both arms under mine, and gone straight up. He'd brought Mara, Lohn and Sonn with us, and Auron followed after a moment's shock. Ruuel was moving as quickly as he could fly and I slid helplessly down, clamping my arms over his and trying not to panic until he bound our suits and I stopped sliding, just as a wave of purplish light washed out the dawn, filling the air with the scent of burning metal.

Both of the outer segments had blasted us, one up at Maze's group, the other direct at mine. We'd managed to move in time, Auron just barely clearing the upper edge of the purple, but the interface showed me Zee's location plummeting in a way which was absolutely wrong.

Maze and Ferus dove after her. Ruuel, breathing hard from the effort of moving everyone so quickly, said: "Swoops from mark four. Auron, take over carriage and bring us rapidly over it and down. Sonn, full power into the detached part."

Ferus had caught Zee. He and Maze paused together, then Maze said, voice tight: "Rendezvous with the others."

Lohn took care of the swoops behind us as Sonn dropped another ball of lightning down onto the damaged segment. We descended rapidly, meeting together on another roof. Zee was limp and still, but I knew from the mission display that she was alive. Ruuel let me go and turned to watch the massive, saying: "It's reorienting."

"Restart enhancement rotation," Maze said, brushing a finger against my arm. "Looks like the second ball of lightning has had some impact. We'll work on detaching the other segment. Keep moving. Spel, join us with Gainer and Halla."

Ferus passed Zee to Auron, enhanced, and then he and Maze took off again.

"We'll work on finishing off the injured segment," Ruuel said. "Kettara, use Light element. The rest, whatever minor seems most likely to damage it." Lohn and Mara re-enhanced, and I went back to being Auron's carting-about problem. I was too caught up in the fight and worrying about Zee to spare much attention to the whole grabbed-by-Ruuel thing. I've been thinking about it plenty since. He was going all-out, at his limit of Levitation and Telekinesis talents, and I could feel his chest move as he gasped for air. If I hadn't been panicking, I probably would have enjoyed that a lot.

The damaged segment didn't seem able to produce the purple beam any more, or didn't have a chance before we rained Light and Fire and Ice down on it. The other segment shot at Maze and Ferus, but forewarned they were able to dodge and pelt it with big chunks of the buildings it had been tromping over. The rest of the Setari swung around and toasted that side as well.

The centre section was still alive, though, and still moving, crushing more of the city in the process. We all dropped down to another roof, very close to it, meeting up with Ketzaren, Alay and Halla.

"Take Annan back to the ship," Maze told Ketzaren. "Spel, enhanced Sonics on the main body."

Alay nodded, taking my hand and squeezing it: I've no doubt I was looking wide-eyed and pale. We all moved back behind her then, with the ship behind us, and I found out that Alay's Sonic talent is a really scary thing. Like Ketzaren's Wind, it's something that takes her a long time to build to a seriously destructive level, but even with our ears covered and not being the focus of her attack, my bones started aching. The massive began to wail and rock, and every bird and animal in its direction which hadn't fled already burst from cover and ran.

It died unspectacularly. I expect if it had anything recognisable as a head, blood would have run from its eyes and nose and ears. As it was, it just stopped moving and wailing and settled down on the crushed remains of the buildings below. Alay stopped shredding our ears and let out her breath. She turned her head and just for a moment I saw her face. Naked. I know that Maze lost his wife in the last massive attack, and now I know that Alay must have lost someone too.

"Escort Ionoth are still emerging," Ruuel said, and added either to me or to our audience on the *Diodel*: "Massives are usually trailed by other Ionoth, particularly swoop roamers."

"We'll pause here for recovery and then clear," Maze said.

"Pandora control is sending reinforcements," Tsel Onara added, voice crisp but with just a hint of relief, or respect. Massives are well-named.

Most of the Setari began eating the energy bars Ruuel had handed out earlier. I had mine in a pocket, but ignored it, for all I was really hungry. I figured it wouldn't be that long before we went back to the *Diodel* and had some food which didn't leave a tarry-sweet aftertaste in my mouth.

Lohn came over and gave my shoulders a squeeze. "Remember when you asked if enhancement was worth all the complication of rotations?" he asked. "This is what it comes to – the difference between dozens of us bouncing attacks off one of these things, or a handful with enough impact to penetrate its defences."

I smiled a bit weakly, feeling shakier than I usually do after working with the Setari, and asked: "How bad is Zee injured?"

"Her vitals are steady," Maze said, coming across to give me a quick captain-survey. "The attack seemed to be electricity-based, intended to stun prey and not strong enough to kill a healthy person. Though it would be another matter if we'd not caught her." He gave Ferus an approving glance.

"Surion."

There was something in Ruuel's tone which made us all look at him, and then follow his gaze to a building far up the hill. Two dark figures were watching us. Distance and the thin light of dawn made detail unclear, but I knew them anyway. Cruzatch.

I glanced at Maze, but he was being pure captain, surveying the watching pair before saying: "Any others?"

"Not that I've sensed."

"Out of range of an immediate kill." Maze frowned. "The nearest gate to that location is one street beyond. We'll feint a retreat back toward the ship, then split and attempt to circle and catch them between us."

Ruuel nodded, and the Setari broke into two groups, Auron tucking me under his arm again. They were very intent, grim. I guess, since Maze thinks the Cruzatch are organised and actively working against the Setari, he didn't want to give them a chance to report back.

When we split, Fourth Squad headed straight for the gate while First took a swift, circling loop toward the Cruzatch. One of them launched itself at First, while the other did as Maze had predicted and went for the nearest gate.

I'd not seen a Cruzatch fighting before. There's an eerie similarity to the Setari in their speed and the way they grow weapons – though the Cruzatch Ruuel fought created long claws from its fingertips rather than a sword from its arm. It was very fast, too, if no match for Ruuel, especially Ruuel enhanced. The thing I hated, though, was the way it almost seemed to be getting off on fighting him, like it knew it would just come back if he won.

"Clear the emergents and rendezvous back at the *Diodel*," Maze ordered, and we spent another half hour chasing down swoops and one of those stilt things. Then it was hot showers and hot food and First and Fourth Squad were just about recovered from their wake-up call when two shuttles from Pandora arrived. It had a bunch of greysuits who wanted to investigate the massive, and more greensuits, and Ninth Squad, which I'd had nothing to do with before.

I took the opportunity of everyone being distracted by their arrival to go see Zee. She was still unconscious, looking very crumpled and bruised for such a tall, fit woman. The doctor's letting me sit with her, and they think she should wake up soon, but I've managed to write this entire diary entry without her so much as twitching.

Setari Musical Chairs

Zee woke up. I'd fallen asleep – one of those post-too-much-enhancement power naps I'm getting used to taking – and when I opened my eyes she was lying on her side watching me.

"Just a few moments too slow," she said, voice dragging a little. "Nasty shock to the system. I'll be joining Alay in rehabilitation for a while."

"Alay's nearly better," I said, and squeezed her hand. "Dodge faster next time. Scared me half to death."

Zee smiled and mumbled something I didn't understand. She was pretty out of it. I watched her failing to stay awake, and for a while wished I was still living with the Lents, that I'd never seen any of the Setari after being rescued. They live such dangerous lives, and the chance of all of them surviving is so slim. That may be another reason the Setari as a group are so competitive and distant with each other outside of their squads: having too many friends would mean having too many people you care about constantly in danger.

That was after midday, while the two extra shuttles were still here. The greysuits wanted to record as much detail of the massive as they could before it vanished, which it did a couple of hours later. The vanishing thing really worries me, actually: it makes all this a little too like a computer game for me to be entirely certain that the nutter-in-a-straightjacket option isn't the right explanation for everything I do and see. Monsters that respawn infinitely, whose bodies despawn after they're killed. And me being some mysterious touchstone thing with bunches of incredibly hot people looking after me. It's all a little too wish-fulfilment.

I would really hate it if I was insane. Though if this is a psychotic episode, at least it came on suddenly and doesn't make me face up to the fragmentation of my own mind. It would be far worse to be insane only some of the time.

But if this was all my own private fantasy, I think I would make more people like me. The captain of Ninth Squad is called Desa Kaeline, and she has wonderful smoky eyelashes and unusually pale skin for a Taren. And was extremely correct and polite to me in a way that suggested that I gave her a headache but she didn't want to admit it. And there was another girl in her squad, Kahl Anya, who gave me this absolute viper-look. I've got to stop reviewing my own logs: it was only a quick glance and I wouldn't have caught it at all if I hadn't looked back over the reinforcements leaving just before sunset.

They took First Squad away with them, and left Ninth Squad behind. Today sucked.

Monday, April 7

Team Drama Queen

Ruuel made us all get up early to do enhancement testing and training, since Ninth Squad has never worked with me at all. Setari pecking order seems to be based on active duty seniority, so when the squads work together, the captain of the squad with the smaller number is treated as being in charge. Ninth Squad doesn't seem to resent this, though I noticed during this morning's session that Ruuel had Ninth do a lot more repetition of the multiple-squad enhancement rotation and the intricacies of carrying me around than he bothered with when Fourth Squad was testing. I don't know whether that's because he thinks they're slower on the uptake, or he just isn't sure another squad member would ask to go over things again if they needed to. It's pretty clear squads hate looking bad in front of other squads.

Ninth Squad is another generalist squad: a little more big-hitting than First, since the older Setari for the most part aren't quite as powerful as the younger. Desa Kaeline turned out to be easy enough to work with; maybe she simply did have a headache when she was introduced to me yesterday. The rest of the squad seemed to settle into two groups: Kahl Anya and her two best buddies, and two people who really don't like Kahl Anya. I began to see why Kaeline might be prone to headaches.

Not that they were squabbling or glaring at each other. I doubt they'd do that where Fourth could see. They just had this tendency to stand in two different groups, and Anya and her groupies would exchange little smirks, while the other two looked unhappy. I was glad my 'ride' in Ninth was one of the non-groupies – a bean-pole guy named Rebar Dolas. Other than an undertone of being in a bit of a mood, he seemed nice. He asked me where I prefer he put his hands, anyway, gave me a sympathetic smile, and kept an eye on my reaction when we changed directions abruptly.

I was pretty tired. Napping half the morning yesterday meant I'd stayed up very late, doing school work in my pod since I hadn't felt like chatting. Fortunately Fourth Squad was on babysitting duty, so I didn't have to walk half the day. Islen Duffen kept making aggrieved comments about all the damage to the buildings, but she wasn't blaming the Setari particularly.

I sat with Glade and Mori at lunch and dinner. I'm liking Mori more and more. She has a wry sense of humour, which she mostly only indulges when Ruuel isn't around, and she and Glade both watch *The Hidden War* devotedly, just to pick apart the things that don't make sense. They say that some of the characters who show up later in the series are based on leaked details of the real Setari. I'm still only up to the second year of it: I like it, but I've found I can only stand watching it sporadically, and prefer *Super Sight Six*. *The Hidden War* is often quite a dark show, and just now I don't want to think about how First has had two close calls in a handful of weeks.

I'm glad I'm settling into Fourth, that I'm able to chat and laugh with some of them, because otherwise I'd feel pretty alone without First, dealing with Ninth. Of course, no-one's about to discuss Ninth Squad with me. By this stage I know to not even consider asking. I don't know what Anya has against me. I figure the best thing I can do is just not be interested in the opinions of people who've never even spoken to me.

Nor is anyone willing to discuss whether the Cruzatch could really have driven that massive to attack us. People are discussing it, but the idea makes everyone desperately uneasy, and they shut up when I'm nearby with my ever-present second level monitoring.

I keep thinking of Zee, falling out of the sky.

Tuesday, April 8

Chinese Mountains

Halfway between midnight and dawn I woke feeling fretful and uneasy. I thought maybe I'd had a nightmare, and lay for a while not able to sleep, then eventually got up to go to the bathroom. The pods have quite a lot of shielding on them, much like my room back on Tare, and it was only after I'd opened mine that I started to properly register what had woken me.

It was the "mmmnnnnnnnnnnnnnnnnnnnnnnnnnn" noise, the one I associated with the Ddura attacking or hunting, but very far away. I could barely hear it, and spent the time it took to go to the bathroom and then to get a drink to decide whether or not it was just my imagination. I'd been told I had to immediately report if I heard the Ddura, but hearing a noise which might be the Ddura in the middle of the night meant my own interpretation of immediately. Especially when the person on night watch was the prima donna from Ninth Squad.

Still, I was assigned to Fourth Squad and all Anya would be able to do, beyond act like I was wasting her time, was report to the captains. So, with a squeamish mix of feelings, I sent Ruuel an override saying: "Can hear Ddura."

He didn't treat me to any sleep-fuelled incoherencies, responding within maybe ten seconds with: "At what distance?"

"Very far away," I said, watching as his pod cover lifted and he sat up. Facing away from me, fortunately, so I could enjoy the sight of him with his uniform converted to a tank top and knee-length arrangement. He scrubbed a hand over his close-cut hair, his uniform starting to return to standard configuration, and I looked away, feeling oddly uncomfortable. "Can only just hear," I added, out loud this time instead of over the interface. "It making noise it makes when it attack things."

"Outside," was all of his response, and I followed him to the aft lock.

The Setari on watch is posted with a greensuit just inside the lock; there's seats, and they don't have to stand, but usually seem to be. Anya and the greensuit were both standing, and the greensuit looked like she had a headache, heh.

"Any movement?" Ruuel asked, and they both said no, tensing because we wouldn't have been there if nothing was happening.

Ruuel opened the outer hatch and lifted us both on to the roof of the ship. He used straight Levitation, which I much prefer to being hauled about clinging on to people, but the Setari can only lift me directly if they're not enhanced.

"Try to gauge a direction while I arrange clearance," he said, and then I guess sent an override in turn to the *Diodel*'s captain.

It's really hard to work out the direction of a distant noise. Shadowed by Ruuel, I walked around the roof of the ship, trying to ignore the chilly wind, and eventually decided that I could hear it best on the aft end. By that time, a couple of greensuits were preparing the ship's transports for a night-time excursion, and Fourth and Ninth were all up and ready.

There's a lot of different types of smaller transports, and the name of the two the *Diodel* carried would roughly translate to 'skimmers'. They hold eight people and are more complex than the flat, hovering sleds we used crossing the lake at Pandora, with low seats wrapped around the edge and a flat area in the middle: flying rafts. No visible controls or console or anything like that. They can only go about forty feet up, but scudded along at a brisk pace.

Each skimmer had two greensuits, and five Setari, with two of Ninth Squad left at the *Diodel*, including one unimpressed drama queen. I sat up front opposite the greensuit, feeling very silly, and we flew in the direction I'd indicated. I was picturing the reaction if I'd chosen the wrong direction, but as we got closer I could tell it was more to one side, and re-directed the greensuit, and kept making corrections the louder the Ddura became.

Nurioth sprawls over two rivers which drain into another fresh-water lake – the westernmost of a chain of huge lakes including Pandora's lake. After a while, as the Ddura grew louder, I stopped feeling so self-conscious about playing native guide, and enjoyed looking at the stars and the reflections in the lake and the spooky gloom of the city. After we left it behind us, I was expecting to arrive at another of the small settlements marked by the circle symbols on roofs, but there was just forest beside the lake, and small mountains which reminded me of those pictures you see on old Chinese pictures – conical pointed arrangements.

"Very near here," I said, looking back confusedly. "Think we passed." There was no sign of any settlement, just the gleam of an old road.

"Take us lower," Ruuel said to the greensuit, then touched my arm and added to Auron and Mori: "Try to locate another of the communication devices."

The moon was three-quarters full above us as we dropped to nearly ground-level among the steep mountainettes. All three of the path-finders turned slowly in the same direction, glanced at each other and nodded. We moved back the way we came, until we were in the middle of a triangle formed by three of the conical mountains, with the lake to our left and patches of whitestone paving poking through the dirt and plants beneath. There was something distinctly unnatural about the shadowy near-vertical slopes of the mountains around us, the moonlight picking out too-regular shapes among bright-edged shadows.

"We need more *light*," said Ormeral, the sole greysuit who'd been sent along.

Ruuel said: "Halla," and she obediently sent a huge Pillar of flame into the air above us, startling a flock of birds (or bats) into flight and revealing large stone doors surrounded by decorative carving, firmly sealed and very impressive. Before the flame died away I saw that all three mountainettes had the same sort of entrance.

"Set down by the lake," Ruuel said. We were well out of what he'd said was normal interface range, but I guess the skimmers would include communication links, since he got that talking-to-someone-else expression and, when we set down, said: "The *Diodel* will relocate, and we'll wait for daylight. What's the status of the Ddura?"

"Still hunting." It was loud, but not as loud as it was on the surface at Pandora, let alone at the communication platform.

Ruuel nodded. "We'll scout for gate locations external to the site while we wait."

He split us into two groups, putting me in the "sit in the skimmers and don't move" half, and then divided the rest into pairs who vanished off into the night. Pairs meant he didn't sense a major threat nearby, which I guess isn't that surprising since the Ddura had been hunting through the area for the last half hour. Ormeral began taking readings using a bulky machine he'd lugged along, looking tremendously excited. I watched the lake.

This is such a beautiful world. I pretended, just for a few minutes, that I was here on a family holiday. Mum and the aunts and the cousins, maybe even Dad. We'd fish, and only Nick would catch anything. Mum would go off on a long rambling walk, and bring back a huge bouquet of interesting leaves and flowers. Jules would be everywhere, complaining half the time of X-Box deprivation, and then would fall out of a tree, scrape every limb raw, and be all pleased with himself. Maybe I'd go canoeing – I've never tried that, but it looks like it might be fun. We'd have a campfire and cook the fish, with potatoes in the coals, and tell ghost stories. Everyone would argue just a little, and laugh a lot, and be comfortable and relaxed and no matter what planet it was I would belong because that's what being with your family does.

Thinking about all this of course made me feel intensely miserable. I was surprised when Auron patted my shoulder and when I looked at him he gave me this shy, sympathetic smile. I smiled back, appreciating the gesture, which was uncharacteristic for him: he's even more taciturn than Ruuel, though in a very different way. Ruuel had swapped him for Glade as my primary babysitter pretty early on, maybe just because he's so tall it makes it easier for him to tuck me under his arm. I'm more comfortable clinging to Auron, anyway. Glade, though he was always correct, was I think endlessly tempted to tease me about it.

Halla and Sonn are still pretty formal, but I think even they accept me as a temporary part of Fourth Squad; they're certainly not hostile. Mori and Glade are becoming friends, and Auron (Par) sort of comes as an added extra with Glade. And their acceptance and growing willingness to talk to me makes it a lot easier to be around Ruuel so much. I really don't enjoy the way I feel about him a lot of the time. Too vulnerable.

The arrival of the *Diodel* interrupted all my introspection, and now I'm back on the ship and everyone's sitting around waiting for it to be dawn. One of the main things all this exploration is for is to find information about the Pillars, and I guess Ruuel has decided there might be some here. This means the place is going to be searched really carefully, with especial emphasis on not accidentally standing on vital bits of evidence. Most of it will be inside the mountains, though, so I find it funny that they're waiting for dawn just so they can sift through the debris outside the doors.

I think I'll try and get a little more sleep now that I'm no longer so keyed up.

Seeing too much

Mori woke me around mid-morning. "We've finally reached the stage where we're going to open the doors," she said. "Or try to – they seem to be a complicated arrangement."

A hot shower and breakfast were first on my schedule. I was surprised to realise that all of Fourth Squad had gone back to sleep as well, but of course it made sense to not have the ship's entire Setari complement sitting around waiting for dawn, and then watching the greysuits take pictures and measurements and search the overgrown paved area for artefacts.

As I was finishing breakfast, a vibration ran through the ship and on cue Mori reappeared, hair damp. "That's the *Litara*. Initial scans have shown there's an extensive underground complex here. Between that, the presence of a communication platform, and the fact that the doors appear to be charged with aether, this is going to be a major site, perhaps even our second settlement. Let's go look before we're overwhelmed by reinforcements."

"Why expedition in Nurioth so relatively few people?" I asked. "Such a large city; barely chipped the edges."

"Well, our primary purpose there was to find something like this place," Mori said. "The archaeological survey and analysis of the city – all the cities – will take decades. What work was done in Nurioth will be useful, of course, but this whole expedition was focused toward finding active Lantaren technology, particularly more platform towns. Not only because we want to analyse such technology, but because we want to concentrate the archaeological analysis on these sites in the hopes that the builders left records of the Pillar construction."

We'd reached the port lock, where the rest of Fourth Squad was waiting on a sled. I really don't know why they get themselves ferried to shore instead of flying: some kind of protocol? Or just careful conservation of energy when on duty. I've come to realise how prone to exhaustion the Setari are.

"I don't care to guess how long it would have taken us to uncover this, though," Mori continued, as we started across. "It's not something aerial surveys would easily detect, and far out of our Sight range."

"Seems different style of decorative tradition, too," I said, staring ahead to what I could see of the carved face of one of the mountains. Everyone was quiet and tense as the sled left the lake and slid smoothly between the curving base of the steep-sided mountains.

It reminded me vaguely of – I've forgotten the name – that building which is carved into the face of a gorge. It's not only the size of the thing which makes an impression, it's the frame of natural rock, in this case not of sheer, baked yellow stone, but of grey and black rocks, worn into rounded piles and heavily decorated with lichen, ferns, shrubs and small trees sprawling down and sideways. A big contrast to the clean, curving lines of pointed arches, maybe twelve or fifteen metres up to the tip. Between a simple inner and outer border were carvings with a faint resemblance to Mayan decorations or even Celtic knot work. The doors were rectangular, not pointed, and the space above their lintel and the point of the arch was full of figurative carvings.

The three mountainettes were close, like a circle of people holding hands. The gap in the centre wasn't more than a couple of hundred metres across, a lop-sided circle which the greysuits had been busy sectioning with stakes exactly as you'd see at a dig on Earth, except they projected an electronic grid in the interface rather than using string. A few areas had been cleared, exposing circular paths and a tumble of whitestone in the centre which looked like something had fallen on it. They'd made a lot of progress in the last few hours, obviously intent on ensuring nothing was trampled underfoot when people tried to examine and access the doorways.

Kaeline from Ninth met us at a small tent which had been set up just outside this central area, and there was a lot of talk of readings and measurements and where we were allowed to walk. I stood staring at the triangle of carving above each of the doors. Each had a central figure of the head and shoulders of a person – the face was androgynous, idealised, and the arms outstretched, something trickling from cupped hands down on little people below. God-kings. The Egyptians had them and I'm willing to bet that's what the Lantarens who built this place considered themselves.

Things started getting crowded then, as the reinforcements from the *Litara* began arriving. I was surprised to see Tsur Selkie among them, though he seemed to be playing observer rather than person in charge. As soon as he showed up all the Setari forgot how to talk and focused on standing very straight, while Islen Duffen called a halt to her team's work and we all gathered near the tent to discuss what would happen next.

The person in charge was a woman called Tsen Helada (so many Ts titles), a whip-thin, narrow-eyed lady with streaks of grey in frizzy black hair, and an air of barely suppressed energy. She reeled off lists of detail, about how the greensuits would examine the nearby area and decide the site of the settlement while Islen Duffen would continue to coordinate the archaeological side, and a man called Islen Tezart would manage investigation into what amounted to 'psychic technology'. We were to consider the site dangerous, not only because of Ionoth and aether, but because we had no idea what the potential dangers of active Lantaren technology might be. And we were to above all else be thorough, to miss nothing.

Islen Tezart had a very different attitude toward Sight talents compared to Islen Duffen. He wanted the Place Sight talents to assist in the investigation of the doors, which didn't seem to have any moving parts. He was hoping they might be able to see a way to unlock it without damaging it, or discover if it was something which could be commanded using Ena manipulation, like the communication platforms.

More dullness after this, with everyone standing around talking and waiting while different machines took readings. Ninth Squad was off being guard-like, and Tsur Selkie was with Fourth, watching silently. I kept staring up at the image of the person above the door and thinking of that Shelley poem, *Ozymandias*.

"Is there something familiar about the carving?" Tsur Selkie asked me while they were performing the last of the machine scans. "Does this have a correlation to structures on your world?"

I shook my head. "Doesn't really match anything. If wasn't for communication device inside, would think this was tomb though."

"Tomb?"

I'd had to use the English word. Tarens cremate their dead and toss the ashes into the ocean. Necessary given their space issues, and better than the soylent green option. They have a word for grave, but not for a building for dead bodies, which I guess means that the Muinans didn't use tombs either. "Cross between monument to the dead and a grave," I said. "There was Earth people called Egyptians, built huge pyramids and sealed bodies of their god-kings inside."

"God-kings." Tsur Selkie glanced up at the carving, at the sightless face gazing at us from the past. Not even Tsur Selkie could win a staring competition with a statue, though, so he looked away.

They finished the last of the machine-based tests then, and moved on to trying Place Sight. Place Sight hasn't really been very helpful in the explorations so far, because the events the Tarens are interested in happened so long ago that the 'impressions' have faded. But Place Sight is a really broad and adaptable Sight, and there was a chance they'd be able to understand the mechanism of the doors.

Ruuel, Halla and Tsur Selkie enhanced. I'm not sure if Tsur Selkie has Place Sight, but Sight Sight is no doubt just as useful here. They told Halla to go first, and remembering what had happened with the platforms the first time someone touched them, I was a bit nervous, but there was no reaction and no Ddura or anything else turning up. Halla closed her eyes, pressing her hand flat against the smooth stone and, I think, holding her breath.

"It only has the appearance of doors," she said, after a long pause. "As the scans suggested, the stone has been fashioned as a solid panel. The aether–" She paused. "It appears to be maintaining the structure. If we damaged it, it is very likely it would reform."

Dropping her hand, she stepped away, being all super-professional. But when Ruuel nodded she relaxed a little, relieved and pleased. It's so interesting how the squads react to their captains. These are people that they've grown up with, known almost all their lives, and probably competed with for the captaincy. But Fourth Squad, even Glade, who really doesn't seem the type, act like Ruuel's approval is tremendously important to them. Third Squad's the same with Taarel. It's a combination of respect and trust, I guess. I found out today that Fourth also treat Ruuel much as First Squad does Maze.

Once Halla had stepped back, Ruuel moved forward, making his gloves go away. It made me think of what he looked like this morning – such a long time ago now – and I had to work to not be too distracted by the memory of bare shoulders and neck. I really don't ever see most of the Setari in anything but all-covering uniforms, so it seems like a lot more than I guess it really was: nothing compared to Lohn walking in on me. Like Halla, Ruuel closed his eyes, then carefully touched the tips of his fingers to the stone and I was looking at the length of his lashes and wondering if he plucked his eyebrows when I realised that he was slowly going white.

I looked from his face to his squad's, and found them all with variations of the same worried expression. Tsur Selkie was more evaluating, but he was also watching Ruuel's face with a hint of tension, as if he was ready to step forward and catch someone about to faint. Which Ruuel didn't do, just opening his eyes again. But there were beads of sweat on his forehead, and he looked like he'd taken a fist to the stomach and refused to admit it.

"They were trying to escape," he said, voice steady in a way which took effort. "It sealed, and they could not open it."

He stepped away, recovering enough to shut down into a professional mask, and Tsur Selkie moved forward without comment, doing little more than to confirm Halla's evaluation of the door with an addendum that he suspected the 'seal' extended at least to the corridor beyond and possibly through the entire complex.

First Squad is quietly protective of Maze. And Fourth Squad's the same about Ruuel. They spent the rest of the day pretending they weren't keeping a watchful eye on him. And Ruuel spent the day looking distracted, still caught up in whatever he'd seen or felt about the last moments of the people sealed inside. Not so bad that Selkie took him off duty, but a visible difference to his usual observant and distant air.

The whole thing made me think a lot of Zan, too. Does anyone in her squad respect her? Want to protect her? That prompted me to write a long email to her talking about the things we'd been doing on the mission. The satellite isn't positioned to directly connect us to Pandora, but she'll have it already if she's still there, or will with the next ship if she's back on Tare. I hope she's okay.

The rest of the day was filled with even longer doses of dull. The Setari tried to open the seal using Ena manipulation, without any effect, and even had me try. Glade whispered to me afterwards that it was very tactless of me to look so glad I failed. And now they're bringing some equipment in to try and set up a field to interrupt the flow of aether, or drain it off. They really don't want to smash their way in, or do anything by force.

Still, the horde of archaeologists are cleaning up the central area very nicely.

Thursday, April 10

Kolarens and crypts

I do wonder where the Tarens get all these tents. Their own planet is totally unsuited to tents as a form of accommodation: too incredibly windy. I suppose they might use tents inside the few caves they haven't filled with whitestone. Whatever they usually use them for, they certainly have a lot of them. By sunset yesterday, the greensuits had constructed a little canvas city around the outer slope of the northern mountain. Currently the mountains are being referred to (in Taren) as North, South and East, even though I think they've been given more official names. North is the mountain on the Nurioth side, and East is the one furthest from the lake. The south mountain has the equipment and 'finds' tents at its base, though the main finds so far have been the fragmentary remains of two skeletons which turned up under the tumble of whitestone in the centre of the circular paths.

Because of the wait for the *Litara* to return with the equipment to try on the seals, the central circle's been getting a lot of attention and is looking increasingly bare – great patches of raw earth and freshly cleaned pathway. It's not a bulls-eye pattern, but a more complex set of part-circles and radial lines, and I think it would make a nice garden. The greysuits are talking about trying to reconstruct the central structure.

I spent the morning doing school work, since Fourth Squad had left right after breakfast to map out all the nearby gates. They found some buildings, too, off under the trees a ways down south, which the greysuits are hoping are related to this site. Ninth Squad is stuck with the more boring guard duty, broken into pairs assigned to different shifts, since the Ddura seems to have taken care of any active threats in the area. With so many people here, I decided to stay out of the way and found myself a natural seat on a big stony shelf overlooking the mess tent. It was an unusually warm day compared to recent temperatures, nice and sunny.

Having grown a little more used to how long it takes the greysuits to do anything, my only reaction to the *Litara* arriving with the new equipment was to access the latest news feeds: little parcels of the latest public infocasts collected each time one of the ships returns to Tare. There's a ton in them about Muina, of course, but very little of depth, and I was more interested in whether the Ionoth incursions back on Tare had gone back to normal levels. The Setari have re-established most of their rotations, and the only story I could find was about long-term upward trends.

When I was first given access, I used to close my eyes when using the interface. Now I'm more able to watch *and* see the world around me at the same time, but I by no means pay attention to my surroundings. And thus I was very confused by sudden movement right next to me and the soft sound of an impact. Suspending the news feed, I saw a couple of people standing over me, wearing a dark green and black uniform. My brain sluggishly caught up to what my eyes had recorded, and I realised one of them had tried to kick me and another had stepped in the way, catching her foot.

"Don't start this, Katzyen," said the catcher, a guy who sounded more resigned than annoyed. "It's not what we're here for." I found it very hard to understand what he was saying, but didn't immediately realise they were talking in a different dialect.

"If they'd had their way we wouldn't be here at all." The second speaker was a small woman with sparking-hot green eyes, whose temper seemed set to nuclear smoulder. "Wouldn't you say it's only in the spirit of our alliance to test their level of combat training?" She shot a disparaging glance at me. "If you're an example of the standard we're constantly tested against, there's nothing to Taren Setari except their reputation. Can you prove yourself the better?"

That was my introduction to Kolar's Setari. Kolarens started out with the same language as Tarens, but it's become quite a distinct dialect. They pronounced the words oddly enough that my translation suggestions weren't being very helpful. Anyway, my response was to stare at her blankly, finally figure out that she wanted me to spar with her, and say: "Would be short fight."

This made her look even more annoyed, and some other Kolarens who'd been approaching stopped where they were. I guess they thought I was saying I could take Katzyen with one hand tied behind my back.

Before I'd done more than realise I was about to get a fist in the face, rescue showed up in the form of Tsur Selkie, who did one of those suddenly-just-there-in-the-way appearances that people with Speed talent are so good at. One of Ninth Squad – a guy called Thomasal – zipped up a moment later. It's not as if my seat wasn't in the full sight of half the camp, after all, and Thomasal was camp guard of the moment. I'd been expecting him to show up, but not Selkie.

The Kolarens had the same reaction to Selkie as the Taren Setari. They went all upright and parade-ground. He didn't act like he'd interrupted a scene, just glanced over them, then said: "This is Caszandra Devlin. Your briefing material will include the requirements regarding interaction with her. Remember two points. First: Devlin's system cannot handle contact with multiple talent users. The seizures such contact causes would be fatal without medical intervention. Second: as part of this detachment your priority, above all else, is to keep her alive." He looked at me, adding: "You have a security alert for a reason," then signalled for Thomasal to follow him and left.

The Kolarens had gone interesting colours. They're a great deal more tanned than Tarens, and tend more to brown and blonde hair than black, though they still appear to have a combination of Asian and Caucasian ancestry. They all looked to be around twenty. The guy who'd stopped Katzyen from hitting me reminded me immensely of the movie version of Lawrence of Arabia, except younger and without the flowing robes and headgear. I turned on my interface name display to see that he was called Arad Nalaz.

"I couldn't fight my way out of wet paper bag," I told Katzyen, feeling sorry for her now she'd stopped being aggressive and had gone dull red. "Would be very short fight because I lose straight away. Maybe we start this conversation over again?"

One of the Kolarens, golden-brown and medium-tall, began to laugh. "We've certainly managed a strong first impression." He came closer, and did a quick hand to chest bow. "I'm Raiten Shaf and I think it's very unfortunate of you to be dressed as a Taren Setari if you're not."

"Assigned to Setari," I explained. "Sometimes go into Ena with them so need uniform's protection." The Kolaren Setari weren't wearing nanosuits, though, and have to carry actual weapons for close combat instead of growing them.

"You're the, ah, displaced person from the world called Earth?" asked a very burnished woman named Laram Diav.

"Yes. Is Kolaren Setari here to baby-sit archaeologist horde too?"

"That's – well, probably not an inaccurate description." Shaf grinned. "So you have seizures if people touch you? That's quite an allergy."

"Only if too many people touch me at once," I said, then my face went hot. "Pretend that didn't sound strange. You think Taren Setari not want you here?"

Shaf gave Katzyen an exasperated glance. "No. But we have spent what felt a short eternity being told that technical details of our contribution needed to be finalised."

"Excuse after excuse, delaying any of us from coming to Muina," Katzyen said. "We wouldn't even know that a settlement had been established, if they'd had their way."

"No-one on Tare would either, probably. But Setari don't make that decision." I shrugged. "Give you unofficial welcome, anyway. Is beautiful place."

That produced the classic exiled-Muinan expression, and the Kolaren Setari ended up spending the rest of the morning up on my rock shelf having a discussion about Earth and Muina and how I'd ended up at Pandora and then Tare. They seemed like nice people. Less formal than Taren Setari; or more like the older squads. It was impossible to miss the deep resentment they hold toward Tarens. Tare basically showed up fifty years ago and started messing with their world. Kolar was in something like the Gaslight era while Tarens had had the interface for decades, and advanced nanotech for something like seventy years. Other than the Kolaren Setari program and the whitestone building material, Tare hasn't yet allowed Kolar anything like the full extent of their technology – only their Setari program had been allowed use of the interface. It sounds like their approach has been a little on the paternalist side, with a strong eye to profit. Almost guaranteed to cause offence.

I'd love to know what Tsur Selkie's reasons were for leaving me to be the Kolaren Setari's introduction to this site. It didn't last too long: the arrival of the *Litara* had been Fourth Squad's signal to head back and Ruuel sent me one of his characteristically word-stingy messages: "Testing before lunch." He must have sent one to Shaf as well (he's the Kolaren squad's captain) since he reacted at the same time. Hopefully he got a little more explanation, but he did look kind of quizzical when he said: "Time to move, it seems."

We went down to meet Fourth Squad, who were waiting near the finds tent, watching the construction of some really complicated machine around the door of South Mountain. As usual, Ruuel brought everyone into mission channel as soon as we were in sight of each other, and began briefing and leading us all further south, to an area which was mainly low bushes.

"Contact with Devlin enhances and sometimes warps talents. This session is to verify the effect of Devlin on your available talent sets, then to practice movement and multiple squad enhancement rotations in combat simulation. We don't have adequate test shielding here, so push elementals to far range. Sonn."

"Unenhanced," Sonn said, and shot a lightning bolt outward and upwards. She touched the tips of her fingers to my arm. "Enhanced."

I guess no-one had mentioned the enhancement effects to the Kolarens. A few of them looked briefly incredulous as the ball of lightning arced and spat in the air, drifting slowly away.

"The distortion has been consistent, and observed effects on each talent are listed in the briefing material." Ruuel gave Shaf one of his captain-nods and Fourth Squad stepped back, obviously handing over to him.

Fourth Squad was an interesting choice to end up first to work with a bunch of Kolarens with chips on their shoulders. There's plenty of squads which might have soothed some of that resentment; certainly First Squad could put anyone at their ease. And some who wouldn't want to: it was a damn good thing that it wasn't Fifth Squad, who would have guaranteed that interplanetary relations developed an Ice Age. But Ruuel – Ruuel is always so focused on getting the job done, as quickly and painlessly as possible, and obviously doesn't see any point measuring himself or his squad against other people, or trying to prove anything at all. He behaved exactly as if the Kolarens were any squad who hadn't worked with me before, with every expectation that they would just get on with it.

Shaf's obviously good at adapting to the unexpected, and had Nalaz start out with Wind, buying himself some time to review the briefing material they won't let me see. They tested without anything odd happening, and then there was a precise, exacting session of enhancement, whizzing about with Telekinesis, and fake combat, and I was very amused to see Katzyen trying not to look pleased because she'd earned one of Ruuel's brief, approving nods. He has that effect on people.

He was back to being his usual focused self today, but there were dark shadows under his eyes. I don't think he slept much last night. He's asleep two pods away from me right now, and I hope he has a better night.

The training session was winding down when I started hearing the Ddura. It says something for my chances of hiding my feelings for Ruuel that he always seems to know when I'm debating telling him something. He said, "Hold," to the squads, then looked at me. "The Ddura?"

I nodded. "Sounds anxious."

"Hunting?"

"No. The confused noise." I transmitted what I was hearing into the squad channel, and watched his eyes narrow.

He added Tsur Selkie to the channel, then said: "Either a reaction to the machine itself, or to a threat to the site's integrity."

"Continue the relay, Devlin," was all Selkie said to us, but he obviously said a whole lot on other channels since there was a sudden exodus of people out of the central circle toward the edge of the lake.

The tone of the Ddura's call changed almost immediately. "Now partly question noise, but mainly unhappy noise," I said helpfully over the interface, then asked Shaf aloud: "Kolar has dogs, right?"

He wasn't surprised by my hearing the Ddura, so I guessed he'd gotten through my 'briefing material', and just nodded in answer to my question.

"Ddura acts like very big dog." I looked back at Ruuel. "This sounds like one not know Muinans back. Ddura at Pandora stopped making this cry."

"Security identification has been reapplied," Tsur Selkie said. "Stand by."

The Ddura paused mid-moan, making the confused sound again, then the question noise. But then it switched back to being mournful.

"Security identification had been placed on the power unit," Selkie said, sounding satisfied. "Evidently that isn't sufficient to cover a machine using that power unit. The device looks as if it will be successful, however."

He left the channel, and Ruuel said: "Keep lunch brief. If the site is opened, both squads will go in as point team."

I'm guessing he had a private channel open to Shaf, since they walked off together. I dropped out of mission channel as well, and glanced at two squads of Setari who were going to go on being super-correct at each other, but at least didn't seem to be openly hostile. I've no doubt Fourth Squad knew that Katzyen had started out spoiling for a fight, but they would follow Ruuel's lead. Ruuel's lead wasn't exactly chatty, though, and everyone was silent as we started walking back to the mess tent.

"Are Kolaren squads numbered as well?" I asked Taranza, who looked to be around my age rather than the couple of years older the other Kolarens seemed to be. She had short, streaky blonde hair and less of a tan than the others, and a way of looking around with wide-eyed appreciation which I liked. "Like this is Fourth Squad, and the other squad here is Ninth Squad?"

"We're First Squad," Taranza said, with a faintly apologetic glance at the Taren Setari. "That *is* going to cause some confusion."

Both squads ended up talking that over during lunch, even Sonn making one or two suggestions. The Ninth Squad captain, whose watch was about to start and who was eating breakfast when we reached the mess tent, ended up deciding that we could use a variation which was the equivalent of 'Squad One' and it would still mean the same thing and the Kolarens seemed okay with that, though I expect they'll keeping calling themselves 'First Squad' in their own dialect.

Islen Tezart explained that the machine his team had been building created a counter field of aether to hold the site's own aether field back from the doorway around South Mountain. Then they used the same sort of nanotech which they create their buildings with to eat the seal – and only the seal – away. The counter field machine formed an ugly frame about the opening, but it was done.

Going in as 'point team' was delayed by what was on the far side of the seal. Ruuel's initial reaction had prepared me a little and I'd expected there would be the skeletons of the people who'd been trapped inside, but no-one had guessed at the sheer number. Dozens, maybe hundreds, packed into a short entry corridor and hexagonal room beyond. How many were crushed by the panicked press trying to escape? The seal had preserved them well, too: leathery skin stretched over grey bone, cloth still whole, although so fragile a touch would probably destroy it. They were almost all lying facing outward, withered hands stretched forward or covering their heads. I guess it was the Ddura which they were running from. Something which caught and killed them all together.

Imaging from scans had already shown us the general outline of the underground rooms: five ring-like levels, each smaller than the previous one until finally there was what seemed to be a single room, sitting at the centre point between the three mountains. Once I'd seen how huge the place was I wasn't surprised the Tarens had thrown a big portion of their resources at this place. The site commander wanted the Setari to sweep the rooms of this part of this level for anything which sparked their Combat Sight – monsters, traps, invisible lurking death – and if possible locate the communication platform and maybe whatever was generating the aether field. Islen Duffen wasn't very pleased with the Setari going in first, even though they were under orders to levitate as much as possible to avoid disturbing anything. But since the massive battle she seems more inclined to listen to what the Setari have to say, at least where safety is concerned. She wants me to tell her more about Earth history when she has time, but since we found this site she's worked non-stop and looks ready to drop, so I don't know when that will happen.

The walls inside the site glowed: the same sort of glow made in Pandora during moonfall, but with no free-flowing aether. It meant we didn't have to worry about lights, at least. Fourth and 'Squad One' split into their respective teams, and worked their way along a main central passage, moving apart to follow side-corridors and enter rooms, and then joining up again. One thing they found out almost immediately was that the ramps down were sealed like the entrances, and when we met a longer connecting passageway on this level, it was also sealed. So we've only gained access to one third of the top level.

It was a town, not a tomb. I've no idea why any of the old Muinans would want to live underground – the issue of ventilation alone would be enough to make it less than ideal – but every room we looked in seemed to be living quarters, except for occasional ones which were water sources or gathering areas. Nothing leapt out at us and there were no traps. The communication platform was in the room at the end of the long 'spoke' passage and after a tedious amount of back and forth discussion they had Sonn try to use the platform to deactivate the seals. Didn't work, did produce an ecstatic Ddura, but fortunately going back outside was next on our schedule.

The technology group spent the afternoon constructing another machine around the entrance to North Mountain, while the archaeologists broke into two teams: one painstakingly untangling the human wreckage just within the entrance, and the other working on the nearest of the rooms. The archaeologists are so tremendously excited. It's not that everything was perfectly preserved or anything, but there had been very few places at Pandora and Nurioth which hadn't been exposed to wind and rain and been pulled about by animals. And, of course, it's working old Lantaren technology. I don't know if this is the big break we need to fix the spaces, but it's the first major find since Tare gained 'security clearance'.

My Ddura-headache wasn't too bad, but I was feeling tired as well, so I was glad when Ruuel sent us back to the *Diodel*. Squad One is sleeping on the *Litara*, which is staying for the night. Most of the expedition is sleeping in the tent city, but while the Taren Setari are more accustomed to being outside because they're trained to go into the spaces, the Sight talents especially find it difficult to sleep without the shielding on our pods or their rooms back on Tare. Combat Sight reacts to people coming near them, for a start.

Ruuel was absent, as he often is during meals, and I had a feeling Fourth Squad would probably talk about Squad One if I wasn't there, so I headed for a shower and bed straight after dinner.

I was sitting sideways on my pod seat braiding my hair when Ruuel showed up from wherever he'd been. "Devlin. Have you seen the cat Ionoth since the infirmary?"

This wasn't a question I wanted to answer. But it also seemed weird for him to suddenly bring it up. I blinked, then guessed why he was asking. "You've been warning Kolaren captain about silly things I might do that he has to watch out for?"

"Yes." Very straightforward, very typical. "You've sighted it, I take it? Report it next time."

If there's ever a time I really do need to lie to Ruuel, I'm going to have no chance at all. And I didn't think I could just pretend I was going to do what he said, either. "I do most things told to because either make sense to me, or don't see any choice. Ghost I handed over once, so tests could be run, but not going to do again."

Other than a couple of fits of temper I've had with the medics, I think that was the first time I've refused to do what I was told since I was rescued – and Ruuel is really the last person I want to say no to. I felt pretty nervous about his reaction, but he just looked steadily at me a moment, then said: "And if it proves less innocuous than you believe? You will not be able to undo any damage it causes."

"Just because she not turn into evil, people-eating kitten in the past not mean she won't one day? May as well lock me back up in case I decide run around stab people."

"The cat has a better chance of landing a blow," he said, totally straight-faced, and shook his head, apparently deciding it wasn't worth pressing the point. "Get some rest."

I felt like telling him to practice what he preached, since the shadows under his eyes were worse than ever, but I was too disconcerted by more evidence of a sense of humour (or, just possibly, proof that he is totally bereft of one and is saying these things without a shred of irony). Besides, he was already walking away.

I'm finding I like waking up a lot earlier than everyone else, not least because it gives me a chance to write up the day in this diary without anyone looking at me curiously, but today I wish I'd stayed in the dream I was having. I was lying curled up with Ruuel, not talking or doing anything, just curled up in a dark, quiet place listening to him breathe, to his heart beating. It was an uneventful but intense dream, and incredibly real. When I woke up I felt so content, so happy, I wanted to go straight back to sleep.

Must find cure for besotted goopiness.

Sweat

Each of the main entrances are open now, and each third was very much the same inside. Corpses just inside the seal, and then living quarters beyond. We haven't found anything which was obviously controlling the seal, and won't be opening any more levels until more machine parts arrive. The technicians weren't expecting to have to build dozens of the things. The *Litara*'s gone off to fetch that and other construction-related items, as they've begun the first stages of building the settlement, which is going to be called Arenrhon after some Taren historical figure.

Ruuel decided his squad was getting out of shape and started them on an evil training regimen. Being in good physical condition lessens the strain of using their talents, and these constantly 'on-mission' days without their usual training facilities means Fourth haven't had much opportunity for strength training. So they did lots of jogging and chin lifts and things like that. And since I'm assigned to Fourth, I got to do it as well, except – thankfully – only about a quarter of what Ruuel put everyone else through. That still nearly killed me.

It was bearable, though. Things I could obviously not do – like chin lifts – he didn't make me stick at, and had me do milder versions instead. I didn't enjoy the day, but I got through it, and Fourth Squad were good at not making me feel embarrassed about being comparatively pathetic.

Friday, April 11

It's all a question of angles

Today I taught a handful of greensuits and greysuits and three Setari squads how to skip stones. I was waiting around for Fourth to come back from their longer-than-mine training run, and since it was a very still day and this lakeshore is even pebblier than Pandora's, I entertained myself by collecting a bunch of stones and seeing if I could best my record (seven skips).

My arms were tired from push-ups, though, and the best I could manage was four skips, and was looking around for more stones when I realised I had a small audience: two greensuits and a greysuit looking immensely puzzled. Their question – "But, how?" – says something about how different their planets are from Earth. Kolar isn't entirely desert, but it's a dry world and most of its water is in underground Springs, while Tare is all massively violent oceans. By the time Fourth got back I had most of Squad One and two from Ninth lined up in a row.

Ruuel let Fourth have a break to play around, but didn't try himself, going off to be captainly. Glade easily beat my own record, and asked what the maximum was people could do on Earth, but I didn't know. I think when he taught me Dad said something about people doing over thirty skips, but that always seemed a bit much to be right. Par Auron took the record today – eight skips. At least half the Setari could skip better than me on their second or third try. They're just good at physical tasks, not to mention strong.

Then it was more exercise: stretches and lifting big water containers Ruuel had borrowed from the greensuits. Fortunately we're doing all this training in a clearing a little north of the tents, so I didn't have to deal with an audience. I think every muscle I have is sore.

Saturday, April 12

Museum exhibit

Uneventful day. You'd think exploring lost alien underground cities would be more dramatic, but going through the second level of the installation, which required another three machines to hold open the entrances, was very much a repetition of the first level. More living quarters, larger ones. Fewer bodies. Wood well-preserved, metal tarnished, cloth fragile. Not much writing. The Lantaren caste of the Muinans did use a written language, but non-Lantarens apparently weren't literate. Other than a couple of inscriptions on pots and statues (possibly the names of people – the alphabet has mutated a fair deal and I can only half read it), I didn't spot anything written down. Definitely no library, or manual of instructions, or super-secret plans. No field projector we could turn off, either.

One thing all this has made clear to me is I would not have made a good archaeologist. I don't have nearly the patience for it. I concentrated on my school work during the waiting about, and watched a handful of greensuits who seem to have fallen in love with stone skipping. And tried not to look at the smooth white scar of the new settlement. I don't like to think too much about the impact I've had on this world.

Sunday, April 13

Large and loud

This morning Fourth Squad and I went into near-space, trying to work our way down to the lowest levels of the installation through the gaps in the walls that only exist in near-space. But the aether shield exists there as well, and though we did go down to the second level through the holes the machines were maintaining, we couldn't find any way through to the lower levels.

And the Ddura came and looked at us while we were there, which was really disconcerting. It's just like a humungous cloud of coloured light, and felt like tingly ice crystals on my face. And was tremendously happy about the Setari, who all could hear it in near-space. It Hhhaaaa'd enough that even Ruuel couldn't hide how much he wished it would shut up. The greysuits were tremendously interested in the data we brought back about the Ddura, and Fourth

Squad all went and lay down for a while. The technology group is growing concerned about having so many of the field-disrupting machines operating together and is going to undo a few of them and open a single path downward in only the first of the thirds. Lots of standing about guarding them while they do that for the Setari.

I stuck with the lying down.

Monday, April 14

Worship

The third level of the installation seems to be some kind of church. Maybe. It was empty of anything resembling furniture, just had carved images of the same woman all over the walls, and mosaics all over the floors. Everywhere the same beautiful, idealised woman, with rivers flowing from her tears, and animals (pippins!) hiding in the folds of her skirts, and forests unwinding from her long flowing hair.

Fourth Squad went very expressionless when looking through this area, and no-one is entirely certain if this is meant to represent their world mother-goddess. There are three entrances to the facility, and the faces above each entrance look different. This woman matches the face above the door for this third, so everyone is wondering, if this is Muina, who are the other two faces meant to be?

Since the levels have been decreasing in size, they'd been expecting to clear down to the lowest level today, but they don't seem to be able to get their machine to work on the next shield. After spending the entire afternoon standing around watching them not be able to figure out how to get through, Ruuel decided his squad could do with some close-combat training to get the kinks out. This unfortunately included me, with Sonn as my partner. But though she gave me a heck of a bruise on my leg because she expected me to have some faint ability to dodge, Sonn was otherwise a methodical and practical teacher.

Squad One joined in after a while. They haven't all magically stopped resenting Tarens, but they've decided Fourth Squad are decent enough at their jobs and not to blame for a few decades of interplanetary politics. Or, more importantly, Fourth Squad don't act like they think Kolaren Setari aren't as good as Taren Setari, and so Squad One don't constantly have their hackles up.

That didn't mean both squads weren't interested in how they measured up to each other at close combat. Particularly Katzyen (her first name is Meral). And Fourth Squad is after all still human and took the matches seriously. Neither squad seemed definitively better. As he usually does, Ruuel was instructing rather than participating – I think he avoids competitive situations – but I wasn't at all surprised when Katzyen asked him to spar with her.

He agreed matter-of-factly, since it was one thing to avoid competition and another to put her back up by treating her as no competition at all. I doubt he wants too many Kajals obsessing over him. In a way he got that anyway, though not in a hostile way. After countering and avoiding Katzyen's attacks for a while, as she pushed to even come near him, he ended the fight with what looked like tidy and untroubled efficiency. And told her to work on attacks from the left, since she was weaker with those.

She's barely taken her eyes off him since. Being comprehensively bettered at hand-to-hand combat isn't my idea of a turn-on, but it obviously worked for Katzyen. I think it might have worked for Diav as well, and a couple of the greensuits who'd been watching from a distance. Unsurprisingly, Ruuel failed to show any awareness of newly-earned admiration. His squad all noticed: Glade highly amused, Mori tolerant, Sonn dismissive, Halla distant, and Par just a little pink.

I'm getting to know them, settling into a new 'my' squad. Four months since I was rescued. Five months since I was walking home from my last exam and took a wrong turning. I'd be well into my first year of university by now – presuming I did well enough to get in. Jules' birthday soon, and then Mother's Day. The days add up.

Tuesday, April 15

Uncomfortable belief

Lately I've been dreaming consistently of Ruuel: vaguer versions of the dream I had of being curled up with him asleep, which has made me look forward to heading off to bed. Last night, though, I dreamed that Fourth Squad had been transferred out overnight, and I was now assigned to Seventh Squad. No-one even told me they were gone: I just found Forel and her cronies having breakfast. And then...it was all a confused jumble, but involved more of the training I've been doing the last couple of days, except with Seventh Squad making smart-ass comments at my expense. And I was all crushed and humiliated and hurt because Fourth had gone without saying goodbye. Not Ruuel so much, since he's always so captain with me, but Mori and Glade and Par – even Halla's chatting with me a little now, and Sonn doesn't disapprove of me quite so much. And they were just gone without a word, on to their next assignment.

I guess the dream is a reaction to working so much with Fourth these last weeks, to starting to feel like I belong with them. My subconscious was reminding me I'm not part of any squad, that I will always be a temporary assignment. That Mori and Glade probably chat to me because Ruuel told them to.

Fortunately I'm still waking up long before most everyone else. After a shower and a morning spent writing email to Zee and Mara and Zan, I'd gained enough perspective to not look obviously depressed. And it's not as if I think they're planning to change my assignment in the near future, since Fourth is the only squad with a Sight Sight talent. It's funny how the Nuran's attempt to warn me off prompted the Tarens to drag me around Muina's ruins on the off-chance that they can figure out what he meant.

No progress on breaking through to the next level today, so they opened up the other parts of the third level instead. It was all more murals and carvings and mosaics, but with two different people playing the role of god-like being: a man and a different woman. All a little confronting for ex-Muinans. So far as they know, the Lantarens enjoyed an unquestioned right to rule, but were not considered gods, and the Tarens are very uncomfortable with imagery which so obviously treats them *as* gods. Well, presuming these were meant to be Lantarens and not some gods that the Tarens don't remember anyone believing in. Maybe this is the not-very-secret base of a cult or something.

Muinan culture must have been very unified before they had to leave. Given the similarity of Kolar, Nuri and Tare's languages, they must have all started out speaking the same way. But I guess the similarity was partly a result of having a single ruling class which could teleport and travel through wormholes and, according to Katha, were all raised and taught to control their powers at some kind of central imperial training city. Not Nurioth – a place called Kalasa, though the Tarens don't know much more than the name. Figuring out which of the ruined cities is Kalasa is another expedition priority.

The greysuits had some heartfelt discussions about the murals. Dase and Katha, who I only occasionally get a chance to talk to now that they've been moved out of the *Diodel* to the tent city, were divided on the question. Dase thinks the murals must be representations of Muina and two unknown gods, or possibly even aspects of Muina. Katha thinks it's three Lantarens. Since the Lantarens aren't held in great esteem on Tare, I'm not precisely sure why it's so upsetting for her to see images showing they were incredibly narcissistic. But then, Tare and Kolar both have a fairly unified view of what a god is (or rather they don't believe in gods, they believe planets have spirits).

Anya from Ninth, who has been stuck on night watch since Ninth Squad was rotated here, unfortunately has been moved to day watch. Urg. She and Katzyen really aren't benefiting by being on the same schedule, and though they're not openly glaring at each other, there's a distinct frost which seems to be extending to all the Taren Setari.

Which is the main reason I was eating dinner with Dase and Katha.

Wednesday, April 16

Killing time

Fourth Squad's gone off gate-mapping again today, since there's been no progress in getting to the next level of Creepy Undercity. I had one of my regularly scheduled medical exams in the morning, during which the medic noted I had a big bruise on my leg from training and a few random minor bruises and sore bits, but otherwise was the healthiest I'd been since the last time I nearly died. The amount of sitting-about I get through continues to benefit my school work, and I've moved on to marginally more interesting classes. Even though my spelling is pathetic, my comprehension has increased enough that I can push through most lessons super-quick. But it's still frustrating, rather like this site, which everyone thought was such a big discovery, but which hasn't given us any explanations at all.

The day's growing cloudy and win–

–

Okay, pissed off now. I was sitting at the outside tables in the mess area writing when I heard someone gasp and stumble next to me, nearly dropping the drinks they were carrying. I didn't hear the crunch, but I glanced up to see a couple of greysuits looking guiltily at the ground at my thoroughly trodden-on watch.

My face must have shown exactly what I felt – kicked in the guts – because they went from sorry to stricken, the one not holding the drinks rushing to pick up my watch and turn it over hopefully, only to have the back fall off. It was just an el cheapo digital, $20. The face was cracked and dead and I totally felt like crying.

But I didn't. I'm proud of that in retrospect, of holding it together enough to look around me, just a log-capture in every direction. I told the greysuits that it was okay – not that they believed me for a second – and took the bits of my watch and went back to the *Diodel*. I had my schoolbag with me, tucked into the end of my pod, and grabbed out my long-neglected mobile. The battery had run down ages ago, and I hadn't chased up finding out how it had been charged since I'd copied the music into my interface already. Then I found one of the science greysuits and asked if she had any idea how it had been recharged.

Her name was Elless Royara and she took my phone like it was a brand new toy, but all she had to do was look up the records of whatever they'd done before, then put it in a thing which looked like a microwave, but recharged instead of frying my mobile. It seems it wasn't really a difficult thing to do: the Tarens have gone through a few centuries of equipment becoming obsolete, and have plenty of practice working out ways to recharge older, 'museum' pieces.

After thanking Elless I went back to the *Diodel* and turned on my phone. It had been so long the date and time needed to be reset, but I could at least make a rough guesstimate of what proper Sydney time would be, and of course the date hadn't changed from when I'd started writing in my diary.

Only then did I let myself relax, and review my log.

I almost always wear my watch underneath my uniform, unless it's a mission or some other situation where I think I might get soaked. But I often take it off when I'm writing, because the buckle presses into my wrist. I'd set it on the corner of the table, near my elbow. It wasn't in my peripheral vision, and I suppose it's within the bounds of possibility that I'd knocked it off and it had bounced onto the rocky ground next to me and got itself crushed.

But I didn't really believe that, and a careful review of my log showed me Terel Revv from Ninth watching. Revv's one of Anya's cronies, and a telekinetic. Not proof, of course, and he was actually looking pretty unhappy.

They probably didn't realise how important it is to me, to know what date it is on Earth. To know when I should be wishing my family happy birthday, to mark the dates of the year back home. To be able to keep track of my own age.

I don't see that there's anything to gain from making a fuss. I'll be more careful not to give people opportunities, and certainly won't sit out in public writing my diary again, or leave my mobile exposed. I need to remember that I'm someone who total strangers will feel strongly about: whether to be grateful I unlocked their world, or to hate me for threatening their ideas of Muina's past, or whatever Anya has against me.

The Setari needs fewer assholes.

Pass/Fail

Fuss happens, whether I want it to or not.

After venting in my diary, I hung about the deserted 'passenger lounge' of the *Diodel* fooling with my newly revived mobile, listening to proper played-out-loud songs while it grew darker and windier outside. Then Tsur Selkie showed up with Ruuel in tow. Time for a pause in the music.

"Do you have your damaged wrist-piece with you?" Tsur Selkie asked, without preliminaries. He and Ruuel are alike in more than looks; since he considered it obvious why he was there, he didn't think it necessary to explain.

I was momentarily tempted to pretend I'd thrown it away, but even in the unlikely event they believed me, they could have just used Path Sight. I expect I didn't look very keen as I pulled it out of the little pocket I'd made for it, though.

"How did you know?" I asked, dropping it into his outstretched hand.

"The technician who crushed it was concerned about the strength of your reaction, and reported to his senior. One of the site guards on duty had you on log, including your survey of the area." Selkie wore gloves on both hands, one of them fingerless, and looked down as he touched a bare fingertip to the cracked face of my watch. He didn't take more than a moment or two, and his face didn't give anything away as he handed the watch to Ruuel, but I knew he must have seen something to confirm my suspicions because he went on to ask: "Have there been other incidents?"

I shook my head. "It was just I didn't think I knocked it on ground." Then, because neither of them looked like he believed me, I shrugged and added: "There's squads I rather not be assigned to, but no-one tried to break my things or hurt me or anything before."

"Which squads?" Selkie asked immediately.

"Expect you have good idea," I said, annoyed.

"Indulge me."

I thought about it, then decided it was nothing I wasn't prepared to say if I were assigned to them. "Fifth and Seventh so far. Wouldn't feel safe going into Ena with either captain, so would rather not. Ninth, I didn't feel that way about." Ruuel handed back my watch and I looked down at it, remembering the sick stabbing feeling in my stomach. "They probably not realise what it mean to me."

"Not the object but the function, yes?" Selkie said, reaching to pick up my mobile. "This device can replace it?"

"Both have the date on Earth. That needs recharging every five or six days."

Selkie gave it back to me, added a little nod and left.

"What will happen now?" I asked, since Ruuel hadn't gone immediately after him.

"Reprimand for any involved. The squad will return to Tare for review, then likely be stood down and reformed with personnel changes."

All for knocking my watch onto the ground. I felt ill.

Ruuel gave me an impatient look. "Don't overreact. Ninth has needed to be rebalanced since it was formed. Failing this assignment is only the trigger."

I was confused what assignment he was talking about, until I realised he meant me. Protecting me is the Setari's primary assignment here. I expect that emotionally screwing over someone you're supposed to be looking after would count as failing.

"They forgot the psychological aspects," I said, letting myself find it funny.

I've no doubt Ruuel knew I was quoting him, but he didn't break out of serious captain mode. "Concentrating on a practical solution was a good response," he said. "But you continue to hesitate to communicate when you most need to. It's not only your own welfare you put at risk."

"Today more choosing not to speak," I pointed out. "But generally don't see how to decide what's important."

"Don't try. If anything prompts you to wonder if you should inform us, or ask for help, then always assume the answer is yes. The same rule should serve for speculation about these sites. Parallels with Earth's cultures could be misleading, but we cannot judge their worth if we do not hear them."

I looked out the long view port, to the triangle of mountain and camp which I could see from that part of the ship. It wasn't raining yet, but people were getting under cover, the greensuits making sure all the tents were secure. It was true I'd been stopping myself from sharing any more guesses about the installation, not wanting to waste the historians' time.

"What did you feel when you touched that door?" I asked. Ruuel didn't answer, and I turned back to find him even more than usually shuttered. Rather than make a point about people communicating, I continued: "Could you tell if it was Ddura which kill them?"

"No." He paused. "Fear, panic, anger, overwhelming betrayal. A sense of something approaching, but no tangible impression of its form."

"Was talking to Dase and Katha yesterday about how whole thing doesn't make sense to the historians," I said. "Accepted Taren history says Lantarens decided to make space travel easier, built Pillars. Pillars tore gates everywhere including between real-space and near-space, and Ionoth started killing people on Muina. Lantarens built Ddura to kill Ionoth and to try and make it easier to get to the Pillars. Something happened that made them lose control of the Ddura, and lots people start dropping dead. Before finding Arenrhon installation, technicians had decided that it was combination of aether and Ddura killing people because their 'security clearance' revoked. All historians here having big argument about how long did that all take? They all thought it was quick – was maybe around a Taren year from turning on Pillars to running away from Muina. This place fits that timeline wrong.

"When saw there was a town inside, historians thought maybe must be intended to be a kind of bunker, a place intended to keep the Ionoth out, but that didn't work on Ddura and Ddura killed them. But whole place built in less than one Taren year, everyone moved in? Could Lantarens do that as quickly as Tarens can? If emergency shelter built quick, why spend time covering walls with pictures? And Ddura – whenever we touch the platforms, the Ddura have responded so quick. Don't get impression it takes them long to kill things. Whole town would have died in moments if it was Ddura. And only me can hear anyway. Would not have had time to try and run away and get packed into exits and crushed. But if it was big wave of aether, then would have just collapsed in piles like Setari did. If was slow drift of aether, wouldn't they all barricaded themselves in rooms with doors shut? And the air shafts they've uncovered are sealed by the aether stone too – so doesn't seem like people meant to survive in this place once aether shield up."

I don't usually try speaking Taren in such big blocks, and was a little tangled by this point. I'm pretty sure Ruuel had heard most of those theories already anyway; the Taren historians had been arguing about it for the past few days. He listened without impatience, though, and said: "We can't overlook the possibility of there being another source of danger here, something the Lantarens could not defend against."

I shook my head. "You said it before. Betrayal. I think maybe the Lantarens killed the people here."

He didn't give away what he thought of the idea, just said: "Why?"

"Being underground with a seal covering even air vents. And especially all the worshipful imagery. The Egyptians did this with their God-kings: preserved their bodies, built massive monuments to put them in, surrounded them with their treasures, covered the walls with images of the stories of their lives. And provided them with a household to serve them in afterlife."

That made his eyes narrow. "A household?"

"Servants. They would kill them, or just seal in tomb alive." I sighed. "It doesn't quite fit, because if that was what was happening here, it would be well-known culturally. And not normal to build houses for the servants in the tomb. But if they were told it was a shelter beforehand, and then sealed inside and killed by whatever the Lantarens were doing, it does seem to match more than anything else I can guess."

"We may learn more tomorrow. They've been making progress on the fourth level seal." Ruuel had the distracted look of interface-conversation, so I wasn't surprised when he only added: "Go get some lunch," and left.

I blatantly disobeyed orders. The idea of meeting any of Ninth Squad made me feel too ill to eat. But there's never any escape, and Kaeline brought Anya and Revv in to apologise to me. Anya did so with a complete lack of grace or sincerity, but I think Revv meant it. I'd been wondering if only Revv would take the blame, but it seems everyone else has as much trouble lying to Tsur Selkie as I do, and it was obvious to anyone who'd seen anything of Ninth Squad that Anya would be behind a game of tease the stray. Kaeline sent them off, then apologised to me on her own behalf.

"Would rather no-one had noticed," I told her. "Caused all these problems for rest of Ninth Squad."

"We brought our problem with us," she said. "I hope to work with you again one day."

She left, and I felt slightly better because I noticed as she went that for once she looked as if she didn't have a headache. I wasn't surprised when Mori turned up and made me go have lunch. Ruuel doesn't forget the psychological aspects.

We spent the afternoon in near-space trying to map a path to Pandora, but though the path Par was following did seem to lead there, one of the gates was a rotational which seemed likely to shift soon, so

Ruuel decided we'd look for a better route another day. By the time we returned, Ninth Squad had left with the *Litara*, and I was no longer feeling too embarrassed to talk even to Fourth Squad.

I'd rather the whole day hadn't happened, though.

Friday, April 18

Creepy

It took the greysuits well into mid-morning to finally solve what they decided was a deliberate layer of extra security around the lower levels. I went in with only Fourth Squad, since Squad One's now stuck with covering watches. The good news was that there were no more shield walls, so we were able to travel freely through the three rooms of the fourth level, and down to the fifth level. The bad news was there was still no handy library, or big wall of explanation in stone, or any writing.

Except the names carved on all the sarcophagi.

I might have felt tempted to be smug if the place hadn't freaked me out so much. I wasn't too bad on the fourth floor, just felt kind of squashed when we went in, but I thought that was because we were deeper underground and the place was creepy. The fourth level rooms were wedge-shaped, taking up a third of a circle each with the outer wall arranged in a tier. It reminded me of the audience of an auditorium except instead of seats there were all these not-quite-upright sarcophagi. Smaller, and far less stylistically rendered than Egyptian ones, so that it was like there was a room full of tilted, metallic people looking down at us.

When we've been doing these initial searches, Sonn's log has been 'streamed' back to the ever-growing audience of greysuits, but only the people in charge (in this case Tsen Helada, Islen Duffen, Islen Tezart and Tsur Selkie) have been in channel and able to make comments. Islen Duffen, sounding considerably startled, wanted a closer examination of the sarcophagi, and I had my first opportunity to obediently err on the side of interrupting.

"Are they blurry to anyone else?" I asked, sounding fantastically apologetic – I've grown far too used to making sure to keep my mouth shut when we're on-mission to feel at all comfortable piping up whenever the notion strikes me.

"Show us," was all Ruuel said, signalling for Fourth Squad to hold.

I streamed my log to the mission channel. It's pretty hard to describe the blurriness. It was like each sarcophagus was layered over the top of itself over and over again, except not quite lined up. Not all of them were blurry, and some were far blurrier than others.

"Scan the whole room," Tsur Selkie said, and I looked slowly around, finding a few other blurry things, though nothing nearly so bad as the sarcophagi. There were lots of carvings on the walls, of upright, stiffly posed people gazing up proudly at the three familiar god wanna-be's, and that bit was particularly blurry. Even Halla went blurry a couple of times.

"Vitals are raised," Ruuel said. "Return?"

"Not yet. Keep that stream open, Devlin, and report any further developments."

We wandered around the fourth level, finding it all much the same: spectacular and spooky and in my case blurry. Since I hadn't shown any negative reaction other than signs of mild effort, we went down to the final room.

I was by no means surprised to see three final sarcophagi, facing what looked like the top third of a car-sized malachite marble rising out of the floor in the very centre of the room. By see, I mean peer through a blur of white and grey and gold, trying to make out the shapes. I went over the mission log later to see what it looked like to everyone else. Ruuel's and Halla's view of it was almost as confusing as they switched through their Sights, but very different to mine, involving dark mists and shadowy human figures. The sarcophagi were very beautiful renditions of the three who were featured so gloriously on the third level, slightly stylised, with lots of gold and silver and black metal.

"Impressions?" Selkie asked.

"The central stone is the power source of the shield," Ruuel said. "Beyond that...there is a great deal beyond that, but I cannot interpret it."

"Danger," Halla added. "Almost – almost, I would call it active menace."

Ruuel turned his head to me to remind me to speak and also, I think, to check how I was holding up. The interface would be showing how hard my heart was thumping. I felt like I was jogging slowly uphill.

"It's heavy," I said, and hated how stupid that sounded, but went on confusedly: "Like gravity is heavy. Like it's pulling everything around it down. Warping it."

"Return Devlin to the surface," Selkie ordered crisply. "And then act as escort to the technicians. Nothing is to be approached until we have every scan imaginable."

I was sent straight to medical, where I was told that I'd been using some sort of Sight talent, probably, maybe. I'd developed a ripping headache by the time we were back on the surface, which is apparently a common symptom of people learning how to use their talents, and made me feel even sorrier for kids inducted into the Setari program. I was stuck with having brain scans for much of the day, but it's not as if anything much else happened. The technicians were escorted very cautiously down and spent the rest of the day running scans and trying to work out what the heck the room was doing.

And now it's morning again. I stayed in the *Diodel's* medical section under close monitoring overnight, but they've let me go. They haven't the foggiest idea what blurry overlays mean.

Reinforcements

The *Litara* arrived just after breakfast with what seemed like ten thousand people, including Eighth Squad. I'd had no problems with Eighth when I tested with them or when they were on the Pandora mission, and was glad it was at least a squad I'd worked with. Still, I felt stupidly embarrassed saying hello to them, because I knew that before coming to this assignment they'd have heard all about how someone from Ninth had teased the stray too much and were reprimanded for it. I know that everyone in the Setari must have heard some variation of the story, since the entirety of First Squad sent me worried emails telling me to always let them know if I needed anything, and even Zan sent me a long email updating me on what's been happening with her, which is Zan's way of being supportive without poking at my psychological aspects. Zee is much better, and both First and Twelfth Squad are back on Tare doing rotations. They're no longer posting Setari to guard Pandora because the Ddura does such a good job keeping it safe.

The *Litara* also brought more Kolarens: mainly archaeologists. There'd been a Kolaren who arrived with Squad One whose job appears to be to watch and report back to Kolar's government, but before today there wasn't a significant percentage of Kolarens on site. I'm not certain how this will impact on the balance of the expedition, but it complicated my morning. Islen Duffen had 'booked me' for the morning to tell one of her senior minions everything I knew about tombs, Egyptian burial practices, sarcophagi, and from the sounds of it the complete mythical beliefs of the whole of the Earth. I was already too aware of how little I knew, and particularly worried about mixing up what was history, what was mythology, and what were things I'd seen on Stargate. It did not make it any easier to find myself being interrogated by half a dozen people (four Kolarens, two Tarens) who kept breaking off to argue with each other, and also occasionally disputing the things I was saying, or being impatient and critical because I couldn't answer all their questions, and still speak relatively slowly and disjointedly.

Arad Nalaz from Squad One was on guard duty, and chose to do his guarding from the rock next to my seat. He really helped a lot. If the interrogation squad got too over the top he'd just turn his head and fix them with this thousand-mile stare with those Lawrence of Arabia eyes and even though it hadn't seemed like they were paying attention to him at all, they'd abruptly quiet down and remember to be polite to me and at least civil with each other. I made sure to thank him afterwards, and he looked briefly amused but pretended he hadn't been doing anything at all.

I don't think my ramblings about Earth myths really helped very much, anyway. I mean, though there's some similarities, what happened at this site is obviously far different from pyramids with mummified pharaohs sealed inside.

After spending all of yesterday and the whole morning scanning, they decided to leave the fifth level alone until they had analysed the readings which were coming from the central stone, and concentrate on the fourth level. They had Fourth Squad and me play observer while they opened some of the sarcophagi. From which we learned that some had nothing in them, and some had bodies in them which the greysuits think were perhaps burned before being placed in the sarcophagus. The odd thing was that the sarcophagi which weren't blurry were the ones which had bodies in them.

I still haven't the faintest idea what the blurriness means. Ruuel told me that I needed to learn how *not* to use the Sight, and so I had to spend my time trying to get the blurriness to go away. I ended up tired and frustrated. All my so-called talents – of which I seem to have accrued a large and indefinable number – don't seem to be at all interested in doing anything on *my* say-so. They just happen.

So do headaches.

Saturday, April 19

Malachite Marbles

Beaten up by Sonn all morning. My bruise collection is growing nicely.

While we trained, Squad One kept one eye on the archaeologists. The sarcophagi on the fifth level were empty as well, and in the afternoon they decided they were going to look closer at the 'malachite marble', as I think of it. The greysuits call it the power stone.

They couldn't decide what it did, other than maintain the seal. Because they were very dubious about what would happen if someone touched or tried to manipulate the malachite marble, they had everyone evacuate the whole of the installation, all the way down to the shore. Fortunately the weather was much better today. Then they sent Sonn (for Ena manipulation) and Mori (for teleportation) down to the fifth level alone, carrying an emergency supply of food and water. The idea was that Sonn would use Ena manipulation to try and get the marble to stop maintaining the shield. If the shield responded by overloading the entrances the greysuits had made – or by causing the facility to explode amusingly – Mori would try to teleport them out.

Ruuel hated this plan. He didn't openly object to it, or look annoyed or anything. But he kept his eyes almost closed the entire time, and what few orders he gave were even more clear and precise than usual. I don't think Kanato of Eighth liked it either, maybe because he and Mori spent a lot of time yesterday evening talking quietly to each other. I didn't enjoy the idea of Mori being trapped among the sarcophagi any more than they did – nor Sonn. Sonn doesn't make it easy for me to like her, but I appreciate the way she approaches my combat training. Well, I wouldn't like for anyone to be trapped under a mountain, even Fifth Squad.

But nothing bad happened. Whatever else the malachite marble might or might not do, it was obedient enough about removing the seal. Ruuel opened his eyes to half-mast again and nearly caught me watching him (who am I kidding – I've really got to stop watching him because I already know how effortlessly he spots such things).

After the seal was gone they did another round of readings and had the various Sight talents touch the marble to try and figure out what it's for. They all seemed unsettled by it, particularly Halla, and all said pretty much the same thing: dominance. Somehow the marble would give power. Halla said over others, Selkie said over the world around us, and Ruuel wouldn't say more than just power.

Then, of course, they had me touch it and it gave me a headache. And made *everything* go blurry. I felt like my bones were vibrating, and had a hard time not vomiting all over the mysterious mystic stone. This was one of the days when I had to struggle to not have a tantrum. Obviously they wanted lots of readings – and because of the Nuran calling me a touchstone and this being a big stone (which makes me feel sick) they spent ages (well, it wasn't that long, but it felt like forever) until finally Tsur Selkie said I could go back to the ship and have my brain scanned for the ten-hundred-millionth time.

When the medics let me go I still felt sick so I went back to my pod and sulked until I fell asleep and now, of course, I've woken up just after everyone's gone to bed. Must try to get back to sleep so I don't konk out halfway through tomorrow.

Sunday, April 20

Belonging

So I'm back on Tare.

This whole day has done my head in, starting out with another of the Ruuel-dreams. I was half-awake and knew he was there, but I didn't have that proper dream-logic which lets you just accept everything no matter how unlikely. I really thought he'd for some reason gotten into my pod with me, and was lying curled against my back. My thoughts were this escalating stream of wtfwtfwtfwtfWTF! and then he leaned forward and I thought he was going to kiss the back of my neck, and I took a great gasping breath, and woke up. I was lying in the same position as I'd been in the dream, just with no Ruuel. And my nanosuit was completely withdrawn into a pad onto my back, so I was wearing only underwear and the uniform harness. The interface isn't supposed to respond to your commands when you're asleep, but I guess I must have been just awake enough. I'm so glad I didn't make the lid of my pod transparent as well.

I went and hid in the shower, thinking about all the ways I could humiliate myself half-asleep, and horrified by the idea of going anywhere near Ruuel. I don't really know why. Sight Sight is a difficult talent to define, but nothing I've seen or read suggests he'd be able to know what I was dreaming when I was inside a shielded pod. It almost certainly shows him that I'm highly embarrassed when I'm around him, but it's not "Omniscience Sight" or anything close to it.

And it didn't matter. After half my shower I managed to spare a glance out of Angst Central at the day's schedule and saw that Fourth had just headed off on another attempt to find a good route through the spaces to Pandora. And then the *Litara* arrived and Tsur Selkie sent me a message that I was being assigned back to Tare. The wrong dream had come true, in reverse.

I had hardly any time, since the *Litara* was leaving after a quick drop-off of equipment, and could only numbly dry my hair and grab my bag and something to eat. I did send an email to Fourth saying not much more than goodbye and good luck, which they would have received as soon as they were back in real-space. I'm so glad I've been preparing myself and not letting myself think of Fourth as 'my' team again. If nothing else, I can pretend to be pleased to be proven right. But I felt very alone and disconnected on the trip back to Tare, with a whole 'pod room' to myself.

Not quite left to my own devices however, since a greysuit had obviously been assigned to make sure I didn't go off the rails during the trip. There always seems to be someone now: usually one of the squads, or a greensuit or a greysuit who will pop by and pretend they're not checking me over for signs of imminent meltdown. It's hugely annoying, but I guess they felt they'd been forgetting my psychological aspects too much lately. Why they think reassigning the useful stray without warning is a good way of dealing with me is another question.

Not just a useful stray: I'm a *multi-purpose* stray. I enhance, hear LOUD noises, act as a key to lost civilisations, and see blurry! From the looks of my calendar, I'm going to be Third Squad's babysitting problem now. Pass the bloody parcel.

There was one good point to counter my gloomy morning. Tsur Selkie had organised a techie guy called Voiz Euka to recreate Earth's calendar, and I spent an hour with him after my inevitable medical exam, explaining the way Earth measures time, letting him measure the time units from my phone, and working through all the variations of the calendar. He seemed to think it not too difficult an exercise, once we'd properly compared my phone's seconds and minutes to Tare's time units, and so now I won't have to fret about losing my phone. A whole clock and calendar program, written specifically to keep me happy. I even remembered leap years.

And as soon as First Squad heard I was back, they arranged to meet up. They were heading out on rotation soon after I arrived, and I was on a slightly earlier shift to them, but we met at Mara's quarters when they finished their rotation and had nuna (crepes) for dinner.

It was great to be off-duty and off-record. As off-record as second level monitoring lets me be, anyway. Also fun to not have to wear my uniform, and to eat food which involved a lot of sweetness and not a lot of attention to nutritional value. To be teased by Lohn and hugged by Mara and have Maze be kind and a little worried.

I wasn't even close to surprised when Zee took me back to my room and interrogated me mercilessly about the whole thing with Ninth Squad. And, to my dismay, about what exactly Fifth and Seventh Squad had done to make me not want to work with them. But she said that my squad preferences weren't general knowledge, that Maze gets told stuff like that because he's senior captain, and that she was asking on his behalf.

I really didn't want to bring Zan into it – I don't think she'd be at all happy about me talking about the way they bully her – so I just said I'd seen how nasty Kajal and Forel were toward other Setari, and explained about the testing session I'd had with Fifth Squad.

"It's not that I think they *do* anything to me," I said. "Just that I think they find it funny if I scared or embarrassed. Going into spaces, need to trust squad more than that."

Zee was more than a little annoyed after reviewing my testing session with Fifth, and said I should have told someone, at least about the part where they went ahead of me in the Ena. And then she asked me if anyone or anything else had made me uncomfortable or unhappy. I gave her an entertaining description of my meeting of Squad One, and she seemed satisfied that I was getting along with most of the Setari.

I'm so glad Zee's okay. They all looked tired, but I couldn't spot any new injuries. It's so messed up that when I meet up with my closest friends here, I check them for damage.

Oh, and it's Jules' birthday. Happy birthday, brat. Hope you scored lots of loot.

Monday, April 21

Something a little different

Taarel from Third had me meet her for breakfast, and explained what we'd be doing for the next few days. One of the gates from near-space to real-space is in a tremendously inconvenient spot on Unara: a major travel junction. Over the past few decades it's slowly been growing, and they've continually had to increase the size of the lock around it. It's nearing the point that they're going to have to do some major infrastructure rejigging if it grows any further, and it already causes a huge amount of blockage and trouble.

Ever since they figured out that with my enhancement there was a possibility of actually closing gates, there's been an increasing amount of pressure to assign Taarel and me to "closing really annoying gates" duty. The 'mayor' (Lahanti) of Unara, one of the most powerful people on Tare, finally ordered KOTIS to give this particular gate highest priority and get it done. Guess that explains my abrupt reassignment.

The problem was that even with my enhancement, it's exhausting work and they estimated it would take just Taarel and me weeks to get this Rana Junction gate closed. They decided multiple talents assisting would speed it up, if Taarel initiated a closure, but they couldn't take off rotation every strong Ena manipulation talent, particularly now KOTIS is posting squads to Muina as well, so they're using the strongest of the Kalrani Ena manipulation talents instead.

Today was a test day, to see whether a mass effort would work, so after breakfast we met up with the Kalrani who had been selected for the experiment. There were ten, all very correct in their brown and cream uniforms. The youngest looked about twelve and the oldest the same age as me: probably one of the candidates for Fourteenth Squad. Thirteenth Squad has already been chosen and is on 'pre-rotation training' and has moved into the rooms on the same floor as me, though I haven't seen any of them about yet.

They all seemed to know Taarel, at least to say 'good day Tsee Taarel' to. I hadn't thought about it, but the 'graduated' Setari would be the logical candidates to give the Kalrani some expert tutoring. And of course before the Setari had qualified for their squads, they'd been Kalrani as well. Since it was Taarel, I wasn't surprised that most of them couldn't quite hide being awestruck by her presence, and were more than a little nervous and determined to be excellent for her.

They didn't know how to treat me. I'm a curiosity and the prospect of a massive increase of power. I wondered if they'd heard about Ninth Squad, and politely said hello back when they greeted me, and otherwise kept my mouth shut, even when I saw that the test session was in my old room in the medical facility, and the gate they were testing closure techniques on was the one I'd torn into near-space. It was very strange seeing my old room-with-a-view with a thick metal gate-lock built around where my bed had been. They'd removed one of the walls, but there still wasn't much room for the twelve of us, and I had to be careful about where I was standing.

Taarel took them through the touching-the-stray rules, then enhanced herself and started the closing process. Once she'd demonstrated, she had each of the Kalrani enhance and try in turn to close the gate just by themselves. I found this very dull, even with a projection of the gate for me to look at, and so it was simply a procession of serious kids frowning at the air. One of the Kalrani, a boy about fourteen called Dayn, managed to start it closing. It meant so much to him, and he was trying so hard not to show it that he went white and then red when Taarel gave him one of those brief, approving nods which Ruuel does so well, except Taarel adds a warm smile. Taarel is definitely charisma-plus.

After that, she enhanced again and started working on closing the gate properly, telling each of the Kalrani to enhance and join in one by one. They can't work on it continuously, needing to rest sooner than the five minutes my enhancement lasts, with long recovery times. But still, in less than a kasse they'd completely closed the thing, and were all looking tremendously exhausted. But very pleased.

After that were medical tests for all, heh, and Taarel told me that we were likely to be cleared to head to Unara tomorrow. Then I slept all afternoon and for the second time since I came back to Tare I dreamed of wandering around KOTIS, through endless empty corridors, looking for Ruuel.

Back in Year 10, Alyssa fell for a guy named Kyle Marcus. He was the sort who ends up Dux of the school, playing violin recitals, and winning debating prizes, but fun enough that hardly anyone hated him for it. Alyssa and Kyle were both on the student group helping organise the joint Year 10 Formal with Agowla and the Boy's Tech, and she spent the entire term being her brightest, funniest self: chatting with him, putting up all the signals. But when the term was over, and he'd passed up going to the after-party she'd arranged, she gave up. She said it would be embarrassing for them both if she ran after him like a dog in heat.

I don't want to run after someone who doesn't want me. And I've been trying very hard not to think about Ruuel, or write about him, and I try to avoid sitting around looking at log images of him because I'm sure what files I access is part of second level monitoring as well. But I keep having these dreams and when I wake up all I can think about is that he's not there. That he's not just one pod over. That he's not even on the same planet as me, and if I cried out for him he wouldn't come. It's so pathetic.

Ruuel has never encouraged me in the remotest way, never shown any interest in me beyond carrying out his captain-duties. Unfortunately, I can't simply make a sane, logical decision to not want him, and so I've spent the past couple of days feeling miserable and being frustrated with myself. Because Ruuel, who has never sat down to chat with me or spent any effort trying to socialise with me, isn't here. I miss just being near him.

Taarel is too good a captain not to notice I'm down, but she's also smart enough not to push. She keeps an eye on me, treats me with consideration, but otherwise just gives me opportunities to talk to her. Of course, Taarel's the last person I'd tell about my feelings for Ruuel. Too humiliating if she had to gently break it to me that she's engaged to him. If Taarel and Ruuel are a couple, right now I just don't want to know.

Ghost was with me when I woke, which helped considerably. I have as much hope of smuggling her with me to Unara as I did to Muina, but I wish I could. Even though she's only the echo of a memory, she's such a normal cat: smart and mischievous, loves being scratched behind her ears, purrs and acts like she missed me. And she's mine, in a way very little is here. Petting her was the best stupid thing I ever did.

Tuesday, April 22

What would Wikipedia say?

In among the make-believe there seems to now be a handful of truth about me in the public domain. I read all about myself this morning, finding dozens of interface 'spaces' devoted to me, just like the Setari watch sites. And I have an encyclopaedia entry. No 'real' pictures of me at all, thankfully, although there's some quite accurate drawings. I wasn't surprised to see that some of Nenna's friends had recorded meeting Nenna's guest stray, but it seems that you can't record images of strays any more than you can images of Setari. Strays count as 'protected incompetents' until they've passed various tests. But they could record my voice, and the 'outline' of me, and it was squirmy awful hearing me trying to speak in Taren back then. I was so slow, and my pronunciation was dreadful and I kept using the wrong words and totally wrong grammar. It's a wonder anyone could understand me at all. I'm still not close to fluent, and wouldn't be able to speak it properly without the interface, but I'm clear enough now.

My encyclopaedia entry says:

"Kaszandra Devlin. Born approximately 15 Denn 3732, city of Oztralya, planet Urth. Passed through natural gate to Muina approximately 40 Ord 3785. Located by Setari exploratory team on 2 Arn 3785, at ruins site Goralath, and processed as displaced person. Identified as enhancement talent and assigned to assist Setari. On 32 Nayz 3786 provided identification clearance to Setari squad under attack by Ddura at Goralath, effectively unlocking the planet of Muina for resettlement."

I had a good laugh at the 'city of Oztralya' and read through the entries for 'Urth' and Pandora, which sadly did not include anything about releasing all the evils of the world. There was tons more on the less official sites. A good deal of the initial hostility toward me seems to have died down after the 'sister planet' explanation, but it's a thousand percent obvious I'm never going to have anything remotely resembling a normal life on this planet. If I were at all unclear on that point.

KOTIS has released a handful of statements about my discovery on Muina, and how I'd been working with the Setari, but what I'd been doing recently was definitely not public knowledge. In fact, there was nothing on the public networks about the Arenrhon installation at all, let alone the Nuran. I'm betting they'll keep it quiet as long as they can.

Tons on Pandora, though. The settlement has grown enormously: multiple buildings up and running, and more under construction. Even some that aren't blocky squares. Pandora's focus has become more about learning to live on the planet, rather than unlocking the secrets of its past, and they're cataloguing the plants and the animals and testing out crops. It looks utterly gorgeous, with the leaves vivid reds and golds and the lake a slate-blue colour. Everyone not too freaked out by the thought of being outside really wants to go there. There's even a competition, where the prize is getting to visit.

We're starting for Unara late this afternoon. I've been in a very non-talky mood. I need to deliver Pollyanna instead of Gloomzilla.

Into the breach

We didn't start out for Unara until quite late in my day, and it felt very much like a school outing with the Kalrani in their cream and brown uniforms lined up before the entrance of a small arrowhead-shaped tanz. Space-aged school bus. The Kalrani were, if anything, even more stiff and upright than yesterday, making Rite Orla and Tol Sefen from Third look positively laidback as they strolled up just before me. The half of Third without Combat Sight gets to go on leave, but Orla and Sefen are stuck with helping baby-sit – guarding against any Ionoth which have been missed by the sweeps and come lurching out of the gate at us. There were also a handful of greysuits and greensuits, but Taarel was most definitely in charge, and started us out with a crisp briefing about the arrangements for getting us to and from the gate-lock, and what we should do if anyone somehow gets separated. She thinks the job will take one to two weeks (twelve days).

One of the oldest Kalrani, a girl named Pen Alaz, piped up at the end of the briefing and asked Taarel if it was true gate closure would become a regular task. I could see from the way a few of the Kalrani leaned forward that this was an important question to them. I expect, given how long they've trained to go into the Ena and fight Ionoth, the idea of a career in world-wall repairs was as dull as it sounded to me.

"It won't happen," Taarel replied, clear, crisp and serious. "Rana Junction is a useful exercise for us, but those who propose more have not fully appreciated the current situation. New gates are tearing at increased rates. Ionoth numbers are multiplying. On some rotations we're facing doubled, even tripled populations. That is a situation which is only going to get worse, and we need to throw everything we have into a solution, because if the current rate is maintained, in a five-year KOTIS will be building locks not around gates, but around the few places without gates."

"Is the increase because of the shutdown of the Pillar?" Alaz asked.

"No," Taarel said, before I could do more than mentally flinch. "If anything, turning off that Pillar appears to have bought us a minor reprieve, as well as giving us the first real evidence that the Pillars are connected to the continuing fragmentation of the wall between near-space and real-space. In all the time we've kept exact records of them, there has been a slight yearly increase in the number of new gates formed, and the widening of existing gates. Fractional amounts, but undeniable. This past five-year there's been a marked rise, accompanied by a surge in Ionoth population. Inconveniently located gates are nothing to the need to arrest this deterioration, so don't concern yourself with talk of gate-closing assignments. There isn't time for that."

Taarel doesn't pussyfoot around. Though the increase in gate and Ionoth numbers isn't a secret, and has been reported in the news outside KOTIS, this was the first time I'd heard anyone be quite so blunt in their assessment of what it meant. No wonder they're throwing everything at Muina, pouring people and resources onto a planet they wouldn't even set foot on a few months ago. KOTIS is racing disaster.

Wednesday, April 23

A bit of an audience

Taarel's talk yesterday put my he-doesn't-like-me whine into perspective, and I at least partially succeeded in throwing off my gloom. It helped that Orla and Sefen from Third are willing to chat to me while they sit around being vaguely alert for attack. The Kalrani all listened intently to our rambling conversation, but for whatever reason they haven't said a word to me other than when we were introduced.

Rana Junction went way beyond my expectations of busy. Located in the very centre of Unara, it's a mega-city's worth of Grand Central Station. If you want to get from one major segment of the city to another you travel in to Rana Junction and then out to wherever. All roads lead to Rana Junction, basically. So having a metal box the size of a two-story suburban house crowding out one of the main concourses in the Junction – where people travel from one line to another – is a complete pain in the ass for everyone involved. While their nanotech allows the Tarens to reshape sections of their city comparatively easily, changing Rana Junction would make for major headaches.

There's little private transport in Unara: it's all 'trains' and elevators and travelator walkways. Emergency and military services and a few very rich people have these zippy individual carriages which can whiz around on any of the lines in between the normal services, and shunt off into special short slots to get them out of the way. We travelled from the place we're staying – a weird 'government' hotel – in one of these solo carriages and walked fifty or so metres under an escort of Unara's police force to where the lock around the gate was waiting for us, the entrance under a little tent. They hadn't officially announced anything about Setari trying to close gates, but we were all in uniform and the reaction from the crowd was intense. Unlike the Setari's home island, most people on Unara have never had a chance to glimpse a flesh-and-blood Setari, and even on Konna it's rare to see them in uniform. Usually the only time the Setari go out in Tare's cities in uniform is when they're killing Ionoth which have reached real-space, and that involves a lot of alerts and evacuations.

Having hundreds of people double-take, walk slower, or just plain stop and stare made for some serious congestion. The person in charge of the set-up – a fussy, bearded guy called Marda who worked for the transport department – ushered us hurriedly into the big tent and spent a lot of time quacking to the long-suffering woman in charge of the police detachment about making sure the foot traffic kept flowing. I'm pretty sure Marda didn't believe the Setari would be able to close the gate, and thought the entire exercise just an unnecessary complication of his already complicated job.

The gate-lock was a larger version of the usual metal box with bonus scanning equipment and what I presume is weaponry, but they'd prepared for the several days we'd have to spend in it by decking it out with low, soft chairs, and tables with food and hot drinks, and even a porta-potty in one corner. It looked truly odd, arranged around the big empty patch left by the gate.

One of the first things Taarel did was have Anasi – a delicate-looking boy of fifteen – use Illusion to show the current outline of the gate. She could have just used the interface to show everyone what she was seeing with Gate Sight, but I think this may have been more effective for our observers. The gate was enormous, much larger than the one they'd closed yesterday, and was starting to break through the floor of the gate-lock, like an invisible tree root.

The fuss outside grew the entire time we were there. I kept an eye on the gossip channels and Setari-devotee channels, and almost immediately had outside views of the tent entrance and its guards. We hadn't been there more than ten minutes before the transit authority switched the entire concourse to a no loitering zone, which meant that if you stayed in the area they wanted kept clear for more than five minutes without special clearance, or kept coming back to the area, a deterrent noise would start playing through your interface, growing in volume the longer you hung about. The rare few who could stand that were flagged personal escort out of the area.

There were a couple of cafés on the far side of the concourse which didn't fall into the keep-clear area and they abruptly became the busiest cafés on the planet, eventually needing police assistance to control their customer volume. The news channels began reporting the story within five minutes of our arrival, and managed to wring an official statement from the transit authority about the gate-closing (which didn't mention me, but speculation about me being here immediately reached the point of unofficially confirmed – people have a very good idea of the limits of the Setari's strength, and obviously they've never been known to close gates before). Some people were excited by the idea of seeing me, but most were far more interested in the Setari. And I think the Kalrani were considered even more exciting. There's no recorded sightings of them outside KOTIS in uniform.

Taarel, totally unconcerned by the fuss outside, kept today's session to one and a half kasse, dropping out the younger Kalrani after the first kasse. When she called a stop, and had Anasi display the current size of the gate, it was maybe a little more than a fifth gone.

"Another four sessions," she said to Marda, who was staring up at the revised gate outline as if he'd only just decided that this might work.

There was a delay while they made arrangements for us to leave: moving our carriage so that it could zip out and slot behind whatever train was arriving at the nearby platform, and having the police set up this very handy containment wall involving a double row of seven-foot sticks on stands which produced a blurring shield. This, of course, totally gave away our imminent departure and abruptly absolute thousands of people started to flood onto the concourse. The news channels later said that they'd been waiting in surrounding 'streets'. The noise was incredible, this echoing excited chatter. The police had been given plenty of opportunity to assess the potential fuss, and we were in no danger of being overrun, but I feel sorry for them handling the security headache this is causing.

The crowd roared and cheered when we emerged. Taarel responded with a brief smile and nod in the general direction of the masses, but then kept us moving the short distance to the platform and through the door to the private section. She kept her attention on the Kalrani, making sure they weren't too overwhelmed and didn't lag, while Orla and Sefen bracketed me. It seemed a much longer walk than it had on the way in.

Everyone except Orla and Sefen was exhausted. I managed not to fall asleep on the train back, but as soon as I reached my hotel room I dropped and slept for four hours – as I expect all the Ena manipulation talents did, except Taarel, who paid the price of being captain and had to talk to people first. Fortunately, it's not just us along: with a half-dozen KOTIS support staff we've plenty of people to keep things running through the frequent napping. There's an evening meal scheduled half an hour from now, and then medical exams, bleh.

I was vaguely hoping that maybe I could go shopping while we were here – buying things over the interface just doesn't compare – but I don't see how it'll be possible.

Thursday, April 24

Zzz

Today was a repeat of yesterday, except that the crowds were expecting us back. We went several hours earlier in an attempt to avoid the worst and tomorrow we're going during a later shift to give the Ena manipulation talents more rest. They're even considering skipping a day if necessary. I do wonder why they didn't try and disguise everyone, rather than cause such a circus, but I guess the interface makes that kind of difficult, and certainly the location of the gate and the fact that Tare doesn't have a 'night' when most everyone goes home means that not wearing our uniforms wouldn't have hidden very much at all after the first day.

I spent a large part of today feeling very self-conscious. Yesterday gave a huge number of people a chance to look at the stray who unlocked Muina. And air their opinions about her. They couldn't get too close, and don't seem to have spotted that my eyes are different colours, but there was a lot of talk about me being so 'suyul', and it was amazing how uncomfortable that made me.

A suyul is a droopy, pale pink flower, and by calling me that they were saying I acted shy. Just as on Earth there's a stereotype of people who are red-headed being temperamental, on Tare people who are white-skinned are stereotyped as shy and bashful and a bit wimpy. It didn't help that after the first appalled glance yesterday I kept my eyes down and blushed madly. It was just too many people, too loud, and too overwhelming.

I couldn't make myself not read all these comments about me. And it left me weirdly conscious not of how I looked, but of how everyone else does. Practically everyone I know here looks Asian. Of the people I'm close to, only Lohn and Zan look primarily Caucasian, with maybe a hint of mix around their eyes. It wasn't something I'd given more than an occasional thought to until all these comments about *my* skin colour.

I've spent way too much of today trying to work out if I'm racist, or just annoyed because I *am* a bit shy and not good at fighting.

Friday, April 25

Something to Say

At the end of today's shift I walked into my hotel room wanting only a shower and then to curl up for a thousand hours, and there was a man waiting for me.

That startled the hell out of me, more because I was tired and wasn't expecting it than anything he did, which was smile and start talking. I froze for a moment, then stepped backward out of my room, for once remembering to set off my alert. Only after I did that did his words filter through to me: he was introducing himself and saying he wanted to interview me, to give me an opportunity to speak outside the control of KOTIS. And seconds later Sefen and Taarel were there, suit weapons out and looking extremely dangerous. Orla arrived a few moments after that, then one of our greensuit escort, and then a half dozen more people: a hotel security woman and more of our escort and most of the Kalrani.

I ended up feeling sorry for the reporter guy. The Setari didn't attack him, being more intent on making sure they were between me and him. Combat Sight obviously didn't classify him as a threat. He put his hands out palm up to show he wasn't planning anything, but the greensuit wrestled him to the ground anyway, and put a knee in his back. Then hotel security and one of the pinksuits helpfully piled into the room and I think he was stood on a bit.

Taarel began to usher me away, but I said: "Wait," to her and stood my ground until there was a lull in the noise, then said: "Am not under duress. But thanks for the offer." I'm not entirely sure he heard me.

Taarel gathered all of the Kalrani up as she went, some of them looking painfully tired, and stowed us in a big lounge. She disappeared for a few minutes, leaving Sefen and Orla still alertly on guard in case any more attack reporters showed up, then came back and said we were going to be moved to another floor. She gave the Kalrani a thorough survey – they were being all wide-eyed and battle-ready, which was more than disconcerting from the younger ones – then corralled me off to a couch to one side and asked me if he'd touched me, if I was hurt. Since we'd gone 'off-mission' I didn't have a log Taarel could access with her security level.

"He just want to talk, I think," I said, helpfully sending her the segment of my non-mission log which showed me walking in and back out of my room. "Sorry about alert. I was surprised and didn't realise he was just reporter."

"The alert was exactly the right reaction," Taarel said, eyes abstract as she reviewed my log. "Reporter or not: to get into your room he has to have by-passed security in ways that are by no definition legal."

"Moving so that rooms can be scanned?"

"And also because our location isn't supposed to be known. They will make it appear that we have relocated to another building entirely, but it will only be to a different floor."

The adrenaline surge wore off very rapidly, and I fell asleep on the couch, waking up hours later in a different room. I don't like being shifted about while I'm asleep. Or people touching my bag. I don't know if the reporter pawed through my stuff, but nothing was missing, and my diary and phone seemed fine. I presume it had all been scanned as well. Fortunately there were no delays or extra security before eating, because I was absolutely starving. And the day's drama even prompted a couple of the Kalrani to talk to me, started off by one of the oldest two, a girl my age named Pen Alaz, asking: "Why did you thank him?"

Alaz isn't exactly friendly and cheery, but she doesn't give off a malicious vibe either. She's a bit like Jenny from my maths class – super-smart, but not quite socialised, with a tendency to ask abrupt questions without any thought to whether they're rude or not, but just because it's occurred to her to want to know.

I swallowed my mouthful (really weird brown sticky bread that tasted like congealed vegemite). "Because he was offering to help me if I needed it. Mostly wanted good story, I expect, but I appreciated the gesture."

"A would-be rescuer, in fact," said the other of the oldest Kalrani, a guy called Tahan Morel. He's tall with sharp brown eyes under straight dark brows, and a very expressive wide mouth. Not hostile, but with an edge of sarcastic challenge which is pretty refreshing compared to the way most people treat me. "You didn't have anything you wanted to tell the world?"

I thought about it. "Only that that official encyclopaedia spells Australia really badly."

He laughed. "That's not the story that reporter was looking for, I'd bet."

"You really have nothing to complain of?" Alaz asked, sounding disbelieving.

"Sure. Complain lots about combat training. Hate that can't go anywhere by myself. Loathe second level monitoring. Don't see what good would do telling any of that to reporter."

"I don't recall anyone noting complaints about your combat training," Taarel said, looking amused.

"Mara said pulling faces counted as complaining."

Unfortunately that made Taarel schedule some combat training for us tomorrow morning, though she has to find a suitable room for it. It was good to have more people willing to talk to me. I wonder whether it will be Alaz or Morel who ends up in Fourteenth Squad.

The whole thing with the reporter made me realise that hordes of them have probably asked to interview me. That random people were surely trying to contact me, for whatever reason, and that KOTIS just doesn't pass any of that on to me. I'm not sure if that bothers me or not.

Saturday, April 26

Positive outcomes

Maze opened a channel to me last night after dinner. Mainly to chat about the reporter, but also about me generally and what was likely to happen to me over the next few years. Not that he can be really certain what will happen, but he could confirm that there wasn't a chance in hell that I'd be going anywhere without minders. I talked a little about the complete lack of control I have over anything I do, and how I understood that the restrictions were for my protection, but it was just occasionally it got to me.

Happily we moved on to the work being done on Muina, and it was nice to realise that Maze was excited by what's been happening there. A little confused by Arenrhon, but not upset by the implication that the Lantarens were even more arrogant than everyone had realised. Like the discovery of the Pillar, he saw Arenrhon as a chance to uncover the mechanics of the problem. It was, he said, better to learn more before turning off any more Pillars, because we really had no idea whether turning off the Pillars would necessarily fix the problem. But while he agreed with Taarel's assessment of the need for urgency, they now at least had the prospect of achieving more than simply fighting continually increasing numbers of Ionoth.

"And," he added just before saying goodbye, "locating your planet hasn't stopped being a high priority simply because the Nuran told us your talent set is beyond rare. Since we know there's a natural gate in Pandora's general region, there are standing orders for any Path Sight talents to try to locate it."

Maze was upbeat, but I could tell he was tired. I'm continuing to try to keep my dramas down to a minimum, because I'm one of the things which worries him a lot.

This morning was combat training in a conference room, squished between a small stage and chairs stacked along one wall. I'm sure Taarel simply wanted the Kalrani to get a little exercise to balance all the exhausting themselves with Ena manipulation they've been doing, but that didn't mean she went easy on us.

I'm at such a basic level, still trying to consistently block a simple attack. The twelve year-olds could have taken me down easily, but Taarel partnered me herself. I can't tell how good she is – everyone seems so deadly to me – but she was a patient teacher, encouraging but relentless in pushing me to be more aggressive. She told me afterwards that I needed to overcome my reluctance to hit people. I hadn't thought about it that way before, but I think she's right: I do flinch away from the idea of landing blows. I like working with Taarel, though she acts as if I'm a couple of years younger than I am.

We've grown used to the fuss at the Junction, which shows no sign of dying down, no matter how we move our arrival and departure times, or how brief our actual appearance is. The atmosphere inside the tent has changed: we're all chatting a little more. Muina remains the main topic of conversation, and we talk over the latest news releases. The exploratory teams are constantly expanding the 'known world' of Muina, sending back some spectacular visuals from their aerial surveys. It's a beautiful world, and most of it lush and green with fewer of the dry, arid sections so common on Earth. Not so much huge interrupted ocean, either, but a more even distribution of land and lakes.

One day of this left, and tomorrow looks to be a short day. There's maybe a tenth to go and we plan to finish it off just after breakfast.

Sunday, April 27

Unara thanks you

It's done. I think the people most relieved are the police security detail, though I'll bet the Kalrani are also glad to see the end of it. The area will be closely monitored for years, in case the gate re-opens, but by the time we were back at the hotel in the middle of our post-session medical exams they were already dismantling the big metal lock which has been taking up half the concourse for decades. The news services had plenty of happy warbling by officials in interviews, and excited comments from Setari-watchers about what everyone had looked like, and the fact that as we trailed off for the last time Kinear – one of a set of twelve year-old twins who would be mischievous if they weren't Kalrani – turned and waved goodbye to the humungous audience.

And just when I thought it was all over, Taarel came to tell me that the Lahanti (mayor of Unara) has invited us to dinner, although it will be more afternoon teatime for us. We're going off to shop for clothes in a few minutes.

Monday, April 28

Dinner Conversation

Yesterday was one part fun, two parts uncomfortable. Pampering and fuss and then the kind of glitzy meal which would make Mum produce dry comments, but with people I didn't know or particularly like.

I'm not altogether sure why we couldn't just wear our uniforms to dinner, but I by no means minded going off to a boutique store opposite our hotel to try on dresses, despite the fusspot aide from the Lahanti's office who was in charge of making us suitable. Tare might be a meritocracy, but that doesn't mean everyone's all sunshine and equality. Being rich is still a bigger thing than being smart.

The aide – Nona Maersk – didn't seem to think much of the Setari, but it took Taarel maybe two minutes to get the woman eating out of her hand. Taarel has a kind of radiant self-confidence and warmth of spirit which is very difficult to resist. That looks weird written down, but it's the best I can describe Taarel. She also looked phenomenally awesome in a dark green, velvety-textured dress, with her hair done up in a curling knot. I had something which shimmered between purple and blue and red depending on the angle, and I liked the way I looked in it, except that it made my repaired eye look even more purple.

Maersk's attitude towards me was disjointed. She treated me as the guest of honour (Taarel, Sefen, Orla, Morel, Alaz and I were going), but she also treated me like I was five. Speaking very clearly and slowly, and also sometimes talking to Taarel about me as if I wasn't in the room. I amused myself by pretending that I could barely understand her, and speaking incredibly fractured Taren – at least until Taarel opened a private channel and told me to stop.

I considered not doing as I was told, just to see how she'd go about getting me to be good, but instead replied over the channel: "Can I ask you possibly impolite question?"

"Ask, always. My response will depend on the question."

"Why do you wear your hair in such difficult style? Doesn't it take a lot effort to keep up, especially when spaces flooded or rain on you?"

Taarel laughed, not offended. On Tare, no-one finds it strange at all if you suddenly smile or laugh at nothing. The voices in your head are quite real here.

"It's an exercise in Ena manipulation," she told me. My hair had been brushed out but not styled yet, and she reached over a finger and made a long strand of it curl just by touching it. "Ena manipulation is primarily used on the gates, but if we wanted to spend the time and effort we could effect the structure of the spaces themselves. More difficult is to alter that which is not of the Ena. It is possible, but takes a great deal of strength and control. Once it was beyond me to move a single strand, and to arrange my hair became not only something of a boast, but a daily practice." She looked amused, and added out loud: "Sometimes I don't style it as I normally do, and my squad does not recognise me."

"I don't recognise you now," Sefen said, and blushed bright red. He totally worships Taarel. "Nor myself," he added.

Formal clothing for guys on Tare doesn't resemble Earth's penguin suit at all. It's mostly in pale natural colours, with long narrow-leg pants, soft shoes, and a shift and coat which goes down to about knee-length. Vaguely Middle-Eastern, but no turbans that I've seen yet. Female dresses are more what I'm used to, except with a tendency for multiple layers.

I returned to the private channel and asked: "Is there anything Unara Lahanti doesn't know about, which I should not talk about?"

"The Lahanti will have been kept fully apprised," Taarel said, sounding thoughtful. "But as for other guests – it would be best to follow the Lahanti's lead. Discuss any topic she raises. Remember, if anything happens that concerns or confuses you, open a channel to me."

I spent the rest of the time asking about table manners, just as I would if I were sent to have dinner with the Queen on half a day's notice. A single-carriage train even plusher than my hotel room took us to the official residence's own station, and the Kalrani and Setari, except for the unshakeably at-ease Taarel, went extremely po-faced and upright, like they were on parade, which looked very odd when they weren't in uniform. The room we were taken to was already crowded with people, and I think I was introduced to all of them. Only my log is going to remember any of that.

The Lahanti of Unara is called Sebreth Tanay. She looked younger than I expected, in her forties, and had disconcertingly clear grey eyes, very unusual on Tare. She reminded me a little of Isten Notra, with the same incisive intelligence, though I didn't feel nearly as drawn to her or comfortable with her.

Not that the Lahanti was nasty to me or anything, and I wasn't sitting there thinking she was evil. But she wasn't interested in me so much as my effect on her world and the problems and benefits I represented. I was placed next to her for dinner and after the usual questions about my first few weeks on Muina, she interrogated me about Earth. Population, form of government, weapons capability, complete lack of verifiable psychic talents, likely reaction to Tarens showing up. Most of her questions I'd been asked before, and my answers were probably in reports she'd read, but I speak Taren better than the first time I was asked, so I suppose it wasn't a complete waste to grill me directly. The thing I had to keep emphasising was how disparate Earth was, that there would be no unified response to the Tarens, even from a single country, let alone the entire planet. I kept barely getting a chance to taste each of the courses they brought out because the Lahanti kept me struggling to answer the entire time.

The dinner seemed to be serving two purposes: to let the Lahanti and a couple of other government types get a better handle of what Earth was like, and to let the Lahanti's children talk to real live Setari. I didn't hear much of what they were chatting about, but the son was laying some full-on charm on Taarel and I think the two daughters were thinking of renaming Morel 'morsel' and having him for dinner.

I'm glad I didn't have to face today back when I could barely speak the language. I'm pretty sure most of my answers used the right words and only slightly idiotic grammar. I'm also glad that the Kalrani were so obviously tired, so we didn't have to stick it out too long.

And we can keep the dresses! I am *so* tempted to draw my lab rat on mine, just to see people's reactions, but my role has mutated enough that my lab rat doesn't really fit anymore. I'm an enhancing dousing rod now – they poke me at alien ruins and see what happens. We're flying back to KOTIS headquarters, and I'll be glad to be in my apartment again. I hope Ghost's waiting for me.

Tuesday, April 29

Here and There

My schedule for the next week has been set: I'm flying back to Muina tomorrow, as are Third Squad. Third Squad are going to Arenrhon to relieve Fourth, who've been on continuous duty for a very long time now. Third is dropping me off at Pandora on the way, to take part in an intensive investigation of the platform there and how it works as a communicator. Which means lots of headaches for me, which I can't say I'm at all pleased about.

I spent a big chunk of my day curled up in bed, having Ghost purr for me and thinking about a life scheduled and arranged by committee. The only person who has offered me a choice since the Nuran is a reporter I ended up getting arrested. If I pushed, could I get more say in what I do and where I go?

Must keep in mind that obediently standing where I'm put is still far better than independent and starving on Muina.

Wednesday, April 30

Now and Then

Eeli is so funny. She's been home visiting her family (Kalrani and Setari do get proper holidays and to visit their families and so forth – KOTIS is like a big strict military boarding school, not a prison) and was in a fever of joy about seeing her younger brother and sister. But she was so chagrined that she missed out on playing dress-ups, and seeing half her squad in fancy clothes, that she could barely manage two sentences without looking at the log images again and wishing she'd been there and saying how wonderful everyone looked.

I was given a little present before the *Litara* started out – Euka had finished my Earth clock and calendar program and it's all installed. He told me that I should make comparisons with the clock on my phone to make sure he had everything right, and to let him know if there were any adjustments. He'd mimicked the look of my phone's clock and calendar very exactly, although using Tare-characters instead of Earth-characters. Hard to believe it's the end of April already. More than five months, now.

I'm a different person. Yet I'm still me. A lot of the things I used to think were interesting seem so stupid in retrospect. All that time wasted watching reality TV. I still miss Earth music, though I'm getting a little more into Taren songs now that the language isn't such a chore. I miss my favourite books, and I wish I knew what happened next on a lot of TV shows and web comics, and there were a few movies coming up that I wanted to see. I'm feeling more and more disconnected from my own world, and yet still in no way Taren.

It bugs me that I'm basically swapping planets with Fourth Squad. Not just because of Ruuel. I'm still dreaming about Ruuel every night, but I'm hoping that a long patch of not seeing him will cure me. The problem is Fourth is the squad I've connected with the most outside of First. Particularly Mori, who I think was becoming a sort of friend. But between shifts, and assignments on different planets, and assignments to different squads, I'm not sure I'm going to be able to overcome the barrier that second level monitoring already raises.

Thinking about that, and wishing I could send Alyssa a letter asking how she's going, prompted me to write to Nenna again, even though she didn't answer me last time. We're about to arrive at Pandora, so she won't get it till tomorrow at the earliest, but I hope she writes back. The Lents were so nice to me, and it'll never stop bothering me that I ended up hurting them.

Time to go be poked at mysterious alien installations. Hopefully they won't expect me to stand about getting headaches for too long.

MAY

Saturday, May 3

Two Steps Forward, Ten Steps Back

New resolutions:

1. Always carry full Setari equipment.
2. Find a lighter.
3. Be careful what I wish for.

Monday, May 5

Extended dodging and swimming practice

It was just on dawn at Pandora when I arrived with Third Squad. My labrattery session wasn't for a couple of hours, so Taarel handed me over to two greensuits who were to be my primary babysitters: Esem and Hetz. They were a younger and older guy, polite, but super po-faced, making me sorry that Third Squad left almost immediately with the *Litara*. I would have loved to listen to Eeli's reaction to Pandora's changes. It's grown so big, I could hardly believe it: still plenty of tents, but dozens of buildings in varying stages of growth and fit-out. My greensuits showed me to a room in the main building, just a bed and a shelf, but with a window looking over the lake. I left my things, ate a little lunch/breakfast, and asked if I could go for a walk along the lake since I wanted to visit my otters, to make sure their stream was undisturbed. Esem nixed that idea – I'd have to schedule any departure from Pandora – but was quite amenable to taking me to look at my old tower while we were waiting for my first appointment.

It gave me a very eerie feeling to explore the old village, to check out how far the cleaning-up project has advanced. They've been concentrating on the buildings around the central amphitheatre section, removing encroaching plants and encrusting dirt, cataloguing the objects but leaving all but the most fragile in place. I kept peering through the windows expecting to see people who belong here, instead of greysuits and greensuits. They're even planning to restore the gardens, because the whole town is going to be a museum site. So is my tower, but as Fort Cass, part of the history of the stray who unlocked the world. That spun me out, and I'm still not sure whether to be upset or amused that they're turning a piece of me into a tourist site. My blanket, mats and pots look incredibly pathetic.

Far too soon, Esem and Hetz herded me to the amphitheatre, where I was introduced to the small group of technicians who were going to give me headaches. They were all eager to start work: it seems they've been waiting for some considerable time to get their hands on me. The cats have all moved out, off to a part of the town which isn't being worked on yet. But I'd noticed two or three in Pandora: kittens kidnapped and adopted, and one or two slightly less feral adults on the look-out for food.

The technicians explained that they were investigating how the platform operated and where the aether went when it flowed down to it. Since I could hear the Ddura, they were hoping that they'd be able to get clearer or different reading of the platform's operation when I was in contact with it.

"Simply try to communicate with the Ddura as you have previously," said Jelan Scal, the geeky guy in charge. "I know that the volume of the Ddura is painful for you, so we'll keep the sessions as short as possible. What we want is quality, not quantity. We've found that we take much clearer readings from subjects standing on the platform, so we'll monitor the platform's reactions with you there until the Ddura arrives, and then we'll keep you for only a brief exchange. Ready?"

I nodded, and walked up the stair onto the platform, betting that the 'brief exchange' would end up much longer and hoping that the Ddura was by now so used to there being Muinans again that it would listen to me when I told it to shut up. I turned to Jelan Scal, who looked pleased and started to say something, and then he disappeared.

For a moment I really thought that Scal – and everyone else in the room and all the machinery – had just vanished. But of course it was the other way around, as glowing walls and the big hole in the back of the room made obvious. It was a different platform room, broken and split, with a chunk of floor and back wall missing so I could see I was perched beside a drop to a big flooded chamber. I walked to the edge of the platform, peering down, and could see what looked like some kind of cistern system, the water quite clear, with low outlet tunnels.

Not inviting. I shook my head and tried to work out how to leave. Just wanting to go didn't work. I walked back into the centre of the platform and wanted very hard, and that didn't work either. And then I looked up, feeling uncomfortable, and there was a Cruzatch crawling along the ceiling toward me.

Wanting really, really a lot to leave didn't help either.

The Cruzatch was moving quickly, completely upside-down: Spiderman with a burning Cheshire Cat grin. I didn't have a whole lot of choices. I sure as hell wasn't going to fight it. I didn't seem able to conveniently teleport back to Pandora. So I turned and dived into the water.

It was a long drop, and the water shockingly cold, but I entered clean, angling toward one of rectangular outlets. They were a fair distance and I knew I wouldn't be able to reach them, let alone swim through one, without surfacing for air. I paused, floating underwater as I peered upward, and couldn't see anything behind or above me. The ceiling and the wall above the outlet was empty of grinning black shapes and so I swam hastily upward, surfaced just long enough to take a huge breath, then dove again.

I felt a jolt on my heel, then a grip on my ankle, and I was hauled backward out of the water, straight upward. The Cruzatch didn't need to cling to the ceiling or wall, flying easily, and its hold was both painfully tight and so hot it felt like even my very resistant nanoliquid suit was having trouble. Coughing because water had gone up my nose, I kicked upward with my free foot, connecting twice but not seeming to bother it much until I made a nanoliquid spike extend out the bottom of my boot to spear into its arm. It let go, white light spurting.

It was a longish drop back to the water, but that was good because it gave me a chance to twist into a diving position, to orient myself and take a breath, and the velocity to shoot into the nearest outlet and swim as hard and quickly as I could, and fortunately it wasn't too far and I surfaced in a tall round chamber, only about three metres across, with a clutch of underwater outlets but no other openings I could see.

All that sounds very calm and ordered and deliberate, but my head was nothing but Gah-ahhhhhhh!!! I half died from shock when it grabbed me. The kicking and the stabbing was total panic and my log is full of the coughing sobbing noise I'm making while I'm trying to get free. When I reached the round chamber I was gasping and staring in every direction, looking to see if the Cruzatch was coming after me.

It took a while for me to calm down, but once it was obvious that the Cruzatch wasn't coming I started taking long, deep breaths and my heart rate gradually settled. I noticed there was a submerged ledge around the edge of the room and swam over to float above it since it was too deep to sit on properly. I just felt so overwhelmed. I'd spent a month alone on Muina, and been terrified more than once, could definitely have died a few times. But nothing had involved me being grabbed and having to fight to get away. And I was alone. No Setari. I was somewhere which might or might not be Muina, with my interface telling me there was no connection.

Deep shit, meet Cassandra.

I didn't even have the normal gear the Setari go into the Ena with – and if there was one thing I could have done with it was the breather mouthpiece. The water was very cold: not ice, but the kind of thing you wouldn't want to be in for long without a wet suit, and my breath was coming out with just the faintest hint of mist. As soon I'd calmed down enough, I made my suit impermeable, but it was still unpleasant. So: cold, wet, no food, with at least one Cruzatch roaming around.

I immediately knew that unless the technicians pulled a miracle of analysis out of their asses, no-one was going to be coming through the platform after me. It was obviously one of these everything-works-different-for-Devlin things. Nor could I simply call for help. The Tarens currently had two satellites above Muina: one in an orbit which allows for continual communication between the two settlements, and the other scanning. But my interface, powered just by my body's electricity, only has a range of a few miles. And obviously I was out of range. Or behind a seal like in Arenrhon.

Having decided that I could absolutely not sit in the round chamber and hope someone came and rescued me, I lifted my right foot out of the water and made the suit draw back from it. There was an impressive set of fingerprints around my ankle – bruised, burned and with a couple of deep, seared scratches. My suit hadn't been able to hold up to the heat, though it had reformed once the Cruzatch dropped me.

Since I hadn't prepared for an Ena mission, I didn't have a medical kit, but the injury wasn't that bad and the cold was at least numbing the pain. Having settled that, I regrew my boot, then made them both extend out into a reasonable facsimile of flippers. And also grew webbing between my fingers. I love my nanosuit.

As ready as I could be for moving on, I replayed my log, trying to work out which of the four identical inlets was the one I'd come in through. I was on both mission log and my second level monitoring log, so everything I did was thoroughly recorded at least.

The walls were scummy with a green algae, and eventually I matched up the blotches on the first wall I'd seen in my log with one of the walls, which made that wall immediately opposite the one with the inlet I'd come through. I created a nanoliquid sword and scored a one in a circle in the algae above that inlet. Then I opened a drawing application in my interface and started making a map. I couldn't go back through that inlet, not when I knew that Cruzatch was there. I wouldn't survive another encounter and wasn't even sure if I could get out of the water through the broken floor to the platform. So I had to find a second way out.

Picking the wall to the right, I drew a circle with a two in the algae, then began taking deep breaths – both to calm myself and to get a lot of oxygen in my lungs – and set out.

Looking back, I can hardly bear to think about what the next few hours were like. The cistern system was huge: an endless series of inlets and enormous tanks and nothing better to stop and rest on than the too-low ledges around the endless circular junction rooms. There were two saving graces. There didn't seem to be any animals except for some fish and little turtles. And it glowed, very much like the walls in Arenrhon. Though that worried me immensely, because I suspected it meant I was behind a seal.

The nanosuit saved me from freezing to death, but the longer I went on the colder and slower and heavier I felt. I soon felt like I'd been swimming my entire life, through an endless maze of dimly glowing rooms, and that I would never be able to stop. Once I started to get really tired, I became convinced that I'd made a mistake in my mapping, or that I'd turned myself around swimming across the larger cisterns, but the numbers I was scratching on the walls, no matter how faintly, reassured me whenever I found one which matched my map. The inlet tunnels were hell – long, low passages that I had to swim down into and get through as quickly as possible and once or twice they were extra long and I'd barely make it, especially when my swimming slowed. I would never have made it through some of them without my nano-flippers. One near the end, my lungs were burning and my vision started to fill with wriggling white squiggles and even when I reached the surface and could finally *breathe* I felt so tired that the idea of going on seemed impossible and I floated on my back until finally I had to go on or just go under.

And then there was a current of water. Warm water.

I stopped in the middle of the cistern I was swimming across, brought alive by the sheer difference of it. A current of warm water. I swam toward it, of course, and followed another inlet and found myself in a small square room with very warm water pouring down from above and – joy – a way up.

I was stupid, too tired and soaked to think of more than standing in that stream of glorious warmth and then climbing straight up. It was almost like a spiral stair made of blocks, with warm water flowing down it, and way too slick for my first effort. I was only halfway up when I slipped, and was rewarded with a bad smack on the side of my head and a bruised side in return for my haste. The second time, I made ridges for traction on the surface of my suit and inched my way up until I found a round metal grate which miraculously could be lifted out of the way so I could oh-so-carefully ease myself through.

It was a bath house, vaguely Roman-style, about twice the size of my bedroom back home. The water was coming from a sunken pool in the middle of the room, which was being made to overflow by a constantly pouring flood coming through an ornately carved hole in the wall. There were big double doors – closed – leading out.

I was so tired I couldn't stand without shaking, and when I finally managed to do that I went and as quietly as I could moved a green corroded metal thing (maybe a brazier) and wedged it under the handles of the doors. I'm not sure if it would have stopped anything determined to get in, but it would certainly have made a lot of noise and at least given me a chance to try and throw myself back into the cisterns.

Standing in the pool for a few minutes drove away the chill, but after that all I could do was tuck myself into the driest corner of the room, close my eyes and shake. I'd been swimming for over five hours, and was starved and weary beyond imagining. I was too tired to even cry properly, just sat there quivering until I passed out for ten hours straight. No-one came and rescued me, but no Cruzatch showed up either. I had endless nightmares about swimming in the cold and felt battered and starved when I woke up, but at least I could move about without wobbling.

Then I had to decide what to do. Obviously the Cruzatch hadn't been able to follow me through the water, but exploring would take me away from liquid safety. After all that hellish swimming, I could get halfway down the corridor, run into a horde of Ionoth, and game over.

Sitting in a bathroom starving to death wasn't that attractive an alternative.

I had a hot bath while I thought, withdrawing my uniform partially and studying my skin, which had wrinkled amazingly where water had been trapped beneath the nanoliquid. Mara had shown me how to block my mission log for privacy – it doesn't stop recording, just means you have to have super-high security clearance to watch the blocked bit – but I don't trust whoever it is with that clearance to not look simply because I've flagged some tiny part of my life as private. And I'd been told not to turn off my mission log while I was technically on mission. Being constantly recorded makes bathroom breaks tremendously embarrassing, but at least my nanosuit helps me be discreet.

As ready as I could be, I nerved myself to go through those doors.

The balcony walkway outside was deserted. And cracked, dropping half a foot to my left. There were no Cruzatch in sight, but there was a clear view outside, and I crossed carefully over, hid behind a Pillar, and stared out.

A mountainside, three mountainsides, with a valley between them covered in white buildings, palatial and grand, with swooping, impossible-looking arches criss-crossing in the air. I could see the sky, but it looked unreal, pearly. Bright enough for daytime, though. I slowly turned my head side to side, keeping behind the Pillar as much as possible in case there was anything out there looking back. My aim was to get a good solid survey into my log and then to look at it in detail somewhere less exposed. I was at the very bottom of the valley, and decided that was a good sign. The cisterns had obviously all been of a level, and I'd climbed up about as much as I'd jumped down from the platform, so I was probably on the right level for that platform. I concentrated on studying the buildings on this lowest level, which were still a large number since the valley had a broad, flat bottom.

There was plenty of damage. Cracks, and rocks and rubble from higher up which had smashed into buildings. Try as I might, I couldn't decide which direction I'd come from. I'd swum for so long, but had had to keep retracing my steps, and my mapping had gone very skewiff. There were no visible platforms, but I did see that there was a circle of small buildings in the centre of the valley. Pandora's platform had taken me here, and I knew there were other towns with platforms. Since it seemed to be a transport system more than a communication device (got THAT one wrong, Sight talents) then a central circle of them would make a lot of sense, just as Rana Junction is central in Unara. But to check that out, I had to get to the nearest one without anything seeing me.

It all looked horribly exposed and open. And Cruzatch could fly. As if to underscore that thought, I saw one, drifting slowly up the far mountainside.

Sliding down out of sight, I reviewed my log of the buildings near me and plotted out a route which took advantage of fallen rubble, shadows, and anything that had overhangs and avoided open patches of ground as much as possible, but really it was all going to come down to luck. Anything that happened to be looking in the right direction would see me easily, even when crawling on my hands and knees as I did getting out of that balcony walkway. Black is not a good fashion choice for sneaking among whitestone buildings.

I can review my logs and feel silly for the way I peered around every corner and in every direction each time I moved, but it didn't seem remotely foolish at the time. I did see Cruzatch twice, and lay still in whatever spot I was in, ready to run madly if spotted. The closer I got, the more I believed I'd make it, and then I started worrying about what if I got to the buildings and there were no platforms, or if I got to a platform and it didn't take me anywhere.

But when I reached that central circle of buildings, I hit a bigger snag. Other than some fallen rubble and parched bushes, most of the central space was quite clear and flat. There were fifteen buildings, all facing inwards, some with big double doors opened outwards, some with them sealed. Each set of doors sat at the top of a short flight of stairs behind a few not very concealing Pillars holding up porticos, continuing the vaguely Roman theme. And drifting about the steps of the fifth building to the right were a little clutch of Cruzatch.

In some ways that was encouraging. There had been a Cruzatch at the platform I'd come through, and a cluster of them suggested they were guarding the area. After a brief peek and an extensive review of my log, I crept around behind the buildings in the opposite direction, aiming for the building which was six buildings away from the Cruzatch cluster. It had open doors, and its angle was good for concealment as I hauled my way up onto the landing at the top of the steps directly from the ground so that I was sheltered by the open door. Then I peered around the door, hoping they would all conveniently face away from me, but it wasn't to be, so I bit my lip, chose a moment, and slipped not too quickly and not too slowly out and then inside.

Once through the door I ran. I knew that the platform, if it was there, couldn't be too far in, since the buildings weren't that large. And when I had a choice of ramp up or ramp down I took down, since that matched the platforms I'd encountered before.

I don't think I've ever run faster. I'd seen from the corner of my eye the reaction of the Cruzatch. They'd seen me. If I'd chosen the wrong direction I'd...not be writing this now, I guess. As it was, there was a platform, and I ran up on to it, and I wanted to be anywhere but there, and all the lights went out.

I sat down hard, panting. The place I was in was hot, and closed in, and too dark for me to make out any shapes at all immediately. The platform was gritty. After a few gulping breaths, I slid to one side, worried about the Cruzatch being able to come after me, but then the Ddura arrived: a new one making the question noise. Not ecstatic, because I wasn't Muinan, but pleased and asking for orders. Head pounding instantly, I laughed, and slid over the side of the platform so I couldn't accidentally teleport anywhere else, and then sat there in the stifling dark and bawled.

Eventually my eyes adjusted enough to see shades of grey, and I worked out that the entrance corridor was almost completely blocked by sand. After I'd recovered from all the running and crying, I wriggled and dug my way out through the gap near the ceiling, and staggered up into too-bright sunlight.

My head felt all the better for getting away from the Ddura, but my heart fell the more I looked about me. After all that water, I'd ended up in one of the few desert areas on the planet. The town was almost completely swallowed by a drifting dune, with only a few roofs poking above the sand, and those were well-covered with a scatter of gold. The Tarens had been analysing years of satellite surveys and locating all the 'patterned roof' ruins. I was sure they would have immediately sent ships to the ruins they hadn't already stationed relay drones at, to check whether I'd ended up there. This was not one which was going to be visible from the air.

My interface still said 'no connection', of course.

It was baking hot, and dry, and just climbing up to the top of the tallest tower to get a good look around had me dripping with sweat. I converted my nanosuit to a rather scanty arrangement. You can detach bits and they'll hold their form, so I kept my boots – reinforcing them for fear of snakes and scorpions – and made the rest into a thin layer in shorts and tank-top form, with the rest of the nanoliquid in a pad on my back.

The village seemed to be on the edge of the desert, but the land which wasn't covered in sand was a parched wreck for as far as I could see. At one time it must have been a forest of long, thin trees, but I couldn't see any that looked even remotely alive, and very few that were even upright.

After that I went inside the top room of the tower and sat in the shade, waiting. I read a book, actually – one of the glories of the interface is that I'll never be short of entertainment while I'm stranded on alien planets, since I've downloaded a few decades of TV and books. It was perhaps early afternoon when I'd arrived, and after a couple of hours the extreme heat let up and I went back up on the roof to take another look.

I'd been thinking about what to do in between reading. There was no sign of anything green, of any hint of water. Not even cactus. It wasn't a place anyone would last long. But trailing off on a cross-country march in this kind of country would be suicidal. And, more to the point–

My ankle had been hurting more, and I reconnected my boots to my suit and withdrew my right one to inspect the bruises and burns and cuts. The entire area around them was swollen and flushed red. It didn't look up to a cross-country march.

I debated trying to use the platform to go back and get to another platform, but the chances of me avoiding any Cruzatch waiting for me was only marginally higher than a snowflake in my current hell. Instead, I relocated to the closest exposed building to all the dead trees, collected some wood, and made a fire. Sounds nuts, I know, and I didn't enjoy doing it, but I knew how much energy fire-lighting took from my attempts at Pandora, so knew I needed to start with it. It was also considerably easier than it was at Pandora – bone-dry wood, I guess. It caught within minutes, and I fed it up into a nice smoky bonfire, one which would last for hours. Then, after a little rest, I began hauling long, thin sapling trunks out onto the sand. Even at full size it didn't look like these trees grew that large, but I focused on the thinner ones because I needed to not exhaust myself lugging serious weight.

I made an arrow, the biggest arrow I could stand to complete, working until sunset. It was about half a metre thick for its entire length and it felt unbearably long. I was a wreck by the time it was done: covered in sweat, sunburned, limping and parched beyond belief. My ankle hurt so much, I had a raging fever, and struggled to keep myself focused until the sun went down. By then I almost couldn't bring myself to stand up again and limp along the entire length of that huge arrow setting the bushes I'd pinned under the logs alight – getting myself thoroughly smoked along the way.

I almost lost myself on the way back, too, which is quite a feat when you've built a huge burning arrow to point out the direction. But I started staggering off into the night and stood in the dark for a long time, not sure where I was. Eventually I managed to reorient on my original bonfire and reached the building there, and after that nothing much makes sense in my memories. It was endless nightmares of swimming and running and being trapped and then escaping and Cruzatch everywhere and constantly feeling cold and burning up at the same time. Ducking out of that Cruzatch's reach at the Pillar mixed itself in as well, and I actually remember that more than I used to now.

I didn't need to remember how afraid I was.

And then, running through an endless maze with Cheshire monsters always just behind me, I came face to face with Ruuel. He said "Devlin," and lifted one hand and pressed it – the back of his hand – to my cheek. I can remember that really distinctly, how cool his hand felt, and how he said: "You're with us. Stop running."

I blinked up at him. I was in a bed and could feel his hand against my cheek, and I said: "Thanks," and my log tells me I really did say that (in English), and sounded so completely astonished that it makes me laugh to listen to it. And he looked amused. Just faintly, barely a shift in the line of his mouth, but that's in my log too and it's very hard not to watch it over and over.

I passed out again, but was spared any more dreams, and next time I had anything resembling a coherent thought I was back in the infirmary at Setari headquarters on Tare, and that was two days ago.

And, eh, it's taken me all day to write this. I'll pick it up again tomorrow.

Tuesday, May 6

Strayed

From everyone else's point of view, I walked onto the platform at Pandora and vanished. I have to feel sorry for my two greensuit minders, and Jelan Scal, who'd had to report that I'd gone. I'm also rather glad I wasn't assigned to any of the Setari squads when this happened, because I guess it would count as a severe assignment failure.

So they started a planet-wide search for me. Like I'd thought, they'd assumed I'd been teleported to another village, or possibly to a sealed place like Arenrhon. It was a massive search effort and I'm glad that they treated my being off by myself as an absolute emergency, even though I'd survived perfectly well alone on Muina for a month. The first thing they did was visit the known pattern-roof villages which hadn't yet had drones planted at them, and put drones there. Then any known settlement. Putting scan and relay drones all over the planet was something they were intending to do anyway, but they brought forward the schedule on it by a factor of ten. Third and Fourth Squads were sent into the Ena to see if Path Sight through the spaces could locate me, and Second and Eleventh Squad were also sent to Muina, since they also have strong Path Sight talents.

Most of the time of the initial search, I was in the cisterns or asleep in that bathroom. After I woke up, played hide-and-seek across the centre of the city, and made my last-ditch dash for the platform, I'd been missing for nearly seventeen hours. I was just over twenty-four hours gone when I lit up my arrow and passed into fever dreams.

I'm not sure if my arrow would have been spotted if one of the technicians hadn't noticed that the placement of the pattern-roof villages had its own pattern. It wasn't a precise one, but it seemed that the villages are pretty evenly-spaced across the planet, so there were particular regions that the Tarens were concentrating on searching. And the satellites were looking specifically for fires, even though it seems there are an awful lot of natural fires. A satellite taking a closer look at a dying fire in one of the search regions found that it was, well, an arrow, and everyone celebrated. Arrows mean the same thing on Tare as they do on Earth.

The nearest ship was sent post-haste to that location: they were over an hour away, and from what I can tell reached me about three hours after sunset.

Eeli sent me a nice get-well email full of highly vivid descriptions of the drama of the search. Since she's the most powerful of the pathfinders, she'd been very determined to find me herself and it sounds like Taarel had pretty much needed to have her sedated to get her to get some rest during the middle of it all. Third had just returned from a second, very long attempt to locate me through the Ena when the nearest shuttle came within range of my interface and confirmed that I was there. The excitement was dampened by me being non-responsive and in really bad shape – dehydration on top of infection – and then of course they uplifted my log and saw what I'd been doing.

They took me to Pandora until I was out of critical condition, and then back to Tare. My only memory of the first two days was Ruuel telling me to stop running, and once looking up at the lid of a pod. The third day I kept waking for ten or so minutes, then falling back to sleep. Every time I woke, someone different was with me. Mostly First Squad, but Zan, Mori, Glade, even Nils from Second Squad. Lots of hugs, but I was too out of it to hold any real conversation – I'm surprised I managed to write anything in my diary. The medics were doing a lot of work with my leg and it seemed every time I could put two thoughts together they'd come and inject me with something.

The next day was better. My mind was a lot less fuzzy when I was woken by my primary medic, who gave me a 'follow this light with your eyes' test which is becoming very familiar, then took the tubes out of me, and let me eat mush. They checked how I was at sitting up, and helped me to the bathroom and back. I napped again after the medics had cleared me, and next time I woke Maze was with me.

"First Squad have roster to sit with me?" I asked, and he looked over and gave me one of his superb smiles.

"Not that formal, but we are taking turns, yes. You're more yourself than last time we spoke."

That confused me. "Don't remember last time." I reviewed my log later and Maze had been sitting with me very early on, and I'd said a few disconnected things to him in English which don't make sense even to me.

"Doesn't matter." He gave me another smile, and I could tell he was weighing up what kind of state I was in mentally. "The arrow was a very clever idea."

"I thought that until started building it. Too hot there. Luck not very good in picking which platform escape through."

"Anything that let you get away from the Cruzatch was a good choice," he said, looking away from me briefly. He hates the Cruzatch so much. "Do you feel up to answering some questions? Things the log couldn't cover."

I shrugged. "Nothing else in my schedule."

"All right. Did you actively try to use the first platform, or feel any sensation of effort when using it?"

"No. Was just standing there hoping the Ddura would be not as loud as usual, and then everyone vanished. Didn't feel effort at all." I anticipated his next question, adding: "When I got there, I looked into water, then tried to go back. Then Cruzatch turned up and I tried to go back more, and then I ran away. Not sure why didn't work. When on next platform, didn't feel any effort, but I was trying to make it work."

He asked me a few other questions – why I'd changed direction toward the bathroom, and how I'd decided where to look for the other platforms – watching me carefully the entire time. Very worried about me.

Eventually I said: "Not going to break down."

His expression was wry. "Do you know, just watching your log was an ordeal? You can't expect to come through something like that without after effects."

"If you sat through whole thing, will know did plenty breaking down already." But I sighed, and looked away from him. "Going to have more nightmares. And, that probably Lantaren school-city Kalasa, yes? Place most want find."

"Your grammar deteriorates when you're upset."

He said it with an air of discovery, which *did* upset me, and I gave him an angry glance.

"We're not going to let you get into a situation like that again, Caszandra." He touched my cheek and I realised I'd started crying without even noticing, and then of course I cried all over him, which I'd particularly wanted not to do. I ended up feeling thoroughly sick and exhausted, but somehow better.

Not that I believe for a moment that they won't stand me back up on a platform if they can't find Kalasa any other way. I know the Setari will be with me, but there's no way to be sure I won't end up in the same place, alone.

I'm working on not thinking about that, about being comforted and relaxed, since I'm hoping to be allowed out of infirmary tomorrow and they're not going to clear me if I act even a little like I'm scared to be alone.

Wednesday, May 7

Annivarming

A week with nothing but medical appointments and some mild training in my schedule. My skin is still peeling thanks to my thorough sunburning, and the infection took a day or two to kill off, but while I'm physically run down (again), and my ankle is covered in this blue spray-on bandage because of the deeper burns there, I wasn't badly injured this time around. They've been feeding me horrible-tasting nanite 'restorative' drinks which seem to have helped a lot, and thankfully Zee was allowed to spring me from the medical facility this morning. I'm so sick of constant monitoring. She also brought me a change of clothes and told me she had a surprise for me.

"What kind of surprise?" I asked. Not, to tell the truth, at all keen on surprises at the moment.

"How is it a surprise if I describe it to you first? Get dressed and you'll find out all the sooner."

The clothes were new – a pair of black Capri-style pants, sandals, and a really nice silky top with a gorgeous print of a bird with blue and black wings.

"Is this yours?" I asked, pulling open the door of the ensuite. "So pretty."

"It's yours," Zee said, pleased. "That's my part of the surprise."

"Thank you," I said, startled and a bit doubtful. "Congratulations on not dying present?"

"Anniversary," she said, flicking my chin lightly for making silly comments. "It's been a year since you were found on Muina. Well, a year and three days, but we figured you'd prefer to do this when you could get out of bed."

Taren years: a little over four months. "Seems like longer," I said, and hugged her. "Thank you. I promise not to draw on it."

"You'll be hearing from me if you do." She led me out of the medical facility back to the living quarters. We got off the elevator on the level where First Squad's quarters were, but instead of heading straight down the corridor, we circled to the other side of the elevator shaft.

"They've moved up activating Fourteenth Squad to next week," Zee said. "Since they've finished your quarters."

"Different quarters?" On the same level as First Squad. I liked that idea, more than being on a floor where I hadn't been introduced to anyone.

"It's the same pattern as ours still, just with even more shielding. We brought your things down."

"Is an anniversary and a housewarming all at same time."

"Housewarming?"

"When move into new house, friends come over and have a party."

"Then, yes, a housewarming."

It was, too, and more than First Squad were waiting for me. Zan was there, and parts of Fourth Squad, Second Squad and Eighth Squad. We barely all fit in my new apartment. And the apartment wasn't quite the same pattern as everyone else's, because it had a big round window (not openable or anything) with the wall cut into a smooth cup underneath it: a window seat. And there were rugs, and masses of really lush cushions, which were presents from everyone. Zan gave me a set of actual, physical books by an author she said she thought might be one I would like – that was very cool because books still don't really seem like mine if there's not paper involved. And Sonn produced a familiar statue and handed it to me.

"My pippin!" I must have sounded totally astonished, because they laughed. "Thought weren't allowed to take anything from Muinan sites?"

Sonn looked highly embarrassed, but pleased that I was so pleased. "An exemption was given for this piece," she said. "I gather you're meant to think of it as a permanent loan rather than a possession."

I was really happy. I would have asked for my pippin ages ago if I thought they were willing to give it to me. And there was not-healthy food and tingly drinks, and everyone was all relaxed and chatty and made me embarrassed by being so nice to me and of course I fell asleep in the middle of it. I woke late in the afternoon in my new bedroom (half-buried in all the big soft cushions) and lay there for a while looking at my pippin statue, which had been set on the bedside table almost as if it was watching over me. I really like having *things*. So much of Tare is interface-only.

Ruuel wasn't at my party. He and Halla have been sent off to Unara to be psychic detectives, and the rest of Fourth Squad is killing time giving guidance training to the elder Kalrani, taking them into the spaces. Then they have some belated leave, a whole week to do whatever they want. I guess most will visit their families. I don't know if Ruuel would have come to the housewarming if he'd been at KOTIS headquarters. I'm pretty sure he's trying to quietly discourage me by keeping me at a distance. And yet, I'm also almost certain that he was the one who knew that I regretted not bringing my pippin statue, and arranged for me to have it back.

I haven't been dreaming of him lately, because I've been having so many nightmares, but I consistently wake up feeling his absence, knowing that he's not anywhere near me. Stupid of me, but I've stopped fighting it. Wanting Ruuel to be there is just a part of who I am right now. It's hardly the first time I've liked someone who didn't like me back.

If I had any sense I would have fallen hard for Maze. He's got to be the nicest guy I've ever met, and certainly one of the best looking. He always makes me feel accepted and safe and makes me smile and he coped with me crying all over him really well, and I have to admit that I didn't mind being squeezed against his chest. But I can't imagine kissing him.

Well, yeah, I can, but it doesn't make me feel the same way as I do thinking about Ruuel. Not even close.

When I list reasons for liking Ruuel, the first thing that comes to mind is that he doesn't hesitate to criticise me, which sounds wrong, but just means he treats me as adult enough and smart enough to be told when to lift my game. And Maze treats me like a younger sister that he really wants to protect.

That's kind of overstating it. Ruuel also gives a lot of leeway to my psychological aspects, I suspect, and Maze does go all captain on me occasionally. I don't know. It's not as if wanting Maze would be a good idea either.

Thursday, May 8

Scar

Very mild training with Mara today, quite similar to what I was originally doing with Zan. It's almost Tai Chi. Afterwards she went with me to my medical appointment, and talked about the hand mark burned into the skin around my ankle. Taren medical technology is more than equal to healing it without a scar, and there shouldn't be a trace within a month.

I like chatting to Mara. She probably has to report on our conversations afterwards, but at least she doesn't act like she's just waiting for me to get upset. But she also said she's not going to go so easy on me in combat training from now on, because I obviously can fight when I want to. I think that's tremendously unfair.

Friday, May 9

In the ducts

I made a huge mistake watching a documentary about how Unara's air-conditioning works. Such a big city requires really serious, complex and fail-safe systems. Not only to make sure clean air gets in, but so all the fumes and smells and heat don't get trapped. All that was interesting, and I recognised one of the wind tunnels from a rotation, but then they explained how they keep the ducting clean. To prevent dust clogging it all up, they've made these nanotech slime mold things which live in the ducts sort of constantly licking them. That's bad enough, but it's not just the ducting which is kept clean that way - it's all the rest of the Taren's cities as well. When apartments are unoccupied, the slime crawls out of the air inlets and eats all the dust and grot in the rooms. People call them *yannar*, which is a Taren slang word for 'snot', and fits way too well.

I did NOT need to know that. I'm so glad there's no outlets right above my bed. I'm so sorry I even glanced in the direction of the countless horror movies based on things yannar might try to clean. Taren horror movies are almost all about Ionoth or nanotech.

While not staring obsessively at ducting, I've been curled up reading the books Zan bought me. I wasn't really into the first one at the start, but the main characters grew on me. It's set on a world called Lithia, and though the people are ex-Muinan and psychic, they're dealing with the problems of their new world, not Ionoth, and there's a nice dose of magic and mysticism mixed in with the science. I don't know if she was thinking of my psychological aspects or not, but Zan hit on a gift which really made me feel settled, and less keyed up. Even though it's in a different language, holding a book is such a familiar, comfortable thing for me. Like crying all over Maze, I guess it was something I needed.

It didn't take Ghost long to find my new apartment. She seems to like it, especially the window seat, and buried herself in the cushions, keeping a watch on the storms. It's still night on Tare, but there's been some spectacular lightning. Even though all the sound is blocked out so I can't hear the thunder, I love having a window.

Saturday, May 10

Stressing

Horrible nightmares last night. Of drowning, and then being so thirsty. I gave up in the middle of my sleep shift and watched the first few hours of dawn and wished Ghost hadn't gone off somewhere. Training again with Mara today, and more medical exams than seems really necessary. They've moved on to brain scans, and there's yet another greysuit trying to 'debrief' me. Really, if they want to check how I'm coping mentally they'd be far better off having Ista Tremmar chat with me, instead of some woman I've never met before.

The more nightmares I have, the less I want to talk.

Sunday, May 11

Flinch

Today I had lunch with Zan and the only other girl in her squad, Dess Charn. Just a chat about Arenrhon and how I survived my visit to Kalasa. Dess, who doesn't like swimming at all, was very struck by my flippers and webbed fingers and doesn't see why they should do swimming training without using such a useful modification.

Zan listened to her thoughtfully, and said they would include the flippers in their next underwater manoeuvres training, but was absolute about the need to increase speed with surface, non-enhanced swimming. Zan's very good at giving orders. She took my afternoon training session instead of Mara, too, which felt very strange to me. It's been so long since those early sessions with Zan, and I found myself occasionally glancing up at the observation window half-expecting to see people looking down at me.

I'm a lot improved physically. Not halfway fit or anything, but I'm well past getting shaky just because I'm walking. Zan said as I left that she'd be glad to go swimming with me next time I went, and can't know how what she said struck me. I don't want to go swimming. The idea gets me all upset.

And that bothers me a lot.

Monday, May 12

Desensitisation

After this morning's medical tests, today was a free day for me, since First and Twelfth were both on rotation. I brooded in my room for a while, watching it raining outside, the ocean pounding thunderously, then booked the pool and went swimming.

I took a breather with me, but at the start just swam around the surface. It was a long time before I could make myself use the breather and slowly swim down through the obstacle course to the bottom of the pool. It wasn't easy: I had to constantly fight down this urge to kick frantically for the surface. But I'd gotten angry at myself for being like that, and stuck it out until I was all the way at the bottom and then I lay there for a little while taking deep breaths and telling myself I was okay with swimming now.

"Come to the surface."

A text from Ruuel, curt as usual, and unexpected enough that I didn't move immediately. With a sense that I was about to get a lecture, I started back up, only just remembering to stop at the marked spots where you have to wait to avoid getting decompression sickness, though I'm not sure if the pool is so deep you would really get the bends from it. It takes over five minutes if you stop at these points for as long as it says, which gave me plenty of time to make guesses on what he was going to say, wonder why I had to come to the surface for him to say it, and to school myself not to just look totally happy that I got to see him.

I could see a blurry black shape, standing on one side the pool, but remembering how at a disadvantage I'd felt looking up at Kajal, I surfaced a few metres back from the edge only to find he'd dropped to his heels to avoid towering over me. He studied me as I moved a little closer, eyes their usual half open flatness, then said: "Why do this when the squads you're working with are in the Ena?"

I don't know whether it's his Sights or simply being very smart which allows him to jump ahead like that. He didn't need to be told what I was trying to do, and so went straight to the things which were less obvious.

"Because I feel safer when Setari are with me," I said. "Would defeat purpose."

"So would fainting at the bottom of the practice pool."

That annoyed me: it's not as if I'd have gone in the pool if I was feeling tired or sick. "Haven't fainted in days," I said. "Fourth Squad not on leave any more?"

"Another five days."

"Just like wearing uniform?"

He glanced down, well aware that I was moving ground to avoid more lecture, but only said: "This is the middle of my sleep shift."

He meant he was wearing the uniform because it was quick to put on, and he'd been woken up and sent down here to get me to stop putting myself at risk. I felt my face go really hot.

"Sorry."

Ruuel shook his head, then stood. "Confine yourself to the upper five delar," he said, and walked off.

He was out of the room before I remembered I wanted to thank him for my pippin. I could have just sent him a message through the interface, but it wasn't the same, so I put my breather back in and dropped back under water and spent about ten minutes being massively upset.

It wasn't a particularly rational response. After all, instead of telling me I had to have people with me when I went swimming, or telling me off for doing things which someone had obviously considered dangerous, he'd just put a sensible limit on it and left me to it. But I felt bad that he'd been woken up on his holiday because I need babysitting.

And because I do need babysitting right now.

After a while it occurred to me that being upset had distracted me from being underwater. I'm still not keen to go swimming, but I didn't think I was going to achieve anything more hanging around in the pool. Plus I felt really exhausted by then, so I went back to my room and fell asleep. And had horrible nightmares about being chased.

And now I'm wondering if I've stopped being on second level monitoring and have been switched to third level: someone watching me all the time. What, after all, had made them send Ruuel to get me to stop experimenting if they hadn't been watching me do it? And that's upset me even worse than before and I have to think of some way to calm myself down before Maze inevitably shows up and wants to talk over yesterday. I'm lucky I was asleep when First Squad finished their rotation.

Tuesday, May 13

Facing facts

About five minutes after he woke up, Maze sent me a chat message asking if he could come talk to me. I said 'Sure', but as soon as he walked in, I asked: "Have I been put on a higher level of monitoring?"

"You're on a live vitals monitor," he said, not missing a step as he came to sit with me in my window seat. "And locations monitor. A greatly elevated heartbeat at the bottom of the training pool was guaranteed to gain attention."

"Extra monitoring permanent?"

"Few things are permanent." He sighed, looking me over. "I know it chafes you, Caszandra. And that you're used to a great deal more independence than we're likely to ever permit you. But even if you were fully recovered, I'd prefer you not try such experiments alone."

"Needed to do that alone, in case *have* to do it alone," I said, stubbornly. "Agree probably shouldn't have gone so far down."

I could see him decide not to argue the point, instead shifting to the reason I had to think about it at all. "The aerial search for Kalasa has only just begun," he said. "Are you so certain we'll fail to find it?"

"Fairly sure," I said. "Would rather not pretend it's not strong possibility that will have to get back on platform. Easier to prepare for worst and then be glad if doesn't happen."

He had to concede that was common sense, and we talked a while about the likely approach if they can't find Kalasa any way except through me. Finding Kalasa as quickly as possible is one of the highest priority tasks on Muina, because if there's one place that's sure to have information about the platforms and Pillars, it's the place the platforms all lead.

If they do decide to try and use the platforms to get there, they'll first see if it's another level of 'security clearance' and whether it's possible for me to give the Setari clearance. If that doesn't work, it will get a good deal more chancy, and most likely they'd give me some kind of weapon (and food and water and a breather and a really powerful location booster), and then see if I can bring through a Setari in physical contact with me.

They're not keen on that option. But Maze admitted that it was possible I would be asked to do it. We went off to breakfast, and then he had to go do captainly things and I had medical appointments and later training with Mara. I'm feeling better than yesterday. Going into the water was a hurdle I needed to get through, and though I think it'll be a while before I go swimming for fun, I at least know I can handle it.

I'm coping.

Wednesday, May 14

Yesterday, Today, Tomorrow

I think last Sunday was Mother's Day. I was so caught up I forgot all about it. So happy belated Mother's Day, Mum. I probably would have bought you another flowering plant, since I know you like them better than cut flowers. Francesca, maybe, since the last one met a sudden death by Jules.

I've thrown myself back into my school work. For one thing, passing certain tests are a requirement for 'adulthood' here. It's a combination of age and ability. They're not particularly difficult tests, apparently, but I'd hate to be permanently considered to require special care.

And I don't see why I have to have medical tests every single damn day. First Squad are making sure I eat most of my meals with at least one of them, which strikes me as a sufficient stray health check.

Thursday, May 15

Traces of me

They chose Fourteenth Squad today. Alaz was made their Ena Manipulation specialist. Fourteenth is another exploration specialty squad, and I've been booked in to test with them tomorrow.

Their Captain is called Kin Lara, and I feel a little weird that he has my old room. Especially since he has four Sights (not Sight Sight) and who knows what he'll pick up sleeping in my old bed? I'm glad I haven't really been using that room for a while.

I hope it's a squad I get along with. At least there's someone I know already. Alaz wasn't exactly friendly with me during the Rana Junction expedition, but at least she'll be familiar.

Friday, May 16

Fourteenth Squad

A good session today.

We met in the usual test room. I went a little earlier than usual to meet up with Nils Sayate from Second, who is trying to teach me how to make illusions. Lessons are my present from him: he gave me a choice between foot rubs and lessons and I chose the lessons because I don't really trust Nils to give me foot rubs. I mean, I think he's in love with Zee, but sometimes I'm not altogether sure he's just teasing when he flirts with me.

Occasionally the only thing which keeps me from flirting back is that I'm pretty sure Zee is in love with him too. But I do think about it sometimes. In a way I think a couple of nights with Nils would be good for me. It would certainly be educational.

He's very professional about the lessons though, which have all been visualisation exercises so far. He's got a great voice for talking through what you're supposed to be visualising: smoky and evocative. I completely failed to make any illusions, possibly because I'm far less professional and kept thinking about foot rubs. But Nils told me that Illusion-casting is one of the hardest talents to master and that I shouldn't give up, and he'd try talking me through every few weeks. I'm still not entirely convinced I have any kind of Illusion talent, but I don't mind trying. It would be nice to be able to *show* the things I'm talking about when trying to describe Earth.

Fourteenth Squad arrived in a group, and came across to introduce themselves. Their captain, Lara, was so very relaxed he was almost unconscious, and I really liked the sleepy smile he gave me. He totally didn't act like someone who'd only been a captain for a single day, taking his squad through the tests as if he'd been doing the same thing every day for the last year.

It was interesting working with a squad where everyone was my age or a year younger. Except for Lara, they were still tremendously correct and upright during the session, but I felt less like a pet or mascot and more of a peer. I liked them. I hope all my future test sessions are so comfortable.

Saturday, May 17

Slowly shifting back to normal

Mara stepped up my training today, and also took me on a tour of the gym facilities the Setari use. I knew they had to be doing weights training somewhere. She explained how to use the machines, but doesn't want me to use the place without someone with me. No fear of that: although there were only a couple of people from Tenth Squad there today, the chances of me ending up alone in a gym with Fifth or Seventh Squad are too great for me to ever risk using the place without minders.

I'm due to test with Thirteenth Squad tomorrow, and my next week has been mapped out with testing with the few squads I haven't worked with. Mara says they still don't know if I'll be put back on rotations or not, and surprised me by asking my preferences. I usually don't get to have any input on these decisions, so suspect this is more catering to my psychological aspects. Since my excursion to Kalasa, everyone's pretty much decided I'm a delicate little flower on the verge of collapse. Even Mara is more careful with me than she used to be. That's what I get for crying on a mission log.

I said I'd prefer to go on rotation so long as it was with First Squad. It's a more positive thing to do than fretting about nightmares, and I worry about them. They're looking tired.

Sunday, May 18

Fifteen minutes plus

A little after "my" midnight, just as I was settling into bed for the night, Mori sent me a text channel request: "You may be interested in this."

Surprised, I opened the channel to find Mori, Glade, and Par, as well as Seeli Henaz from Eighth Squad in channel. I don't know Henaz well, but I think she's Mori's particular friend and maybe Glade's almost-girlfriend.

"Which?"

"This is an extra-length special episode," Mori said, popping up a link in channel, and I opened it to find the middle of the opening credits of *The Hidden War*.

"Still years behind on show," I said, though I was beginning to suspect why Mori had felt the need to call me.

"From the episode preview, we think they've based a character on you," Glade said.

"Inevitable, I guess," I said, making sure to sound totally unfussed about it. And I wasn't, really. It's nothing that wouldn't happen on Earth. "Kind of used to people making up things about me."

"You can tell us what they've gotten wrong," Mori said, sounding pleased. "We comment in text, and chat during the breaks."

I thought it sweet of her to have made sure I knew about it, so stuck around even though it would mess up my sleep schedule again. Taren entertainments have two release 'broadcasts' in different shifts which have commercials in them but are free, and then the show is available to watch for a fee (like twenty cents), without commercials. It was very common for people to watch the release in channel groups, though not necessarily to make fun of the show like Mori and Glade. I'm not sure if Par watches it because he likes it or just to keep Glade company. It's one of the most successful entertainments on Tare at the moment, and I've been enjoying watching it, though I'd taken a break from it because it was full of the main character being picked on by other Kalrani competing to be selected for the next Setari squad, and I kept getting stuck on the thought of people bullying Zan. I can only guess what Zan would think of me thinking about her that way. It's not like she's not incredibly deadly and competent in her own right.

The special episode started with a girl walking out of nowhere onto a hill and being all astonished, staring about her. She was tallish, with brown hair, but that's where the resemblance to me ended. This girl was much, much (much) better looking. Pointed chin, huge, dark eyes, gorgeous bones and skin and figure: a kind of Russian look, which I think is very rare here. I was totally distracted by the way she was dressed, with a vaguely correct school blazer and a white shirt, but no tie, and a micro-miniskirt with long dark blue socks that came up to mid-thigh. Seems *The Hidden War* isn't above a little fan service.

"Would get sent home if turned up to school wearing skirt that short," was all I said in channel, and moved on to wondering if they'd gone to Muina to film this, since it was quite obviously hills in the same region as Pandora, except just starting to turn colours – wherever they'd sourced the images from, it wasn't in the late Autumn of the last few weeks. I could hardly believe they'd managed to produce a whole program about me in the short time since news of my existence was released.

Other than the silly outfit, I didn't mind the way they were portraying me. Upset, but not totally hysterical, calling out in a nonsense-language and looking bewildered and sitting down for a while before growing resolute. She picked a direction and started out that way, scoring marks on the trees with a rock, which I hadn't thought to do. I was impressed with the relative correctness of her school bag and how the first problem she ran into was blisters, and they even had her doing an inventory of what she was carrying, and writing in a diary as the sun set.

Her writing was nonsense characters which looked like shorthand to me, with subtitles translating fragments such as: "Where is this place? I'm sure this isn't Urth. All I can do is keep pushing on until I find civilisation – but what if I'm the only one here?"

There was a commercial break after that, and we chatted in-channel about how the actress was good at looking scared and lost and determined, and the things I'd done which they obviously hadn't thought about (mainly checking my mobile, and finding out that I had not nearly enough tissues to serve as toilet paper on an alien world – though I didn't bother to mention that to everyone), and we made guesses at the mechanics of how they'd created the program, since they were all sure that no on-location filming had or would be permitted for some time. Glade was full of explanations of how they'd have done the computer simulations based on the officially released surveys.

After that fake-me's journey was 'fast forwarded', cutting several days into a series of shots of worse blisters, and trying random berries and nuts, attempting to weave a basket and a mat and make a hat, and avoiding animals, then staring at the moon with its very un-Earth-like hole. I started to be less impressed about the accuracy of the show around the time the actress climbed up a tree to avoid a pack of small yellow dogs, and they went to the next break after a longer scene where she was lying under a mat of woven reeds, the 'screen' filled with darkness and all you could hear was something walking toward her, the crackle of the reed mat bending under the unseen thing's weight, and its breathing as it stood above her and she tried to hold her own breath and not to cry. Extremely effective.

I couldn't even talk after that. Not for the bad memories but because I'd told only Isten Notra about the yellow dogs, and only Lohn and Mara about that horrible night when I nearly died from the sheer anticipation of being eaten. That was the same time I'd talked to them about how upset it would make me to be cloned. Mori and Glade were being impressed with the show, but when they started to chat I said in text: "That really happen. Only told that two people. Lots of this happen."

There was a brief pause, then Glade said: "Are you in quarters, Caszandra?" He wouldn't know because Fourth's still on leave and most people don't have the rights to do pinpoint location tracking.

"Yes. Supposed to be asleep. How many people can access complete KOTIS file about me?"

"I'll ask," he said. "Don't leave the channel, all right?"

The ad break had only just finished when Ketzaren – the only member of First Squad not asleep – sent me a text saying: "Can I come in?"

I released the door and made the lights go from black to dim. I didn't feel like getting out of bed – I felt sick and awful and hot – but didn't want to wait there like a kid clutching a teddy bear, so I met her at the door and she took one look at me and made me sit on the couch. She was dressed in a shirt and shorts, had obviously been in bed herself, and she sat down with me and squeezed me hard as Mori brought her into the channel we were sharing.

"I think mainly I'm angry they didn't warn me they were going to release so much," I said out loud, but that was a mistake because my voice sounded nearly as rawly betrayed as I felt and I missed a lot of the next bit because I was concentrating on not crying. It was about finding Pandora, and searching out my tower and setting up a home there. I began to calm down, for while it was still accurate, except for a dramatic Ming Cat stalking which hadn't happened at all, there wasn't anything in it which I hadn't described to several different people. Ketzaren rubbed my shoulder and watched, and when the next ad break came, just after the first moonfall, she said: "Mara's bringing us something hot to drink."

"Didn't want to wake people up," I said, unhappily. Part of the reason I was upset by then was because I'd *gotten* upset and caused a fuss, instead of just asking Maze about it the next day. "Feel like an overwrought baby lately, always having dramas."

"Stop holding yourself to such an impossibly high standard," Ketzaren said. "This whole year has been an extreme for you. You've adapted better than we could have hoped, but being lost again, hurt and alone and in such danger – you're not going to just get over it. Why are you expecting that of yourself? Are you still having nightmares?"

"Not as many."

"But too many, right? And now this. Believe me, this goes well beyond the limits of what's been officially released about you. And you end up feeling violated, feeling you can't even trust us, to talk to us and not have what you say repeated. And yet we're the only people you know enough to want to talk about it, and then you feel like you're burdening us by being upset."

"That transparent?"

"You're a straightforward person." She tugged at a wisp of my hair. "Myself, I'd be furious and want to hit things, but you don't seem to respond that way. Are you sure you want to watch the rest of this?"

"Will never get to sleep without knowing what else is in there." But then there would be next episode, and next episode. I realised I was shaking, literally sitting there shaking because of a TV show, and there was no way to hide that from Ketzaren.

The show played up the drama of me slowly getting sicker while trying to do practical survivor stuff. Mara arrived with some mugs of a hot drink which bore a vague resemblance to tea. Lots of sweetener. She and Ketzaren squeezed me between them even though they're not supposed to both touch me at once and we watched the improbably pretty girl decline into a exhausted and ill but possibly even prettier girl, and apparently have some prophetic visions of Pillars and stone gates during the second moonfall. Mara and Ketzaren felt me react to that, too, but there was no way I was explaining.

"It amazes me that she's still wearing those socks," I said into the shared channel during the next ad break, and my voice was almost normal. "The number of useful things I could have done with thigh-length socks, and all she does is wear them."

"Useful things like what?" Mori asked, sounding greatly relieved that I'd stopped having a breakdown.

"Could probably have made a sling – a way to throw rocks and things really hard and fast as a weapon. Or used one as a bag. Make good straps, too. She didn't even double them over as padding when she had blisters."

"Part of the image they're marketing," Glade said. "I expect the entire outfit can be purchased as cross-promotion."

The idea of thousands of Taren teenagers running around in sexed-up versions of my school uniform was pretty mind boggling. I shook my head, hoping that if ever Tare established communication with Earth they'll have lost all copies of this program before then.

It was hard to watch the next part. I've always been scared by the idea of madness, and those days after the second moonfall, when I grew increasingly convinced that there were things lurking around every corner, were still a confusing and unpleasant haze. I was very weak and felt like my mind was falling apart along with my body. I'd skimmed over this when talking to Isten Notra, but had obviously revealed more than I'd wanted. And then the Ddura, which I realise must have saved my life from the Ionoth trying to reach me, or whatever was going on before it arrived. Then a hazy still morning, and the scene was shown through the actress' eyes – two black-clad figures standing in her refuge looking down at her. They hadn't exactly matched Sonn and Ruuel in looks, but there was a definite similarity, particularly in the half-lidded eyes of the guy.

Then the viewpoint drew back, showed the three from the side, and switched to Sonn's viewpoint, looking down at a sick and unkempt (but still very beautiful) girl who was gazing up at them, fear and shock turning to joy on her face.

"Filthy creature," commented the fake Ruuel.

My jaw dropped. I could imagine Par, Mori and Glade's reactions.

"What do we do with her?" asked the fake Sonn (their names, according to the Setari mission overlay, were Lastier and Chane). "We don't have the time to waste on a stray."

"Put her down by the lake for collection. She's not our problem."

He went up the stairs to the roof, leaving 'Chane' to herd a frightened kittenish girl downstairs, making a big point of avoiding any attempt by the 'filthy creature' to touch her. The show finished with a scene of the girl sitting abandoned on a rock by the shore, clutching school bag to chest and staring at the ship out on the lake.

After 'Lastier' made his nasty comment, Mori had said hastily in text: "Ruuel didn't say anything like that, Caszandra," and I'd replied: "I know – I read mission report." When the closing credits began to run, she and Glade exploded, outraged. Even Par said something half-audible about it being so wrong. All of Fourth are totally loyal to Ruuel, and they couldn't stand him being shown in a false light.

"Poor Sonn," I said, when they paused for breath. "Ruuel not likely even blink at this, but Sonn will be really hurt. If you talk to her, make sure she knows I didn't think they were being nasty to me: they just looked like they were busy and hadn't expected to find me." When I'd watched the mission report, I'd realised it was more they hadn't expected to find me *alive*, after tracking my movements to the tower.

"Fourth is an unusual squad to have cast in the role of villain," Henaz said, sounding like she was trying very hard not to laugh. "But this is the most obvious and deliberate reflection of a real squad I've ever seen."

"And portions of that were an exact copy of the scene recorded on the mission log," Ketzaren added. "Which is the issue at hand. You'll hear the results of the investigation presently. Be assured that there is no suggestion that Fourth Squad's conduct was anything but correct."

"And on that note, we're well into our sleep shift," Mara put in. "Good night to you all." She dropped out of the channel, and after adding "Thanks for letting me know," I followed suit.

"Funny how two extra words can change tone of entire scene," I said. "That's almost exactly how Fourth did deal with me, but by adding two words it made it so they were horrible instead of just really busy."

"You've recovered a little," Ketzaren said, smiling. "No longer so shaken up?"

I shrugged and ducked my head. "It was the surprise, seeing that without any warning. I was expecting the story to be all wrong and totally made up."

"Instead of including something frightening you'd only told Lohn and I?" Mara asked, voice tight. "I'm so angry about this I could scream. Maze has been looking for ways to increase your sense of security and privacy, not destroy it. We did log that conversation, Caszandra, and Maze attached it to an evaluation report, but even Lohn and I can't look at the report. Outside the higher hierarchy, only captains can look at evaluation information, and then only on their own squad members, which in your case means three captains. None of it should be forming the basis of public broadcasts. I really don't know what's going on, but both you and Fourth Squad have every reason to be furious."

"Too tired now to get angry," I said. "Sorry to have made fuss in middle of sleep cycle."

"You think it would be better to work yourself into a state alone?" Ketzaren asked. "Part of being in a squad is supporting each other."

"I'll be sitting with you for a few hours," Mara added. "No arguments. Besides, it means Ketz gets to be the one to wake Maze and tell him there's been a security breach. It'll be easier on all of us if someone's with you."

I didn't really have the energy to argue, to try to convince Mara that I was fine, that I was coping. I'm starting to have to admit, at least to myself, that because of Kalasa, or just everything which has happened since my last day of exams, I'm not nearly okay.

I'm so glad Mara stayed, because I had the most horrendous nightmares, and it seemed like I could escape from them because she would hold my hand when I started thrashing around. Some time toward the end, Zee replaced Mara, and I woke up from this really awful dream – of being in a Roman colosseum with thousands of people watching me being eaten by lions – to find Zee sitting on the edge of my bed, a steadying hand on my arm.

She watched me blink at her, then felt my forehead. "Medical for you today, I think," she said, "and don't pull that face. I don't know if it's the fever causing the nightmares, or the nightmares causing the fever, but your temperature's definitely elevated. Did you dream so violently on Earth?"

"No. I used to have bad dreams when I was young, but nothing like this. Not even on Muina, though I did have nightmares. Started on really bad dreams after turning off Pillar – kind of remembering what happened, the bits I couldn't remember when I was awake. It had gone away, though–" I paused, flushing.

"Though should I talk about it in case it ends up turned into entertainment?"

More that I'd started having very intense dreams about Ruuel, which had made up for the nightmares, but this wasn't something I was going to admit, security breach or not. I shrugged and said: "I think I generally dream more intensely now. Or remember them better when I wake up. Did investigation into program get anywhere?"

"I've heard rumours, but there's nothing official. Get dressed and we'll have breakfast."

We ate in Zee's quarters. Maze came and joined us to talk over the program and how I felt about it. I said pretty bluntly that it made me want to not tell anyone anything, but that I knew that was an overreaction. I totally refused to talk to a psychologist though. I have nightmares because scary monsters were chasing me. If I have to talk about that, I'd far rather talk to Zee or Mara, not some random stranger.

Maze told me I shouldn't watch *The Hidden War* any more but I said there was no way I was going to miss Fourth Squad playing villains, and couldn't wait for the episode where the Nuran shows up and tries to save me. He knew I was teasing him, but I think I will watch it anyway, just not with other people watching with me. I get the feeling Maze has a good idea of how the people who make the program got the information, but he's not going to tell me anything until it's official. I hope he's right about nothing more leaking out.

Right now I'm stuck on a sense-bed in medical, while they run more scans on me. They want me to go to sleep later so they can scan me while I'm having a dream, but I'm seriously not keen on that because what if I dream about Ruuel?

I hope I was right about him not caring about the show. He'll probably be annoyed because it will upset his squad, but would surely shrug off anything else. I'm so glad I'd watched the mission log, and knew immediately that he hadn't said that. I find it difficult to imagine him actually saying something gratuitous and insulting, whether he thought it or not.

I *was* really grubby, after all. Just thinking about it makes me want a hot bath and lots of scented soap.

Monday, May 19

Careful what you say

Nothing useful from all the scanning and testing. My temperature went down, and though I was tired I found it hard to fall asleep. They eventually gave me a mild sedative and I'm not sure I dreamed at all. They had me come back today as well and this time I could fall asleep naturally. My sleep schedule is completely messed up. I dreamed about being lost in a shopping mall, I think – it was a bit of a jumble. They've cleared me to go back to what I was doing, anyway, and my scheduled testing with the remaining squads is on again (though Thirteenth has been pushed to the end instead of the beginning).

I think the sleep tests were skewed for failure. First because I didn't *want* to have any intense dreams and was consciously or subconsciously trying not to. And second, I wasn't really upset any more, and I mostly have the worst nightmares when I'm upset or stressed out. That's the reason people usually have bad nightmares, anyway.

Mori came and visited me this afternoon – Fourth Squad is back on duty tomorrow. She's still really pissed off, and was worked up about an interview with the actor who is playing fake Ruuel. In the interview he talked about the incredible schedule they'd been keeping to produce the show so quickly, and how much he enjoyed the role, and that one of the reasons *The Hidden War* was so powerful was because it refused to show the Setari as bland, one-sided heroes without any faults. That even out-and-out villains can risk their lives protecting others.

I thought this terribly funny, but tried not to show it too much because Mori was genuinely upset on Ruuel's behalf. I'm willing to bet Ruuel's the least upset in Fourth right now. The main reason the squad's so worked up is that it's so similar to what happened, and certainly within KOTIS everyone knows it was Fourth Squad who found me. Plus, the kittenish actress is playing 'Caszandra Devlin'. In the interview with her she said that the producers had decided it would be foolish to rename such a major historical figure. And *The Hidden War* has portrayed the people who found me as being severe pricks. I can only hope that they're just playing up 'villain aspects' for drama, and will tone it down later. After all, Ruuel did save my life when I wandered off into the spaces.

After Mori left, Maze and Zee dropped in to tell me the results of the investigation. Apparently one of KOTIS' publicity officers, a woman named Intena Jun, decided to use me to build her career. Part of her duties was the release of information about the Setari and lately about me and the developments on Muina. That includes giving technical advice to shows like *The Hidden War* when they ask for it. And it seems she fancies herself a bit of a scriptwriter, and just happened to have resigned the day before the episode featuring me was broadcast – and then bobs up in a press release as a former KOTIS member joining the scriptwriting team.

That was a far from ideal situation, but still shouldn't have meant that my conversation with Lohn and Mara ended up forming the basis of anything: you can't join KOTIS without signing an inch-thick nondisclosure agreement, and publicity officers certainly don't have access to anyone's evaluation file, or even the mission reports. But it turns out that Jun is using the completely transparent excuse that it's all fiction based around the publicly-released information about me, and that her family in the past has been known to produce minor Sight Sight talents, and she was simply intuiting very well. Of course, since the press release there's been tons of rumours about just how much of the script is fiction, which is exactly what the producers wanted. The episode was a wild success, and the discussion groups are filled with anticipation of a season they hope will reveal details of real Setari.

The episode was a critical success, too, with lots of admiration for the actress (a newcomer named Se-Ahn Surat, who did after all carry a kasse-long program as the nearly sole character, practically never speaking). Almost all the reviews rave about the night scene, the way something as simple as an animal breathing brought home the peril and horror 'this valiant child suffered through'.

It took KOTIS an extra day to figure out how Jun had accessed the files. Maze stayed vague about the details, but it boiled down to some very senior and high-up bluesuit who *did* have access to just about everything, also having 'an inappropriate relationship' with Jun. So lots of nasty consequences for him for the breach of security, and less clear-cut consequences for Jun. Although the legal system here isn't as insane as Earth's, KOTIS is merely a body of government, not all-powerful. They can, and probably will, prosecute and try and get Jun punished (fines, loss of all but the most basic interface function, or possibly confinement). Tare doesn't have capital punishment, but in extreme circumstances they can do particularly awful things to you using the interface. Stealing my file isn't nearly extreme enough a circumstance.

It sounds like Jun is ambitious enough to consider a few years of freedom or privileges or even citizenship a price worth paying for highly lucrative employment.

"Our ability to control media access to KOTIS and the Setari is waning," Maze said, rubbing his eyes. He's looking tired again. "Previously, we succeeded in retaining our anonymity because to a degree outside KOTIS we were all the same. A uniform and a talent set: there was no need to release anything about our personal lives. Which means programs such as this one would be freely provided with details of how we balance squad make up, the limitations of talent sets, and information about the rotations and the Ionoth, but names and our lives off-duty and the minutiae of actual missions: we simply allowed nothing at all out, so into these situations they would place invented characters. Even the squads in these fictions are named for colours, so that a character in Green Squad cannot be taken as a member of Fourth, or Eighth or Tenth. Occasionally someone's family would grant interviews, and most of our names are in public domain, but they cannot match the names to squads, faces or events. Only in death are we known." He glanced at me, nothing on his face showing whether he was thinking about his wife.

"But now, because of the opening of Muina, the ground is shifting," Zee added. "Our efforts in the Ena lessened deaths on Tare, but we had made no substantial progress toward a solution. There were no critical events to attach to us as individuals. Until Fourth Squad found you. Something so significant that this show's producers chose to upset the established rules, obtain actual information about the squad, and introduce characters based on Fourth. Worse, a distortion of Fourth. Even if they used already-established characters, those characters would become associated with the squads who have worked with you."

"If they follow my story very close, that means Zan would be next." I didn't like that idea at all.

"The classification of information about Muina is also being called into question," Maze said. "The discovery of Arenrhon, your time in Kalasa – all of this is known to hundreds, thousands. Details are starting to leak, many are asking what right KOTIS, the government, what right anyone has to classify matters which are important to all descendants of Muina." He sighed and shrugged. "It's difficult to justify keeping secret the existence of Arenrhon purely because it might upset people. These things cannot be hidden forever."

"Which is a long-winded way of saying that KOTIS may not be able to quash these programs," Zee added. "At most delay them, but however the information was obtained, your personal journey can't be argued to be a military secret."

"And through me, parts of Setari become known too." I turned over the possibilities, and felt a little ill. "Is squads I don't want to work with in file?"

"Selkie kept that entirely out of the reports," Maze said. "It will go no further than himself, Ruuel and us. Fifth and Seventh are very effective squads who need to learn to control their egos. We won't achieve that by letting anyone know just why it is you will never again be assigned to them. If we handle them properly, they should come to understand and regret that of their own accord."

I relaxed, then sighed. "Can still be a mess, though, yes? Because they mix extra drama in with true, and Setari won't always know which has come from my file." I paused, eyes widening. "Is lab rat explanation in file?" I tugged at my shirt, one of the drawn-on ones. I make a point of wearing them to my test sessions in the medical section.

I saw from Maze's expression that it was, and couldn't help it, bursting out laughing. "Did you put in bit where Ruuel says calling myself experimental animal was right?" I asked, trying (maybe not very hard) to hold back my grin. "Set himself up for this. Oh, wish I dared tease him about it."

Maze and Zee told me that I should remember that Fourth Squad wouldn't find it nearly as funny, but I think they were mainly glad that I was able to laugh. Zee offered to sit with me tonight while I sleep, but I think I'm past the worst of it. I seem to have these bad dreams after a shock or surprise. Must figure out how to trigger the good dreams instead.

Given the chance, I would love to give that publicity woman a good slapping. Maybe I should tell Taarel that I think it would help me overcome my reluctance to hit people.

Tuesday, May 20

Ticking off the rest

I've been scheduled to test with Sixth, Tenth, Eleventh, Twelfth and Thirteenth Squads, and that will finish me for general squad testing until they form some new ones. Today was Twelfth Squad, which was nice. Lenton was carefully correct while a relaxed Zan chatted with me before starting the session log. Afterwards, we all went to lunch, and talked about Kalasa. Zan kept a watchful eye on me, ready to stop if I looked distressed, and when a couple of them moved on to *The Hidden War,* particularly how hilarious it was that Fourth Squad were evil, she quashed that conversation with a word.

I think active service has let Twelfth settle down and accept Zan more. I still have no idea why they were so hostile to her, but don't like to ask.

Fourth Squad's back on duty, and I spent all day being a little extra attentive in case I could catch a glimpse of Ruuel. And was so annoyed with myself for doing that. I had my usual post-testing session nap, and when I woke the sense of him not being there was so strong that I had to spend a lot of effort making myself not get upset. He's on a different shift to me now, so there's not a lot of chance I'll see him.

Time to have dinner with Lohn and Mara.

Wednesday, May 21

Trashy Mags For the Win

I went up to the roof today: it's the first time the weather's been good enough since I was released from the infirmary. Tare doesn't really seem to have seasons, just storms. It still bothers me to be shut inside so much, but having a window makes a huge difference. I wonder if I have any chance at all of convincing them to make me one which opens.

I'd been there a while, reading an explanation of why everyone on Tare isn't chalk white and suffering from vitamin E deficiency (special lighting, basically), when Zee showed up and sat down with me.

"That looks like your 'time for a serious talk' expression. Something happen?"

"You'll make me self-conscious," Zee said (with the easy confidence of a gorgeous, super-deadly woman). "And, yes, something is happening. A media storm about Arenrhon, via Kolar. Previously we've controlled information by allowing very few to return to Tare or Kolar after visiting Muina, and vetting outgoing communication. But that was always going to be a short-term solution as more and more people became involved. And Kolaren devices don't connect to the interface, and thus don't have the censor controls. One was smuggled back there, containing very complete details of the expeditions, Arenrhon–"

"Cass's visit to Kalasa."

"There are many images of the Arenrhon site, including images of Third, Fourth and Eighth Squad, and you. It's all over Kolar's news networks, and is about to hit here. The fact that information between the planets depends on ships means we have a little warning."

"Setari losing more and more anonymity." I sighed. "You feel like doing some training or playing a game or something? Would rather not sit waiting for the initial reaction."

"You're very calm about this," Zee said, sounding approving.

"Knew this one was coming. Too many people at Arenrhon who very interested in me – and Setari. Don't like it, but not so upsetting as someone making lot of money off things they stole out of my file, or without warning seeing some girl pretending to go through that."

We went to the gymnasium and Zee put me through some mild resistance training and stretches, and then a short stint of fast walking on a treadmill. I'm not really up to jogging yet. I had switched my interface status to 'busy', which meant that while people could send me messages they shouldn't expect me to respond. Zan and Mori both sent me messages, but I didn't even look at them until Zee had decided I would fall over if I trained more, and we showered and took lunches back to her rooms to look the news over.

I check out the news about the Setari first, which was basically a frenzy of joy. Actual pictures of real Setari. No matter how accurate the drawings of those who had enjoyed a personal Setari sighting, they could not compare to proper images. They were nice quality pictures, too – clear and sharp, often close-ups of faces. They were already matched up to the dossiers which had been compiled from sightings over the years, and I noticed with amusement that the only person who didn't have a clear picture was Ruuel, who seemed to have always been turned away.

The reaction to Arenrhon was unsurprising: upset about the implications of the worshipful imagery, anger that none of this had been communicated to the public.

I'd been avoiding any of the links that appeared to lead to me, but finally started browsing. Some of them were really great photos, making me look not half-bad looking, but it was very disconcerting how many were close-up. They'd used a zoom function to great effect. Much was being made of the fact that my eyes were different colours.

My favourite picture was one where I had one brow pulled a bit down and the corner of my mouth screwed up and an air of absolute incredulity – the kind of expression I'm sure I was wearing when Maze told me to put on a dress to meet the Nuran. I couldn't resist one link titled 'Interplanetary Love!', and opened it to find a Kolaren trashy infozine with a picture of me smiling up at Arad Nalaz of Kolar's Squad One, who was looking down at me in a kindly sort of way. That had been just after I'd been grilled by all those Kolaren archaeologists.

"I hope Nalaz doesn't have a really jealous girlfriend," I said, speaking for the first time since Zee and I had ventured into the wilds of interface fervour. "I'll have to remember not to smile in public at anything male in future. And, wow, there's a lot of pictures of me. These were all taken in my last couple of days at Arenrhon, too. Whoever took these could qualify as a full-blown stalker."

There was no fooling Zee, who rubbed the back of my neck gently. "That looks like your 'pretending not to be upset' expression."

I shrugged, though my face went hot. "I'm not saying I like this, because I don't. But it's...kind of distant from me. And it's just pictures and information that everyone on Muina already knew: that I react weirdly but not usefully to the ruins, and that I can use the platforms to get myself in bad situations, was injured and taken back to Tare. A thousand people already knew that. The only real difference with that number changing to a billion is that I can read about their opinion of what I look like. Though – did you see all that stuff about how KOTIS was being too careless with me and that an oversight committee needs to be established to ensure I'm properly handled? What chance is there that actually happen?"

"Hard to say. There's an oversight committee for the Setari and that's been beneficial for us over the years. Do you feel KOTIS has been too careless with you?"

I had to think it over. After all, I've been hospitalised a half-dozen times since I was rescued.

"It's like when I first arrived on Muina, and was trying to find something to eat. I looked for fruit that I could see animals were willing to eat, then did taste test, and ate more if it didn't kill me. One of things I ate made me so sick. Was that too careless? I saw a bird eating some, and it looked and tasted, well, as non-poisonous as anything can look. I look like ordinary stray, so KOTIS treat me like one. Then find out have enhancing talent, so KOTIS test what enhancing talent does. Couldn't know in advance that three Setari touching me at once give me heart attack. Obviously wouldn't have arranged that test if had known, any more than I would eat fruit that make me vomit. Same with teleporting about on platforms. If platforms did that for anyone else, no way they would have had me stand on it. Is not to say that I don't dislike some things. I drew my lab rat on clothes for a reason. Never consulted or told about almost anything, especially at start. Never agreed to follow anyone's orders; just do so because seemed best option for me. Oversight committee...sounds like more people who get to read my file."

Zee stayed with me for my very low-impact training session with Mara, and then the whole squad came together for dinner. We ate something resembling doubled-over pizza in Maze's quarters, the first time I'd been in there. I thought initially that he had no decoration in his public space at all, but every so often a bird flies across the room or patters around the floor, and treats the walls like they're curtains it can hide behind. And there was a picture spot, which flicked through images of a whole bunch of people who looked like Maze, reminding me that the Setari all have families outside KOTIS. A few excess objects, a nice bowl on the table, an odd-looking wire statue. If there was anything which had belonged to his wife, I couldn't tell.

None of First Squad seems to think all the revelation of the day will have any major consequences. I made sure to not act upset, and I didn't really need to act. It does seem very distant and not part of my life and at least most of it is positive. The spin KOTIS put out about Earth being Muina's 'sister' planet seems to have held. But the pictures were another reminder that even ignoring second level monitoring, I don't have any real privacy and I'm coming under more and more scrutiny. Everything I do, everything I say and see and hear, is recorded. Even this diary, well-protected by its barrier of foreign words, will stop being any kind of secret if the Tarens learn English from me (or other people from Earth).

I did figure out a solution to my worries about the record made of files I access. I just watch my conversation with my family over and over again. Not only does it make me feel better to see Mum, but anyone compiling statistics on my access patterns will be sure to put it down to 'watches encounter with family' not 'gazes mournfully at Kaoren Ruuel'. I always make sure to stop as soon as I move away from my family, then start again from the first time I see them.

This makes me sound really lame. But it does help to be able to look at him, and I would find it pretty unbearable to have my pathetic, one-sided crush exposed for everyone in KOTIS to laugh about, let alone risking it becoming public gossip. I don't care at all if gossips make up patently false stories about me and every second Kolaren I talk to, but Ruuel *matters*.

It seems like forever since I had one of the really good dreams about him, but every damn day I wake up knowing he's not there.

Thursday, May 22

Eleventh Squad

Eleventh Squad today: a team I'd only seen the once at the big parade where they demonstrated me to all the Setari. Didn't go too badly. Their captain is a girl called Seq Endaran, who contacted me before the testing session and introduced herself before walking down to the test room with me to meet her squad members: Couran – Path Sight, Gate Sight; Genera – Ena manipulation; Wen, Seeth, Dava – combat. They're a big-hitting squad, lots of big elemental talents. I started out giving Endaran points for good manners and feeling very positive, and she didn't do anything to change my mind, but she also seemed kind of pleased with herself. I don't know, maybe it's just that so many of the big hitting squads love being able to hit even harder. The only person in the squad who really stood out for me was Wen, who just was very calm and cheerful, watching the testing session like it was a good special effects movie.

I've tested with so many squads now the faces are beginning to blur together.

Enhancing elemental talents takes a lot more out of me than Speed and Sights. I don't even seem to get tired after a session which doesn't involve elementals, but bring on a big-hitting squad and it's a guaranteed afternoon nap.

Incredible storm outside. Black as pitch, lots of lightning, horizontal rain trying to pound the world to dust. I'm amazed the Tarens survived their early years here.

Friday, May 23

A little light gossip

Tomorrow's the next episode of *The Hidden War* (the week here is six days). Mori asked me if I'd like to join them in watching it, but I said I'd pass. Not that I'm not going to watch it, but I plan to keep my breakdowns to myself from now on. We chatted about the big media storm, and how strange it was for some of the squads to have their images out there properly and how some of the drawings that people had made (Tare isn't above fan art of every variety) had once bothered Mori a great deal, but she'd grown to care about it a lot less.

Mori also said that I was right about Sonn being very upset. The episode had shown her as an obedient henchman to Ruuel's villain, and though no words were put in her mouth she was taking it badly. Ruuel's only comment, apparently, has been to say that he expected them to have more sense. He's been working Fourth unusually hard, though, which is the same tactic Mara uses on me when she thinks I'm fretting.

I wondered if the other squads – particularly Fifth – had been openly enjoying themselves at Fourth's expense, but Mori hasn't reached the point of being willing to talk about other squads with me. And I, in turn, am far too cautious to ever directly question her about Ruuel.

Generally a quiet day for me. Training with Mara, and medical tests, which are fortunately becoming a trifle less frequent. Lots of reading about me, and also about Arenrhon. Since the Lantarens were very unpopular on Tare and Kolar anyway, all this has done has confuse people and confirm their opinions that the Lantarens were to blame for the loss of Muina.

Saturday, May 24

Tenth Squad

Tenth Squad today. Tenth was the squad who went with Twelfth to rescue everyone at the Pillar. It brought a lot of memories back to work with them again. Their squad leader, Haral, is this calm, soft-spoken guy and I'd already had a demonstration of him being very good in an emergency.

We went through the testing quite thoroughly, even though all of Tenth had enhanced with me during the retrieval, and then did a bit of managing-the-stray combat training 'since we're here'. Tenth has a Telekinesis talent, Mane, and a Levitation talent, Tens, who are both female and shorter than me and we were all finding it funny working out comfortable ways for them to cart me about.

Another team lunch afterwards, and again lots of questions about Kalasa. It's always easy to the spot the captain in the squad: the one keeping a watchful eye on me to see if I'm going to burst into tears. I don't particularly mind talking about Kalasa, though I do wonder why the Setari feel the need to ask me questions when they've obviously all watched the log of me stumbling around the place. I was glad when it turned into a more general discussion about the Lantarens, and whether the people at Arenrhon were some kind of weird sub-cult or something known to all Lantarens.

I started to fall asleep, so Haral sent his squad off and escorted me back to my quarters.

"Thank you for indulging them," he said, as we rode the elevator down. "Are you facing the same interrogation from every squad you test with?"

"Some still in the must-be-very-proper stage," I said, and he gave me an amused smile.

"We're working to adapt. We've been very well trained to deal with Ionoth, and each other, but not extraordinary girls from other worlds who keep completely altering the scope of our lives."

"Am pretty typical Australian," I said, opening my door to hide my embarrassment.

"Oztralya must be a disconcerting place, then," he said, then was distracted by a really spectacular lightning bolt outside. "There's certainly few on Tare who could bear that in their living quarters, for instance. Let alone survive what you've endured."

His voice was still soft and calm, but very definite, and I was all of a sudden aware that he was an attractive person my own age, and these were my rooms. But I pushed all that aside and just said: "Is a thick window." Blushing madly, of course.

He smiled again, nodded, and left. After the door closed, I shut off the lights and sat in my window seat, watching another incredible lightning bolt.

I couldn't decide if Haral was just being straightforwardly complimentary, or quietly indicating that he rather liked and admired me. Something in the way he'd said it just felt...charged. He is a Lightning talent, heh.

It's hard to decide how I feel about the possibility. I was impressed by Haral during the retrieval, and I liked the comfortable way he worked with me today. He's sort of relaxing, made me feel at ease. He's fairly typical Taren in looks: golden skin and black hair, though with just the faintest hint of a curl, and his eyes are a clear, light brown. Like all the Setari, he looks very fit and impressive in his uniform. I would have felt immensely happy, back on Earth, if someone like him had shown any sign of liking me.

I fell asleep on my window seat, under the lightning, and dreamed of Ruuel. Not one of the good dreams, but of being in a palace full of towers and balconies, looking for him. I'd see him through a window and spend a small forever finding my way to where he was, but by the time I got there he was gone. Over and over, and I knew he was doing it deliberately, leaving whenever I came near him, and I woke up crying and ashamed.

Frankly, I'd rather have the dreams about lions. I really need to accept what my subconscious seems to be trying to tell me. Wish I could figure out how to do that, and stop working myself up like this.

I slept way too long – it's quite late. The next episode of *The Hidden War* is in a few hours. I don't know if I'll watch it after all.

Sunday, May 25

Endorphins

I wasn't paying enough attention in training today and got a big whack on my shoulder. Mara made me do push-ups for punishment, which I was oddly pleased about, since it means she considers me recovered enough to punish.

I'm in a more optimistic mood today than I have been for a while. I read back through a lot of my diary last night, and decided that, after all, I haven't been chasing after Ruuel. I've never gone looking for him, or bugged him. I just think about him a lot and who does that hurt? Him being woken up because of my swimming experiment was bothering me, I suspect. The higher-ups seem to consider him my assigned captain when First Squad isn't around, but I can be careful not to do anything which might require a lecture when First is on rotation, and that should fix that problem. I'm damned if I'm going to keep feeling bad about liking Ruuel if I do absolutely nothing to bother him.

My overall health really effects my mood too. Concentrating on school and training helps, and though the training leaves me sore and wiped out, it's also an active, positive thing. I felt so sporty today, having one of the Setari's physiotherapists rubbing their equivalent of Tiger Balm onto my back and doing some painful poking-fingers-into-muscles which hurt in a good way. And I doubt I would have survived all that swimming if I hadn't been fitter than I was on Earth, so I'll focus on at least getting back to that level as my next goal.

The Hidden War episode turned out to be uneventful, switching back to the characters from the main cast doing another mission. There was a brief mention of 'Squad Indigo' and a mission to Muina to investigate a Ddura. They called Lastier 'that cold bastard' and mentioned that all Indigo had achieved on the trip was to find a stray, but the episode's focus was firmly on other things.

It's really hard not to compare the various squads of *The Hidden War* to the real ones. The main character reminds me of Mori.

Monday, May 26

Sixth Squad

Sixth Squad today. They were the squad who'd been stationed outside the Pillar space when it all went pear-shaped. They'd sent Quane to get help, and went in to try and rescue people and fight off the Ionoth, only to all succumb. Ammas, their Telekinesis talent, had died. All that made me a little nervous about testing with them.

Their captain is a girl named Cormin, who had a touch of Taarel about her in terms of her air of command. She looked more Amerind than Asian, and was very decisive and efficient. Her attitude toward me was quietly polite but distant, and her squad followed her lead and were all very courteous but not remotely inclined to chat. A girl called Jorion has replaced Ammas, and she kept glancing at me when she thought I was turned away, a puzzled, evaluating look. I wonder if I'll ever find out why. I never found out why Anya found me so annoying. I think it's probably best not to spend too much energy trying to work these things out unless I'm assigned to a squad. There's eighty-four active Setari, and every one of them is going to have an opinion about the enhancing stray.

Only Thirteenth left now, and nothing at all in my calendar next week. They obviously haven't decided what to do with me. All this testing, but I'm not entirely sure they'll allow me back into the spaces, even with First Squad. I also think they've had orders not to take me out into the city – First collected me for dinner again tonight, but in Mara's quarters.

Tuesday, May 27

World of Mystery

I bought some fancy interface games today. I've been hesitating over joining an online game, but most them use voice chat, and I just can't make myself sound enough like a Taren to risk that, even with the cool voice modifiers you can use to get in-character.

I'm also entirely uncertain whether I would be allowed to join: I've never tried to post on a public forum or communicate outside KOTIS, and that's not just because I'm worried about the reaction of whoever I talk to. I've never been specifically forbidden to, but the Setari aren't allowed to reveal their identities, and the Kalrani aren't allowed to post on public forums at all. I don't particularly want to deal with being ordered not to talk to people. I'm a lot more settled than I was, but I'm avoiding confrontations and upsets. I really don't like how I've been feeling since Kalasa, and I don't want to push myself just now.

The games I bought were single-player puzzle/adventure games. The first one I'm playing is a noir-ish murder mystery, set on Tare before computers, let alone the interface. It works as a really interesting history lesson for me, and is letting me dip my toe into the virtual worlds so many Tarens consider daily entertainment. In the game I look down at myself and I'm this six-foot guy. I reach out a hand and I'm missing my little finger. It's very disorienting, and is only the tip of Tare's virtual entertainments, and probably as full-on as I can manage at the moment. I'm still way too big a wuss to try any of the games which are in-skin. Sight and sound is more than enough.

Otherwise, full squad hand-to-hand training. I concentrated hard, and Mara said nice things about the effort I was putting in, but the gulf between me and First Squad is so monumental. At the same time, I'm better than I was. If I went back to Earth and some random thug tried to attack me I might have a chance of tripping him and making him fall down.

Thursday, May 29

Great Wall of Astroturf

I was nearly late for my session with Thirteenth Squad (thanks to my new game, which is very engrossing). The captain of Thirteenth is called Teer Alare, and he's this absolute baby-face. He looks about fifteen – taller than me, but like he's not old enough to shave. I could totally picture him sitting in front of the TV with Jules, playing *Halo* or some stupid skateboarding game. I was half expecting him to be wearing a goofy grin, and for every second word he used to be 'cool', but he was curtly professional and started us out at a spanking pace.

Thirteenth is a big hitting squad, so we were in the highly shielded training room, starting on the second person – a very grim-faced girl named Dry – when KOTIS went to full alert. Everyone went still, waiting, then a broadcast message appeared in the interface (red words in the mid-distance of my field of vision): "Massive at the Dohl Array."

Before any of us could react, Grif, the captain of Second Squad, brought me into a mission channel with his squad, and began rapidly adding squads. Fourth, Fifth, Eighth, Tenth, Eleventh and Thirteenth. Most of them were on their sleep shifts, more than a few only just struggling to consciousness. Everyone else was in the spaces or on Muina.

"Gather at Green Lock," Grif said. "We'll be going through the spaces to Gorra, possibly collecting Sixth on the way, and then using transports to the Array. No delay."

That seemed to mean run. Alare gave his squad a hand signal, cast me a glance to make sure I understood, and it was a quick dash down a couple of corridors, a short elevator ride, another dash along a major travelator with lots of greysuits and pinksuits hopping hastily off it out of our way, then another elevator and another corridor. The elevators made it easier, giving me a chance to catch my breath. Everyone else was barely breathing quicker.

Eighth Squad went 'no connection' before we were halfway there, and Fifth just as we arrived. All of Second Squad was waiting by the gate, along with a mixed crowd of partial squads.

"Thirteenth, go straight through," Grif said as we came up. "Further briefing once we're at Gorra. Devlin, you're with Fourth."

I promptly sat down on a seat I suspect had been deliberately left empty for me, and hoped I wasn't too red in the face. A greysuit came disconcertingly out of nowhere and gave me a once-over. They can monitor my heartbeat, temperature, various chemical levels and so forth using the interface, but the greysuits are very fond of peering into my eyes and asking me whether I feel lethargic. Thirteenth went through, and then Fourth arrived all in a group.

Ruuel nodded at Grif, gave me a five-second glance which I interpreted as 'usual formation', and headed into the gate-lock. Auron paused beside me, offering me one of his shy smiles, and I stood and went in with him. The location of the gate appeared as a triangle in the interface and we went through without pause, not even waiting for the gate-lock to close.

Ruuel gave typically abbreviated orders once we were all through. "Auron, your sole role will be moving Devlin. Stay unenhanced for greater flexibility. Eyse, paired with Auron. Steady speed."

Auron lifted me off the ground with Levitation, and they began jogging at something just short of an all-out run. I'd never been on the Gorra rotation – it was five spaces long, but they were still empty from the last time they'd been cleared – and then we were in Gorra's near-space which looked, unsurprisingly, just like Unara's near-space. Tarens don't go in for a great deal of architectural experimentation. We were through into a gate-lock about twenty minutes after setting out, which is pretty impressive time for reaching the other side of the planet.

We beat Eighth Squad, which confused me considerably until they arrived with Sixth. They'd detoured once they'd reached Gorra's near-space and gone into the rotation Sixth was scheduled to clear, collecting them. Gorra had a KOTIS facility, barely, and we went straight to two tanz which were being prepped for us. These were flat things about three times the length of a bus, very similar to the transport I'd ridden in with Sa Lents to Unara: wedge-arrowhead airplanes.

My transport had Second, Fourth, Sixth and Eighth, and the other Fifth, Tenth, Eleventh and Thirteenth. There was a brief wait until we were all seated and the pre-flight routine underway before beginning our briefing, but there was already tons of massive news on the interface. I started out by looking Dohl Array up in the encyclopaedia.

'Dohl Teva' in Taren, and I'm not quite sure if 'array' is the right word to translate to. It's a gigantic series of underwater farms. Huge flexible clear tubes lifting from the ocean floor, bending and twisting in currents, their insides filled with different sorts of seaweeds and plants tended and harvested by drones. The ocean in the area is relatively shallow, and very clear and the place is one of the mainstays of food production on Tare. There are several fly-speck islands nearby given over to processing, and one slightly larger one, Kalane, with a population of nearly ten thousand. Tiny by Tare's standards.

Tsur Selkie and a couple of bluesuits were brought into the mission channel as Second Squad arrived, and Selkie began the briefing as soon as all squads were seated

"First sighting was of swoops, and air units were detailed. While they were en route, a drone mechanic made this report."

A recording was relayed direct into the channel, a woman's shaking voice: "This is Gensen XY, Dohl East Axis. There's a – I don't even have the words to describe it. Some kind of creature in the Array. Forwarding images from our external monitors."

I could see why the woman didn't want to try describing it. The closest I can manage is a giant piece of black Astroturf – smooth on one side, all bristly on the other. But big in a way which was beyond things like football fields and more into golf courses. It was shaped like a frilly almond, swirling and twisting an impossible ballet through the vertical farms, the wake of its passing making them sway and wrench about madly. Occasionally a vein-like network of blue lines would light up across its non-bristly side and it looked quite beautiful. It reminded me a little of a smaller Ionoth First had killed on the Unstable Rotation.

The Astroturf wrapped itself around one of the vertical farms, like a carpet giving free hugs. And then the image changed to a shot of what was obviously the inside of the farm tube as it was squeezed and crushed, and a thousand wriggly black things tried to get inside, only to draw away.

"The aerial units made a surface sighting after dispatching the swoops," Selkie went on, "and an evaluation strike was ordered."

We were relayed an image of dark, oily-looking water and I searched for the massive only to realise *everything* was the massive. It was floating just under the surface. Two small wedge-shaped ships which moved rather like hummingbirds drifted into view, and one dropped abruptly down low, bolts of light peppering the darkness below. Puffs of steam rose from the water, and at first the only response was a sudden crowding of blue light to the area, then the whole vast surface of the massive roiled and bucked, tossing water into the air. The ship was already darting away, and the other one had released a more Earth-type weapon – some kind of missile – which hurtled toward it...then wobbled, paused, and reversed direction, shooting directly back the way it came. By the time it had exploded in mid-air, the massive had sunk out of sight.

"Drones from the Array were redeployed to track, but the next sighting was again from the air." Selkie gave us another image log. This was of a small island, a miniature pile of white blocks standing perched on a spar of rock poking out of the sea. I'd barely taken that in when a wall of black rose out of the ocean, reminding me of a waterfall in reverse, or a whale breaching insanely high. It came down on the island, covering it completely, and contracted as it had around the vertical farm.

"Therouk Island," Selkie said, clipped voice moving inexorably onward. "Processing, and residential. Two hundred and seventy-four on site. The structure began fracturing immediately. Currently eighty-nine alive. Most deaths have been from crushing."

He followed this with another log, one which I really wish I hadn't watched. It was from a person on the island, trapped uncomfortably in a partially collapsed room, describing in a horrified tone the noises above him, grinding, scraping. And then black tentacles broke through the ceiling above and wrapped around him and pulled him upward and he was screaming in agony and struggling and there was nothing at all to be done.

Nils, who was sitting behind me, leaned forward and squeezed my shoulder. I smiled at him, glad to be sitting down, and tried not to show how sick I felt. I was hardly the only one. Par had gone quite grey. I doubt any of the Setari watched that without their stomach clenching.

"Air units attempted to draw it off, strafing with energy attacks, but it responded only by tightening its grip on the structure. The majority of survivors are gathered in a reinforced vault on the lowest level, with a handful of others scattered throughout. While evaluation is underway Charal, Palanty, and Eyse will attempt retrieval. Other assignments pending evaluation. Visual range in eight. Environmental conditions deteriorating."

"Eat something," Grif added.

Jeh Omai, Ketzaren's friend from Second, handed me a molasses bar and for a short while everyone just ate, had a few mouthfuls of water, and cycled through the four toilets at the back of the half-empty transport. Sonn was assigned as my secondary babysitter, and Grif, Ruuel and Halla enhanced and sat studying the logs.

We reached the massive way too quickly, barely an hour after the alert was sounded. Not soon enough for another four people on Therouk Island. I started to look at the public media channels and saw that the other islands in the area were all frantically evacuating – escalating into wild panic on the largest, Kalane – and one was broadcasting an open link to a girl trapped alone in her room on Therouk, injured and begging for help. That was too hard, and I switched to watching the transport's external feed, of ocean and sky paling into late afternoon, and a huge front of black storm clouds not quite in the direction we were flying.

"Third level monitoring established for the survivors," Grif said, as the faint hum of the tanz changed. "Destination ship incoming, primary contact Vichie. Charal, you're coordinator."

Charal of Second, who is a quiet guy with eyes which droop down giving him a mournful look, nodded once and then he, Palanty of Fifth, and Mori dropped out of the main mission channel. KOTIS is still not willing to test teleportation enhanced – it's apparently a very reliable talent so long as the person teleporting has seen or can see the location – but the potential consequences of it distorting are so great they'd rather not risk testing it with me. In this situation, I could guess that they weren't entirely certain if the massive would have any impact, but the greater risk was exhaustion, trying to move over eighty people as quickly as possible.

As the three teleporters vanished, the two ships slowed to a hover. "All to the roof," Grif said, as exits to either side and in the ceiling opened.

It was chilly with a light wind outside, and I'm never really going to get used to floating high in the air. Therouk Island was not quite directly below us, much closer than I'd expected, and looked as if it had been wrapped in wet leather. Then Par set us both down on the reassuringly broad and almost flat roof of the transport and I had to switch back to using the transport's external feed to see what was going on.

No surprise that Ruuel was primarily responsible for evaluation. He stayed floating off to one side, gazing down at the massive for a short eternity of unbroken contemplation. When he started speaking it was the same focused, exacting tone he uses for just about everything official.

"Electricity will be useless. Other elementals should all be effective, with Ice our best approach. In addition to repelling projectiles, the outer side is strongly absorbent of elemental attacks. We need to force it to lift if we're to have any chance. No apparent central brain or weak point. Status on retrievals?"

"Still working on primary group." Grif began breaking the available Setari into three groups: the main attack force, a group of close-range or electric-focused talents who would be hunting any 'escort' Ionoth, and the Devlin handlers who would make sure I didn't fall off the transport or get eaten by a straying swoop. Beyond the evaluation, they weren't using me to enhance anyone yet, and spent some time on technical details of which telekinetics would be carting who about, and what the order of enhancement would be.

"Primary group retrieved," Grif said, after tote-duty was settled.

"Air support unit en route to your location," Selkie put in. "We've isolated an intact upper chamber with active visual feed. Placement of charges at that point should achieve considerable damage, but it's critical that we prevent it fleeing once injured."

"Use Ice to fix it, at least temporarily?" Grif suggested.

They went with that plan, and repositioned the ship while we waited for the air support unit with its explosives. As soon as it was close the three teleporters were recalled, even though they'd not been able to retrieve four unconscious people – a thing which no-one commented on, but which I could see they hated. The escort hunters had already gone, and everyone else gathered on the roof of the one ship, positioning themselves in order of who would enhance first. The three teleporters looked completely exhausted, drenched with sweat, and Grif had someone bring them one of the horrid super-energy drinks that are all salty and sweet at the same time, and make you instantly long for a chaser of water. I watched the storm, tiny flickers playing among the blackness. It was still far away, but the wind was picking up, and I could tell by the way a few of the Setari kept glancing at it that they didn't want to wait too long.

"Air support on approach," Grif said, moments before one of the hummingbird fliers lifted into view. "Nise, retrieve the charges to the rear of this transport." He glanced at the three limp teleporters. "Palanty, Eyse – straightforward placement and then off-mission."

Charal went below straight away – he didn't have the strength of the younger Setari and was very grey – while Nise from Fifth whisked across to the opening hatch of the flier and lifted out two warning-plastered crates, lowering them carefully onto the roof of our transport. Mori and Bayen Palanty teleported one each; Mori first, then Palanty. That barely took a minute, but we paused again in the increasing wind to make sure that everyone's timing was exact. The Ice talents would all enhance, and race down to the 'rear' of the massive where it was still partially in the water. While they moved, the rest of the main attack force would enhance as the transport circled us around and down to a strike location. The Setari would attack while the transport moved on to a second point.

They expected the Ice squad to have commenced freezing as much as possible of the water and rock and massive together by the time the ship hit the strike point and the charges Mori and Palanty had teleported onto the island would be detonated as soon as the transport darted past the immediate danger zone. It would circle around to the 'rear' to be close to the Ice squad for a second enhancement and then they – presuming the massive hadn't broken loose – would continue their freezing from the front.

A great deal was dependant on the massive not breaking loose, which was why the Ice squad was so focused on holding it in place. Setari are far less effective under water, and the thing was so quick below the surface that there was too much chance of it getting away.

Grif was frowning, not toward the storm front but toward a flicker and glimmer some distance away which I realised was the group of

Setari assigned to fighting escort Ionoth. But then he said: "At ready, Kajal."

"Commencing," Kajal replied, fingertips barely brushing my shoulder. He looked tense, and also a little hyped, but at least not interested in showing me his opinion of strays. There were eight Setari with us who had strong Ice talents, and they had two telekinetics assigned to cart about the ones who couldn't manage that themselves. They'd barely taken off before the ship moved into a glide which forced me to change my stance to keep upright.

The second attack squad began enhancing, while Grif murmured to me: "Call a stop to the enhancements immediately if it starts to overwhelm you." The look he gave Par and Sonn underlined the order, and then he signalled for the surrounding Setari to take off and said: "Clear."

Kajal's voice came over the interface: "Attack begins."

The transport was at the wrong angle for me to see the start of the ice, but when Selkie said: "Detonate," I couldn't miss the reaction of the massive. The top of it bulged upward – in one or two places fragments of white stone actually flying through it – but to my disappointment it hadn't ended up with a huge hole in the middle. For a moment it didn't react at all, and then it started scrunching backward like a big flat caterPillar.

"Nise, use rubble to try and knock it upward," Grif ordered. "Kanato, take your group forward and target the edge to gauge effect."

Five Setari dropped down, setting the retreating edge of the thing blazing. But it was like destroying only the fringy bits of a carpet, and the thing showed no sign of lifting as they wanted. It was so huge.

By this time the transport had circled around to the rear and I could see the work of the ice. I was really surprised at how much they'd made so quickly, like a mini-glacier rising out of the water. I found out later that while Ice talents can produce it apparently out of nothing, the amount of water in the air makes a huge difference, and having an ocean to draw on is as good as being enhanced. The ice was cracking, though, as the thing tried to pull free. It couldn't immediately manage it, and the folds began to gather and bunch up. The Ice group took advantage of that, catching the folds in the growing trap.

"Attack wherever it's slightly raised," Grif said, and the main attack split to either side, blasting into the folds. The Ice group began to return to the transport in pairs to enhance, darting back quickly to continue to reinforce the glacier as parts of it shattered and crumbled. The transport moved around to the side as the massive changed tack, hunching down and trying to seal all access to its underside.

The nearest group took the opportunity to enhance, and then Ruuel, who was floating somewhere underneath the ship, said: "It's preparing an offensive attack. Gain distance and circle to the front, all forces."

Brilliant blue lines were gathering on the massive's exposed back. My attention was distracted by Sonn, telling me to kneel for balance and grip the edge of the hatch as the transport put on a sudden burst of speed, causing more than a few of the returning Setari to stagger and follow Sonn's lead.

The massive was folding itself vertically, still trying to keep its sides sealed. I'm not sure it could even tell if the Setari had retreated as it began to produce such an intensity of power it burned little vein-like afterimages into everything I was seeing.

"After the blast, it intends to leap forward," Ruuel said. "On my signal, go low, strafe the underside with everything you have. Ice, you will have the barest chance to retrap it."

The massive's brightness climaxed in a tremendous arcing halo, a display of lightning to put anything the Setari could do to shame. The wind brought the scent of ozone so strong it felt like my nose was being scoured, and I had my eyes squeezed shut when Ruuel said: "Go."

I haven't watched the mission report showing them fly underneath the thing as it leaped forward. The whole idea of it makes me nervous, because it could so easily have crushed them. I stayed down, resting back on my heels, and didn't even let myself look using the transport's view until I heard the faint relieved sound Sonn made.

Caught a second time, with its underside blasted from below, the massive reared up perilously and then flipped backward, trying to jerk itself free. If it had managed it in the first lunge it would probably have escaped, but instead it exposed itself in the worst way to further layers of ice, was pinned wrong-side out and unprotected from unrelenting pounding. The fliers carefully manoeuvred in to join the Setari, blasting away with their weapons.

The thing was just so damn large, and didn't have any kind of head or heart they could concentrate on. It took ten full minutes of relentless hammering before it stopped trying to break free. The last enhancement cycle, I really started to feel it, a painful effort every time anyone so much as brushed against me and they weren't even halfway through the cycle before I looked up at Sonn and didn't have to say anything at all. I think she'd been about to call it anyway, immediately saying: "Devlin's at her limit. Returning below."

Par levitated me down, then he and Sonn were called away to support the escort-chasing group, who were close to being overwhelmed by something like fifty swoops, but had held off reporting numbers until the massive was beyond escape. Everyone who wasn't in a state of collapse went off to help them. One of our entourage of greysuits made me drink something which tasted like caramel and hot milk, and I even felt her touch as effort and protested a little incoherently before passing out in the seat next to where Mori was already sleeping.

Zzz.

I woke on a very flat, hard bed in a nook hidden by a curtain. A girl of about eleven was standing clutching the corner of the bed by my foot, staring at me. She was totally Wednesday Addams: tight black braids, big forehead, huge eyes. It took me a minute of staring back at her to decide I wasn't hallucinating.

"Are you just going to lie there?" she asked, when I didn't do anything.

"Are you just going to stand there?" I asked. It was so disorienting, to be on the ship, and then somewhere else with someone I'd never seen before, and no sense of transition at all.

"No. But I can't interview you while you're lying down. It would look bad."

I blinked at the impatient tone, and rubbed sleep out of my eyes. "I under impression that random junior reporters not able record my image."

"I can log your outline." Scornful now. "Hurry and sit up. I've a lot of questions and hardly any time."

"I tell you what," I said, propping myself on one elbow. "I trade you question for question. You first: where is here?"

"Timesa. My turn. What do you miss most about your home world?"

"My family."

"*Other* than your family."

"That a different question." I smiled at her provokingly, shifting to prop my back against the wall while looking up Timesa in the encyclopaedia. It was another of the little food-processing settlements scattered through the Array. The interface told me it was two kasse (about five hours) since the massive battle. "We're waiting out that storm here?"

"Uhuh. What, *other than your family*, do you miss most about your home world?"

"My friends," I said, grinned at the look on her face, and added: "And the food, the music, the stories. I miss a lot some of the things I was reading, because I don't get to find out how end."

"What's the biggest difference between the people on your world and the people here?"

I considered pointing out that it was my turn, but instead glanced at the team lists to see who was awake. Most everyone was out of it though, here and back at base. First Squad was back from their rotation, but asleep. I had some emails from them waiting for me. "Tare less diverse than Earth," I said, after thinking about it. "Everyone here speak same language; Earth has hundreds. On Earth, more variety in the way people look. Many more different customs." And more misunderstandings and wars as a result. "But no psychic people."

Ruuel was awake, but I'm being very strict with myself about contacting him, so settled on Nils instead. I sent him a text: "Need to be saved from precocious little girl."

"You get to work with the Setari, right? What talents do you have?"

"Talent for getting headaches, mainly. Do you have any talents?"

Nils, sounding like he was laughing, opened a channel and said: "Glad to see you're awake. What's this dire peril?"

"Levitation," the girl said tightly, though I couldn't tell if she was annoyed at me for being facetious or for the question. She tilted her head, and I realised that like me she was having a conversation with someone else at the same time – people feeding her questions, judging from her expression as she asked: "Which Setari is the best looking?"

"Third Squad captain," I said without hesitation, adding: "Being able to fly one of best talents. Would like to have that one. Is that how you got in here?" To Nils I said: "Intrepid girl reporter woke me up for exclusive interview. Being very indiscreet."

"How much of *The Hidden War* episode about you was correct?" the girl asked, ignoring my question. "And did you like it?"

"There was a lot of made-up stuff," I said. "But some of it was real, like that bit where I was nearly stood on by something in the middle of the night. Don't think I could ever really enjoy watching that. At the time was very upset because someone had taken the things which had happened to me and turned into entertainment, just so they could make money." I thought about adding a stalwart defence of Fourth Squad, but was spared having to decide if that was a good idea by the faint shushing noise of a door.

The girl glanced around, then crossed her arms and waited defiantly as the curtain pulled back to reveal both Nils and Ruuel. "You're interrupting," she snapped, totally unfazed by six-foot-something, black-suited, uber-dangerous psychics.

Nils laughed, sounding surprised but unbothered. "I'm often told I have no sense of timing," he said easily. He gestured with his hand and the girl rose a couple of feet off the ground. "But I *am* irresistible," he added, and walked off with her, ignoring her outraged demand to be put down.

Highly amused, I looked at Ruuel and realised he was annoyed, his eyes narrowed and his mouth very flat. It's such a rare thing for him to show anything but his captain expression that I felt sick with dismay, and said in an embarrassingly plaintive tone: "Would have felt silly sound alert on little girl."

"You've forgotten the lesson of the cat," he said, but something had shifted in his eyes and he suddenly seemed more his usual self.

"Ghost kind of a mixed lesson," I pointed out, trying not to show how relieved I was. "And if she'd wanted to hurt me, she could have done it before waking me up and asking me questions. Is everyone all right? I fell asleep before fight was over."

"No fatalities." He stepped back as one of our attendant greysuits showed up. "Food down the hall when you're done."

The greysuit – one from Gorra who didn't usually have a chance to test his theories on the stray – was really interested in whether being pushed to my enhancing limits had had any effect on me, but frustrated that they didn't have any of their fancier scanning equipment on hand. I was distracted by the rest of what proved to be Timesa's small medical facility, which was overcrowded with seven injured Setari, and me in for observation. I was surrounded by little alcoves with curtains and wanted to see if any of my friends were behind them, but the only person I could see enough of was Hasen from Eighth, her nanosuit partially withdrawn and the exposed skin of her shoulder covered with liquid bandage.

After locating the nearest bathroom first, I found Nils, and Endaran from Eleventh, waiting in a largish conference room along with another greysuit, two greensuits, and the bluesuit in charge off in one corner talking to someone I assumed was local to the island. I gave them all a vague and general smile before helping myself to the little buffet laid out on the table, sitting down next to Endaran. I was seriously starving.

While I ate, Nils tried to tease me about my interview, which had taken about two minutes to reach worldwide transmission. The girl, Palan Leoda, had levitated up the shaft of something like a dumb-waiter to win a bet that she could get in to talk to me. The other children in her class had promptly begun feeding her questions, and now half the planet was dissecting my answers. Everyone seems to have leapt to the conclusion that Nils is the Third Squad captain and that I'm desperately in love with him. He *does* have a very sexy voice.

I was still pretty tired, and went back to the medical facility to sleep again until Mori woke me when it was time to go. Most everyone was awake by then (another kasse along). All but the injured had been sleeping on the transports. Ironically they'd brought me into the facility so I could be under closer medical observation, but there's no way Wednesday could have reached me if they'd just left me with everyone else.

A few of the injured would be returning all the way to the main KOTIS facility using transports rather than through the spaces from Gorra. Eighth Squad came out worst from the clean-up of the swoops. Bryze had a broken leg and Hasen was speared by a beak almost through her shoulder.

The trip to Gorra wasn't very relaxing, since it had stopped raining but was still extremely windy, and occasionally the engines of the transport rose to an audible whine, or we would gain or drop altitude alarmingly. I hate to imagine how bad it must have been to ground us altogether. Everyone was quiet and grim, probably, like me, reviewing the post-storm images of the little island with the massive half falling off what little remained of the buildings underneath. It had been treating the buildings like barnacles, breaking them open and picking out the flesh inside, then chipping down further for more. Add a few explosives on to that and there wasn't much remaining of the processing facility.

Rather than look at it, I said to Mori: "Realised another reason why Setari hunt Ionoth in spaces instead of in real-space. Much better weather."

"Absolutely," she said. "We would have trouble surviving the battleground, let alone the battle. Does Earth ever face storms this bad?"

I had no idea how to measure them comparatively, and shrugged. "Think it's more frequency that's the issue. Earth has destructive storms, but we don't have them every week all over the planet."

"An extreme rather than the normal state. What about Earth compared to Muina?"

"Hard to say – only ever saw a bit of rain there. No really violent storms. Think it must be a lot more geologically stable, though, since your language doesn't even have words for things like volcanos or tsunamis."

"Volcanos?" Par repeated curiously.

"When burning liquid rock is pushed up to the surface, out of the planet's core."

Par gave me a very uncertain look, and Mori frowned. Nils, behind me again, leaned forward to ask: "Are you being serious?"

The short remainder of the flight back to Gorra involved my feeble explanations of tectonic plates, earthquakes, tsunamis, hot springs, bubbling mud pools, pyroclastic clouds, Pompeii, and the prospect of California falling into the ocean. They weren't quite sure whether to believe me, and now have a distortedly dramatic view of what life on Earth is like. I've been describing Earth to people for months, but there's still so much I've never even mentioned, or have given only half-assed explanations for. It's like the story of the group of blind people trying to get an image of an elephant by touch.

I think I also helped distract them from the recent fight which, though it didn't involve any Setari deaths, was not by any means easy and had as its prelude the death of nearly two hundred people. It's the second massive to emerge on Tare in a short few years, and the number of escort Ionoth was by far the most they've ever seen. Without me along it would have taken them a lot longer to kill the massive, and with the storm and swoops factored in, any number of little islands might have been crunched before they'd finished it off. For all the killing they'd done, for all they could now go to Muina, they were no further along to finding a solution to the tearing of the spaces. And the problem was getting worse.

We walked rather than ran back from Gorra to the main KOTIS facility on Konna, with the usual brisk care Fourth Squad takes to everything. When we finally arrived, Ruuel gave everyone a nod and said: "Free time until the rotations have been rearranged. Devlin, report to medical."

I expected that, so didn't pull a face at him, just made sure to detour back to my rooms for a shower and to grab my diary first. The greysuits love to add to their collection of stray's brain scans. And I have nothing in my calendar any more, and aren't assigned to anything.

I think I figured out why Ruuel was so annoyed with me, though. I was assigned to Fourth Squad, at least nominally, yet reported Wednesday Addams to Nils instead of my captain-of-the-moment. And Fourth Squad's had enough grief lately about their fictional treatment of me. Any hint that I preferred not to be working with them was pretty much guaranteed to get me a black mark in Ruuel's books.

Can't risk showing any hint of how much I want to be around Ruuel. Can't let anyone think I don't want to be around Ruuel. Can't win.

Friday, May 30

Long Term

I spent a lot of today on the roof. It was windy and overcast, but nothing dramatic. After I escaped from medical yesterday, Ketzaren and Alay took me for a 'jog' around the stairs training course (in other words, we started out jogging, and then there was a lot of walking involved while I caught my breath), and later First Squad had me for dinner again.

We had a pretty frank discussion about the increasing number of Ionoth. Just as Taarel had said, all squads are reporting increased populations in the known spaces, and larger numbers of roamers. More new gates are tearing, too. It's not like Tare's going to be overwhelmed next week or anything, but First didn't hide that the long-term situation wasn't looking great.

Zee put it most bluntly. "Even if we do succeed in gaining access to Kalasa, there's no guarantee that there are explanations there. No guarantee that there is any kind of solution. And the timeframe is beginning to tighten."

Nor did they pretend that experiments with me trying to get someone into Kalasa weren't likely to happen sooner rather than later, though they haven't been scheduled yet. I'm glad I've been preparing myself.

Saturday, May 31

Tentacles v Otters

Exceptionally horrible night. I'd been relieved when I hadn't suffered through any memorable nightmares after the battle with the massive, but I guess I was just saving it up because it completely took me over last night. Not the battle itself, but I dreamed of waking up hearing a grinding noise above me and then these black tentacles would break through the ceiling and grab me and my skin would be burning, melting with acid and it would lift me up and I'd be screaming and then I'd wake up and be in my bed panting and upset and then there would be this grinding noise above me –

I don't know how many times it repeated. When I finally did wake up properly, I was so freaked out I was convinced that I was still dreaming, and pretty much crawled out of the room trying to escape the next onslaught. Then I broke down clutching one of my couches and ended up crying in my shower for half an hour straight. I'd only been asleep a couple of hours, too, and felt sick and exhausted, but would rather have died than go back to bed.

Everyone I would have wanted to talk to was either asleep or on rotation. Even Ghost wasn't around, and eventually I contacted Ista Chemie, the greysuit Zee had taken me to for tests last time I'd had really bad nightmares. She was happy to tape monitors all over me in medical. Not that I cared about their tests; I just couldn't stand to go back to my room, and was hoping that being monitored would have the same effect as last time and mean I slept normally.

No such luck. The only difference to my dream was the setting, and I dreamed that I was lying in medical waiting to get to sleep when the massive came, and that it ate the greysuits along with me. It kept repeating, a half-dozen times I think, and then the next time it reset Ruuel walked into the examining room, gave me a stern look and said: "Stop this." The scraping, grinding noise started above him, but though he glanced up, he just said: "You're doing it yourself. Wake up."

I stared at him, and saw that I was holding his hand, gripping it so tightly my knuckles were white. And opened my eyes to find that I was.

"Well done."

I looked past him at the ceiling, and while there was no grinding I was totally convinced it was only a matter of time, and I think if he'd let my hand go I would have had complete hysterics. As it was I lay there and shook and didn't take in whatever Ista Chemie was saying to me and eventually she went away and came back with something for me to drink which tasted so awful I snapped out of it a little.

"Really hope that was a stimulant," I said, after I'd stopped choking on it.

"A fortifier," she said, sounding a bit like she needed one herself. She, and the two other technicians I could see, were all white and upset looking.

I looked up at Ruuel – still entirely unwilling to let go of his hand – and he said: "Watch this," and gave me a log file.

It was from a scanner's view, not from the technicians', and showed me lying on the couch, eyes closed and breathing deeply. Ista Chemie and another of the technicians were beside me, probably talking over the interface so as not to disturb me. I started to shift and move, but the two greysuits looked up, confused, at this grinding noise coming from above them. Then Ista Chemie staggered and fell, clutching her side and the other technician grabbed his face and doubled over. I writhed about violently, and thick red marks appeared wherever my skin was exposed by the cut-offs and t-shirt I'd worn to testing, and then I went limp, panting, the marks fading.

The greysuits, astonished and panicked, retreated out of the room, and I just lay there – no doubt until the dream started again, but I didn't watch that long.

"Sorry," I said to Ista Chemie. "More than you bargained for."

She gave me a rather strained smile. "We think it's a variety of Ena manipulation. You are trying to make your dream reality."

"'Trying' not the right word," I said.

"This may be related to the ability which took you back to your own world's near-space," Ruuel said. "Although it appears actually bringing a massive into being is beyond you. You haven't been dreaming like this since Annan brought you for testing?"

"No."

"Not immediately after the recent battle?" Ista Chemie asked.

"No." Being careful not to look at Ruuel, and yet not loosening my death-grip on his hand, I added: "Think maybe this started after I went home. To Earth. Had a really strong dream while still in medical wing, but remember feeling mainly angry at the time, not scared–"

Ruuel broke in: "What was the dream about?"

"People doing medical things to me that I really didn't want them to do," I said, very neutrally. "And then dreams after the Pillar – not specifically about the Cruzatch, but really bad dreams of ducking under things, over and over. Next really strong dreams were after assigned to Muina – they weren't nightmares. Mainly had dreams about being asleep on the *Litara*, peaceful sorts of dreams, but very real. Maybe for a week every night."

I could feel my face heating up, and had no doubt Ruuel at least could tell I was leaving something out of 'peaceful sorts of dreams', but nothing could have made me describe them.

"After that, was having awful fever-dreams of being chased waiting to be rescued after Kalasa, and then that time after my file was made so entertaining. Tonight's been the worst, though. Couldn't wake up." I tightened my grip on Ruuel's hand, then finally forced myself to let go.

He was wearing full gloves, but I don't know if they would have completely protected him from the raw, gibbering terror I must have been projecting. He never made the slightest move to pull away, and I was humiliatingly grateful for that. Even then I couldn't stop myself from looking up at the ceiling, just in case, then said as calmly as I could manage: "Not very keen on sleeping now."

"You seem at least marginally aware of your surroundings while you dream," Ruuel said. "Annan noted that you were reassured by her presence?"

I nodded. "It's like she – and you just then – come into my dream. Tell me I'm safe."

"While we technicians are not so reassuring," Ista Chemie said, a little greyly. I think she'll be having a few nightmares on my account. "Quite aside from the effects you were producing – which were painful but not life-threatening – that is a sleep which has the potential to kill you. Your energy use was beyond healthy limits."

I glanced at Ruuel, but he was gazing into the middle-distance, discussing me with somebody. My head was throbbing, so I asked Ista Chemie if I could have something for it, and was glad she didn't tell me I'd have to wait until they'd done more tests. I was desperately tired, too, and getting stressed out about falling back to sleep, or maybe still being asleep, and the memory of it all filled me up so that I started staring at the ceiling again until Ruuel put his hand on my shoulder and told me: "Stop that."

"Am trying," I said, sounding very doubtful. "New useful talents to add to getting headaches, and seeing blurry things. Extra strength dreams."

"Strong talents left untrained and undirected are often self-destructive," he said, unimpressed by my pity party. "This seems to be a combination of a formidable Ena manipulation ability and the Sight talent we've seen hints of previously. The obvious course is to train you in the techniques used for other Sight talents, many of whom also have issues with dreams. Until you've reached some measure of self-control, we'll return you to a higher level of vitals monitoring." He gave me a steady look in return for my unenthusiastic reaction. "The monitor will be active only while you're asleep. If your heart rate spikes, one of your squad members will be given access to your quarters to sit with you, and attempt to wake you if their presence alone is not sufficient."

That was a more bearable approach than I'd been fearing. I'd half expected to be stuck back in medical having nightmares for dozens of interested greysuits. I think Ruuel felt me relax a little, because he nodded, then waited while Ista Chemie pressed a cold tube – headache stuff – against my arm.

"To which end, we'll start with a visualisation technique," he said. "Close your eyes." He waited until I (reluctantly) did, his hand still on my shoulder. "Now, think of a place which you associate with calm and safety." He paused, then with a slightly different note to his voice, said: "Think of the stream with otters, near Pandora. Picture walking along the shore of the lake toward it. The stones beneath your feet crunch and click, and there is a cool mist against your skin. A bird makes a noise to your right, the sound lifting into the air. There is a tumble of rock ahead, marked by a small pile of pebbles. You approach in silence, seeing the stream, shaded and half-real. You sit carefully on the rock. It is rough beneath one hand, and through the cold you take in the scent of some unknown greenery you crushed on your last step. The water murmurs as you wait, and you keep yourself still, searching for movement in the liquid shadows."

I dreamed of otters. Of sitting watching otters, with Ruuel beside me, just as had really happened, except he had his hand on my shoulder, and I could feel the warmth of him. The tight, sick dread faded completely out of memory. After a long while Maze came and sat on my other side, and Ruuel went away. Then Alay swapped for Maze, and then Mara curling an arm around my waist. Then I woke up and Mara was there, sitting on a chair which had been brought into the test room.

"Bet you never guessed how much babysitting involved in this job," I said.

"Tch – there's so many reports to read that an excuse to sit down is never a bad thing." She looked me over as I wriggled out of the embrace of the sense-bed (which always tends to mould itself around me a little too tightly if I lay too still for too long). "Feeling better?"

I nodded, though couldn't quite resist a glance at the ceiling. "Just really hungry. We allowed to leave?"

"I knew those dreams had to be serious for you to volunteer to go anywhere near medical," she said. "Yes, they've cleared you for the moment."

Happy to escape, I detoured back to my quarters to shower and change (and, to be honest, so Mara was with me when I went back there). Then to the canteen, where I was intent on eating two or three breakfasts. Going to the canteen these days is a big contrast to my first few weeks of visits, because now that I've tested with all the squads it's rare that people don't at least say hello. Mara picked at a light lunch until I came up for air, watching me critically.

"The technicians, once they'd recovered from the shock, managed to identify two synapse patterns active while you were sleeping. One is very similar to Ena manipulation, though they don't believe it is quite the same talent. The other you continued to use, even when you stopped dreaming of the massive. It's the same area of your brain which was active when your sight was blurring at Arenrhon. What was your last dream about?"

"Watching otters – exactly what Ruuel told me to picture. Guess I'm pretty easily influenced." I paused, draining the last of the tangy drink I like. "Did Maze come and sit with me after Ruuel? And then Alay, and then you?"

"Well, that confirms that you can tell we're there."

"That's what I dreamed. But I don't seem to notice the technicians."

"The strength of the Setari's affinity to the Ena is probably the deciding factor. First and Fourth will be primarily assigned to, ah, babysitting you, with Second and Third in reserve. Anyone else you're comfortable enough with to include?"

"Zan. Think training really make me stop having nightmares?"

"Possibly. Some Sight talents are plagued by dreams, and Sights discipline at least isn't likely to hurt you. There's been some hesitation about actively training you with the Ena manipulation talent in case it strengthens whatever you did to return to your home world."

"Or lets me make real tentacles, instead of just noises."

"That too." Mara shook her head. "The thought that you might dream yourself to death is hardly comforting. At any rate, we're going to increase your fitness training, and add fairly intensive Sights training – even though we're not entirely certain what Sight it is we're training you for. Between that, some weapons training, in case they do go ahead with attempting to locate Kalasa through you." She grinned. "And you're not to listen to any of Nils' offers to help you get to sleep."

"Zee wouldn't forgive me," I said, trying to be all nonchalant, though I could feel myself blushing.

"Zee isn't involved with Nils Sayate," Mara said, lifting her eyebrows.

"Would still matter to her."

Mara didn't comment about that, but she didn't deny it either. Instead she spent the day working me into the ground – and making me really regret eating such a large breakfast. She and Ketzaren tag-teamed me till well into the afternoon, with the rest of First Squad showing up for dinner, and then we all played an interface game, a memory game with puzzles. I wasn't too bad at the memory, but hopeless at half of the puzzles. It was really a lot of fun, though.

Mara asked me if I wanted her to stay when I went to bed, and I was more than a little tempted, but I told her that I was going to try thinking of otters and see if that worked.

"But glad knowing someone come wake me up if gets bad," I said.

She gave me a strange smile and hugged me. "I'm glad you still trust us enough to talk to," she said, and her voice was angry. "That wretched program, so badly timed–" She made an exasperated noise and drew back. "Just remember that you're with friends. There's never a need to hide when you're hurting."

It's hard not to be pleased that Mara considers me a friend. Not so good is how obviously worried about me she is. I'm not doing a good enough job hiding how close I am to falling apart. Because I'm back to being more than a useful enhancing stray. I'm yet again an irreplaceable key to part of Muina. Worse, I'm someone who can hurt people. I don't want to be someone who can hurt people. I don't know if I can even stop myself from hurting *me*. Talking about it a little to Mara helped, but if I let anyone know that being alone in my quarters outright scares me, they might park me permanently in medical.

As it is, I'm going to sleep in my window seat.

Fortunately, a few minutes ago Third Squad arrived back from Muina. Eeli sent a channel request and then overwhelmed me with excited burble trying to update me on everything they'd been doing (mainly continuing the exploration of Nurioth, and surveying widely around Pandora), and also asking me all these questions about the massive fight. Eventually I figured out that she was particularly happy that I'd said that the Third Squad captain was the best-looking Setari. She adores Taarel so.

It's hard not to feel upbeat after talking to Eeli.

There's a new *The Hidden War* episode tonight, but even though I slept really late into my shift, all the exercise makes me doubtful I'll be able to hold out till it airs. Far more interesting to me is that my calendar filled up while I was chatting to Eeli. The inevitable medical exams, lots of exercising with First Squad, and a couple of sessions of weapons training with someone called Perrin Drake. And Sights training every day with Ruuel.

Strangely enough, my first reaction wasn't positive. Not that I like him any less – more than ever, in fact – and I don't doubt he'll be as good a teacher as he is a captain. But it will be like when I was attached to Fourth Squad on Muina. I'll be an assignment and the assignment will end and I'll be someone else's problem for a while. I can't think of any way to guard against that.

And I don't want to associate Ruuel with tests and experiments, for him to ring a bell and see if I drool on cue. I don't want him to be the one treating me as a lab rat.

Not that I get any choice. Tonight I'll replay him telling me to think about otters, and probably feel just as surprised and glad that he remembered that so distinctly.

I can still feel his hand.

JUNE

Sunday, June 1

Pedestal, schmedestal

I was right to worry about being treated as an experiment by Ruuel.

The day started well enough. I was pleased with myself for succeeding in dreaming of otters, and in a calm frame of mind. There was an email from Nenna waiting for me, and after I read it I had to go and watch last night's *The Hidden War* episode, because Nenna's email was an apology for it.

To think I used to think it would be cool to go on reality TV. Nothing makes me feel less like myself than to watch my introduction to Tare turned into entertainment.

It wasn't as bad as Nenna obviously felt. The entire episode was from Nenna's point of view (or a thinly disguised version of Nenna called Senna) and was all about her Dad bringing home a stray to foster. Since most of my time with the Lents wouldn't have been detailed on my file, it was pretty obvious the scriptwriters had sat down with Nenna, and maybe the rest of her family, and had her describe everything I'd said and done while I was there. From the level of embarrassment in Nenna's email, I'm presuming she got paid for it.

The episode was really about Nenna, about what it had been like for an ordinary Taren girl to have an alien stray added to her family. They'd even written in a boyfriend for her, just so he could be caught ogling the stray's legs and make 'Senna' feel conflicted. And there were all these conversations I'd never heard, so didn't know if they were true. Did Nenna's sister protest the idea of her father taking in a stray in the first place? Did the Lents really have a doubtful discussion about my difficulties with the language and how little I seemed to be progressing? The actress's very fractured Taren is being used as a source of comedy and cuteness, far more appealing than the reality – it helps when the person saying things backward and being barely comprehendible is a gorgeous, kittenish girl with huge eyes, and the words she uses incorrectly tend to be mild double entendres or accidentally witty.

I wonder what Earth's copyright position is on the songs I'd played to people from my phone being used in Taren television shows? It was very weird to hear Gwen Stefani and the Portal closing credits song being used in a Taren show. I could tell from the brief explanation given for the Portal song that my lab rat is definitely going to feature in upcoming episodes.

They showed Nenna and me falling and getting hurt, and then it stayed with Nenna for her first few days in hospital, scared and guilty and angry, and facing arduous rehabilitation work. If she'd been relying on Earth's level of medical technology, she'd be in a wheelchair for life and that would be my fault. Of course, on Earth people don't teleport and neither of us would have been hurt.

Instead of replying to Nenna's email, I sent her a channel request and ended up chatting to her for half an hour. The fact that she'd spoken to the writers didn't bother me nearly as much as the thought of her hating me, and I was incredibly relieved that blaming me for her injuries wasn't the reason she hadn't returned my emails. [I was also more than a little relieved to know that KOTIS wasn't blocking my emails, which had occurred to me more than once.]

Once she was sure that I really wasn't upset, Nenna reverted to the girl I was more familiar with, and immediately started trying to pump me about the Setari. I did tell her there was someone in Third Squad who reminded me so much of her, but figured it was best to wriggle out of telling her any real detail.

First Squad were on rotation today, but that didn't stop Mara from snaffling me before they were due to go out and throwing balls at me, and then ordering me to go through some of the junior grade combat exercises after lunch (there's lots of interfaced-based training I can follow – I don't actually need any of the Setari to stand over me to do it). And in this case I was glad to do it because I really needed to not concentrate on upcoming training with Ruuel.

I may as well have been fourteen and going on my first date, I was so keyed up. Since Fourth Squad's on the next shift from mine, my Sights training is scheduled for late afternoon for me, and first thing in the 'morning' for Ruuel. It's so hard to be sensible about getting to see him. I ended up taking a needle-cold shower to distract me from the waiting, and filled in the last of the time brushing my hair a few thousand strokes and braiding it into a French braid so that I could at least look all efficient and businesslike.

The area where I was supposed to meet him was a new one to me, a series of rooms off a single corridor, all with observation windows. 'Sights Training'. I was booked in room five, but was distracted by room three, which had two Kalrani weaving their way through it. It was a kind of obstacle course, but with moving sections. I can only suppose it helps train Combat Sight. Suitably padded, but I bet it was no fun being hit by swinging beams – let alone falling to the ground from the more aerial parts. I can only hope that none of my training ever takes me into such a room, because the gymnastic expertise required looks to be Olympic level.

I'd been watching a couple of minutes when Ruuel arrived, standing to my right and just a little behind. I'd been having grim and dramatic thoughts about the reasons the Kalrani were pushing themselves so hard and asked: "How many have died in training?"

"Five. Put this on."

He looked like he was in a bad mood, which was not the way to make me look forward to the session. Ruuel with his eyes nearly shut is best avoided, especially when he hands you a blindfold by way of greeting. Nanoliquid too, so that when I reluctantly held it up to my eyes and touched the ends together it oozed under my fingers, then flowed down to cover my ears as well. Yuck. It was extremely effective, and very disorienting. All I could hear was my heartbeat, and I could see nothing at all.

"Your interface will be reduced to minimal function during testing," he said in text, and immediately cut it back so I couldn't do anything at all. Then I was levitated off my feet and moved. It was hugely disconcerting. I'd come to expect brevity from Ruuel, but this made me feel way too powerless, especially when I wasn't put down, but kept floating in the air. All I could see was blackness, and a square text box floating in front of me which said: "Test 1" and the date.

It changed to: "You will be given a series of containers. Attempt to divine the contents of each container. If you cannot make a clear identification of the content of the container, use the first word or image which came to mind when you touched the container. Responses are to be verbal. Signal that you understand."

"...understood," I said, making an effort not to show I was annoyed. After all, sensory deprivation was logical in the context. I lifted my hands up obligingly, and something cool and round dropped in them: it felt like a glass ball, about softball size.

The first word which came into my head was softball, which is not a kind of ball I've seen on Tare and obviously wrong and related more to the container than the contents. I was shuffling through all the random other words which came after that when it occurred to me that I didn't feel like I was with Ruuel. Now, I feel a lot of different things when I'm with Ruuel – right then I was pissed at him, with a touch of fretting about embarrassing myself and lowering his opinion of me – but there's simply a level of him being present which I'm always very aware of. Or absent, as when I wake up each morning knowing he's not there. Today he was standing beside me, and I'd put the blindfold on, and been lifted up, and after that I hadn't really felt like I was with him. I could tell that I was moving; even a blindfold and earplugs can't disguise the sense of being moved, of travelling maybe thirty or fifty metres. I'd assumed it was Ruuel levitating me, but it was obviously someone else.

It's a good thing those containers weren't fragile because I squeezed that first one violently. I felt like the butt of a practical joke, with everyone laughing at me secretly and waiting for me to twig. But after a few seconds of silent temper I turned my attention to who it was if it wasn't Ruuel. I could sort of tell where they were, a fact that I found very interesting, and which went a long way toward distracting me from being angry. Not within reach, and a little below me – I guess I was floating higher in the air than I'd expected. And it was Par, felt like Par. There didn't seem to be anyone really close, but the more I concentrated on Par, the more I had the impression that there were people at a distance, but out of reach like a word you know you know but can't quite remember.

It had been a long time since I'd been given the container. I made a genuine effort to try to divine what was inside, but couldn't tell if it was working or not. I didn't have any kind of certainty, nothing like knowing Ruuel wasn't there.

Finally I gave up and said: "Is test to try and guess object, or to see if I can tell that Auron has kidnapped me?"

"Both observations are relevant. Continue the container test."

I hadn't recovered from being annoyed, so decided to be very literal in following instructions and said: "Softball," and held it out.

There was a slight pause, then the container lifted out of my hands and another one the same size and shape replaced it.

I kept my responses strictly to English after that. I don't think in Taren, after all, and if they wanted the first word that came into my head they were going to get it. I'm not sure how much Symbol Sight would assist in interpreting my answers: things like "Daffodil" or "McDonalds" or "Stefani". I did censor myself a few times, when I went through a spate of sex terms which there was no way I was going to risk to Symbol Sight or possibly being asked to translate it later. Most of my answers I knew had to be wrong, because there was no way an elephant would fit in a globe the size of a softball.

After a couple of dozen globes, the interface switched to saying: "Test 2", then: "Describe your surroundings, including all objects and persons."

I thought it over. I expected I was in Sight Training Room 5, but I hadn't actually seen it. Although it was probably as bland and white-walled as practically everywhere in KOTIS, saying that would be an assumption. The only thing I was really sure of was people.

"Auron is down there," I said, moving an open-palmed hand toward him. "There are four – five? – people over there." I indicated what was probably the direction of the corridor, but I wasn't entirely certain about that. "One person over there?" I pointed to my right, feeling a bit uncertain. Whoever it was was moving about. "Everything else just guess."

After a moment, the floor came back below my feet – Par had lowered me to the ground. I managed not to stagger and was feeling pleased about that, then had another message: "Test 3. Identify and track the location of room occupants."

Par began to move around the room and I pointed to him as he did. If he went too fast I would lose track of him, and if he kept moving quickly I'd lose him altogether and only know that he was near. Then one of the group of five came closer and turned out to be Glade. He and Par stood together a moment, then split up, but I had no trouble telling them apart so long as they didn't move too quickly.

A third person came in. I could track them just as distinctly, but didn't know who it was. The fourth person, I almost missed. It was a lot harder to tell she was there, but I eventually recognised her as Ista Chemie.

All this time I'd been working on a headache, which grew steadily worse until it was at Ddura-level pounding, and I was thoroughly relieved when the next message was: "Test session concluded." I straight away lifted my hands to my head, trying to figure out how to take the blindfold off, but the nanocloth was smooth and unresponsive to my touch, then abruptly melted back into a single strip. Not designed to be removed by the wearer, which made me like it even less. My interface functions were restored a moment later.

The person I hadn't been able to identify was a Kalrani, someone I hadn't met. I could make that much out while squinting through my headache and sudden exposure to light. Ruuel said in text over the interface: "Report to medical. If they clear you, practice sensing your surroundings before the next session, but do not push yourself."

Par very kindly levitated me down to the medical section, and I only had to wait through the shortest of scans before Ista Chemie gave me something for my headache. I fell asleep there, but didn't dream, and Zee came and collected me for a quiet dinner in her quarters. I told her I felt even sorrier for the Kalrani and Setari if they had to keep giving themselves headaches when they were only little kids. She said the first few times are usually the worst – it sounds like it works a bit like having your ears pierced – when you start using talents actively, pushing them beyond a 'passive' state, it opens pathways, but repetition strengthens rather than continuing to hurt.

I had a long bubble bath after dinner, and let the water get cold thinking about myself. Not the weirdness of being this touchstone-psychic-mysterious whatever. To tell the truth, I think staying on Muina turned me psychic. Maybe it's something in the pears. I sure as hell couldn't do any of this before I got stuck there. No, during my bath I was trying to remember if I used to hate surprises. I don't think I did. No-one's keen on unpleasant stuff being sprung on them, but these days I just hate it if anyone does something without warning me. Really hate it.

It's hard to believe Ruuel had forgotten the psychological aspects. He's far too sharp to not understand that blinding me and then switching places with Par would leave me confused and vulnerable. I'm sure it helped with the test, pushing me into a more sensitive state, and really it was logical and not something I should make a fuss over. But it made me so angry.

I'm telling myself it's a good thing, though. I'm an assignment to Ruuel, and I had an unhealthy level of faith in him. Maybe over the next week he'll keep pissing me off, and I'll end up thinking him on par with that ass Kajal.

Well, okay, that's not very likely. But I don't even want to listen to him telling me to think of otters now, and I would never have guessed that I'd feel that way.

Monday, June 2

Second in Command

So last night I dreamed I was arguing with Ruuel. He was being very cold and cutting, saying things about how worthless my trust is if it takes such a small thing to shatter it. I was saying that trusting someone was like being a little bit pregnant. You either are or you aren't. You either trust or you don't.

It wasn't as bad as the tentacle nightmare. I kept waking up, instead of being unable to, and was just unhappy rather than nearly having a heart attack, but I could do without having dreams like that. When I woke the last time I had an email from Selkie with the draft report from yesterday's session linked and instructions to fill in translations of what I'd been saying for my object identification attempts. I'm not entirely sure if this means it was Selkie conducting the testing session, or if he was just reviewing the report, but how much difference would it make if Ruuel was playing tricks on me under orders? It doesn't make me feel any better about it. I filled in the report results, unsurprised to discover that I'd been wrong for every single one of them. Reading the rest of the report didn't tell me anything I hadn't already concluded about my ability to know who is near me, but I did discover that part of the test had involved Glade and Par feinting blows at me to see if I reacted to that. I'm going to end up not wanting to be around all of Fourth Squad at this rate.

I was feeling very down and tired-eyed when I went for my first session of weapons training. The greensuit in charge of my training, Drake, looked like a poster-boy drill sergeant: fortyish, world-weary, no-nonsense. I started out half-expecting him to yell at me, but he was carefully correct and just a trifle indulgent – I bet he'd be the type of guy who calls women "Little Lady" back on Earth. The weapon he was training me with today was some kind of laser pistol, and I was hopeless with it. It's got to be the easiest gun in the world to use, but while I was okay (not dreadfully accurate, but okay) with shooting big, unmoving targets, as soon as he started me on moving or pop-up targets (all generated by the interface), I rarely hit anything. I've never had very good aim with ball sports and the like. Plus – maybe it's an Australian thing – but it just felt wrong having a gun. I've never even touched one before, and I'm too convinced I'll accidentally shoot someone.

After seeing how useless I am, Drake booked me in for more practice sessions, but since I don't think he expected me to be any good at it in the first place, he was all very relaxed about it. There's some other weapon he has to train me in as well called a 'pulse', which is what we'll focus on in the next training session. I guess all I can do about this is practice a lot.

I had a relatively light exercise session with Mara after lunch, weights and resistance. The gym's one of the few places you see Setari out of uniform – well, in a 'training' uniform which is basically shorts and a Singlet. They also use a light-weight outfit when doing combat training which doesn't involve weapons. There were quite a few people in the gym today, and I found it very distracting that they weren't dressed in form-fitting black. None of the Setari are body-builder muscular – they work out for strength but not mass and I gather too much muscle impedes agility. Mara could tell I was down, I think, but since I like being with her I cheered up a bit, and then Lohn came and joined us and he can always make me smile so it was an okay afternoon.

I ended up going to the Sights training area early, mainly because I think if I hadn't I would have given in to the temptation to wear one of my lab rat shirts. I was still annoyed and distrustful, but I didn't want to make a big fuss over what everyone else probably thought was nothing. Nor did I want to start a fight with Ruuel, or spend my time sulking or having tantrums. At the same time, I didn't want to be made to feel like that again, and I figured I'd have a better chance of avoiding it if I took a proactive, rational approach. The session was booked for Room 6 this time, a smaller room with a few brown square things scattered randomly about which I decided were some kind of blockish, backless chair. I sat cross-legged on one, listening to music until he showed up, also very early.

As soon as he came in I said: "If have to be blindfolded, can I have one I can take off myself? Really didn't like that thing yesterday."

"There's no need," he said. "This session is training, not testing."

I was relieved, but couldn't quite relax, and tried not to look obviously nervous as he made one of the squares slide across so it was opposite mine. He sat, one foot hooked under the opposite knee, relaxed like someone who'd never even thought about being in a bad mood.

"These are visualisation exercises," he said. "They are designed for attempting to pre-select which dreams you have, rather than changing the course of a dream you wish to escape. There are techniques for that, but these are a first step. You succeeded with the otters?"

I nodded, and he went on to explain the different things you could think when you were trying to get to sleep. It was a bit like counting sheep, really. Think of the details of a safe place. Construct something you liked, piece by piece. Follow a familiar routine. Do something which step-by-step focuses your mind on a particular thing, so that other things, like tentacles, don't slip in.

As I'd expected, Ruuel was a good teacher, giving examples of each of the techniques in a clear and really quite evocative way. He told me to try a different one each night, and use the most effective ones, even when I hadn't been stressed or suffering from nightmares. An entirely non-annoying session but, even though he did nothing but talk, I stayed tense and wary the entire time, not able to convince myself that there wouldn't be some test or trick, and struggling not to dwell too much on how I felt yesterday.

I let out a little relieved breath when he told me that was enough for the day, which I should have known better than to think he wouldn't notice. Probably he'd had a fair idea all along how I was feeling, but that made his eyebrows draw together slightly.

"Your dreams are too potentially destructive for you to not fully engage with this," he said, going into extra-captainly captain mode. "While I did not agree with the approach to yesterday's testing, I did carry it out. If that isn't possible for you to overcome, I can arrange for another person to oversee your training."

I'd hate to get into a real argument with Ruuel – I get the feeling I'd be outmanoeuvred at every turn. As it was, I felt my face burn, but I managed to meet his eyes steadily. "What was making me upset supposed to achieve?"

"Stress is a primary trigger to talent development." He was channelling his inner humourless robot, with no hint of expression. "In your case it mixes very badly with how you came to be here, and why you choose to tolerate being used by us. Do you want me to arrange for a different trainer?"

"Would they be more likely to disobey orders than you?" I asked, and was glad my voice was dry instead of hurt. Then I shook my head and stood up. "No. But thanks for the offer."

I left, needing to think about how I felt, somewhere away from Ruuel and all his Sights. I still haven't decided, really, other than to know I was happier for the explanation. For Ruuel that probably passes as an apology, too, and I wonder if that was the reason he'd seemed in such a bad mood: knowing that playing games with me would make me angry, and yet told to do it anyway.

I thought Selkie understood me better, too...and I just looked up his schedule, and saw that he'd been away on Muina again, and arrived back a few hours before he emailed me the report to complete.

Ah well – hopefully I won't have dreams about arguing with Ruuel tonight. If my visualisation works properly, I should dream about being in my room, cleaning it up. I'm kind of looking forward to that.

Tuesday, June 3

One Thousand Cranes

It occurred to me before going to bed last night that trying to dream about home was probably not a good idea. I really don't want to end up in Earth's near-space needing to be rescued. The otters really are the ideal 'safe place' visualisation for me, but I either have to disassociate it with Ruuel, or fully get over being upset with him before I use it again.

I decided to go with the 'think of making something' example, and went to sleep remembering Noriko Yamada teaching me how to make origami cranes. She was making a thousand of them, which she sewed onto long strings and was going to give as a present to her grandmother. I didn't make that many, but I remember the pattern well, and so I curled up in my window seat and thought through the steps of making origami cranes, and I had a dream about the day I met Noriko in the library at school, and made cranes over lunch.

After a while, Mori and Ruuel came and stood down by the far end of the table, but then Ruuel went away again almost immediately. I made cranes and listened to Noriko telling me about how the strings of cranes would be strung up in her grandmother's garden and as they fell to pieces they'd take the wish she made for her grandmother on the wind.

Then Ruuel and Taarel came in together, standing by my chair. "Do you want me to show you how to make one?" I asked Ruuel, handing him the crane I'd just made.

He held it up for Taarel to look at, and she touched a wing and said: "Impressive. Caszandra, do you know where you are?"

"The library?" I looked around, but started to think at the same time and said: "Oh, I'm dreaming," and woke up, still curled on my window seat. The lights were on, about three-quarter strength, and Mori was standing watching me. "But it wasn't a nightmare," I said.

"No. You were pouring out energy at an excessive rate, and that triggered the alert." She perched on one arm of one my couches. "What were you dreaming about?"

"Doing one of the sleeping exercises, making things." I sat up and looked around the room, surprised Ruuel and Taarel weren't there, because they'd felt very real to me. "Kind of have a headache," I said, finding that movement didn't agree with me much.

"We'll head down to medical in a minute. Just waiting on the captains to return."

"Ruuel and Taarel were here then?" I actually found their absence very disorienting, and my head pounded more as I tried to reconcile them talking to me and then not being there.

She smiled. "They went into the Ena, to this point in near-space, to follow a theory. They shouldn't be long."

I went and dressed, since even though I'd added long pyjama pants to my nightwear after my excursion to Earth, I still felt at a disadvantage dressed for bed when people came to talk to me, or when I had to go to medical.

Mori was watching the rain pounding steadily down outside the window. "What was the theory?" I asked her, but she said it would probably save repetition to wait till the captains were back, and instead we chatted about the last *The Hidden War* episode, and I found myself explaining a little about how I felt about hurting Nenna. Mori was in great agreement with this, and said that the main fear of practically every Setari was letting their squad down and getting them killed. Then Taarel brought me and Mori into a channel with her, Ruuel, Selkie and (to my mild pleasure) Isten Notra.

"This is the location in near-space," Ruuel said, and gave us a fragment of his own log, a rapid ascent up the outer wall of the KOTIS facility, Taarel just visible in peripheral vision, and then something very odd ahead – a swirling blurriness centred around the outlines of a building apparently poking out the whitestone wall. I recognised it immediately. My school library building.

It didn't have the sketchy quality of near-space – there were no holes in the walls – but there was a soap-bubble intangibility about it, like it was a mirage which would pop if you touched it. Still, Ruuel and Taarel had to push open the heavy swing door to get inside. There was a suggestion of a library assistant behind the front counter, but she didn't seem to see them, and they turned right and went past long rows of shelves to the tables at the back of the main room, where a ghost of me was sitting with a ghost of Noriko, folding origami cranes.

There were two me's. One sitting there folding cranes, and a glowing outline of me in roughly the same spot, curled up in my window seat. Ruuel and Taarel had to detour slightly to get inside the Taren near-space room as well as the library room, and Ruuel did a lot of Sight-switching, which really didn't help my headache.

"Do you want me to show you how to make one?" the ghost me asked Ruuel, handing him one of the cranes.

He switched through his Sights again, and held it up for Taarel to look at, and she touched a wing and said: "Impressive. Caszandra, do you know where you are?"

"The library?" The ghost me looked around, then said: "Oh, I'm dreaming," and then the whole thing vanished and Ruuel and Taarel were standing alone in the near-space version of my apartment, looking at a faint afterimage of the sleeping me fading away, and a dozen origami cranes scattered across the floor.

The log extract ended and I opened my eyes to find Taarel and Ruuel had arrived, each holding a handful of cranes of all different colours, some patterned like the fancy paper Noriko had been using.

"What do the paper birds represent?" Isten Notra asked.

"A wish of good luck," I said, closing my eyes again because my head was pounding. "Noriko, the girl who was with me, is from a part of Earth called Japan. They have an art form there called origami: making things out of folded paper. The bird is called a crane, which is considered a kind of magical beast in Japan. Japanese tradition to fold a thousand origami cranes, as a luck-wish."

I opened my eyes again, and since Taarel was within reach I leaned forward and took one of the cranes she was holding, and unfolded it. "It feels like ordinary paper," I said.

"Analysis will tell us more on that level," Isten Notra said. "Caszandra, we're going to place a drone in near-space at the location of your room to monitor the development of your dreams on the Ena." Before I could be more than totally horrified she went on: "The visual component will be locked to my viewing only, unless I deem there to be some critical value in releasing it further, and otherwise deleted after my review. Is that acceptable to you?"

I couldn't hide the DO NOT WANT on my face, and there was a long, painful pause before I could say: "I guess," sounding anything but happy about it. The idea of anyone watching my dreams is beyond awful. But that it would be Isten Notra made it just, just bearable, so I added: "Yes."

"Good girl."

"Medical now," Ruuel said, and I was dropped out of the channel. He gave Mori his handful of origami cranes, and waited to see whether I was going to walk myself or needed to be carted about. I managed to walk, just a bit slow and wobbly, but getting to medical mainly involves elevators anyway.

"Do you sleep there because of the window, or because you're frightened of the other room?" Ruuel asked, just before we reached my home away from home.

"Both," I said shortly, knowing it would be useless to lie to him. "Getting better about going into the bedroom though." I no longer had to nerve myself up to fetch my clothes, at least.

He didn't comment. Ruuel's good at knowing when to shut up, and he left me to the familiar routine of having my brain scanned and mapped to the last neuron.

I don't seem to have dreamed at all the rest of my sleep shift – no doubt Ista Chemie was privately relieved about that – and was collected by Maze this morning.

"You're having fewer unbroken nights," he said, after we'd settled in the canteen over breakfast. "And I know you must be far from happy about this latest development."

"Would you want anyone watching your dreams?"

"Not for a moment," he said, so firmly I immediately wondered what he dreamed about. "I'm glad Isten Notra found an approach which is bearable for you, since it's clear your talent development is accelerating. What you managed last night is well outside what we would call Ena manipulation, startling enough that the details are being kept within the squads working directly with you."

"Dream talent might be what a touchstone is?"

He nodded. "We haven't found anything like you mentioned in any of the histories, but it's becoming apparent that enhancement is the least of your talents. For the moment we're going to concentrate on trying to understand more about what it is you're doing, and helping you learn to *not* use it."

"Was easier just watching First Squad fight," I said, with a sigh. "Did you watch my shooting training session? So hopeless."

"You'll improve with practice." He gave me a captain-look to underline that I better take the sessions seriously, but then couldn't help but smile. "Though I concede that you're not a natural fighter. It doesn't sit well with me that we're even considering you having a need for weapons training."

"Are there lots arguments?"

"Little but. For the most part over timing, about how urgently we move forward on Muina. I can't pretend that there isn't a huge amount of pressure to find a way to the city you visited."

"I get to say I told you so?"

"Perhaps. The argument isn't settled yet." He studied my face. "You've had a run of difficult weeks, Caszandra. I can push to delay the decision, give you more time—"

"Would rather get it over with," I said, feeling oddly cross and embarrassed. "Don't want to do it at all, but Ionoth numbers still increasing, yes? Thought of someone I know dying more horrible than standing on platform. And won't have to worry about it once it's done, can go back to being enhancing stray."

"I'm not sure that's possible," he said, seriously. "What you did last night is something with wide-reaching implications, and it can't be left uninvestigated. Fortunately the tie to the Ena brings you into Isten Notra's domain. Now that Notra has assumed direct control we should be able to be more consistent with you, and avoid idiocies like subjecting you to one of the standard Sights tests." He made an exasperated face, then waved a hand to dismiss that train of thought, adding: "Today we're going to take you into the Ena to see whether you can directly manipulate it."

So instead of having Sight training with Ruuel, I spent the rest of the day with First Squad. Ketzaren tried, completely unsuccessfully, to teach me to do the most basic Ena manipulation while Alay guarded us and the rest of First Squad cleared whatever space we happened to be in. They did what they considered basic spaces – what apparently is called a 'scatter rotation' because they don't follow a string of joined spaces, but keep going in and out of near-space. I've been given some Ena manipulation homework, with a little cube smaller than a fingernail which I have to will into being green instead of yellow. Changing colour is apparently one of the easiest things to do, but I feel a complete idiot glowering at a little cube while nothing happens.

And I have very particular orders from Maze not to do 'making things' visualisations tonight. I should really do my otters 'safe place', but I don't want to risk anything Ruuel-related. Even if it's only Isten Notra watching, I know the only real secret is one you keep yourself.

Wednesday, June 4

Do Androids Dream?

I dreamed of counting sheep. It was a 'real' dream, but didn't last long enough that people had to come stop me from exhausting myself. While it felt very real – me sitting in the grass on a beautiful sunny day watching these hairy sheep leap over a fence barely bigger than their knees – counting sheep is such a sleep-related thing that I just knew that I must be dreaming.

And there was a drone there, lurking incongruously in the middle of a bush. I found this funny and annoying at the same time, and I waved at it when I noticed it, but for some reason it made me wake up. No headache, and I feel calm and rested, which I'm very glad about. I've hated these days of feeling like I'm barely keeping it together.

My morning appointment had changed to breakfast/dinner with Isten Notra, which was a nice surprise and turned into a fun outing. She lives in a residential section where some of the more important people who work at KOTIS live. It seems to be the equivalent of a gated community and the important thing to me was that it counts as within KOTIS' security and I could go there without an escort. Very cool. I almost didn't arrive on time because I was busy gaping at gardens, and a little café/milk bar that I so wanted to go and buy something from all by myself.

I'm a sad case.

People did recognise me and stare – even in KOTIS few outside the Setari and the medical staff ever see me – but no-one made any move to stop or question me, and I found Isten Notra's home easily enough. It was off a wide, high-ceiling 'plaza' area, which made it feel more like a house to me. No windows, though, which I will always find eternally strange. Apartments on Tare don't have doorbells: you use the interface to tell the door you're there and it lets the person you're there to meet know you're waiting, or just alerts everyone in the apartment. I stood outside feeling incredibly conspicuous until the door was opened by a girl a few years younger than me who started to say something, stopped, and stared in disbelief.

"Isten Notra lives here?" I asked, then paused while another girl, maybe eleven or twelve, came to the door as well, took one look at me, and shrieked.

I swear, I'm starting to want to go back to Earth solely so people don't react to me like that. It's seriously embarrassing. Both me and the older girl went very red, and I tried to say something, but the younger girl shrieked again, pointing at me. The older girl hastily stepped back, gesturing me inside so she could shut the door.

"Kanna, stop it you idiot," she hissed, shaking her sister by the shoulder. "I'm sorry, um, I'll – Kanna didn't–"

"Jor, Kanna, what in the spaces are you–" A guy around my age appeared in the foyer, blinked twice, but managed to neither shriek or be lost for words. "You must be here to see my grandmother," he said. "I'll take you through, but first let me apologise for my sisters. I'd say they're not usually like this, but that wouldn't be entirely honest."

"Shon!" The older girl looked even more embarrassed. The younger girl kicked him in the ankle, but he ignored her and led me further into the apartment.

It was a big place, really nice and comfortably cluttered – Isten Notra lives with her daughter Keel, Keel's husband Fellan, and their children, Shon, Jor and Kanna. She'd told them she was expecting a guest for dinner, but hadn't told them who. I gather Isten Notra likes to keep them on their toes. They were having pancake/crepe things for dinner, and so it worked as well for breakfast for me.

Unsurprisingly, they were all formidably smart. We ended up talking about Earth's space program, about moons and different sorts of planets – they were really interested in Earth's tilt giving us seasons and how that didn't apply to Tare or Kolar, but obviously did for Muina – and then we talked about Mars and Earth science and as usual I wished I'd paid more attention at school, but I didn't make too big an idiot of myself. I wish I'd read more hard science fiction as well as space opera novels, though.

After dinner, and a very yummy gooey toffee dessert which is not precisely what I should be eating for breakfast, Isten Notra asked me if I'd show them how to make origami cranes and so we had an origami session – I can make cranes and a cup and the chatterbox game and paper airplanes and a turtle, which is the most complex thing Noriko taught me. Isten Notra had had a large supply of paper brought to her in preparation, but she didn't have a single pen in the house, and none of them could write anyway, so I couldn't quite explain the chatterbox game properly until one of Isten Notra's minions turned up with a pen. I bet he loved discovering why he'd been sent urgently to find an anachronistic holdover from the pre-interface age, but Kanna adored the chatterbox and had me write several up for her full of the kind of responses an eleven year-old imp thinks is funny, in my slightly strange-looking written Taren (I can write in the Taren alphabet if I concentrate, but I can't write neatly enough to make it look precisely like the standardised letters).

I'd been at the Notra apartment for nearly three hours when Isten Notra dismissed her grandchildren and took me up to her office to talk about what the drone had recorded of my dream last night. I had been projecting into the Ena again, though less strongly it seems, and I didn't make any permanent sheep, unlike my cranes, a dragon-patterned one of which was in Isten Notra's office. She showed me the visual recording, of a mirage-like image of me sitting in nebulous grass watching sheep, and also the white outline of me sleeping in my window seat. A little after I waved at the drone, the whole thing faded away. I explained counting sheep to Isten Notra, and said yes, I had been aware that the drone was there and described what it had looked like to me.

"We are still at the very theoretical stage with this, Caszandra," she said. "I can tell you this is not Ena manipulation. It does not give the same readings at all. My best initial evaluation is that, at least temporarily, you are creating something resembling a space."

That was far more than I'd realised, and I didn't like the thought of it. "Am I likely to get much stronger? Make permanent spaces?"

"Unlikely. While you are still at the beginning of your development, and these cranes of yours demonstrate you are already capable of producing small, simple objects, the energy required to make a permanent space – you simply aren't physically capable of producing such power. Though I would recommend that you vary what you focus on during sleep as much as possible, as there is a possibility that repetition might achieve what you cannot in a single burst." She tucked a stray curl of white hair behind one ear, and shook her head. "We are only beginning to understand you. The drone has been running scans on the barrier between this space and the near-space around your room, but it shows no sign that your dreams have caused it to weaken. Yet your dream of the Array massive produced audible sounds and even physical reactions among the technicians who were in this space. That is a dangerous possibility. That you are capable of producing a thin version of a space is a thing of curiosity with interesting possibilities. But the implications of you causing effects in real-space, that is something else altogether. Not least because you are terribly at risk of injuring yourself."

Isten Notra sent me off with Shon as an escort, which I thought unnecessary until I noticed how many people were lurking about the streets back to KOTIS proper. Not huge crowds – the general public can't come into the area without a pass – but far more than there'd been when I'd arrived. I could see that Shon had noticed them, but he chattered on blithely about exploration on Muina, which made me feel less uncomfortable. Shon's very torn between the work his grandmother has pioneered in Ena studies, and natural sciences. He's David Attenborough at heart.

He also asked if he could email me, if I was willing to talk about the comparisons between Earth's and Muina's wildlife, and left with a wave when we reached the entrance of KOTIS proper. A nice guy, very relaxed and on top of things. I have a faint suspicion Isten Notra was indulging in some matchmaking, but I think I'll pretend that hasn't occurred to me. I liked Shon, but it's easier not to think about romance at all right now. I figure if I can start waking up not missing Ruuel, I can start thinking about the possibility of other guys, but it's pointless until that happens. Even when I was so upset about that testing session, I still woke up knowing he wasn't there.

I had weapons training after lunch, which involved struggling into bulky grey chest armour. I felt like a Stormtrooper. Drake stood me in the middle of a practice room with actual physical targets in it and had me activate the chest armour, which briefly made an energy shield around me, and then let loose a sort of area effect concussion blast, sending the targets flying in pieces in all directions. It has two blasts, and then will slowly recharge. They're relying on it, far more than any ability I might gain shooting blasters, to keep me safe. I hate it.

What if there was someone I didn't see in range when I set it off? I kept thinking of all the terrible accidents I could cause, which made it hard to concentrate on my blaster practice. Drake kept me almost a full kasse practicing in the armour and while I did start to come closer to hitting stationary targets more consistently by the time he let me go, I still suck at moving objects, never notice anything that pops up behind me, and really am kind of sick of the whole exercise.

After that I took a long bath, and went down to the Sights training area early, intending to play my murder mystery game until Ruuel showed up. I'm liking the game more and more, and it helps me de-stress, but it's amazingly huge so I only play it when I have a good wodge of unscheduled time. On the way to the small training room I couldn't help but notice four female Kalrani gathered around the viewing window into the obstacle course area.

"–by far the best," one was saying. "Absolutely edible."

"If you like your meal ice-cold," another snorted. "You're wasting your time anyway. You think you can compete with *her*?"

"People always say that," said a third. "But it's all just rumour."

"Rumours don't go on for years without some basis," the second said. "And–"

"It's about time we got to drill," said the fourth, and I could tell from the way they all straightened and very carefully didn't look around that she'd spotted me and told them I was there. They all headed off down the corridor, and I went to the observation window and looked down.

Ruuel and Taarel. Ruuel was wearing one of the horrid blindfolds, and Taarel was attacking him. Blind and deaf, and he could still avoid her attacks and hop about the moving obstacle course. He couldn't quite counterattack swiftly enough to hit her, but it was a very near thing, and they both kept barely avoiding swinging bars and things which shot out of the walls at them. It all looked incredibly dangerous.

I watched for a minute, then went up to the roof. It was raining, but not too hard, and I stood in it for a while, then went and had a hot shower so I wouldn't catch cold and get lectured. Then I went down and was exactly on time for my appointment so that Ruuel could step me through techniques for what he called 'release triggers'. Every time you go to sleep you have to try and build into your dream something which reminds you that it's a dream, and allows you to wake up. A door, or an alarm clock. He said I shouldn't use the drone as a release because I wouldn't always be sleeping somewhere there was a drone. I stayed really focused, and asked what few questions occurred to me, and he dismissed me quite quickly.

It's not easy to hide things from Ruuel. But all this talk about visualisations and methods of focusing your mind has been very handy. All the time during today's session I was counting. Listening to what he said and keeping count took a lot of effort, and lessened the amount of energy I could devote to feeling stupidly dejected. He at least didn't act as if he could tell I was upset.

All along I've had a sense that he and Taarel are together. They make a great couple, really. And like the Kalrani said, who could compete with her? Even if you ignore little issues of our comparative looks, I'm someone who's still afraid to sleep in her own bedroom. Someone who has to be babysat.

It's stupid to be upset to hear someone say no more than I already knew – that people think they're together, but aren't sure. But I've spent the evening worrying about what I'm going to dream tonight, and stayed up incredibly late and can barely keep my eyes open. Being upset is one of the triggers for my nightmares. And even if Isten Notra is the first person reviewing what I dream, that's no guarantee others won't see it. And I can't talk about it to anyone at all.

Which at least means I have a huge amount of motivation to get this release trigger thing absolutely right first time. I don't think I've ever been so determined to do something in my life.

I'm going to do a counting dots visualisation. And every dot is going to have 'This is a dream' written on it. And every dot will be a release trigger to get me out of the dream. And I will be in a room which is nothing but dots, and every one of them a release trigger.

And I don't care if I wake up a thousand times tonight, kicking myself out of my dreams: that's the only thing I'm going to dream.

Ghost just showed up and got very annoyed with me for squeezing her so tightly.

Thursday, June 5

A short history of

I'm glad I've been told to go back to sheep. I did manage to dream of being surrounded by buttons saying "This is a dream". But they were all paintings of buttons. Corridor after corridor of paintings of buttons, and me wandering endlessly through them trying to find the right one to push. It was a long night of feeling exhausted and alone – and all the time feeling watched, though I couldn't see the drone this time. I wasn't scared, and obviously wasn't churning out enough power to have anyone feel the need to come wake me up, but just because I didn't give myself a heart attack didn't mean I didn't feel totally battered and done in by it all.

And woke missing Ruuel like hell, worse than ever. What is it going to take to stop me feeling this way about him?

At any rate, I had breakfast with Lohn and Mara, since I was supposed to be training with them before they went on rotation. I had to talk Mara out of sending me to medical, but I'm really glad we chatted since with them I find it easier to admit what a wuss I am, and how stressed I'd gotten about not wanting people to see my dreams. I guess it is kind of odd, since it was a private conversation with Lohn and Mara being made into television which had me so upset. Maybe it's all the hugs which makes them easy to talk to.

One thing Lohn said really struck me – that if I can control what I dream about, being able to project my dreams in such intense detail is really an opportunity. I could show him what surfing looked like, for instance. That's a nice idea, changing the drone from an intrusive spy to a handy recording device. The big problem is the presumption that I can manage anything resembling control, given how badly I failed last night.

We did some mild training, and grabbed a light mid-morning meal before First Squad went into rotation. Then I had weapons training, which being drained and tired really did not help with. Drake was very tolerant, which is one good thing about him having low expectations for me. After that, I went up to the roof, and admired the sheer blackness of the approaching thunderclouds while I tried to think up a way to tell Ruuel that maybe someone else should train me after all. It was hard to come up with a reason that didn't sound wildly insulting, or underline that the problem was just that I was too emotionally messed up about him. I'd rather not have to deal with him at all for a while – not until I stop waking up knowing he's not near me.

Everything I could come up with sounded so feeble, and I had just decided that I'd put off changing trainers till tomorrow when I felt someone standing to my left. The Nuran, Inisar.

"Hello again," I said, after a moment. I'm sure if anyone was paying attention to my vitals monitor they would have noticed a huge spike, but since he was just standing there, all I did was add: "Another rescue attempt, or something else this time?"

"Do you no longer choose to aid the Tarens?"

The question was so neutral I couldn't tell if he was simply curious, or was ready to cart me off through the Rift as soon as I said 'yes'. Or kill me if I didn't.

"No." I stayed sitting down, though I had to lean back a little to look up at him. "Situation hasn't gotten better. More Ionoth, more gates. Don't see how I can walk away from that. I had a – well, I have lots of questions, but I particularly wanted to ask what Cruzatch are."

"What do you think they are?" he asked. Totally unhelpful.

"Muinans become Ionoth. Trying to make themselves immortal. Or into gods. Or both. And now trying to stop Tarens because Tarens reached the point where they can move about spaces and find Pillars and turn them off. Do the Cruzatch drive massives to attack Nurans too?"

"I have been forbidden to answer questions."

That made me feel nervous, since if he wasn't here to talk, kidnapping or assassination moved up the list. "Just here to look at the scenery?"

His eyes – rather too like Ruuel's for my comfort – considered me steadily. "I am commanded to observe your development as a touchstone. While I am here I am to avoid all contact with any of the lost children of Muina."

The rules-lawyering made me smile. He wasn't quite answering my questions, and he wasn't talking to a Muinan-descendant.

"Following instructions very exactly. I don't know which bits of what's happening to me are the touchstone part, but just lately I've started projecting my dreams into the Ena. If that's what being a touchstone is, would appreciate a few hints as to how not to have dreams. Or at least stop half-killing myself with them."

"Control is not a thing gained during sleep," he said, and handed me a book. I glanced down at it, very surprised, and when I looked up again he was gone.

"Straight answers not a thing gained from Nurans," I muttered, and sighed, then looked with extreme interest at the book.

It was handmade, the paper creamy and lightly textured, with firmly sewn bindings forming a thick solid edge. The covers were plain wooden boards, fine and undecorated. The whole thing looked newly made, and when I opened it the writing was dark and cleanly written. And in Old Muinan, which I have as much chance of reading and understanding as Old English. I snorted, but carefully went through it page by page, committing them to my log – and hoping for useful illustrations.

Then it was time to face the music. I'd already checked on 'my' captains, but Maze was still on rotation and Ruuel was asleep. I tossed up contacting Taarel or Grif Regan from Second Squad or even Zan, but decided to skip the preliminaries and emailed Selkie the conversation from my log, with a subject heading of "Nurans" and in the body: "Have neat handwriting." I cc'd the email to Maze, Ruuel and Isten Notra and then sat there trying to puzzle out what the damn thing was about. Not, as I'd hoped, "The Idiot's Guide to Touchstones".

I'd just decided it was some kind of history of Muina when Isten Notra sent a channel request to me with the text: "You are an endless source of amusement," making me laugh.

"Hello," I said. "Suspect 'amusement' is not word everyone will use."

"You may well be right. And how cruel of you to only send the first four pages with that log. Pass me the rest."

That was easily done – I'd already separated out the fragment for my own review. "Can you read Old Muinan, Isten Notra? This is Nuran history book?"

"More than that, child. It is a copy of an account written by a Lantaren just after arrival on Nuri. It is a compilation of everything the Muinans who fled to Nuri knew of the disaster and the events leading up to it. It is-" Her voice throbbed. "It is very exciting, and I will leave you now while I devour it. You'd best get yourself to Selkie's office before he finishes reviewing your conversation."

I'd not been to Selkie's office before – it was in a part of KOTIS I think of as 'Command Central'. An area with lots of bluesuits walking about, and an excess of meeting rooms. I could tell when Selkie finished reviewing my log, because an appointment for a meeting with him appeared in my calendar, scheduled for immediately. But I guess Isten Notra had already told him I was on my way, because he simply waited for me to show.

Some offices on Tare have remnants of design from when Tarens used table-top computers, but most of them are like Selkie's – just a meeting room assigned to a particular person, with storage space for equipment, but little to do with desks or paper shuffling. Selkie's had a small rectangular coffee table thing, with four low chairs around it, and a taller café-type round table with two 'upright' chairs with high backs (like wing-back chairs). He was in one of these, and didn't look amused.

"Sit."

I put the book on the table and sat, feeling like I'd been called to the principal's office. Except it was a school I couldn't go home from at the end of the day. For psychic soldiers.

"I've spoken to you on the subject of your alert before," he said. "If I need to do so again, you will have a squad assigned to you permanently. Do you understand?"

Setting off my alert wouldn't have made any difference if the Nuran had wanted to kill me, and I'd been all prepared to say that until I saw the look in Selkie's eyes. Any argument, and he'd assign a squad to me straight away.

"Understood," I said, resigned to having to do it.

"What is the basis for your theory about the Cruzatch?"

"Arenrhon obviously about godhood or immortality. Bodies in the non-blurry sarcophagi were burnt. And Cruzatch keep showing up. Is just a guess – we don't have anything like Cruzatch on Earth. Don't think I've even heard any legends about things like that."

He didn't comment, but didn't look surprised, either. I was hardly the first to speculate on what the people at Arenrhon were trying to achieve.

"Remain here until Notra has reported on this," he said, picking up the book and leaving.

It wasn't a short book, but I'm not altogether sure if having to sit in Selkie's office for a couple of hours was supposed to be punishment, or just that Selkie wanted me somewhere he thought it hard for the Nuran to get to. I mused for a while on where the Nuran was going to sleep on a planet like Tare, where there was so little unoccupied land. Avoiding all contact with the descendants of Muina would be quite a task.

Not that he seemed to have had the least trouble finding me. If he had been sent to kill me, I'd be dead right now. I think in a way I've grown used to the idea of probably dying. That's what spending so much time in intensive care does for you.

Selkie didn't come back straight away, and I ended up playing one of the interface games I'd bought, caught up in the very curious world Tare had been before it had advanced so far technologically. Cave-dwellers, with their whitestone cities under a sky of stone, and thus with an 'outside' they would go out to, of sorts. Ionoth were present, but far less of an issue, and there was not this obsession with the yet-to-be-formed Setari. Instead the focus was on sorties into the surrounding darkness of the caves, and tunnels leading to undiscovered parts. It was Tare's 'Here Be Dragons' stage, and really quite a different world.

When First Squad came back from rotation, Maze replied to my email with: "Urth person is asking for a lecture. I'll see you shortly." But it was Ruuel, not Maze, who showed up first, walking in and sitting opposite me while I was preoccupied with a puzzle. I felt him there, and shut down the game, opening my eyes.

"The trigger technique was not successful?" he asked, presumably having spotted the huge circles under my eyes.

"Long nightmare about looking for triggers," I said, shrugging. "Will try the action variation tonight." That was where a particular action on your own part, like a hand signal, was the trigger to wake up. "Do you think Nuran was actually answering my question, or just being deeply annoying?"

He tilted his head slightly. "It is possible that your abilities are triggering during your dreams purely because you have no control over them waking. Have you been practicing sensing the location of those around you?"

I nodded, though it was not so much practising as I increasingly happened to know people were on the far sides of walls.

"When the Cruzatch first attacked you in Kalasa, did you sense it before you saw it?"

That was hard to answer. "Don't really know. Don't think I heard it, but something made me look up."

"We'll try a visualisation exercise until Isten Notra is ready. Close your eyes."

I gave him a rather wry look, which he didn't react to, and after a moment I obediently shut my eyes, despite knowing my face had gone red. And I was stupidly happy. It's the feeling that I'm an annoyance to him – and the idea that he and Taarel are together – that bothers me. I'm still not pleased that he went along with upsetting me for the purposes of testing, but – yeah, I can't pretend that that or even the high probability that he's in love with Taarel cured me of wanting him.

For the visualisation exercise he described a room. High ceiling, pillars, some low cushioned benches, and a whole bunch of square display cases with different things in them – old weapons and jars and jewellery. I had to hold a picture of what he was describing in my mind, and repeat it back to him with every thing he added. One of those memory games. I was surprised at how easy I found it. Ruuel describes things very vividly, and I could really see the room, so had no trouble repeating back the contents, but started to struggle with an increasing headache.

"This is making my head hurt," I said eventually, opened my eyes and then flinched because everything around me was blurry and seeing that felt like a needle going into my brain. Just faintly, I glimpsed the room he'd described, superimposed on Selkie's office, but then I had to close my eyes and do rather a lot of head-clutching. Ruuel, after a little pause, moved me to another room and called a medic up to drug me to the point where the pain was pushed behind a wall, but didn't really go away. I was very wan and shaky when Maze and Selkie arrived, but at least could open my eyes.

They'd ordered food, and eating did help me a little, but I mainly wanted a dark place to curl up in, and only half paid attention to Ruuel describing the results of the visualisation – not looking at the log file he shared at all – until he started pointing out details in the ghostly image overlaid on Selkie's office which he hadn't mentioned but which were in the museum he'd been describing. And something which he didn't remember being there. Not to mention that the things he *had* described were exactly correct.

"We will obtain a current log of the museum for comparison," Selkie said. He paused a beat, then added to me: "Attempting to use this ability to see your own world would be crass stupidity."

Guess I'd been looking too obviously delighted. "Probably," I agreed, reluctantly. "Will stay away from trying to visualise Earth until have better idea of limits. Dream visualisation I had night before last of sheep was set on Muina though. And one with origami cranes was Earth building. Possibly all the energy isn't in the looking but the reproducing."

"Either way, you will limit visualisations to controlled experiments until further notice. Knowledge of the expansion of these abilities remains restricted to the assigned squads. For the short term, the other events of today are wholly restricted, even within your squads."

He brought Isten Notra into channel with us then, and she gave us a very cheerful run-down of the content of the Nuran history.

"What this book primarily gives us is confirmation of certain assumptions, and a timeline, but also a few discoveries," she said. "The author was not directly involved in the creation of the Pillars, but details her memories of the project from the time it was first proposed by a group called House Dayen. The major revelation is that stabilising travel through deep-space was only a fortuitous additional benefit, while their primary goal was the aether, which was intended to power what is termed as 'great devices'. There was considerable debate between the controlling houses regarding the risks, and it was the unexpected support of a House Zolen which saw the project move forward. The author notes that during the period of construction, House Zolen also built a number of 'insufferably proud' underground dwellings, which is almost certainly a reference to the Arenrhon installation.

"The Pillars project was considered a resounding success until gates began to tear between real-space and near-space. Ionoth became an immediate issue, and after numerous attacks House Dayen created the Ddura using one of these 'great devices'. The disaster followed only five days later. First, news of an attack by unknowns on House Dayen, swiftly followed by loss of contact with Kalasa. And reports were received from those within sight that a wound had appeared on 'Daman', which is one of the names for the Muinan moon.

"Nurioth and Teklata fell silent within hours of Kalasa. Most of what the author terms 'focus towns' were not responding, but one reported that the platforms had ceased to work, and instead 'stung' any who touched them. Those settlements still with mind-speakers shared what little knowledge they had, and there was considerable argument as to whether the Ddura were responsible, as the Ddura cannot access Kalasa, and that was the city which fell first. Within a day of Kalasa's loss, as more and more voices fell silent, a decision was made to flee."

Isten Notra paused, then added: "What remains gives us some more detail on the methods used to access deep-space, and protect a sizeable town's worth of refugees from the aether and Ionoth encountered."

"Thought aether came from platform towns, not deep-space," I said, finding that the more my headache receded, the harder it was to stay awake.

"Indeed," Isten Notra said. "Our observations have certainly shown that aether is generated on Muina. Whether all the aether encountered in the Ena is that same aether is yet to be ascertained."

"How much does this change?" Maze asked.

"In the short term, nothing. The information about the Arenrhon installation usefully establishes that it was not part of the Pillars project, but does not explain its actual purpose. Perhaps it is one of these 'great devices'. But much of the book merely establishes a timeframe and order for information we already have."

"And leaves open the question of why this Inisar of Nuri has been forbidden to speak, yet chooses to pass this on," Ruuel said, and I thought this a fair point, but was too busy falling asleep to even hear the response.

I woke in my apartment – on the window seat, not in the bedroom, and all neatly tucked up. I'm guessing it was Maze who brought me back, but would he know I needed to sleep in the window seat at the moment?

Isten Notra had sent an email with the first few pages of the book translated, and I suppose that fact that they're leaving the translation to her for the moment is a demonstration of the current level of secrecy. I guess that's to protect Inisar, since there was a possibility the Nurans had spies on Tare. The history book becoming public knowledge would basically be a statement to the Nurans that Inisar had betrayed them. I find it more than uncomfortable to not be able to talk about this to the rest of First Squad or Fourth Squad, but I'll make sure to keep my mouth shut.

I've been switched to the same shift as Fourth Squad, with all my appointments being weapons training in the morning and Sights training in the afternoons, with a little physical training wedged in between. And in another week it's back to Muina, so it's obvious they've decided to use me to find Kalasa. First, Second, Third and Fourth will all be part of the same mission.

Just now I'm more worried about six nights of coping with the problems in my head, than anything a whole week away on Muina.

Friday, June 6

Keszen Point Warehouse

No dreams last night. Nor yesterday after the meeting. Not that I can remember, anyway. I'm not quite ready to relax, but I'm starting to hope.

One thing about switching to the later shift is that I'm awake when *The Hidden War* premieres each week, although I'm not going to make the mistake of watching it with company again. Last night's episode was mission-focused and action oriented, except for the last ten minutes or so when Nori, the main character, is called to a testing chamber and – along with the godly-good and lusted-after-by-everyone captain of Squad Emerald – tests the newly-discovered enhancement talents of the wide-eyed and kittenish stray. Then Nori was assigned to give the stray some basic combat training and baby-sit her.

I don't think it's a good thing to have a link made between Zan and the main character. Nori's not her squad's captain, and doesn't look at all like Zan, but just like Zan (so far as I can tell) she's painfully and secretly devoted to the godly-good and lusted-after-by-everyone senior captain. And I bet Zan's going to get all sorts of smirky comments from that bitch Forel thanks to that. I debated contacting her, but I figure Zan was going to be taking a firm attitude of indifference toward anything on *The Hidden War*, and that there was no need to add my voice to the crowd. But I'll make sure to try and chat with her in the next few days.

This morning's shooting practice went much better, since I'd actually had some rest beforehand and wasn't distracted by any imminent meltdown. I'm still terrible at knowing one of the targets is 'sneaking' up behind me – since they're not alive my brand-new people detector doesn't help at all – but I'm getting better at remembering to check occasionally. I still miss moving targets 99% of the time.

I had lunch/dinner with Maze, who confirmed the reason why the Nuran's book is so secret is not wanting to give away that he'd helped us. He doesn't know how long it will be kept from the squads. Apparently Drake has given me a good report for overall improvement, and Maze wants me to focus on getting comfortable with the practice, to try and make shooting an automatic thing.

"Why didn't you share your theories about the Cruzatch?" he asked toward the end of lunch.

I shrugged. "They nothing new. Couple people at Arenrhon saying almost same thing, and no way to confirm it. Don't like it when total guesses mine given weight just because I say it. Asked Nuran because hoping he knew answer. Do you think that what they are?"

"My guess isn't any better than yours," Maze said, and looked sad. Maze knows he's not exactly impartial where Cruzatch are concerned, which is another reason I wasn't keen to start making guesses.

I left to go meet Ruuel, intending to be early but miscalculating how long it would take to get there. Instead of a testing room, we were supposed to meet at Transport Platform 15, which turned out to be a train station deep underneath the island. Ruuel and Ista Chemie were waiting for me, and he started out with his usual terse briefing as we all boarded a lone train carriage.

"We're travelling to Keszen Point, where we'll be conducting testing for this week. For the next two days we'll concentrate on similar visualisations to yesterday – testing whether you will react to a description of a place that is unknown to the person describing it, and how much detail you require. Two talents seem to be in play – the ability to see the place, and then reconstructing it using the Ena – but don't concern yourself with separating the two immediately."

"Testing there because I might damage things?" I asked, and he nodded as the train started off. It was a very zippy one – I think the line might be used to shift freight swiftly around the underneath of the island. I looked Keszen Point up, and found it was an outlying rock off one side of Konna. A big boxy warehouse, with a few side rooms. It was cold and echoey, smelled of ocean and something acrid, and they had rearranged countless packing crates to the edges so that the entire centre was empty except for a couple of tables and chairs, and a scanning chair for me. There was another greysuit waiting – a gadgets type – and a man called Far Dara who I gathered was the person in charge of the warehouse, who I bet just loved having to turn it into a test facility for a week, but who hid his opinion well and was formally polite, showing us the few amenities of the place.

"Is it possible to go outside?" I asked, which seemed a simple request, but involved a lot of blank looks as to why I'd want to, and then checking the weather. But Tsa Dara was willing to show me, and Ruuel didn't object. I had to talk Ista Chemie into coming: she was typically Taren about going outside and maybe she was justified in that given we had to put on a harness with attached safety ropes. Then it was a double-airlock kind of arrangement before we were out and attaching our safety ropes to a railing/fence thing which ran around the edge of the small bit of rock which wasn't building.

It was the final hours of Tare's long dusk and you couldn't see much more than the outlines of the rocks we were standing on, and the shifting of the great waves almost to our height. But you could look up, and that was well worth it. High, black vertical rock, and then white city. I'd already known from my roof-visits that the whitestone wasn't lit, except in one or two points, but it still caught what light there was. And it was so high, so monumental, so unlike Earth that it really reminded me that I was living on an alien planet.

I leaned over the railing and pressed my hand on the top of a waist-high rock, cold and slimy. "I've been on this planet for half an Earth year and this is the first time I've touched it," I said, discovering some furry green moss-like stuff on one slope of the rock. "But best I can tell, most Tarens haven't even done this much. Is so strange for me to understand."

"Would the people of your world be so different?" Ista Chemie asked. I think being outside and looking up at Konna was a big thing for her – her voice was really strange.

"Hard to say how they'd be if they'd come to Tare like Muinans did. But if you transplanted population of Australia to Konna, every time the weather eased up enough not to be fatal, the roofs would be covered with people having picnics, and flying kites and hang-gliding and a few insane people base-jumping." I'd had to use English words, and laughed at how incomprehensible I must be. "In Australia, there's a job called surf life-saver. Spend all day at the beach watching for drowning people."

This was really good timing for one of the waves smacking the rocks below to be extra-large, and to break over the ground we were standing on. It wasn't enough to make any of us fall over, but Ruuel was abruptly a few millimetres away from me, a stabilising hand on my arm. He only said: "We'd best get started," and gestured for us to go back inside, but he hadn't moved away before he spoke, and I stopped being all chatty and started hoping I could get my mind off those few moments of him being so close, of how I'd *felt* his voice as well as heard it. I really didn't want to be projecting anything that was on my mind at that moment, and concentrated on thinking through the Taren alphabet backwards and things like that.

Ista Chemie was distracted by having shoes full of seawater, and Tsa Dara took her off to dry them. Nanosuits are so much better. I sat on the scan chair, and was glad of the other greysuit, who wanted to check the scanner's calibration. From there it was all business, with Ruuel reading out piece by piece details of an indoor garden with fountains and stony artwork. The description wasn't as well-done as when Ruuel used his own words, but it worked the same – and gave me another massive headache. Ruuel didn't let me open my eyes as quickly this time, which meant the headache was worse and I was completely limp and exhausted afterwards. I managed to stay awake for the trip back, though, and ended up sleeping it off in medical because Ista Chemie wanted to monitor me more. No nightmares. Maybe, just maybe, these exercises are exactly the right thing to do to stop me having them.

But I woke from my post-testing nap really knowing Ruuel wasn't there, and lay remembering his hand on my arm, the warmth of him, his breath just faintly stirring my hair.

I'm not succeeding at all in this getting over Ruuel thing.

Saturday, June 7

Echo of a wind chime

Since knowing Ruuel isn't there is still my dominant sensation on waking, I've taken to lying in bed for a while each morning trying to sense his location. My range is expanding, but the Setari quarters –

including my own – all have various levels of shielding on them, and till now I've only be able to feel people if they're in the corridor on this or the next level up. This morning I knew Lohn was in his room, though, so it is possible for me to sense through their shielding.

And I can tell when Ghost is in my room, even when she's invisible. Something I've no intention of admitting.

Today's test was a fictional place, a magnificent underground hall with intricate and gorgeous murals on the walls and an incredible puzzle-pattern floor. Ruuel didn't tell me it was fiction beforehand, and it took longer for me to get any kind of mental image of it, but it still worked, producing a lot more detail than Ruuel had read from the novel the test was based on. I didn't get so immediate and overwhelming a headache the instant I opened my eyes this time, though the world went very blurry – two images overlaid on each other. The hall had an immense floor to ceiling wind chime, but no wind to blow it. Ruuel went over and touched it and it actually shifted in response.

There were people who came along as part of the room, though they hadn't been in Ruuel's description at all. Very grand and noble sorts, who didn't seem able to measure their clothes, which were all hanging sleeves and trains and twice as much fabric as necessary. When Ruuel touched the wind chime, they all looked at him, which startled me enough that I stopped concentrating on maintaining the image – which was good because I really felt myself stop that time. Though I could have lived without the headache afterwards. It felt like someone had smacked a huge gong right behind my eyes, and I had to lie still until Ista Chemie's medicking had taken the edge off.

"The scans are showing four distinct areas of brain activity," Ista Chemie said, while I was sipping one of the horrible restorative drinks she insists on giving me. "One only activates when you open your eyes while the others are in effect. Can you describe what you experience then?"

"Pain."

Ruuel gave me a captain-look, so I shrugged and added: "Two images overlaid, and a sense of...dissonance? It wasn't too bad this time until you touched the wind-chime and they all looked at you."

Ruuel frowned, then said: "Reviewing log."

I'll never get used to someone accessing the world through my eyes. Ruuel didn't give much away, just stared into the distance abstractly for a minute, then said calmly: "The people weren't visible to us. You're seeing both the image in this world, and the one in the Ena. The drone set at this location in near-space should confirm that."

I got a bit quiet after that, thinking things over. On the trip back Ruuel told me that tomorrow we'd start attempting to find a way for me to separate the talents and gain some measure of conscious control of them. If I had been feeling particularly daring I would have asked him if he had had a lot of difficulty untangling six different sights, but I was busy feeling headachy and worried. I never did get around to telling him I thought I should swap teachers. Even though I get all sad and repressed around him at times, I feel reassured knowing that he has no trouble seeing right through me. Right now I need all those Sights to keep me going off the rails. And I figure I can feel sad about him and Taarel, but see him every day, or feel sad about him and Taarel, and miserable because I don't get to see him at all.

Which is not what I'm worried about right now, but a useful distraction. I wish I wasn't so tired, but don't think I can keep myself awake any longer.

Sunday, June 8

Overwrought

I was getting ready for bed after yesterday's session when Mori sent me a channel request. "Feel like some company?" she asked, when I opened the channel. "I've been given a firm suggestion that I might want to sleep on your couch tonight."

My first reaction was to resent the babysitting, to hate being thought of as this weak-ass neurotic liable to fall apart without hand-holding. I almost told Mori that I was fine, but the problem was that I wasn't, so after an overlong silence I told her: "I think I'd be glad if you did."

"I'll be down in a moment, then." She sounded pleased, so at least I didn't have to feel she found being told to sleep on my couch annoying. And she was smart enough not to pretend that the idea was anything but an order, which is one of the things I like about Mori.

She brought a big, cushiony eiderdown with her, and was wearing a singlet, short-shorts and slippers – I'd love to know if anyone saw her in the elevator.

"You had a bad day, huh?" she said, plunking the eider on one of my couches. "I thought the testing was going well."

"I guess it is." I shifted from my window seat to the opposite couch, feeling embarrassed but stupidly relieved someone would be with me when I slept. "I just started thinking things through properly. The tests have been about places, rooms. Even though there was that whole horrible dream about the massive, it hadn't occurred to me that I could make Ionoth that might attack Setari in near-space."

"Really? It's the first thing I thought of. So you're worried you'll summon up something nasty?"

"Earth has some pretty scary stories." I could tell she didn't understand, that she thought I was scared for myself. "It's very annoying, because the more I tell myself not to worry, the more stressed I get about it. I never used to be like this."

I dimmed the lights back down, and told Mori about slumber parties. She told me about what it had been like for her when, at six, she was brought to Konna to be a Kalrani. During the early days, they'd been allowed to talk to their families as much as they wanted over the interface, and the training had focused mainly on physical education. Only the expansion of the interface network had been particularly distressing. After that, interface rights had slowly been pared back, and the training focused more on their talents.

Mori is glad that she became a Setari. She loves being in Fourth Squad, which is a very tight team, and really enjoys the exploration role, of being the first squad to go into a space. She's excited by everything they've done on Muina, and is looking forward to getting into Kalasa. She fell asleep trying to explain how she felt.

It took me a while longer, carefully doing my visualisations – sheep again, because I find that safest. I don't think I dreamed of sheep at all, dreamed instead of sleeping on the couch, comfortably aware of Mori curled up across from me. Right up until Mori suddenly leapt to her feet and sent a small bolt of lightning arcing across the room. She's only a minor electricity talent, and while the thing she hit squealed and jerked, it didn't go down. Lacking her nanosuit, she hoisted up my coffee table, swung it like an abortive hammer-toss, and threw it at the thing as it came at us.

Struggling out of my couch, I saw movement, started to yell a warning, but too late. A cat-sized purple-black bug hit her in the chest and she staggered backward as it hooked spindly legs around her arms and shoulders and stung her over and over. The first one hadn't been stopped by the table and came toward us as Mori went down. I fixated on another bug climbing over the back of the couch I'd been sleeping on, but I knew that I was sleeping, that I'd made it happen, and reached frantically for the bit of my head I'd felt in the wind chime room.

And woke up, Mori standing over me, a hand on my shoulder. "I'm not sure I want to know what you were dreaming," she said.

There were fading red welts on her chin and throat. I stared at them, feeling sick, then said: "Let's go to medical."

Mori was willing to go along with that, waiting for me to dress, then taking me with her up to her rooms so she could put on something over her bed-clothes. I could barely speak I was so upset, wanting to scream at her to hurry. When we finally got to medical and I insisted that she get scanned, telling the greysuits to look for a parasite in her chest, she was watching me with open concern, but told the greysuits to do as I said. And there was nothing, and I fainted.

I woke up in a scan-chair with three of the greysuits fussing over me trying to figure out why I'd passed out, and deciding eventually that it really was just relief. I'd only been unconscious a few minutes, but that had been enough time for one of the Setari to duck out into near-space to download the data recorded by my drone. After making certain I was no more than embarrassed, Mori brought me into a channel with Maze, Ruuel and Isten Notra.

"I'll share the visual on this if you don't mind, Caszandra," Isten Notra said, and linked the images recorded by the drone. I didn't say anything, just watched it, flinching inside and feeling incredibly sick. "These creatures exist on your world?"

"Only in story I was reading before went to Muina. They lay eggs in people. Is it possible to remove a talent from someone? Do brain surgery?"

"It's been done," Isten Notra said. "When the risk is judged great enough. Since your talent is unique, we would be extremely reluctant to go so far, especially when as yet you have not come anywhere close to the kind of power level you would need to produce Ionoth that endure."

"What you're creating in real-space seems closer to a tangible illusion than actual substance," Maze added. "There's no trace of it once you've stopped projecting."

"I don't want to wait until I kill someone to find out whether it's possible," I said, struggling not to sound as upset as I was. But my voice had gone high, and I had to swallow to make myself not shout.

"You're overlooking the important point," Ruuel said, interface 'voice' clipped and sure. "Unlike the dream of the Array massive, you were able to break out of this one. That after only a few days of training. You're now aware when your dreams have taken on a tangible aspect?"

"...yes."

"Then your current exercise, whenever you find yourself dreaming in this way, is to break out of it, no matter if the dream is threatening or not. And in future remember that Eyse is a considerably better fighter than you give her credit for."

He dropped out of channel, leaving me feeling I'd been overreacting, which in retrospect was no doubt exactly what he'd intended. Maze and Isten Notra spoke to me a little longer, just a few questions about the training of the last few days, then told Mori to take me back to my room.

Mori was trying unsuccessfully not to look hugely gratified – outright compliments from Ruuel are rare and preciously hoarded by his squad. "Combat Sight would have told me if I'd had a thing like that in my chest," she told me as we rode the elevator. "Do you think you'll be able to get back to sleep?"

"Maybe. I'll have a shower and read for a while. Fourth is on rotation tomorrow, yes?"

"Yes – but broken nights are half the reason rotations aren't scheduled for first thing."

Mori's a lot better at getting to sleep than me, out of it by the time I was finished in the shower. Instead of reading, I reviewed various bits of my log, mainly time I'd spent alone at Pandora and Arenrhon. Scenery. I fell asleep and didn't dream, and woke mid-morning to find my shooting practice cancelled and one of the 'extra-long and thorough' medical checks put in its place. I sensibly took my diary down. I've arranged lunch with Zan, since I saw she was free, and then it's training when Ruuel's back from rotation.

Eggshells

After my meltdown yesterday, I wasn't surprised when Maze came along for my test session, even though it finished around midnight in his 'day'. I can just picture all the discussions they're having on how to stop me going off the deep end.

Ruuel told me that today I had to try to use my talents separately – to see things without making them happen, to make things happen in the Ena and not in real-space, to make things happen in real-space but not in the Ena. He also said I should expect to fail. What I needed to focus on was becoming aware of the mechanism, concentrating on what I did.

He started out just describing an object, one which was found in many places, to see if I could consciously conjure something a little less over-the-top than an entire place. That worked. It took a lot longer to get an image of what he was describing, but wasn't as exhausting, so this session lasted a lot longer than previous ones. I also ended up with less of a headache, which was nice, but the cumulative effect of several projections in a row left me semi-conscious.

"I'm pleased you haven't given in to the temptation to try to create visions of your own world," Maze said on the trip back.

"Too tired of headaches to give myself more," I said, struggling to stay awake. "Besides, I think Tsur Selkie meant it about assigning a squad to me full-time. Think he'd put interesting far-sight experiments in the same category as chatting with – as not using my alert."

I managed not to look across at Ista Chemie, sitting opposite with Ruuel. It's very difficult to be all secretive about Nurans when you're sleepy.

"Range is part of the test outline," Ruuel said. "Scheduled for when we're on Muina."

For some reason I'd assumed my training would be on hold while chasing Kalasa. I wondered if I'd be sleeping two pods away from Ruuel again – and whether there'd be a drone recording my dreams. And promptly fell asleep. I think I slept on Maze, or dreamed I was sleeping on Maze, but it didn't feel the way it does when I'm projecting. I didn't try and force myself awake, anyway, and was back in my window seat when I did wake up.

Not long now until we head to Kalasa. I'd probably be worked up about that if the prospect of making monsters in my sleep wasn't sucking up all my Emo tendencies.

Monday, June 9

Moving Target

I dreamed of sheep last night, and managed to make myself wake up almost straight away. Which gave me a headache, but was also immensely reassuring. I don't know if I'll always be able to break out of them – or am always sufficiently aware of the dreams which I'm making 'real' as opposed to dreams which just seem real – but it did give me a faint sense that I might gain enough control to not be doing things accidentally all the time.

This morning brought a nice bunch of packages from a spending spree I'd indulged in when they scheduled my return to Muina. Another diary, since I'm past two-thirds on this one, and a little cold environment gear because Pandora is hitting Winter now. It took me forever to find a non-hideous beanie. People on Tare don't have a lot of call for hats, particularly not for the purpose of keeping warm. Most of what I could find was rainproof, heavy-duty, tied-down headgear for the poor bastards who have to venture outside for maintenance in all kinds of weather. Chapstick was a little easier to find, and I managed to put together a couple of tolerable Winter outfits and something which could pass as daywear or nightwear to sleep in. I was thoroughly sick of wearing my uniform all the time when we were at Nurioth and Arenrhon.

Lots of shooting practice. Drake had me in a different training room, with a maze where half a dozen greensuits stalked me. I had fake weapons which registered hits instead of actually working, and had to try and find my way through the maze without dying (having one of the greensuits grab me). As a game it could have been kind of fun, but they were all super-serious, which made me feel stressed out and stupid. I died a lot.

After that Mara had me for some time in the gym. She soon had me talking about how hopeless I felt about ever coming close to being able to do something like get through that maze without dying.

"No-one expects you to," she said. "A couple of weeks of training isn't going to make you capable of picking off Cruzatch with a simple hand weapon. The force vest is what we're counting on to give you a chance, should you be transported alone." She made a face. "The arguments all this is causing are overwhelming, especially since most of those pushing to return you to Muina are unaware of the latest developments in your talent set. The Array massive has only exacerbated the debate, demonstrating to any who weren't already certain just how valuable your enhancement can be. But there's a sense that matters are becoming urgent, that we don't have the luxury to explore Muina at our leisure, and need to access Kalasa as soon as possible. Do you still feel that you'd rather get it over with?"

I shrugged. "Been more worried about killing everyone with nightmares. Do you – do you ever think you can't deal with being a Setari any more?"

Mara straightened on the knee-lift machine she'd been using, then unhooked her feet. "In the early days, when everything was new, we thought we were invincible. When Jorly – the first Setari to die on duty was Jorly Kennez, and if there had been some fault, some error of judgment which we could blame her death on, then perhaps it wouldn't have been so hard. But it was a rotation we had cleared a dozen times, we were all performing well, and still she died. A single lucky blow was all it took. It was only then that I really understood that we were fighting a war of attrition. And their numbers would never decrease. 'Lese – Helese Surion – helped me immensely with that, just by pointing out a few statistics on the number of lives *not* lost to Ionoth since we began."

"And then she died," I said, in a small voice. I hadn't expected Mara to really answer my question.

"Yes. Of the original First Squad, only Alay and I were left. Second, Third, Fourth and Seventh – as they were numbered then – had all lost someone. Lohn was injured, but not badly, and he gave me...more than I'd ever thought to have from him, an anchor that I needed. If I'd been in Maze or Alay's situation, losing the one who mattered most, I doubt I could have continued in the Setari. As it is, they're neither of them the people they once were. Though–" She paused, and made a wry face. "Maze was convinced, immediately convinced, that the Cruzatch were involved, were more than just escort Ionoth in that massive's wake. I thought his focus on them, his determination to prove that they had a level of agency above other Ionoth, was simply something he clung to after losing 'Lese. A way of dealing with his grief. Even after the Pillar – it wasn't until seeing them in Kalasa that I could let myself believe that we really have an enemy to blame. The impact of that is something I can't describe. And, of course, you had already given us the shift of air when you opened Muina."

She said then that I should go eat before my Sights training, but I stopped and hugged her and whispered, "Thanks," before I went, because she'd told me things that were personal to her, despite my second level monitoring, and that meant a lot to me. I had to look up what "shift of air" meant – it's a phrase a bit like "the light at the end of the tunnel", except it grew out of a past living deep underground and was all about being trapped in the crushing dark, suffocating, and then feeling a breeze, a hint of fresh air which told you there was a way out. And that's how Mara felt about being a Setari.

I liked the idea of an anchor. And I'd like to think First Squad is mine: the people I can turn to for comfort and support, who can help me keep it together. But I know it's Ruuel. Even the comfort, when I'm seriously on the edge. Well, sort of. Hand clutching counts.

Sight Sight talents apparently have an overwhelming need to understand. The Sight is always trying to puzzle out the world, and they see a lot of people's secrets, and I guess that's part of why Ruuel works for me – I always feel he sees me very clearly, that I haven't succeeded in hiding anything from him, and so he knows just what to do or say when I need it most. Of course, he's also doing his level best to keep me at a distance, but I'm okay with that at the moment. Right now I'm more interested in not Killing People With My Mind.

Tuesday, June 10

So over testing

Today I spent my Sights training session wondering if Ruuel was having nightmares too, since he looks like he's hardly been sleeping. He'd probably be amused if he knew I was worried about him. The session went well, though, and I'm feeling more confident that I'm not on the verge of self-destructing.

Tomorrow we go to Muina and now that I've stopped having dramatic daily nightmares, I'm having to work at not thinking about standing back on that platform.

Wednesday, June 11

Heading Out

Excellent surprise when I arrived with Lohn and Mara at the hanger to board the *Litara*. Isten Notra is coming with us. She told me that she'd been longing to go since Pandora was established. Shon is coming along to be her minion – nepotism at its finest, she said – and one of her bossy secretaries as well. She'll be living at Pandora for a while.

I worried about her, though I tried not to be all obvious about it. Isten Notra is what Tarens consider past retirement age and though she's incredibly sharp and not as wrinkled as your average ninety year-old from Earth, there's a fine fragility about her which I don't think really needs to be introduced to her first Winter.

I had fun exposing Shon to Eeli while the *Litara* hauled itself through a full-on storm to the rift. The atmosphere on this trip is difficult to define. The four most senior squads, all of them tight and professional, and 'friends' between the respective age groups, and I'm pretty sure they're all absolutely keen to see inside Kalasa. But Maze is tight-lipped and unusually terse, and I've caught people from every squad looking at me strangely. After having a primary assignment of keeping me alive, I think they're all trying to think up some last-minute way to avoid me standing on any platforms. I guess I am too, but I've been preparing myself for weeks because it always seemed inevitable, and the more they watch me for signs of imminent breakdown, the calmer I get. I just want to get it done, and then I can relax.

Nearly through the rift now. Today we're going to try me giving people security clearance. If that doesn't work, tomorrow I try to take Maze to Kalasa.

Big Boxes

The information being shown on the public channels on Tare is well behind the reality of Muina's settlement. They started building Pandora just three months ago and already it's become a living town, with external lighting and sidewalks and bits which will be gardens when it's not Winter. Of course, having buildings which just grow themselves in a few days, so long as they have enough raw material available, really makes it a lot easier, but they still would have had to do a huge amount of designing and planning and working out power and water and connecting up the toilet recycling system and air-conditioning and outfitting the interiors.

Over fifteen hundred people are living and working here.

There's only one or two 'small' individual buildings. The rest are 'blocks' three stories high and something like six suburban houses square. Quite huge, in other words. It reminds me a bit of the university campuses I toured (via website) halfway through last year, when trying to decide where to apply. Each of the blocks is devoted to a particular area of exploration and science – so far they've built blocks for animals, plants, geography, geology, weather, archaeology, devices and Ena research – along with a bigger central command thing, which combines coordination with greensuit barracks and supplies. There's a combination of both dorms and permanent accommodation in the science blocks, along with a few outer blocks which are primarily residential and something called 'services' which appears to be where everyone's food is cooked and laundry is done and stuff like that (though I don't think they have one centralised mess hall any more). And attached to that is the 'greenhouse' – just as much a big white block as all the rest, but devoted to ensuring that the settlement can survive even if the *Litara* stops showing up. I'm told they're already busily producing crops of Muinan plants identified as edible. And a lot of Taren algae which is processed into food.

To my surprise, although there's some similarities to the severely plain central command block, someone has actually put some thought into appearance when designing the rest of them. There's all kinds of etched patterns and designs breaking up the severity of the whitestone, and lots of windows (almost all opaquely shuttered to keep out the cold or the view). And sloping roofs! Just a mild tilt – you could probably walk around on them quite safely, but definitely sloping, with some gorgeous patterns cut into them which also serve to direct drainage. Even the central block had been retrofitted so that its roof slopes.

"I'm impressed," I told Isten Notra, peering out the window of the ten-person shuttle taking us from the *Litara* directly to the central amphitheatre of the old town. "Tarens remembered that buildings have outsides."

"The cities we will one day build on this world..." Isten Notra began, then stopped and hugged me. "We will make it our home again. Thank you for that, Caszandra."

This embarrassed me incredibly, of course, though I am getting more used to people thanking me emotionally for something I did by accident. I distracted myself by digging into my backpack and pulling out the two beanies I'd bought. I gave Isten Notra the blue and purple one and talked about things I'd learned on my two whole trips skiing at Thredbo, particularly that you lose a surprising amount of heat through the top of your head. Isten Notra was very sensibly dressed, but like everyone else who'd been travelling on the *Litara*, had nothing resembling headgear. She thanked me and plonked it on right away, making her secretary act like he'd just eaten a lemon. I think beanies might count as 'little kid hats' on Tare or something. Lohn certainly looked like he was trying not to laugh.

I didn't particularly care, though. My beanie was two shades of green and when they opened the shuttle door I was damn glad I'd brought it. It was cold enough to make my nose hurt, and everyone's breath steamed out in clouds. It hasn't snowed at Pandora yet, but they think it will very soon, and you can see a dusting of white on the higher hills in the distance.

New arrivals to Muina are always taken first thing to a platform to be cleared, and whenever possible are all done at once to avoid making the Ddura anxious. There were about twenty newcomers on this trip, easily handled. I stayed on one side of the arena with First Squad as Shon and Isten Notra became official Muinans. The Ddura showed up midway through the process, and made happy noises, but was far less wildly exuberant than those first days. The question of whether I could give people access to Kalasa was settled as soon as the shuttle took the new arrivals off to the warmth of the buildings. No.

I tried thinking all sorts of commands at the platform, but it didn't react at all as it does when it gets told people are Muinans. And no-one was teleported anywhere standing on it. Maze didn't push against the inevitable once we'd run through the test options, having Mara take me off to the medical section in the main block for the headache the Ddura had given me. It's not as excited as it was, and shuts up more on command, but it does still hang about letting off occasional moans if people play with the platform. He's scheduled the mission for quite early the next day since by then it was evening for me and very late in First Squad's 'day', though only just sunset at Pandora.

After my headache had lifted, Maze sat with me to explain exactly what we'll be trying tomorrow, and was being very calm and reassuring, but with his eyes so unhappy. I wish I could make him feel better about this. They want me bunk down here in medical tonight, thoroughly monitored. I can see they're worried I'll have nightmares about Kalasa, and I can't tell them what's distracted me from tomorrow. You see, it's occurred to me that there's a faint possibility that Ruuel was at least partially aware of the 'good dreams'. If I could make Mori feel she was being stung by giant insects, could Ruuel have spent night after night on the *Diodel* wondering why it felt like there was a girl snuggling up against him?

It's an awful thought. I'm hoping it's just me being paranoid, since I suspect that if he'd been aware of the strangeness of my dreams at Arenrhon he'd have sent me straight for testing. But now that he does know, and now that I definitely am strong enough to make people feel things, I get to be all worried about having a good dream, instead of looking forward to it.

Ruuel has been tied up with something. I glimpsed him once on the *Litara*, but it was only during the platform experiments that I was close enough to see he still looks tired, and I haven't seen him since then. I don't know if the Setari are even in the same building – except for Jeh from Second, who seems to have drawn first babysitting shift, and is in the next room. It's probably best if Ruuel's far away, preferably somewhere shielded.

Unfair. Good dreams about Ruuel had almost made me look forward to this mission. But while I have no problems with me privately having all sorts of fantasies about him, it's totally another ball game making him have dreams about me.

I'll try for otters.

Thursday, June 12

Into Kalasa

I dreamed I was sitting on the side of Ruuel's bed, watching him sleep. My subconscious making a compromise, I guess. It was a little cell of a room, just a single bed and a rack for luggage and a door. There wasn't any light, so I'm not altogether sure how I could see, but it was all very clear.

He wasn't wearing his uniform: the first time I've seen him in anything else. A dark boxer-brief and singlet arrangement. And he was having a nightmare, was shifting fretfully under a half kicked-off blanket. Fully living up to the Place Sight reputation for being 'haunted'. He looked like he was in pain, and I longed to touch him, but instead I made myself wake up. I knew it wasn't fair of me to watch. I don't think I was projecting, just looking, which is a big leap forward in control. Not that I'll mention it to anyone.

Taarel wasn't with him. Stupid thing to be happy about, and I suppose it's terribly unlikely they'd be together during a mission anyway. I didn't dream again after that, and was woken up by Maze, who took me off to an early breakfast with a bunch of greysuit section heads who wanted to ask me about Winter. Being a Sydney girl, I thought this was tremendously funny, but neither Tare nor Kolar have much experience with snow. Tare has a semi-frozen polar region with scarcely any solid ground, while the Kolarens actually live at their poles because the equator area is too hot. So even Australians know things they don't about seasons, and I yabbered on about hibernation and igloos and tree branches breaking off from the weight of snow, and seasonal migration of animals, and then wandered into a tangent about Ice Ages and dinosaurs. I now have an assignment to review all the information being collated about Muina's plants and animals, mark any that seem familiar, like the hairy sheep, and write little essays on everything I know about the Earth equivalent.

After that, Maze took me to be outfitted in my chest armour of ultimate doom, and all the gear I'm expected to carry. A breather, of course, and a good wad of rations and thin water bottles and a firelighter because I'd specifically requested one (I'm so over making fires by rubbing two sticks together). The gun, and a spare charge pack for it. A small *and* a large relay beacon – one I can wear and one I'll be holding which is very powerful but they were worried it wouldn't come through with me. Maze carted that about for me – it must have weighed twenty kilos.

He was very much in control of himself, calm and relaxed on the surface at least, even when he was telling me what he wanted me to do if he didn't come through with me. Basically get off the platform and get back on, since that might be all that was required. If not, head for the next platform. He'd made me read through all the information about Cruzatch before we came to Muina, which hadn't really made me more comfortable about being anywhere near them.

"You're facing up to this very well," he said, finally. "But I know that you must be nervous."

I shrugged. "Would be stupid not to be. But it's got to be easier than last time, after all, even if I get stuck there by myself."

He sighed, and gave me a quick hug (which made me feel hot all over – it's very different when Maze does that to when Lohn does).

"The first few moments after arrival will be critical," he said. "You will have the advantage of surprise – don't waste it."

We met up with the rest of First Squad and levitated over to the amphitheatre, where the other squads were waiting with a mix of greensuits and greysuits. I was totally distracted by tiny flakes of white swirling and drifting around us as we flew. Two trips to Thredbo hasn't made snow any less of a novelty to me and I said as we dropped down to the amphitheatre: "We have to have an epic snowball fight if it gets deep enough."

"The frozen rain?" Lohn asked. Tare doesn't have a word for snow, though I guess old Muinan must. I'd taught them the Earth word for snow instead. "How do you fight with it?"

"You scrunch it into balls and throw it at each other. And you can make forts to hide behind. But for fun," I emphasised, smiling hello to everyone waiting about in the cold. "Not to figure out the most efficient way to kill things in snowy places or anything."

Maze shook his head slightly – I think he thought I was putting on a brave face or something – but said: "All right – if there's enough snow we'll have an epic ball of snow fight. Ready now?"

I nodded, and he brought me into mission channel, adding over it: "We've all been fully briefed. Let's do this."

Four squads are a lot of people, and the amount of machinery which has been installed in the platform room, along with various technicians, made it feel quite close and cramped. But warmer than up top, at least.

"Verifying equipment function," said the one technician who was in the main mission channel.

Maze handed me back the heavier relay, and then had me take the 'carting Cass about' position, and bound our suits together as best he could with my chest armour interfering. Zee got up on the platform with an even more powerful drone, since they were hoping I might bring everything through which was on the platform, whether or not I was touching it.

"Clear to begin," said one of the bluesuits over the mission channel, and Maze lifted us both up and dropped down on the platform.

It worked. Even to the point of bringing Zee and the drone through with us. Maze let his breath out, and he and Zee shared a look of total relief, even as they both reacted to this weird, crystalline web filling the room. It made a little dome over the top of the platform, and was particularly thick on the side which was broken, hiding the cisterns below.

There were two Cruzatch, over by the room's entrance, but before they could do anything they had to hastily dodge the pieces of rubble and shattered wall Maze threw at them. The crystalline stuff snapped and broke apart.

"Blocking the entrance till we know more about what this is," Maze said, already busily doing so. He just shoved the Cruzatch out with the slabs of fallen wall and then piled the stone up.

While he was busy fishing up bits of fallen stone and preventing the Cruzatch from getting back into the room, Zee extruded a bit of her uniform into a thin cloth and wrapped it around one end of a stick of broken crystal, setting it there like a handgrip.

"Three or four dozen in the immediate area," Zee said, taking the heavy relay from me and handing me the stick of crystal. "We'll hold them out of the room. Bring back the rest of the squad, and get some kind of initial impression on this."

Maze swept a corner of the room clear and shifted us and the big drone off the platform. "Satellite signal not reaching," Zee told him, and he nodded and then picked me up physically and dropped me back on the platform.

I shifted back to Pandora immediately, the suddenness of it a bit disorienting since I'd expected a delay. Blinking, I looked around at the circle of waiting Setari, then slid back off the platform, saying rapidly: "Forty Cruzatch, and the room is full of crystal – some kind of trap. Maze wants to know what it is. He's barricaded the entrance."

Ruuel was conveniently nearby, so I handed the stick to him as a greysuit materialised at my elbow and insisted on shining a light in my eyes and making me follow it. The rest of First Squad climbed on the platform and – when the greysuit said they couldn't see any immediate impact on me – Second Squad joined them.

The faintest brush of fingers on my arm brought my attention back to Ruuel, who had enhanced and now touched one bare finger very lightly to the crystal stick. He was still looking tired, but calmly analytical as he gazed down at the crystal.

"Good instinct," he said, at last. "The elementals – fire, light, electricity particularly – will cause it to become a gas. Not poisonous. The intention of this is to capture."

"Understood," Grif Regan from Second Squad said, and I found myself lifted back on the platform, Ketzaren and Alay flanking me even before my feet touched the stone.

The next couple of minutes were pretty frantic. Cruzatch are dangerous close-combat fighters, and their claws can cut through things: not quite as easily as a light-sabre, but enough to mean that Maze's barricade wasn't holding. And there were dozens of the things. The telekinetics took point, using the splintering rock to force them backward, out of the trapped room. I was sent straight back to Pandora, to bring Third and Fourth Squad, and the Setari went full-out once they were out of the range of the crystal.

Ketzaren and Alay kept me close, but moved me out of the platform room, even though Maze had broken up most of the crystal and shoved the pieces off to one side. By the time I got outside the battle was aerial, and the Cruzatch were retreating.

"Don't pursue individually," Maze said, and the Setari dropped down to gather in the very centre of Kalasa, then broke into two – Second and Third staying at the central point with me, while First and Fourth vanished into a big building about four levels up.

I didn't like that: listening to Maze's occasional terse instructions but not able to see what was happening. The Cruzatch tried to ambush them, and it sounded like it got pretty hairy for a couple of moments. I guess my expression mustn't have been particularly guarded – First and Fourth Squad are most of the people I care about on this world – because Taarel put her hand on my shoulder for a moment and smiled at me, eyes full of confidence and reassurance. She really is so very kingly.

It was over relatively quickly, though, and we listened to them discussing what sounded like another malachite marble. The Cruzatch had apparently vanished through it much like I can use the platforms. For the short term the two squads used fallen rubble to block the entrance, then came back down to stand in the central circle.

"We'll report in and move on to phase two," Maze said, but then paused, looking up, and they all gazed up with him – not at any threat, but at Kalasa. Damaged, but still the city of the Lantarens. No-one said a word, they all just took a moment and looked.

I then spent the rest of the day playing taxi. Maze reported in, and I brought through a mixed bag of greensuits and greysuits. The Setari took the drone up to the highest point of the city, while the greysuits tried to decide where to start, and just before we called it a day a satellite finally succeeded in detecting it – it's on the other side of the world from Pandora and slightly south, on an island in one of the biggest lakes. The *Diodel* is on its way there now, stuffed with technicians, and Second Squad along for safety. They're going to start a settlement and try to work out how to get through the city's shield from the outside while another bunch chip away at it from within. The malachite marble/power stone doesn't seem to turn it off like at the Arenrhon installation.

No-one's allowed to stay inside Kalasa overnight ('night' in this case being when I'm off-duty), although there's half a dozen drones there, particularly around the re-sealed Cruzatch escape hatch. It was a long day of tentative exploration, though we did get a break for lunch – whereupon I was hugged by an awful lot of people (Nils blew in my ear for good measure, and laughed very wickedly at my reaction). I gather from something Eeli let slip that the Setari had been under strict orders to not worry me with discussions of how little they wanted me to get on any platforms. I'm back in medical again, but this time because they want to monitor me for aftereffects of being of taxi. I don't much like sleeping in medical because the greysuits insist on popping in and out of the room. I can track their movements, though they're still not as clear to me as the Setari.

There were crystal web traps on every single platform. I don't think standing on the platform would have been easier than last time, if I'd come through alone.

Friday, June 13

Wake up

I outdid myself last night.

It started out unremarkable. I focused on sheep going to sleep, dreamed predictably of sheep and woke myself up almost immediately. Zee was designated babysitter, sitting in the waiting room next door, but later she left and Ruuel came and sat next to me. And then two Cruzatch rose up at the end of the bed, grabbed an ankle each, and hauled.

There's no way to know where I would have ended up if Ruuel hadn't been there. The room's scanner shows him sitting in the half-lit room, relaxed in his chair, then straightening and looking intently at me, and then hurling himself forward and grabbing me as I abruptly upended. He only just managed a hold under my arms, and was almost pulled off his feet. The Cruzatch I was dreaming were very strong.

In my dream I screamed, but I make no sound on the log as blood spatters down over both of us and the sheet tangled with my legs catches alight. A panicking greysuit runs in as Ruuel uses telekinesis to pull the sheet away. Fortunately the second greysuit was less panicky and dropped a silver tinfoil sheet over it. But that was later. First Ruuel said, very clear and urgent into my ear: "It's a dream, Cassandra. Wake up."

I hadn't known. Or, on some level I had, but all this happened in the first few moments of my dream, so I'd barely had time to do more than process shock and pain. And then I made myself wake up and if Ruuel hadn't had incredible reflexes I probably would have face-planted into the floor.

Although I won't have the blood poisoning and chill and exhaustion this time around, I managed to injure myself worse than the real Cruzatch had. I've moved well beyond temporary marks that fade away, anyway, and now have a fine collection of inch-deep gouges, burns and bruises and a dislocated ankle along with hairline fractures. I remember very distinctly one of the greysuits saying in complete disbelief: "She dislocated her own ankle?" and suspect from the indrawn breath which followed that Ruuel must have said something particularly curt over the interface. That's the only thing I have any real recollection of for the first few minutes after breaking out of the dream, beyond feeling rigidly frozen, and absolutely determined not to let go of Ruuel. He just said: "Deep breaths," to me whenever I started to shake, and shifted me about as necessary so the medics could stop me from bleeding everywhere.

By the time they'd pumped me full of painkillers and put my ankle back the way it's supposed to be, both Maze and Mara had arrived. Mara took over the clutchee role for a change of clothes and room: necessary given the blood-spattered and charred state of both. All that and a really horrible drink made me calm down enough for my brain to start working.

Maze and Ruuel came to my new room after the greysuit had finished telling me exactly what I'd done to myself and how long it would take to fix. She was still wide-eyed about it all, and looked a bit regretful when Maze dismissed her with a word of thanks. Mara stayed helping me sit up at the top of the bed, resting me against her shoulder with an arm around my waist. I think I'd quite happily sleep that way if I didn't think it would drive her mad having to stay still half the night.

"Did you know that I was going to dream badly tonight?" I asked Ruuel. My voice gets so little-girl and small when I'm upset. I hate it. At least me speaking made Maze look slightly less concerned – I hadn't managed to do more than nod and shake my head before that.

"I considered it likely," Ruuel said, sounding as correct as usual, but I think he was relieved too. "You dealt with the need to return to Kalasa by facing it, by attempting to take a level of control preparing for it. Because it was necessary for you to not be afraid, you weren't. There was always a high chance that after the hurdle was past, and you were no longer steeled against it, the nightmare of your first visit would recur. Add to that cages, around every platform at Kalasa. After a day thinking through the implications, a nightmare about being kidnapped by Cruzatch."

That little speech put paid to any doubts I had left about Ruuel knowing I'm obsessed with him. He can see right through me. But I wasn't feeling very focused on romance at that moment.

"Cruzatch ever tried to capture Setari?"

"No. Their interest is almost certainly you."

Mara rubbed my arm, but Ruuel was right about me having thought most of this through yesterday. "If Cruzatch show up and offer to rescue me from evil and misguided Tarens, absolutely will set off alert straight away." I allowed myself to enjoy Maze's expression, then sighed. "Not so sure won't accidentally kidnap myself. Thought I was getting better at this."

"You were able to break out of this dream, though," Maze pointed out. "You've consistently broken out of every dream since your dream of the insect creatures in your room, yes?"

I glanced down at my legs, which are very decoratively encased in varying thicknesses of blueish nanocloth.

"There's no way to guarantee you won't do more damage," Ruuel said straightforwardly. "The daily exercises have obviously helped, but now that you've reached the point of being capable of killing yourself or another, the next week will be critical. You're unlikely to have another occurrence tonight. Tomorrow we'll arrange for quarters which put you at a safer distance from other personnel. It's also unlikely we'll go ahead with the planned entry of Kalasa, but expect training if your condition allows. Ista Kyle will sedate you tonight."

He glanced at Maze, nodded at me (or Mara) and left. Though he only went as far as the next room, which is something I wouldn't have known a couple of months ago. Maze looked at me through narrowed eyes, told me Mara would stay with me for the rest of the night, and then went and lurked about the next room as well.

"Ruuel take courses in psychology?" I asked Mara.

"All captain candidates study psychology," Mara said. "I take it he's right in telling us you find it easier to handle issues if we don't downplay them?"

"If I think you're holding back, have to try and guess what you're not telling me," I said. "Got a good imagination."

One of the greysuits came in, asked me a couple of questions about my pain level and shot me full of sedative, which hit me like a cotton-wool tank, but Mara obligingly continued to let me use her as a pillow, at least until I passed out. After that she shifted to the chair by the bed but kept hold of my hand.

I slept most of the day. Ruuel must have decided I wasn't up to training, since I haven't seen him so far. Lots of visitors from the squads, though, and Isten Notra came to see me and left Shon to fill my ears with his thoughts about animals and snow and Kalasa. He's loving it here. I don't think he knows precisely how I was injured – he didn't ask, anyway. I feel vaguely guilty about all those very eager greysuits desperate to get back into Kalasa today and not able to.

Whenever the pain meds wear off my legs tell me that I did a lot of damage. I can walk to the ensuite, but Maze came in while I was creeping back to my bed and gave me a lecture about not asking for help. Then he took me to my new room, in a small building near the lake which either I didn't spot before or they created and outfitted specifically for me overnight. It's crammed full of scanners, and will be a combination of living quarters and test area for me.

Saturday, June 14

Don't shoot the messenger

Back to Kalasa today. Instead of working the entire day as a taxi, they had me bring through everyone in the morning, then took me back to my room to rest. Since the platform won't work if I'm just levitating above it, Par carried me the entire time, very romantically in his arms and rather pink around the ears. Even with that my legs started throbbing, and I was glad to lie down again and get another dose of painkiller. I swear Mum wouldn't be impressed with the amount of drugs I get through. I'm more injured than I properly understood at first – the wounds were deep, and the burns I think would be classed as second-degree. The painkillers they give me are really effective at blocking out what it feels like, but they're deliberately short-term doses so that the greysuits can assess my condition, and when I'm not quite fully medicated I feel awful. Plus they keep giving me restoratives and fortifiers: horrible drinks and injections which really do help with healing, but also leave me absolutely exhausted. It's annoying because I go through good patches and want to move about and feel almost normal, and then I completely run out of steam. Maze made me promise to not try and walk any more, and I've learned my lesson from that already, since that one stumbling trip to the bathroom made the medics re-do all my weird nanotech bandaging and *lower* my pain medication so that I can feel that I'm hurting myself when I walk. I hate having to be carried to the bathroom. Hate catheters more, though.

After playing taxi, I slept the rest of the morning. 'Normal' dreams, fragmentary and not quite logical, and I felt really quite good when I woke up just before lunch. The temperature had risen, and I talked Ista Temen – the greysuit on shift – into letting Par set up a chair and footrest outside so I could look at the view. It was a beautiful day – extremely blue sky, no wind, and the chill gone out of the air. The thin patches of snow which had formed all melted, and the lake looked amazing.

Since Par's slightly more inclined to talk if you get him alone, I asked him about his impressions of Kalasa and wasn't surprised to find that his feelings were mixed. "I'm glad to have seen it," he said. "But it makes me angry. And proud. And ashamed."

"Do you think the solution will be there?"

He shook his head, then added reluctantly: "If they had known the spaces would be shattered, they wouldn't have done it." And didn't add the 'would they?' he was obviously thinking. I wish I could talk to people about what was in the Nuran's book, but it's still being kept very quiet. I also wish I knew if Inisar had followed me to Muina. He's obviously capable of it, but avoiding the Ddura might pose him some difficulties.

The *Litara* arrived then, giving me the usual huge kick out of watching it settle on the lake. I always imagine Jules' reaction, and wish I could at least send postcards. Send Mum a happy snap or two of me relaxing on the shore of a lake on an alien world, watching a spaceship land and, as it turned out, a bunch of psychic space ninjas arriving. Squad One, who had returned briefly to Kolar while their Second Squad represented Kolar on Muina, but now were on Muina shift again. They flew directly from the *Litara* toward the command centre, and must have seen me wave to them since after they'd reported in or dropped off their luggage or whatever they were doing they all came back to say hello. When she found I couldn't stand up Katzyen, being the get-things-done person she is, relocated a bunch of rocks from the very edge of the lake to make a circle of stony seats so that they could stop looming over me. So now I have my own outdoor entertainment area.

"We heard you'd been injured again," Taranza said, eyeing my propped-up legs. I was wearing my uniform for warmth, and the bandaging makes me look like I have double-sized ankles.

"And couldn't find out how," Katzyen added, up-front as usual. "Most anyone would say is an accident in medical."

"I did to myself," I said. "Been developing talent which keep using accidentally when I'm sleeping. Set sheet alight. Really embarrassing."

That usefully kept to the truth and let them assume I was developing a fire talent instead of illusions-which-feel-real or whatever. Squad One asked me about the first time I'd ended up in Kalasa – they don't get access to the Taren Setari mission logs usually, but KOTIS had given them extracts – and they fetched down lunch and we had a bit of a picnic and talked about swimming, which is not a skill found on Kolar, and about Kalasa and Earth, and speculated on what it was that gave only me a security pass to Kalasa.

Katzyen challenged Par to a stone skipping competition, and the rest of Squad One except Shaf and Nalaz joined in. I was wondering if it would be possible to throw stones while Par levitated me when Shaf said: "I've been asked to speak to you on behalf of the government of Kolar."

I pretty much guessed what it would be, and didn't want to go there. But I couldn't think of anything to say to stop him, other than a wild temptation to make a crack about rescuing me from evil and misguided Tarens.

"The government of Kolar would like to extend to you an invitation to aid Kolar's Setari in the planet's defence," Shaf said, his voice quiet and even, his eyes meeting mine very directly. But his tanned cheeks were darker than normal and grew darker still as he went on to talk about what I'd get in return.

He stopped, and there was this awkward little silence where I was working not to gape at him. I could see Nalaz just past him, gazing fiercely out over the lake, rigidly upright. Then I felt incredibly sorry for them both, and said: "You look so mortified."

Shaf dropped his eyes, but Nalaz turned his head toward us and I think he was liking me for saying that.

"Wouldn't this mess up the alliance between Tare and Kolar?"

"Strain it," Shaf said. "But they can't dictate where you choose to live. Not without changing their own laws. And Kolar is suffering badly from attacks by larger Ionoth."

"Can you record an answer to give to the government of Kolar?" I asked, and Shaf nodded. I'm sure he was logging the conversation anyway.

"Okay." I sometimes forget and use English words – things like 'okay' and 'hi' – often enough that a lot of people here now know what I mean. "So, money first. There's nothing for me to spend it on. Everything I could be bribed with is on Earth, and it's not like I have to pay rent. Second, Taren Setari rescued me. If they hadn't, I'd be here alone figuring out how to survive Winter. I'm not going to forget that. Third, Kolar, while it's probably more like my own world than Tare is, has legal cloning. I know Tarens have lots of arguments about me being irreplaceable, but I think so far they're keeping to their laws about cloning. Tarens having enough trouble stopping me from falling apart mentally as it is, without risking me getting all worked up thinking they're cloning me. On Kolar...I wouldn't be as sure. Would probably enjoy visiting Kolar one day when whole problem with gates tearing everywhere is fixed, but fixing the gates is what I'm theoretically helping with now, and that will solve problem for both worlds. And I'm – I'm not for *sale*."

Something of my feelings came through in that, and I shook my head and added: "That's it."

Shaf gave me a strained smile. "Thank you."

"Pretend we didn't have this conversation," I said, and proceeded to do so. Which was easy enough since Ista Temen showed up and gave me another load of injections and I suddenly needed a nanna nap. Thankfully. That was without a doubt the most embarrassing conversation I've ever had.

But when I woke up – a little before I was due to go and play taxi again – I sent an email to Isten Notra attaching the log. I did think long and hard about not telling anyone at all, but it was within the bounds of possibility that the Kolaren government might not drop the subject. Besides, I'm convinced Ruuel would be able to *tell*.

Isten Notra opened a channel. "I needn't warn you that this is something you will not discuss."

"Is Kolar's situation really that bad?" I hadn't been paying a great deal of attention to the news just recently.

"They've been hard-pressed these last few weeks, taking significant losses. Kolar has not officially requested...borrowing you, but a great deal of interest was generated by the battle with the Array massive. I am going to order increased security for you, Caszandra."

"Figured. Can it be for only when I'm out of main KOTIS facility?"

She agreed to this readily enough, and asked me how I was feeling and said that we'd be heading back into Kalasa a little earlier than planned because she couldn't resist going to look and had finally bullied all the people telling her how unwise that would be into submission. They really aren't at all keen on Isten Notra risking herself, since her understanding of the Ena is one of the things they're counting on to find a solution to the fracturing spaces. I think Isten Notra and Inisar should sit down to chat.

The temperature had dropped by the time we headed for Kalasa, and I was pleased that Isten Notra was wearing her beanie. Shon and her secretary were along, of course, and she had arranged for Squad One to come as well, and peppered Shaf with questions, giving no hint that she knew the Kolarens had tried to buy me. I'm not sure if she's even going to tell the squad captains.

It was night all the way on the other side of the world, though soon to be dawn. Glade came down to join Par in walking about with me, and I could see he was brimming over with enthusiasm and excitement. I couldn't really blame him – Kalasa is a fairy castle of a city, cracked around the edges, but gloriously spectacular. On the far side of the shield it was snowing madly, giving a reverse snow dome atmosphere, and all the walls were glowing. A few more ordinary lights had been installed at points of particular activity, but in the context they looked as strange and unreal as all the rest of it. But the city feels more 'claimed' now and doesn't immediately conjure up nightmare memories. Or maybe it was that I was resting against Par's chest most of the time – he's a very comforting guy.

All three Taren Setari squads gathered together, greeting Squad One with nods, and Maze gave a concise report of progress so far. They've found what seems to be a library/training academy, which they're all very excited about, though they haven't done more than stare from the door since the contents seem inclined to fall apart at a glance. The shield has protected the contents of the city, but it hasn't magically preserved them.

The building with the malachite marble has been very rigorously sealed – and the drones stationed there indicate that the Cruzatch did make an attempt to return the previous day. The city is in part still functional, at least with whatever was making the water in my bathroom warm, and there's so much 'everyday' information about the Lantarens that the greysuits are in ecstasy. The Setari have been doing a preliminary evaluation and map of the site, which is taking a lot of time. Maze didn't actually call the place "freakin' huge" but Lohn's expression did. As I'd learned first time out, there's a lot of sub-surface structure.

The shielding makes the one around Arenrhon pale by comparison. It isn't controlled by the malachite marble, and is giving the greysuits something to argue about, since turning it off would leave the city exposed to the Winter storms. But they'd found a door. And wanted to poke me at it, of course. It was situated about halfway up the valley, at a point where two of the mountains came together, and was damn big, obviously designed to impress new arrivals, and gorgeously covered in carvings of leaves and vines and trees and water and animals peeping through, but no godlike people.

"The shielding runs through the walls, but the signature is very different through these doors," Islen Tezart said. "We've tried Ena manipulation with no response. We're hoping it will react to you."

Since everyone had been in the process of packing up and gathering ready to go back, I ended up with quite an audience and felt completely idiotic, especially when I put my hand on the door and nothing happened. "Feels warm," I said. Then added: "Open Sesame" hopefully and was really shocked when it worked.

Well, I don't think the words worked so much as me wanting it to open, giving it some sort of mental order. It opened outward, with a cracking noise I later realised was ice breaking, and I was hit by a full-on gale and everyone was pelted with snowflakes. Par hastily moved me a long way back out of the frigid wind and Second Squad, who had been sitting about in the *Diodel* hoping for a break in the weather, came inside for a brief reunion. Opening the door allowed the drones to communicate clearly with the satellite and they decided that it was better to just block it physically instead of closing it.

Pleased to no longer be the only way into Kalasa, I was a cheerful taxi back to Pandora for the night, and fell asleep in the middle of a big group dinner in the main building. I woke up back in my little building, with Lohn and Mara playing babysitter in the next room.

I didn't know I'd lost my beanie till Ruuel gave it back to me, just after I'd transported Fourth Squad. He told me there'd be training tomorrow, if the medics cleared me, and then walked off with Taarel, but I was in too good a mood to be conflicted and sad, and was distracted trying to remember enough of *Ali Baba and the Forty Thieves* to tell it properly to Isten Notra.

Sunday, June 15

Hot/Cold

After playing taxi this morning for a good half hour, with Glade carrying me, I spent some time in the main building having a very in-depth medicking session. My legs look amazingly horrible. The greysuits seem fairly confident that they'll be able to get me fixed up without significant scarring (after all, they can regrow skin, muscle, bone – probably everything except a missing head) but I'm not to try walking even short distances for a few more days. Part of the problem is I basically did 'everything' to my legs all at once – burns, deep tissue bruising, hairline fractures and massive gouges. All from the knee down, which makes managing it a little easier – though Ruuel did give me a few bruises stopping me from kidnapping myself.

The medics neutralised my pain meds completely during the first bit, which nicely demonstrated to me that my legs hurt an awful lot. It was Mori and Glade's turn to baby-sit me, and Mori did a lot of hand-squeezing and tried to distract me and I tried to pretend my eyes weren't full of tears. My new security arrangements seem to mean I have two Setari with me at all times, even when I'm just sleeping. Not suffocatingly so – they stay mostly in the next room while I sleep and will let me alone to read and things – but they don't allow anyone, even the greysuits, to be alone with me. Even Shon, who came to chat when I woke up for lunch. Fourth Squad is covering my days, and First and Third are rotating through covering the sleep shift. Eeli was part of my babysitting team during the dawn shift last night, and is a quite overwhelming person to have breakfast with.

It's hard to tell what Fourth Squad thinks about being taken off Kalasa-exploration to baby-sit me. Not visibly annoyed, at least, but I wouldn't expect that of them. Nor particularly wary of me, even though I'm probably as dangerous to them as I am to myself at the moment. Mori and Glade patently had no idea that they were guarding me from Kolarens.

After lunch, it was Ruuel and Sonn's turn, and time for some training. Ruuel was at his crispest and most efficient, levitating me into the second room and onto the scan chair after the scarcest of warnings. "Until you've recovered strength, these sessions will be confined to objects in the immediate area," he said. "And concentrate on the manifestations in this world. Keep your eyes open."

He had me try and make a copy of a mug which was sitting right in front of me. Keeping my eyes open was harder than it sounds, almost as bad as keeping your eyes open when sneezing. Every time I started to shut them, Ruuel would say "Eyes." He never sounded impatient, but I came dangerously close to trying to manifest a mug, preferably full of something hot, falling from the ceiling onto his head. Though he probably would have dodged.

But I did do it, eventually. The cup looked exactly the same, and not blurry either, so it probably wasn't floating around out in the Ena at the same time. I felt like I'd been trying to tie knots in cherry stalks with my tongue, but it was there.

And something else was too. I didn't notice it until Ista Temen took a deep breath. Sonn picked up the mug gingerly, and I could see the steam rising off it before I recognised the smell. Unfortunately, that surprised me enough that the mug vanished.

"What was it?" Ista Temen asked as I sat back in disappointment. "It smelled delicious."

"Hot chocolate," I said. "Earth drink. All these planets, and none of them have chocolate. Severe oversight in world creation."

"Was its inclusion deliberate?" Ruuel asked.

"No. Well, I was thinking about hot drinks." I gave him a bland look, but he was being all business as usual and didn't show any sign of knowing my thoughts.

"Repeat the exercise without letting your attention wander," he said, and kept me at it until I could produce the mug without taking ten minutes to manage it, and had the inevitable headache. But they're decreasing in severity.

"Is it warm again today?" I asked Ista Temen while she was giving me another dose of drugs. "Can I go outside?"

It was, fortunately – much warmer than when the morning shift went to Kalasa. Ruuel called the rest of his squad down and had them try and hit each other while he watched, offering the occasional critical comment. No approving nods this time, and I decided it was stupid to feel let down just because he hadn't given me any either. He's very strict with his squad.

I watched for a while, then searched for birds out on the lake, but I think they must have all migrated somewhere warmer. I was wondering how much trouble I'd get in if I tried to make a mug of hot chocolate without permission – and whether it would be possible to drink it – when Ruuel (standing just behind me and not at all where I'd thought he was) asked: "And would you have survived a Winter here alone?"

Barely managing not to jump out of my skin, I tilted my head back to look up at him, surprised he'd asked me a question not related to any assignment. That Isten Notra had obviously shown him the log of my conversation with the Kolarens wasn't unexpected, but I wanted to see if there was any hint of anger in his face. He was looking out, though, not down at me.

"Barring accidents, probably," I said. "The Ddura was keeping the Ionoth away, and the local predators had plenty of more familiar things to hunt. I would have had to stop being so squeamish and try to kill some of the sheep, though. Living on fruit and nuts wasn't doing me a great deal of good, and along with the meat the skins would have given me clothes, blankets and hides to block the windows with. Only had the vaguest idea how to cure hides, though, so probably would have been very smelly." I grinned, remembering the 'filthy creature' comment from *The Hidden War*, then sighed. "But the blood would have attracted predators, and the rams might have attacked me to protect their ewes. I don't think I'd have been able to manage a broken bone, though I suppose it's just barely possible the aether would have helped that heal. Probably wouldn't have survived that chest infection if moonfall had been a day or two later. Very handy."

I paused and looked speculatively toward the old town, but Ruuel said: "You can no longer risk exposure."

Because, like the Setari, I was now too dangerous to get drunk. It's lucky I'd more or less given up drinking already, or I might have had to be annoyed about that. It's moonfall tonight, too. I'm not even allowed to go outside and watch it because it gets very cold once the sun drops.

"I doubt I would have enjoyed surviving Winter very much, though," I said, looking back out at the lake, beautiful and indifferent. "And eventually I'd have gotten sick or hurt myself, and died."

He didn't say anything to that, but he stayed standing behind me for a while, maybe like me thinking about all the things which would have been different. Then he dismissed his squad, and took me to the amphitheatre for the afternoon's taxi service.

It sounds like a minor thing, but he carried me as Par and Glade did, which was mildly embarrassing when it was them, and with Ruuel sufficient to throw me into mute confusion. It's never a small thing for me when Ruuel touches me. Even a finger-brush of enhancement can send a tingle through me, and I'm always aware that Place Sight will tell him way too much about my reactions. It's very rare that he carries me – Par is my Fourth Squad toter. Even the standard carrying position is something I usually have to prepare myself for, so that my heartbeat doesn't skyrocket too obviously. All I could think of when he lifted me today was how close his face was to mine.

They've been carrying me about like that because my legs hurt more if they're not elevated, as well as the need for contact for the platforms. Floating above them won't trigger it, but someone standing on them holding me does.

I could feel every breath. And fell asleep while he was waiting for them to load the platform for the second trip. Kind of contradictory. It was like those dreams on the *Diodel*. Very peaceful, and yet sharply defined. I could hear his heartbeat, since my head was resting on his shoulder, and was almost glad when the Ddura showed up, noisy as it is, since the platform room is chock-full of drones no doubt busily recording a projection of me gazing up at Ruuel in the Ena. The Ddura could certainly see us, and was being all chirpily pleased until I told it to shut up – and was pleased in turn, because it seems more obedient when I'm dreaming.

The platform room in Kalasa looked different, too, quite distractingly so, pulling my attention away from Ruuel until he was flying me back, when I indulged in gazing up at him, enjoying all the tiny fine detail of a close-up view which wouldn't be recorded by drones or second level monitoring. He is so worth looking at.

When we returned to my little building, Ruuel put me carefully on my bed, then said: "Your instructions were to wake yourself whenever you began dreaming lucidly."

No surprise that he'd known. I made myself wake up, winced, then said: "Didn't need the headache."

I drew a breath to tell him about how different Kalasa had been while I was asleep, but he said in a distinctly cooler tone: "Keep to the training plan. You can't have forgotten the consequences of letting your guard down."

"No." My face burned and I looked away. "Sorry."

I pretended to still be very tired while Ista Temen checked me over, and after a while they all went into the next room and I worked on keeping perspective, but still cried just a little, and then did visualisation exercises until I dozed off. Lohn and Mara are babysitting me now, sitting out the evening shift.

I should have accepted Ruuel's offer to change trainers. He's definitely the best person for keeping me calm, but I don't seem able to stop wanting more than that, or ping ponging all over the place after the tiniest, mildest of reprimands.

An anchor doesn't work if it's trying to pull away from you.

Monday, June 16

Day Off

Fretted myself into a fever, having spent the night compulsively forcing myself to wake up, and racking my brains for some way to not ever have to see Ruuel again, yet somehow not let anyone know that's what I wanted. The dreams were all about trying to kill sheep, which I was very glad to stop as soon as I was aware of them.

When Ista Temen decided I should stay safely in bed and not do anything today I relaxed and slept for most of the day. I imagine there were a few frustrated greysuits, but it's not as if they can't get in without me now. I'm sure they're having fun over in those snowstorms. With any luck tomorrow my legs will be improved enough that I can stand and no-one will need to carry me.

I'm tired of all this.

Tuesday, June 17

Say Nothing

Maze and Zee were my dawn shift babysitters – Third Squad and Squad One went to Kalasa via the *Litara* yesterday, so we're down to two squads at Pandora. After Ista Temen had decided I was fit enough, Maze took me over to the amphitheatre for taxi duty. I asked Maze if I could stay upright today, but Ista Temen lowered my pain medication and let me try out standing, and I couldn't cope with it. She says I'm making good progress, but it feels like I've been like this forever.

"We're pushing to be sufficiently set up here to support the investigation without continuing to use you like this," Zee told me, after I'd shuffled everyone through to Kalasa and we'd gone out into the central square for another look.

"How's the exploration going?"

"Still going."

Maze laughed at her tone of voice, and gave me a wry smile. "It's an enormous place, and there's simply so much. We've a site map now, but actually cataloguing and making sense of what we've found could take years. The Sight talents have marked places for early investigation, but the Lantarens recorded on paper, and it's so fragile. We've wanted records so badly, and can hardly complain about having a library to sift through, but the need to do it *slowly* is remarkably frustrating." He paused. "Everywhere there are reminders that this was a school."

I hadn't failed to notice the skeletons scattered about, nor the small size of many of them, but I had something else on my mind. "Have you been in near-space here?" I asked carefully.

"Can't get to it. Even after you opened the door, the shielding keeps us out. And there's a reason you're asking that, isn't there?" Maze isn't slow.

"Fell asleep last time here. I can't be sure, but...just had a vague impression that Kalasa looked different in near-space. Though I didn't see much more than platform room."

"Different how?"

"Lights," I said vaguely. "Wasn't here long enough good look. Also, I guess the Ddura can't come here, because I haven't heard any when in Kalasa, no matter how much fooling around on platform."

Maze thought this well worth looking into, but since I wasn't the least bit tired right then he took me back to Pandora and told me not to have any midday naps so that they could try and recreate the experience this afternoon. He and Zee went to get some rest and Alay and Ketzaren took over babysitting, so I asked if they could help me have a shower. I've really lost all tolerance for being grubby, and the greysuits had told me that my nanotech bandages 'breathe' and thus shouldn't have scads of hot water run over them. Not until the burns are in better condition.

Coping with that took up a lot of the morning, and made all three of us rather giggly, but I felt a lot better afterwards. It was nice to see Alay laugh. She seems to open up a little on Muina, to talk more and hold her head higher. She loves watching the lake, but the daytime temperature's dropping here again, so they decided not to let me sit outside, and instead we watched the latest aerial survey information together and then the latest episode of *The Hidden War*, which had aired right after we came to Muina. It focused on the main character training fake-me and barely being able to understand the garbled Taren, and not being able to talk about her assignment with the rest of her squad. We were having lunch when I had a channel request from Ruuel, something now possible even though he's in Kalasa because the door's been opened and more satellites are in place.

The request had a text opener of "Kalasa near-space," and when I accepted he said without preamble: "Should I interpret 'just a vague impression' as 'very certain but you were cut short last time you tried to tell someone and now need a reason for the delay in mentioning it'?"

It was difficult to tell if he was angry. And everything I thought of in reply made me sound like I was being a smartass, so eventually I just said: "Yes."

"What precisely did you see?"

"The walls have glowing patterns in them, like electrical circuitry. The platform has more. They change colours when people go near them. They reacted to the drones as well as to people. They changed to a different colour near me."

Not a vague impression at all. The uncharacteristically long silence before Ruuel responded told me nothing useful, then he said: "My error. An unnecessary lecture at that juncture."

I wonder how often he does something he considers a mistake. I'm willing to bet he hates being wrong, but always acknowledges it meticulously. And to be fair I had to admit that his lecture hadn't been totally misplaced.

"Spirit of scientific discovery not exactly the initial reason I delayed waking myself up," I said, and dropped out of channel. Not making Ruuel have to deal with my crush is a kind of weird gentleman's agreement we have. He clearly doesn't want to respond to it. Whether because he's in love with Taarel, or just doesn't think I'm attractive, or whatever, the end result is still him carefully keeping me at a distance. So long as it's not open it's something handled relatively easily. But I'm finding it more difficult not to react to him, to want to push him to react to me, which is why he gave me that little reprimand – because I didn't do what I was ordered just to prolong a dream about him. I'm making his job harder.

Time to go back now. I'm definitely going to be able to sleep – between Ista Temen's fortifier, and my general tendency to be kitten-weak at irritating moments, I've barely been able to keep myself conscious to write this.

Friday, June 20

Hard Rest

The Kalasa sleeping experiment was both positive and negative. After ferrying some people and a pile more equipment to Kalasa I was established on the roof of a building one tier up from the flat central valley of the city. A number of seats and a couple of tables had been set on the main portico above the door, sheltered on three sides by higher sections of roof, but with an excellent view out over most of Kalasa. Ista Temen, very excited at being in Kalasa, and Maze and Zee sat with me, just generally chatting. The idea was to keep me feeling comfortable and unstressed and safe, and for me to pay attention to any oddnesses I observed if I had a dream of Kalasa, but to not feel pressured to have one and most particularly to wake myself up if I had a nightmare or felt threatened in any way.

It wasn't very difficult to fall asleep, but I immediately started dreaming of Cruzatch climbing over the edge of the roof, and hurriedly had to wake myself up. I didn't particularly want to go back to sleep after that, and instead sat talking with Maze and Zee about why I sometimes projected what I was seeing into real-space and sometimes only the sounds or 'sensations' – if you could call tearing chunks out of my own legs a sensation – and sometimes I don't seem to project anything at all. Maze said he did get a very strong sense of threat just before I woke myself up, but that it wasn't as distinct and directional as it would be if Cruzatch really were about to attack. He didn't quite say that he was detecting *me* as a threat, but I'm pretty sure that's what he meant.

I dozed off again after a while, but again didn't dream of coloured lights in Kalasa's near-space. Instead I had a very interesting dream about Lantarens in Kalasa. The shield was down and the sky very blue and bright above a clean and sparkling city, with whole bridges and a very remarkable central waterfall which poured straight down from where the bridges met high above. There was a pool in the centre of the city between the platform buildings which is buried in rubble outside of dreams.

Hordes of people lined a major street all the way from the big entrance door to the central circle. Officials and families and guard-types and a few dressed like Inisar had been. And there were masses of kids, all of them dressed in a pale green-white and carrying huge armfuls of flowers, making a long procession from the entrance down to the central pool where they walked over this thin bridge through the water to give their flowers to the people waiting, who gave them a little crown of flowers in return. Those at the front of the lines looked to be around ten, and those toward the end were at least my age. Almost all of them were the same 'type' as Inisar, Ruuel, Taarel and Selkie – very dark eyes and hair and warm golden skin – which I guess suggests their appearance is a reflection of their descent from the Lantarens.

There was music, too: a solemn, measured drumming and swirling, interweaving notes which mixed with the hushing roar of the fountain – pipes, I guess, both high and deep. I glanced about for the musicians, noticing that the Tarens and Kolarens were in my dream as well, very astonished, which made me realise I must be projecting. The Lantarens didn't seem able to see them, but a few near the biggest groups of greysuits were peering confusedly about, as if they sensed something.

I would have liked to watch more – there was so much – but in the time it took for two little green-gowned children to get all soaked and give out their flowers, this great black rock came and sat on my chest and pulled me out of Kalasa and into a sleep which didn't involve dreams or being aware of people around me or anything but nothingness. Kind of refreshing, really. When my mind finally came back, I felt physically blah, but still rested.

The first thing I noticed was that Zan was there. That made me open my eyes, surprised, and then I noticed how heavy my arms and legs felt. I was in my room at Pandora, despite Zan being there. She was watching me – no doubt the interface had told her I'd woken up – and smiled when I turned my head toward her. Zan's really pretty when she stops looking all serious and guarded. She's very fine-boned and delicate – not that I'd care to take her on in a fight.

"Welcome back," she said.

"Did I get injured?" I asked, discovering uncomfortable tubes. Then I looked at my interface and said: "When did it get to be the day after tomorrow? What happened?"

"You don't remember?"

"Dreamed about Lantaren ceremony, but had to go to sleep. More to sleep."

"You exhausted yourself physically." Zan moved aside as Ista Deve (who I like less than Ista Temen because I can almost see her mentally composing research papers about me) started checking me over. I was awfully tired and incredibly hungry, for all that I seem to have been on a feeding drip. "Not a safe use of talent, though usually not fatal if you're in good general condition."

Which doesn't exactly describe me – though sleeping for two days has given my legs more of a chance to heal, and they no longer start throbbing if I don't keep my feet elevated. Twelfth Squad is on medical leave as well: all but Zan and Sora Nels were injured when two stilts turned up in the middle of one of the more difficult rotations. Tahl Kiste is the worst, with lots of broken ribs and a crushed elbow. Although it sounded like actually surviving was a very good result, none of the teams like being invalided out, and rather than have her squad fret over it Zan suggested they assist with babysitting me.

After I had something to eat – confusedly trying to question Zan and respond to half of First and Fourth Squad wanting to talk to me – I slept again until about midnight and now I'm still feeling gluggy but not like lead weights are tied to my arms. Mara and Lohn were in the process of taking over from Maze and Zee so I could chat to them all for a while and hear their reaction to my overdone projection.

"Every historian on site in near-hysterics, practically gibbering," Lohn said. "But at least there were plenty of drones recording the projection and we could distract them with the logs."

Mara snorted. "And then trying to get them to make some sort of decision of whether they were staying or going, since anyone who was going had to come straight away since while you weren't in a critical state, this kind of exhaustion weakens the system far too much for us not to take you somewhere warm and keep you there. We ended up having to station a second ship there to deal with the accommodation. Second, Third and Fourth are still on-site."

"And you are not going anywhere near Kalasa until you're in full health," Maze added. "Even then, given how energy-greedy that projection was, those who want another glimpse into the past are due to be severely disappointed."

"Think it was really true then?" I asked.

"That or you have a remarkable imagination," Zee said, wrinkling her nose. "Did you have any awareness of what was going on beyond the visual?"

I hadn't, other than thinking it beautiful, but enjoyed hearing what First Squad thought about it. Maze and Zee have gone to bed and I'm sitting on the couch in the babysitter's room, snugged between Lohn and Mara while I write this. My legs feel much better and I'm allowed to walk to the bathroom by myself and everything.

Saturday, June 21

Botany

Spent the afternoon talking to Islen Dola, one of the senior greysuits trying to categorise a whole world's worth of plants. He took me (and Zan and Lenton) on a tour of the greenhouse (conservatory?), where they're growing samples of plants – mainly things that they think might be edible, but also other potentially useful sorts of plants. Between Tare and Kolar and Channa (which is a very rocky planet) and Dyess (even more ocean than Tare, with a mass of tropical islands), the greysuits know an awful lot about different sorts of plants and environments, but only Earth is tilted like Muina and experiences the same sort of seasonal shift.

Muina is really an incredibly fertile and inviting planet. Even its oceans are freshwater, with a couple of saltier lakes, and only a few places desert-dry and lacking lush plant life. All the planets the Muinans fled to seem horribly harsh and hostile by comparison. Even with their overpopulation issues, the Tarens didn't leap to try and repopulate Dyess, or take Channa from the people living there because they're far from ideal.

Although Islen Dola was partly just showing the conservatory off to me, he also wanted to pick my brains. As well as identifying any plants which even vaguely resembled Earth plants and saying what little I could about them, anything I could think of about seasons and plants could be useful. I told him about how Mum puts tulip bulbs in the refrigerator so they'll flower properly, and about certain seeds in Australia needing a bushfire to trigger their germination. He found Australian bushfires thoroughly distracting.

Zan levitated me about, which always makes me feel idiotic, but even though I can walk for short distances they prefer me not to stay on my feet for long periods.

Sunday, June 22

Decorative

I've been getting to know Twelfth Squad better. The main surprise is Lenton, who though I've seen him being super-temperamental and who obviously felt he should be Twelfth Squad's captain instead of Zan, turns out to be a pretty okay guy. Full of suppressed energy, but he focuses it on training and doesn't go around being pointlessly nasty or confrontational – except when he loses his temper, which I expect is exactly why he's not captain.

They're rotating through the morning and afternoon babysitting shift, and Zan had her whole squad come down for practice this afternoon, even Kiste, who can't do much more than sit with me and watch. Kiste told me a little about the fight which landed Twelfth on medical leave, and I got a good vibe from him about how Twelfth is feeling about Zan now. There's a kind of confidence squads seem to develop in their captains. Even though these are people who were all raised together, they've decided to trust Zan's judgment, to accept her orders in bad situations. I could never be a captain. I'd loathe having to prove myself to people, and I'd stress out completely with the responsibility of making decisions for other people. Not to mention the whole not being able to fight my way out of a wet paper bag issue.

I've taken to wearing ordinary clothes instead of my uniform, but the temperature dropped enough outside today that I compromised and wore my uniform and my new jacket over the top. It's a parchment-shade fake leather thing with black strips around the edges and I've been working on drawing a pattern of flowers similar to Celtic knot work but looser which I'd seen on the main doors to Kalasa. It took me ages to map it out right using pencils, and my big nikko pen was running dry toward the end of me inking just the main part in, but I think it looks pretty good. Maze says it's a big improvement over pictures of experimental animals.

I was glad to realise today that I don't really have two whole squads (or a squad and a half) devoted purely to babysitting me. In between watching me sleep, First and now Twelfth have been assisting the exploration teams out harvesting specimens, and even with preparing areas for construction. They're really serious about this being the current capital of Muina. Pandora will eventually bracket the old town completely, although it's a long way from that right now.

No near-future plans to expand down to the stream with the otters, I'm glad to say.

Monday, June 23

Sleet

Ista Temen took my bandages off this morning so my legs could 'air'. The main difference is that nothing is oozing any more, but my skin is crinkled and seamed and the burned bits are silvery and feel extremely weird when I poke at them. Kiste, who was on morning shift with Dess Charn, said he's going to have to stop complaining about his elbow. That's exaggeration – his bones were crushed and before Twelfth came to Pandora he'd spent days having surgery on it and even with Taren nanotechnology it will be weeks before it's close to useable and probably months before he's fully recovered. I'm allowed to walk somewhat longer distances, and don't feel quite so much of a cripple any more. Not that I'm *happy* to have amazingly ugly legs. The cosmetic work will take a couple of months, because they're more interested in getting me healthy than making sure I look good in a dress.

Ista Temen has scaled back my pain meds all the way. She says she'll give me something if I need help sleeping, but that if I want to walk about I need to know when I've pushed it too far. I also have these mild stretching exercises I have to do – moving my feet and lower legs about while sitting down.

My babysitter shifts always have at least one girl (Dess Charn this morning, Zan this afternoon, Alay and Ketzaren this evening) and at least one person with Combat Sight. Now that I'm not so sleepy half the day, I feel less tolerant of having two people in constant attendance, but they at least are willing to chat and to not be in 'Ena-mode'. Not that Zan's not incredibly proper still, just not at full alert.

It rained all morning, this icy near-hail, and after it stopped everything froze. So I can walk, but I can also fall over really easily. Lohn and Mara are here now, and we're going to watch some movies and maybe play some of these virtual world interface games.

Tuesday, June 24

Resolution

A day for gabbing about sheep, and then other Earth farm animals with another of the greysuits. I always end up feeling amazingly ignorant of my own world in these conversations.

They've decided I'm recovered enough to risk me going back to Kalasa tomorrow. Not to play taxi or to have any dreams – they don't want me to attempt any dreams till I'm a little more recovered, not even training. Since I haven't been having *any* lucid dreams lately, and theoretically have enough control to wake myself up if I dream lucidly, I'm under orders to not push the development of my talents until further notice.

Tomorrow I'm assigned to First and Fourth to scout out which of the platforms go where. Fifteen buildings, fifteen platforms, but we've only discovered nine pattern-roof villages (and Arenrhon, which has its own platform). And when I was told about that my heart gave this huge thump and then I had to spend time reassuring Maze that no the idea didn't distress me at all.

Ever since the Kalasa dream, when I've woken up I haven't been aware of Ruuel's absence. I'd decided this was a positive sign, that I was accepting the big 'no' he hasn't had to say out loud, and have been very careful not to write about him, look at any logs involving him, or think about him if I could help it. If I did think about him, I'd very deliberately imagine him kissing Taarel, remind myself that he's made it absolutely clear he doesn't want to get close to me, and tell myself that I was so happy I was finally getting over him.

Such a lie.

I had an unplanned nap this afternoon and dreamed of Ruuel. He was standing alone in the dark – levitating just above the snow – watching the horizon. I could see him clearly, even though there didn't seem to be any lights, and his face was very still and peaceful.

I made myself wake up. It wasn't a projecting dream, but I'm not sure if the monitors would have picked up use of my Sight talent. And if I'd looked at him any longer I might have reached out and tried to touch him. I've decided I can want him as much as I want, but no more little lapses. Nothing which makes him have to deal with my feelings, or even think about them. But I'm not going to stop enjoying looking at him.

Wednesday, June 25

World Travel

An early start to today's 'explore the platforms' assignment, since we were trying to mesh together First Squad, Fourth Squad and me all being awake at different times. I wasn't too tired – I'd gone to bed early, woken up in the middle of the night and written in my diary, and slept fairly solidly till Zee woke me a while before Pandora dawn. It was very freezy outside, so I took my beanie, but opted against my jacket since I knew that at least the desert platform would make me wish I was wearing less not more.

I gather that on particularly stormy days the wind chill at Kalasa has been so icy that they increased the amount of nanoliquid going into the Setari uniforms to allow for extra insulation and for wearing of head coverings as well. Mara showed me the option for the head covering and I burst into laughter because instead of the balaclava I was expecting, it resembles cloth wound above and below the eyes and now they really do look like they're space ninjas. The nanosuits are really adaptable – they can even create goggles if they want.

Maze hauled along a half-dozen drones to place at each of the sites which didn't have a drone already, and set them in the central circle of Kalasa where Fourth Squad was waiting. Afternoon there, of course, and it looked like the snowstorms had let up, but Maze was being all mission-mode and efficient, so I didn't ask if I could go look outside at the construction.

"Along with placing drones, we'll be performing a short survey of each site, known and unknown. Blind entry protocol applies." Maze signalled us toward the first of the platform buildings.

Since Alay and Ketzaren were my minders for the day, I asked Ketzaren what blind entry protocol was and she explained that it was how the squads behave when going through gates in the Ena, except when everyone has to go through at once instead of waiting for the leaders to signal them through. With platform travel it meant that people without Combat Sight were positioned toward the centre, with the Combat Sight/speed talents distributed evenly around the edges. My problems with contact with too many people at once makes this a little awkward, but they worked it out by having Alay on the edge, the drone beside me, and Ketzaren on the inside. Levitation helps a lot with getting me on and off platforms without everyone having to edge out of my way.

We went anti-clockwise around the circle of platforms, and spent the day on a tour of very disparate parts of Muina. Six pattern-roof villages, one platform which didn't work, and two cities. The cities were a bit of a surprise. Neither of them were Nurioth, but the drones and satellites allowed us to pinpoint them easily enough and they turned out to be the two next-largest cities other than Nurioth. I particularly liked the first of the cities we went to, which meandered beneath this incredible forest of absolutely massive trees – redwood tall. It was by far the most ruined of all the sites, tree roots and trunks displacing what they hadn't shattered, and full of bird song and the chirring of insects.

Not much in the way of Ionoth, since these were all locations which 'anchored' Ddura, but a few native creatures like the border collies weren't very pleased to see us and snarled and grumbled but stopped short of attacking.

Since everyone was in official patrol mode, there wasn't much in the way of chatting or exclamations. The one exception was when we went to the desert location where I'd been stranded. It was painfully hot there, stifling in the sand-clogged platform room, and worse above. I could only be glad it hadn't been quite this bad when I'd been dragging trees about. I sensibly retracted the sleeves and neck of my uniform even before we'd climbed onto the platform at Kalasa, and Maze and Ruuel told their squads to follow my lead. Even so, the heat hit us like a hammer and everyone was dripping before we were even out in the sun. The squads still punctiliously did the same amount of surveying, though there was fortunately little to see except the blackened remains of my arrow, frayed around the edges where windblown sand had already started to swallow it.

"I just can't believe you did that in this heat," Lohn said, breaking out of professional mode as we paused to stare at charcoal and sand. "I feel like my *lungs* are cooking with every breath."

"Is hotter now," I said, shrugging so I could pretend I wasn't feeling tight-chested remembering. "And I waited till late afternoon. Worst bit was trying to start the fire beforehand." Although, really, I think the worst bit was when I got lost on the way back after lighting the arrow. There was just blackness everywhere until I turned around, and I felt so small and confused and overwhelmed.

"Enough for the day," Maze said, and took us back to the platform without another word. We immediately froze half to death from temperature difference and I was made to drink horrible fortifying drinks and have a medical exam. We'll finish the rest tomorrow. Everyone seems to be convinced I'm going to have screaming nightmares tonight, and I have Taarel and Sefen from Third as first shift babysitters.

I was very good about Ruuel, not self-indulgent or annoying in any way. I only properly looked at him when he spoke, which was exactly twice, and so long as he's not the person whose job it is to haul me about, I should be fine.

Thursday, June 26

Pieces of Sphinx

I did have nightmares last night, but they were nightmare nightmares – no projection involved in real-space or the Ena, and none of the certainty of awareness which is my completely unpredictable Sight talent. I dreamed I was lost in a dark maze, and the only door I could find was being held shut from the other side. Taarel woke me up, her hand on my forehead, but didn't push me to tell her what I'd been dreaming.

It snowed like crazy overnight, and Pandora looked spectacular in the morning, mounded with fluffy brand-new snow. Eeli loved it, even though she'd already been dealing with the snow out at Kalasa. I swear if Maze hadn't come down to collect us she would have romped through it like a puppy. It snowed all day, so that when we came back it was piled up against the door of my building. Everyone in Pandora is learning things about snow and the one we learned today was that we really need something to wipe or scrape the snow off in the airlock part of the door rather than track it into the corridor or the inner rooms, where it promptly melts into chilly puddles.

The last few platforms brought no surprises – just pattern-roof towns. And no Arenrhon, even though there's a platform there. They're not sure if the non-working platform is meant to link there, or if it's possible that Arenrhon is on a different 'network'. All but one of the Ddura 'recognised' us, which suggests that there's maybe five Ddura altogether, each patrolling three platforms. That's the current theory, anyway.

We had lunch at Kalasa, along with Squad One and Second Squad – a great big group of us sitting in the central circle using some of the rubble as chairs. The captains went off with the senior bluesuit, Tsen Sloe, and Islen Duffen and Islen Tezart, who have been transferred to Kalasa from Arenrhon. Everyone else 'talked shop' about the Ionoth they'd been encountering on the island, and also back on their respective planets. This thrilled me so much I fell asleep and dreamed of interesting lights again. Everywhere. I was trying to work out if there was any rhyme or reason when Nalaz pointed out to everyone that I was asleep and Mara reached to wake me up.

"No, wait," I said, which didn't work, but I tried again and got the "Wait" to be audible and Mara stopped with her hand on my shoulder. I knew they'd consult the captains, so busily kept looking about and was ready for them when all four captains set down in front of me.

I considered staying asleep and projecting again, but it felt like using a pulled muscle, so I woke myself up instead, blinked, and said: "Sorry, really hard to stay awake after drinking those fortifier things. Was seeing those lights again. It's—" I paused, struggling with the magnitude of what I wanted to describe. "Don't think I can describe that properly, but did see that circular building sends out pulses occasionally and everything seems to answer it." I pointed toward a building halfway up the opposite slope, then rubbed my temple irritably. "Think I haven't been projecting in my sleep lately because I can't. It's like that bit of me is too tired."

Maze shifted from a faint frown to the abstract expression of someone looking things up over the interface. "Only a preliminary view there," he said, and glanced at Ruuel, who immediately signalled his squad and went for a look. Maze, Grif and Shaf sat down and Maze said: "Even a bad description is a start." He brought all the squads into a mission channel, along with the three senior officers the captains had been talking to.

I wrinkled my nose – it really wasn't something which is easy to put into words – then said: "All of the whitestone has lights in it. Bands of squiggles which branch out – a bit like veins. Dim and really indistinct most of the time, but when anyone goes near it, it reacts and gets brighter. Even these fallen bits." I glanced at the chunks of broken bridge and fountain I'd been resting against. "It reacts with a different colour to me. Twice a pulse of light went out from the circular building, washing over whole city, and everywhere where there are people, it sends a little pulse back. Even these broken bits, for all they don't seem connected."

Islen Tezart, sounding wholly delighted, asked: "Do you mean these lights are made up of symbols? Writing?"

"Not really. Will try and draw." Which I did, using one of the interface drawing applications, which I'm even worse at using than a mouse-operated thing. It looked like a four year-old had tried to draw a flock of boomerangs and pieces of string flying south for the winter. "Not even close," I said apologetically.

"Visual," said Ruuel, streaming what he was seeing to us. The building was one big empty room with a domed ceiling, an empty walkway/border around the edges, and a huge and utterly gorgeous mosaic covering the rest of the floor. Similar imagery to the entrance to Kalasa, it was all flowers and flowing branches, stylised animals and lakes and streams. A picture of the world.

Ruuel began switching through Sights. First the room went all shadowy, and I thought I saw a hint of movement, and then it was like the mosaic became three-dimensional, lifting into a hemisphere of floral shapes and slinking, flitting, drowsing animals. And then flattened down again, and became very like what I'd been seeing: streaming particles of light, particularly centring on two circular areas in the mosaic, one faded yellow and one greyish.

"Considerably more than decorative," Ruuel said. "Function–" He paused, and I suspected he and Halla were talking over their impressions out of channel. Even though he has more Sights than Halla, Ruuel always consults with her on her impressions for things like this. I'm not sure if it's because she's stronger with Place Sight, or if the talent is just so variable that it's like fitting together fragmentary puzzle pieces in hopes of making a picture. "The most distinct impression is one of a place of annunciation, of being judged."

There was a exceptionally boring period following this where bunches of the Setari and greysuits yakked at each other and installed machines and made cautious attempts to work out what the mosaic was for and how to make it react. I stayed where I was, with Lohn and Mara for company, and worked on my Muinan animals project, which was something I could chat to them about. But eventually everyone gave in and decided to poke Devlin at the mosaic to see what happened. They're much less keen to use me for testing since my first excursion to Kalasa, but it's easy to spot the situations where it's going to happen.

The mosaic did seem to react to me, when they plunked me on the yellow circle. The machines picked up a surge in power. But then there was another short age of faffing around, trying to get me to make something, anything, happen. Lots of bright ideas from the greysuits, mostly based around doing the same thing I'd done with the platforms – except theoretically to a higher security level. None of that seemed even remotely inclined to work.

"You don't have any suggestions of your own, Caszandra?" Isten Notra, observing over the interface, asked.

"Trial by combat?" I asked, looking very doubtfully at Ruuel, who had been patiently standing on the other circle for what seemed an eternity. He looked down, which I suspect was to hide how ludicrous he found *that* idea. I sighed. "Don't see why trying to start with me. If judging, shouldn't other person be proving themselves worthy? Kalasa already seems to know what is my place in this world."

I was just being frustrated, but Ruuel looked up, eyes widening. "Phrase that as a question," he said – ordered, it was very much an imperative command.

It took me a moment, since I had already been asking a question. But then I twigged, and said: "What would you be to Muina?"

He didn't answer out loud, but dropped his gaze back to the mosaic, and then closed them, going very still. Everyone else in the room shut up, almost seeming to hold their breath. I've no idea what he was thinking, what he told Kalasa he wanted to be, but I guess it approved. Just for a moment there, I swear the mosaic shifted. I couldn't spot the difference, but I had to wonder if another tiny tile had been added.

After that everyone got really cheerful. Particularly me when a bit of experimentation showed that Kalasa now responded to Ruuel much as it does me: he could activate the platforms and the mosaic. And Maze then Mara then Islen Tezart quickly followed suit. That's the best news I've had for ages. No more playing taxi or being poked at stuff for me. Not everyone 'passes' though – which naturally upsets those who don't – particularly Islen Duffen, who looked like she'd been slapped. I did notice, from the few who failed before I was taken back to Pandora, that it mainly seems to be people who aren't comfortable with Muina itself – being under so much sky, and with sticky plants and bugs and animals all uncontrolled and in every direction. KOTIS has been having to return a reasonable percentage of staff back to Tare just because they can't cope with Muina.

No-one seems to want to talk about what being judged feels like, either. It seems it's a bit more involved than making some kind of life goals statement. None of the Setari have failed so far, but given the squads involved, I'm not surprised. I was glad all the Kolaren Setari managed. They've stopped looking quite so distracted since the news brought word that matters had improved on Kolar, but today was the first time Shaf has smiled at me since his government tried to buy me.

All I've got scheduled is a morning medical appointment tomorrow. I'm willing to bet they're going to send me back to Tare again.

Friday, June 27

Ice

Zan and Lenton were my post-breakfast babysitters. They'd already been to Kalasa earlier that morning and passed, and so were subdued and thoughtful – I couldn't tell if it was mainly because it was their first time in Kalasa, or if it was the test. The most I could get anyone to describe what it's like was Zee, who told me it left her feeling very exposed, like something very large had opened her up and taken a look inside.

Given the whole idea of the planet as a living entity, I can see why this disconcerts them all so much. They're not sure if what's judging them is the planet, or just some device of the Lantarens. I'd love to know why I didn't have to be judged, but I'm glad not to have to try. It would be mortifying to fail.

My medical appointment was over by mid-morning, and Zan told me she had permission for us to go outside Pandora, which I thought a nice surprise. I immediately suggested we go to see whether the otters were still there – I'm pretty sure otters don't move about to avoid Winter.

As we whizzed effortlessly along the lakeshore I was thinking about those first two weeks on Muina, and all that walking. Trying to picture having to do it in my school uniform in snow. Even in the enhanced Setari uniform and my coat and beanie, flying through the chill made me uncomfortably aware of how little chance I would have had. And then I noticed that we'd flown right past the otter stream. I looked over at Zan in confusion and she smiled (so rare for her to smile) and nodded at the ground.

Six squads of Setari make for a lot of people. Against a huge empty field of snow their black uniforms made them look like a flock of crows, with Squad One's green and black a distinct sub-group. Zan set us down in the centre, where the captains were all clustered together with their squads just a little back.

I stared from Zan to Maze, who said: "You wanted an epic fight with snow?"

It's not often that they do something which so totally surprises me. I said "Really?" on a note of disbelief, then blushed, and looked about at them all being amused at me, then back at Maze. And blushed more and said: "Thank you," and tried not to embarrass myself by bursting into tears.

He gave me one of those super-spectacular smiles. "We've been trying to work out what sort of rules would apply. Is there a standard for these games?"

I seriously doubted that standing in the middle of the field shrieking with laughter and madly hurling handfuls of snow at each other would work for Setari. "Not really," I said. Thinking of Dad's paintball games I added: "Could each mark out a base and do rule that if you get hit, you can't participate until next round, and have to wait in team who hits you base until no-one left. Or do a capture the flag where the team in custody of the flag at the end of limit wins. In that, if you get hit you have to return to base, but then can join back in straight away."

"Either of those would work," Maze said, glancing at Grif. "Perhaps one capture in current squads, and then a second round on an individual points basis?"

"What will we use as a flag?" Grif asked.

"Isn't that obvious?" Nils, looking highly amused, patted me on the head. "A flag which can fight back."

"I just throw snowballs at random people?" I asked.

"At all of us. If you manage to hit any of the squad trying to capture you before they get into grabbing distance, they'll all have to go back to their base. And any squad who wants to capture you has to hit you with a ball of snow. Since I'm sure you won't think this half as entertaining if we scrupulously avoid so much as mussing your hair." He plucked off my beanie and pulled it on, dark curls framing his face. It really suited him – totally smexy. "When you're captured, you can aim at attacking squads, but not your current captors."

Something which encouraged the Setari to not baby me seemed a good idea, and the captains quickly settled the final details. Combat Sight and Speed were allowed because they're practically impossible not to use, but no other talents except Levitation or Telekinesis for carrying the flag. The interface could be used for communication which everyone would hear, but not for showing the location of enemies. Rather than a time limit, winning meant getting me back to their base without losing me. Maze quietly told me not to overtax my legs, then brought everyone into one general channel, and airlifted me into the middle of a vast white expanse. And, after double-checking that I was good to go, left me there.

I was at the crest of a small hill, with only a leafless tree and clumps which I realised were nearly buried snow-covered bushes for company. It was, though of course didn't tell any of the Setari, totally not what I'd meant by an epic snowball fight. I'd been picturing a repeat of a family trip, just with First Squad: a shambolic and silly battle where everyone got covered in snow and there was no real point to it all. But I was really touched that they'd go so far for me, and had managed to coordinate all the squads on Muina – presumably they think it's safe to leave the construction on Kalasa with just greensuits on guard. And I was really surprised Ruuel was willing to participate, since he stays away from competitive stuff, but I guess he'd consider it good for his squad's morale. I'd avoided looking particularly at him, but a quick review of my log showed him being the only captain not smiling at my reaction, just his usual detached and alert mode.

Bet he wanted his squad to win, though.

I decided I'd be happy if I could hit someone, anyone, before being captured. While the squads worked out equidistant locations for their bases, and marked the boundaries, I debated hiding versus making a stand and decided I might as well avoid stressing out my legs. We were a bit higher than Pandora, and the snow was deeper. I'd sunk straight past my knees and by the time I'd finished scrunching out a little bunker and building up the walls, it was waist high. I sat down so I wouldn't be visible and made a pile of snowballs while listening to the chatter over the interface.

They weren't being all deadly serious, fortunately. Lohn and Nils kept up a patter of shit-talk aimed at each other, and anyone who was hit usually said something on the lines of 'good shot', or laughed or groaned. Running in snow was also proving a new challenge. It was a while before anyone got anywhere near me – so far as I can tell everyone first tried to ambush the squad nearest to them, before making their way toward me. I certainly had a nice pile of snowballs by the time anyone came close.

Three teams came within range of my senses at almost the same time (I was shamelessly using my own Sight). Second Squad, Squad One and Third Squad. They were all approaching from different directions, but Squad One and Third Squad attempted to cut each other off, giving Second a chance to rush my fort.

They were coming in a tight bunch, which was a big mistake. I waited till they were almost on me then, lying relaxed in my bunker, simply lobbed as many snowballs as possible in a high arc into the middle of them. Combat Sight saved some, but the groans and laughter prompted me to pop my head up to survey the damage – Nils and Keer Charal brushing snow off and the whole squad having to return back to base. Nils gave me back my beanie as a prize, which nearly distracted me from Third Squad and Squad One, who both decided to take opportunistic shots. I fell over my pile of snowballs trying to avoid the shots, and then dissolved into giggles when Nils took one of them in the face.

"Nils dodge worse than I do," I said, trying to control my laughter enough to lob snowballs in something like the right direction for Third Squad and Squad One.

"Depends who's aiming," he said with a super-sexy grin, wiping snow out of his eyes before following his squad back down the slope.

Third Squad and Squad One managed to destroy each other, so that by the time I poked my head out of my fort, only Eeli was left to fight. Eeli's better at dodging than me, and her smile was at nuclear hyper-wattage for the rest of the day after making first capture.

Taarel, looking highly amused, took the rest of Third Squad on a slightly different course back to base so that they couldn't confuse anyone coming after Eeli and me, and Eeli – huge-eyed and vibrating with excitement, but keeping very quiet – had me go ahead of her on a somewhat circuitous route in the same direction, using the cover of half-buried bushes. Since she's not telekinetic, we couldn't move very quickly, but the snow was broken up enough by then that it wouldn't be obvious which direction we'd gone. Combat Sight only shows threats, and the other squads weren't allowed to use Path Sight, so I actually had more of an advantage tracking than the Setari.

First Squad effortlessly took me away from Eeli – though I did almost hit Lohn before Zee got me – but then there was a really tangled battle between fragmented bits of squads returning from their various bases, which First Squad managed to survive losing only Maze and Alay.

Not letting your squad get fragmented was obviously an important tactic, as First and then Fourth proved. Just as First was approaching their base, Fourth ambushed – as much as you can ambush anyone with Combat Sight. Mori got me hard in the back as part of a relentless barrage which took out Ketzaren and Lohn. Mara immediately tried to capture me back, only to have her ball seemingly explode mid-air. I only realised what had happened when Zee's attack went the same way, intercepted by another snowball.

"Nice tactic," Zee said, shaking her head at Ruuel as she picked ice out of her hair.

"Be prepared to have it used against you," Mara added with a grin, and waved at me before they both headed toward their far-too-close base.

Maze was already on his way back, and Ruuel signalled his squad to hurry up, before ducking down and blurring on ahead along a different route. He was smiling. Just ever-so-faintly. I suppose maybe it was more that he looked extra-alert and alive, with his eyes open wide, but definitely enjoying himself. The rest of his squad certainly was: even Sonn was bright-eyed. If Fourth's base hadn't been on the opposite side of the hill they might have won, but they ran up against Third, Squad One and Second, who held off ambushing each other in favour of taking Fourth down. With First coming up behind, there was an inevitable, suitably epic stand-off. I ended up tagged by Nalaz, and he and Taranza hastily hauled me off while Shaf guarded their retreat. And then Twelfth Squad pounced, having waited for the critical moment when almost everyone was heading back to their own bases.

It was great seeing how proud Twelfth Squad were of Zan. Even though half of them are injured, it was her strategy which had let them win. And so funny watching Zan being so very correct, but with her cheeks so pink, as the other captains congratulated her.

After that we had an every-man-for-himself game of hide-and-seek, where we tallied every time we hit someone, and every time we got hit. Ruuel won this effortlessly, which I don't think surprised anyone, although Nalaz and Mara came close at stages. Afterwards we all went and had a big, hot lunch and everyone looked so relaxed and happy and of course I fell asleep.

Lohn and Mara are being my babysitters at the moment, though I've left them alone in the other room because I got the impression they wanted to snuggle. It was a really good day. I wish I could think of some way of thanking them properly in return.

Toward the end of the hide-and-seek, I'd headed off to one side to get a bit of a rest and make a stock of snowballs. For ease I was lying on my back, deep in the snow, watching the sky growing greyer. And Ruuel came near me. I felt him before he knew who I was – he was following my tracks I think. But something must have made him realise. Because he stopped, and then changed direction away from me.

"Too easy?" I said loudly. I was really angry, abruptly understanding just why Kajal is so infuriated by Ruuel's refusal to fight him. And then I was nervous because Ruuel stopped, and came back toward me.

I didn't try and throw snowballs – I knew he'd dodge easily – just lay there and tried not to be too wide-eyed as he stood directly above me, giving me an incredibly foreshortened view of leg and his face. He certainly wasn't smiling that time. My heartbeat went through the roof because it wasn't the efficient squad captain looking down at me, but the person I'd glimpsed during his fight with Kajal, arrogant and annoyed. For that moment he was entirely himself with me.

Then he dropped a snowball directly on my face and walked off while I gasped and choked. But I had to laugh, and said: "Guess so!" as he walked away. I enjoy the oddest things.

After I'd had my nap, Maze told me that I'll be heading back to Tare tomorrow. First and Second Squad's coming with me, and Mara's going to be whipping me into shape, and Zee overseeing my Sight and projection training. I don't know if Ruuel recommended the change of trainers, or if it's just they want the Sights squads here on Muina.

I'm in an accepting kind of mood about it all, like I'm starting to be able to let him go.

Saturday, June 28

Fly-over

I spent a nice relaxed morning with Zan and Dess building a snowman and then constructing some snow armchairs and making amateurish snow sculptures. Telekinetics are definitely very handy to have when you're trying to shift a lot of snow about. Zan's got a real flair for sculpture, too, and I was pleased that indulging me gave her a chance to do something she obviously enjoyed. Twelfth is going to remain assigned to Muina until further notice – their injuries don't prevent even Kiste from fighting, and they should be fine so long as they're not facing large numbers of Ionoth. And, thanks to the strength of her Telekinetic talent, Zan's got a lot of construction work in her near future.

We're on the *Litara* heading back now, having narrowly avoided a bunch of civilians who were off-loaded at Pandora for an overnight visit along with, so far as I could tell, the fittings they'll be using in the new building that's been going up. It's the first time KOTIS has allowed anyone on Muina who was there just to look and exclaim: a one-off PR exercise for a bunch of VIPs, reporters, and contest winners come to 'experience the home world'. There'll be another group from Kolar in a few days, and no more for a while. Pandora's getting larger every day, but KOTIS is very reluctant to spend resources on tourists. Maze said there's a massive disagreement over the question of settling instead of exploring, mainly because of the Ddura. He doesn't want families, kids, here, but there's an argument that Muina might soon be the safest place on any of the planets.

I hadn't known any of this when watching the *Litara* settling on the lake. Otherwise I probably wouldn't have stayed sitting outside when the shuttle went past on its way to the amphitheatre. KOTIS personnel don't as a rule point at you and wave. Fortunately Maze came down and collected me before any of them were finished at the platform. I don't think much of a career as a zoo exhibit.

It's very weird to me that I think of people as 'civilians'.

Snug

So nice to be back in my own rooms. So nice not to have two people making sure they're always within twenty feet of me.

Ghost showed up within half an hour of me being back, purring like mad. She missed me, or whatever my enhancement does for her.

It made me wonder about Muina v Tare in terms of 'home'. I guess Muina would be as much home as here if I had my own quarters, not a glorified medical monitoring facility. Given the choice I'd probably live on Muina, just because there's so much more outside, but I'm feeling very comfy and settled here, curled into my window seat with Ghost purring on my lap.

First and Second Squad are reverting to 'nightmare watch' instead of babysitting, which is fine with me, especially since I'm not having too much trouble at the moment with my dreams. I think the manifestation part of me is still recovering. Tomorrow everyone has a day off, then I'm back on training.

Sunday, June 29

Nice means precise

The Ruuel-not-there sensation has come back, but otherwise non-eventful dreaming. I spent a long time in the bath this morning, looking at my legs and being amazed at how ugly they are, and thinking back over the fifteen seconds or so that it took me to get them in this condition.

It's really hard to go there. Waking like that scared the hell out of me, and it also hurt worse than anything else I've managed to do to myself. But waking aware of Ruuel's absence really brought it back to me. If I'd been less freaked out, I'd think about that night all the time, since I spent who knows how long with my arms in a death-lock around his waist and my face pressed into his stomach. He kept one hand on my shoulder and the other on the back of my head, and didn't even wipe the blood off his face until Mara came and he got me to clutch her instead. And it's only from looking at the log later that I know that he was grey-faced and sweating, battered by the raw terror I was blasting.

Even if it was just because I'm his assignment, I'll always remember him doing that. And saying my name correctly. I have this increasing collection of special memories of things he's done, including dropping a snowball on my face, but my accepting attitude seems to be holding. My crush makes his job harder, a job which could easily get him killed, and I think seeing that has given me the impetus I needed to step back.

I also caught up on the latest episode of *The Hidden War*. It was the confrontation scene, where Lenton discovered Zan wasting her time giving me baby-level training, and all the squads are introduced to me. Looks like Maze didn't put a word-for-word log of the explanation of my lab rat, which only meant the scriptwriters happily made up a scene where Lastier was quite directly insulting. There was also a scene which I wasn't present for, where he was being very smug and superior and insulting to the other squad captains, but also brilliantly competent and incisive.

I wonder if that PR person had a thing about Ruuel, or it was just script decisions which are making them put the knife in. Lastier is close enough to be recognisable, but terribly distorted.

Monday, June 30

Irresolution

Just physical training today, and that mainly in the weights room, since my legs aren't quite up to training which involves impact, and Mara says I need to work on upper body strength anyway. A couple of squads (Eighth, Tenth) passed through during the two long sessions we had, making me feel terribly self-conscious about my scars, since we were in the shorts and singlet arrangement. They were very good about not staring though. The rest of First Squad came and joined us for the session after lunch and demonstrated how much of a wimp I am. By the time Mara was done with me I was a limp noodle.

She's booked me in for swimming tomorrow morning, which I'm allowed to do alone so long as I don't dive and are feeling up to it. Tomorrow afternoon after they're back from rotation, Zee will be resuming my Sights and other-weird-things-Cass-does training. If, that is, I can actually move tomorrow.

There's a new news frenzy sparked by all the 'tourists' who've returned from Muina. Interviews with KOTIS staff and the contest winners and lots of shots of what Pandora looks like right now and tours of the buildings there and talk about making Pandora self-supporting. And KOTIS used their visit to officially release not only news and images of Kalasa, but to take a select few there and to explain the use of the platforms (although not, as yet, exactly how you get to be able to use the platforms). Other than a lot of extreme impatience at the time-frame of more civilians being able to go there, it's all been pretty joyous and exuberant news.

They've named the settlement at Kalasa 'Kaszandra', which is something I find uncomfortable and highly ironic, given the 'inescapable doom' aspects of my name. And of course the reporters managed to get hold of a whole bunch of anonymous gossip about me while they were talking to people at Pandora, and there's images of the snowmen and snowchairs Zan, Dess and I had built. And someone told them I'd been injured (mysteriously), and about how protective the Setari were of me (devoted) and whole bunches of embarrassing stuff which is very much not about me at all, but this little mythos which is being built up around me (wise beyond her years). No-one mentions the amount of sulking I get through.

I wonder if Tare has an equivalent of the tall poppy syndrome, and after all these unlikely stories about me being brave and wonderful they'll recast me for the feet of clay role. It's not that I don't think they should probably be glad I showed up and unlocked their world, but I hate this increasing tendency to build me up into something I'm not: improbably virtuous and clever and brave. The life I'm living is amazing, and I'm not unaware that I've caused a massive change to happen − I did name the settlement Pandora for that exact reason − but they've all tended to be things that have just happened while I was stumbling about trying not to die. And when I re-read my diaries I just sound increasingly whiney and edging toward certified nutjob. I've spent the last few months falling apart and moaning about it.

I was really glad for Mara's training today, because there's no hint of 'fragile little half-insane princess must be placated' when she makes me do an extra ten repetitions. I'm going to go along with that attitude, and throw myself back into my rather neglected schoolwork, and that animal identification assignment. Every month that's gone by since I was rescued, I seem to have become less stable and lost more privacy. Yeah, I've had good reasons for freaking out, and a lot of the guarding has been necessary. But I don't like myself this way, and I'm looking to change how I've been behaving. To take comfort from the people trying to support me, but to get back to standing on my own two feet.

JULY

Tuesday, July 1

Map of the brain

Swimming was okay. It's been long enough, I guess, and it did help loosen up all my complaining muscles. I hope eventually it'll be fun again.

Zee took me back out to Keszen Point, which had obviously reverted to being a warehouse during my absence, since the boxes were different boxes. Ista Chemie was very interested in the Kalasa projection, rumours of which are already rife on the interface, and also the fact that I feel like the manifestation bit of me is still tired. We started out small – another mug, in fact – and though I can picture a mug in my head very easily, I couldn't make one appear, full of cocoa or not. And I don't seem to be causing anything at all to happen in near-space. This is nothing but a good thing from my point of view.

We moved on to a series of visualisations, measuring my energy output and my brain's electrical activity when trying to see a distinct series of rooms of around the same size at increasing distances around Tare. And then a visualisation of a fictional place for contrast. It was a pretty productive session, both for clearly identifying which part of my brain is responsible for the Sight talent, and for me to become more aware of the separate mechanisms. I kept accidentally trying to manifest things, and I could feel myself not able to, and eventually I began to anticipate the twinge and deliberately avoid it. So the Kalasa manifestation cost me a couple of days of unconsciousness, but gave me a little progress in return. And a chance to not be so worried about accidentally making monsters.

This kind of training will be every second day from now on, with nothing but physical training on First Squad's off-rotation days until I'm fit and healthy. Only then, and if they've gained a proper understanding of the limits and costs of my talent set, will they even consider poking me at Muina again.

Zee was very tired by the time we were heading back, and I made jokes about carrying her to her quarters. I told her, as we rode the elevator, that I had been trying in vain to think of a way to thank everyone for my snowball fight, but she thought this tremendously funny, and told me the snowball fight was them thanking me, and besides they'd all enjoyed themselves.

Then I asked her didn't she think my beanie had suited Nils and she tweaked a strand of my hair and told me she'd make sure Mara left me too exhausted to remember what a beanie was.

I much prefer training with the Setari to being babysat.

Wednesday, July 2

Ow

Entire body hurts. Mara carries out Zee's instructions very well.

Thursday, July 3

In a galaxy far, far—

The whole morning went to medical for the beginning of cosmetic work on my legs. Not too bad, though it left the skin feeling numb and oddly hot, and I have bandages again.

This afternoon Zee had me try and visualise what's going on in Pandora. They wanted to do this test while I'm still not able to manifest, because the previous set of tests proved that distance does take more energy (no real surprise there). I could tell they thought it was an extra-serious test because Ista Chemie was very careful and particular about all the medical equipment being on-hand and ready for business.

They'd decided on 'my' building as the target location, Zee carefully describing the already-familiar furnishings. Imagining something and 'seeing' it are very different experiences for me, so I knew that it was working. All that detail. Seeing things using this Sight makes it go almost 'super-real': every tiny smudge stands out, and all the colours seem special.

Seeing Pandora was hard, though. Carrying a person on your back and trying to walk up a flight of stairs hard. My heart-rate skyrocketed, I started to breathe like a steam-train and my throat and chest felt hot, quickly followed by the familiar stabbing headache that tells me I'm pushing myself into new territory. Zee immediately told me to stop, and I lay still with my eyes shut until Ista Chemie's medications came into effect.

"Building growing extra rooms?" I asked, once I felt closer to human again. I'd almost thought I'd visualised the wrong place, because all the furniture had been cleared out and the walls seemed to be wrong.

"It's being expanded. Properly shielded quarters for Setari stationed at Pandora. And that confirms that you can reach over that kind of distance."

"Earth even farther away," I said, sighing.

"Very likely." She gave me an evaluating look, then nodded, apparently deciding I wasn't going to go experimenting with trying to see Earth any time soon. Not that I probably wouldn't try if they gave me a supply of extreme headache medicine. And I probably will, eventually, if they don't include it in my training and testing in the next couple of months. There are limits.

Not soon though. My head is still pounding underneath the blocking.

Friday, July 4

Somebody Wake Up

All morning in medical again – partially the inevitable brain scans, partially fooling with my legs, which are now encased in a different sort of bandage: a waterproof one I'm allowed to get wet, but not to soak, so no swimming or baths for the next couple of days.

I was eating a light lunch in the canteen when the captain of Tenth, Els Haral, slid onto the seat opposite, pulling Fourteenth's captain Kin Lara down beside him.

"It's against captainly protocols to gossip," Haral told me, smiling. "So we're not at all asking you whether it's true that Twelfth won some kind of ice environment combat exercise over all the other squads based on Muina."

"Squads gave me a snowball fight as a present, but is a game, not training," I said firmly. 'Ice environment combat exercise'. Seriously.

Lara, who had briefly looked less sleepy than usual when Haral pulled him into the seat, shook his head, then gave in. "Either way, Twelfth won? Over First and Fourth?"

"And Second, Third, and Kolar's First Squad. Zan picked smart strategy."

"How does the game work?"

Since they gave an impression of being pleased that Twelfth had won, but not in any way negative toward the other squads, I explained. So far as I can tell, First is considered the best close combat team, while Ruuel is probably the best individually, with Maze and Mara both considered almost equally dangerous. Not that I can get anyone to actually tell me that – but neither Haral nor Lara were the slightest bit surprised that Ruuel had won the second game.

It's nice to know that Zan has some allies among the other squads. I had the faintest suspicion that Haral was teasing Lara about Zan, so maybe he'd be more than an ally if Zan gave him a chance. They stayed and chatted to me. Interested in Kalasa of course, but Haral also had lots of questions about Earth: he wanted to know more about volcanos and the things that made Earth different from Muina. They're both very easy to talk to – more relaxed than a lot of the younger Setari – but eventually I had to go be tortured by Mara, who made me do something like Pilates or yoga. Lots of stretching myself and holding positions.

I spent that torture session turning over who Haral reminded me of, and finally worked it out. Not in looks, but that soft-spoken, laid-back thing he does is very similar to the Hicks character in *Aliens*.

Saturday, July 5

Size matters

No dangerous dreams last night, though I have some tangled memories that feel uncomfortable. I have noticed that my ability to tell who is nearby has expanded in range, and asked Zee how many Sights I might have: one or a hundred. Knowing where people are, and seeing coloured lights, and seeing things in the past and seeing fictional places, and seeing what's happening on another planet all seem like rather different things to me. The most she could tell me is that it seems to consistently be the same area of my brain, and that it might be similar to Place Sight, which can be used in a lot of different ways.

I'm glad I don't feel people's emotions when I touch them.

Today we measured the energy output required for me to see different sized things which were all roughly at the same distance. And then fictional as opposed to real things. It made me very tired, and I had a nap before a squad dinner in Ketzaren's rooms. She'd changed her wall display to a slideshow of images of Muina: snow and plains and mountains and streams and different forests and a wetland I hadn't seen before, amazingly full of birds.

First Squad was decompressing after their rotation earlier in the day, and it seems they are finding it a big mental and emotional adjustment to go from the work they'd been doing on Muina to the intensity of rotations, where they are only ever winning battles, and never the war. And it's getting harder. Twelfth isn't the only squad which has hit some bad rotations lately and been injured, mainly due to an increase of deep-space Ionoth. Maze said they're trying to decide between supplementing the existing squads with qualifying Kalrani, or simply having squads work in pairs. The whole reason the current squads are six members is because Ionoth, particularly deep-space Ionoth like swoops, are drawn to larger groups. If they're having to deal with them anyway, then larger groups may gain more than they cost.

Sunday, July 6

Mara is evil

Tired. Sore. Debating taking a sickie tomorrow.

Monday, July 7

All worked up over nothing

Lunch with Haral – Els – again. I guess I wasn't wrong, back when I tested with Tenth Squad, in thinking that maybe he liked me. My withdrawal that time must have just made him decide on a patient approach. He's not overloading me with compliments, but he's taking the opportunity of our lunch shift being at the same time to talk to me. No pressure, just chatting in a group with the rest of his squad, but I could tell he was into me.

So could his squad, judging by the wide-eyed glances a couple of them exchanged.

Els is a very cool and attractive guy and I like him. I can't decide what to think about the possibility of more. I'm definitely giving it a lot of thought, and my training session with Zee didn't go very well because I was distracted. But at least I discovered that if I think about two different things at once and don't concentrate on just the one location I can give myself a really magnificent headache.

I'm trying to decide whether to respond to Els, or avoid him, or just treat him like a friend and pretend I hadn't noticed any overtones of more. I do like him. I can easily imagine being with him. But how is it fair on Els to encourage him if I'm not sure I'd want to go through with it? When I wake up every morning totally focused on the absence of one very particular person? But I don't want to be that either, mooning hopelessly over someone who isn't a type of person I'd ever thought I'd like, is probably in a relationship with someone else, and has done his best to keep me at a distance.

Stupid. Stupid dilemma. I need to stop thinking about this.

Tuesday, July 8

Peering in the windows

Mara eased up on me a little today. She said she couldn't bear my expression of dread any longer. And I sat in on a First and Second Squad group training session – just watching – because Maze and Grif wanted to think more on Rotational dynamics with a doubled squad. Afterwards they actually took me out into the city for dinner, which is the first time for ages and probably only happened because two whole Setari squads is sufficient to not only block me from casual view but to daunt even the most enthusiastic gawker. I did notice that even on their home island the social politeness of people pretending not to recognise them as Setari when they're not in uniform has more or less fallen away, but we were still left to go to the fondue restaurant unharassed.

Nils, in an uncharacteristically non-flirtatious mood, talked to me a lot about the visualisations I've been doing and the difference between them and his illusions. There was an underlying current of concern behind all the conversation, but it was still a nice night.

Wednesday, July 9

Calooh! Callay!

Excellent, excellent day.

It started out routine, racking up another few hours in medical. I hesitated a bit before going to get lunch, still undecided on how I wanted to handle Els, but eventually figured that chatting over lunch could hardly hurt me. And then when I got to the canteen he was already with his squad at a full table, so I sat with Hasen and Henaz from Eighth, who were having breakfast. I'm finding it rare to go to the canteen and there not be someone around who wants to ask me all about some aspect of Muina.

Tenth Squad caught up with me as I was heading off to meet Zee and rather blatantly abandoned me with Els. They're finding the idea of him pursuing me tremendously entertaining, but he's good at not making it awkward. He told me how jealous they all were that Fourteenth has just been assigned to Muina, then asked me how my Sights and oddly real illusions training was going as we rode the elevator down to one of the main junctions. That's all no secret among the Setari now.

"The music from the Kalasa manifestation was particularly interesting," he said, as I headed for a connecting elevator. "A melody, instruments, revived for a moment from extinction. Can you do that with the music of your own world? Manifest how it sounds from memory?"

I stared at him, thinking through the possible differences in picturing something on Earth, and projecting something I remember, then said: "I don't know. But I'm certainly going to try."

He laughed. "I'm relieved I asked that just before you were heading to a monitored session."

I could only nod speechlessly, too excited for words as my lift came. "Thanks for the idea," I said, very glad I'd ended up talking to him, then spotted Third and Fourth getting off one of the opposite lifts and waved just before my doors shut. Fourteenth must be swapping out to relieve the senior exploration squads.

Zee blinked when I showed up bubbling over with Eeli levels of enthusiasm, and gave me a dry look as I tried to sell her on the idea of music being the same as fiction and not at all like me trying to look all the way to Earth and it wasn't even the Sight part that mattered, but manifesting something I remembered already.

"No argument in the world's going to stop you trying, so I won't even bother," she said. "Since you haven't been able to manifest anything lately, it may be a moot point, but so long as you follow orders and don't do this outside the test environment, it's as good a test subject as any other."

I've never looked forward to a test session so much. In truth, I've never really looked forward to a test session – it's hard to look forward to headaches and exhaustion. All the short train journey I was trying to pick which song I'd really really missed and decided on *Hollaback Girls,* not because it was my favourite, but because it reminds me of Alyssa. I've been really wishing I could ask Alyssa what she thought about the whole Els situation. Actually, I already know – Ruuel's really not her type of guy. She'd think me mad for ever preferring him to Els.

Then I fretted about whether or not my manifestation would still be too sore to use, and it did still feel a bit stretched. But useable.

It was tiring to do, but nothing like looking at Muina had been. I didn't get much further than the first chorus, then lost focus and stopped, panting slightly, but smiling hugely. I've never been so happy.

"Can I try something else?" I asked Zee, once Ista Chemie had confirmed that the power cost wasn't exorbitant. "A picture instead of a sound?"

I was lucky that one of the walls of the warehouse was clear of boxes. It made for a really, really huge screen. And I had just the documentary I wanted to show.

"This is my world," I told Zee unsteadily. The glowing blue and green and golden ball revolved slowly. "That's Australia." I wiped at my face, changing what I was trying to project. "This is Sydney. Where I – where I grew up."

I had to have a little emotional break. Zee gave me a hug and Ista Chemie fed me hot drinks, and it was just so nice that all these frustrating and painful talents can finally give me something I actually want.

I was already way too tired, but Zee agreed to let me do one more. I almost couldn't concentrate from trying not to giggle, and made sure to get a good look at Zee's face as I said: "Johnny Depp, playing Captain Jack Sparrow." It was impossible to hold it very long, and I was so tired, but laughing. "Maze going to kill me."

Zee made a deal with me – I can try and manifest any music or images I want once every day after my other training is done, but only if I have at least one person with me and weren't somewhere inconvenient to get to medical. I emailed Els and thanked him for the good idea and then sent him and First Squad and Isten Notra and Shon and Mori and Par and Glade and Zan and Eeli the images which the scanners at the warehouse had recorded of Earth. My own log was useless since crying blurred all the images. The Captain Jack sequence I sent separately just to First Squad, because I think Maze is going to kill me enough already without spreading it everywhere.

I fell asleep on the trip back, of course, and had fun reading everyone's email responses when I woke up, particularly Lohn's about Captain Jack. I'm so happy, and beyond all the feel-good stuff it will just be really useful being able to illustrate some of what I've been trying to explain about Earth. I'm pretty sure some sort of Sight must be involved in the projection, because there's no way my memory is as good as those images.

Excellent, excellent day.

Thursday, July 10

Voyeur

I was just hyped all day, totally looking forward to being allowed to try and visualise something else. Mara said all the enthusiasm was useful for making me do more for my physical training – which is either getting easier or I didn't feel it as much. The bandages are off my legs again, so we could have swimming in the afternoon, which I think Mara chose deliberately so I didn't feel so tired afterwards. All First Squad joined us, and then came back to my rooms afterwards since I particularly wanted to show them things. I think they were all enjoying me being happy instead of the mope monster in the corner. Maze brought along a scanner for me which I can keep in my rooms to record any images or sounds I want to keep since a good scanner has a much less contaminated quality than things filtered by human eyes and ears, but he warned me that if anything involved pirates he may just have to have Mara increase my exercise load. Maze took the whole Jack Sparrow thing pretty well – I think it embarrassed him, but he doesn't mind a bit of teasing. And he agreed that Johnny Depp looks a lot like him (except much older, and Maze doesn't go in for facial hair).

We met Mori riding the elevator, and I invited her along, but she said that Fourth is doing a lot of training catch-up after being away from the training facilities for so long, and had to rush off. She looked really tired, so I guess that was her way of saying Ruuel is working Fourth into the ground.

I was very keen to make sure no-one thought it was too much stress on my system, so kept each image that I was displaying to a relatively brief duration, but I finally got to show Lohn what I meant by surfing and skiing. Then I showed them some Mayan and Egyptian pyramids and Machu Piccu, which was strategy on my part, since I knew that Islen Duffen would be highly encouraging of being able to see pieces of Earth's ancient world. They agreed that there must be some kind of Sight element to me 'remembering' the fragments of documentaries I was replaying, but it didn't seem to be costing me too much energy.

It's still fairly tiring, though, and I can't play a whole song in one hit. Maybe I can put them together bit by bit. I fell asleep leaning on Ketzaren, and woke covered up but still on the couch, with Ghost curled up snugly with me. I've really got to remember to eat dinner before doing stuff I know will make me pass out.

I'm a little worried about doing this, because it might make me stronger. And the stronger I get, the more chance I have of accidentally hurting someone. If I dream about monster insects again, for instance. My Sights have definitely been growing stronger, particularly since I tried looking all the way to Muina. Since then I can sense people four levels up, and the shielding is posing less of a barrier. That has its good points and its bad points, one of which I found when I woke up just now and I wasn't missing Ruuel. Not because Els has succeeded in distracting me, but because he's asleep one floor up. If he's within my senses when I wake, it doesn't ache nearly as much.

The downside is that I really, really don't want to know if he's sleeping with Taarel. I'm trying to let him go, but that would be hard to deal with so I'm working very hard on figuring out a way to not be constantly half-aware of people around me. I need to be able to choose to be looking, or not looking, to not just be absent-mindedly aware. I've already discovered that Mori's sleeping with the Eighth Squad captain (or they're just...chatting...really closely...in the middle of her sleep cycle) and even without my problems with Ruuel I could live without finding out whole bunches of really private stuff about people by accident.

When I was sending my Earth pictures around yesterday, he was actually the first person I addressed the email to. Because he'd been training me, and, well, because I wanted to share them with him and I was very happy. But everyone else I was sending it to was my friend, and I realised I was pushing again, trying to get closer despite all my resolutions, so I removed his name. He'll read Zee's training report, after all.

Wonder if Zee will let me test more Earth-related stuff tomorrow?

Friday, July 11

Getting a message across

Big serious discussion today with Maze about *The Hidden War*. I've been ignoring the legal wrangling about it, although I knew that Evil PR Bitch has been slapped with massive fines and some weird kind of 'house arrest' which severely limits her rights and movements. The question hasn't been so much what happens to her (may she rot), but whether the producers can continue to use the information she provided.

"KOTIS is under a great deal of pressure at the moment," Maze told me. "Unlike our work in the spaces, Muina represents an immense emotional, financial and political...property. The question of whether KOTIS should control what is happening there has been raised again and again by those who see it primarily as a home to reclaim. There is increasing resentment over any attempt to control the information coming out of Muina, a growing sense that there are unnecessary layers of secrecy. KOTIS initially struggled to prevent any use of the information leaked about you altogether, but was met with political opposition as much as legal. It is very difficult to argue that it is not in the public's interest to know these things, when you can scarcely find a person outside of KOTIS who agrees."

"You're not leading up to me having to do interviews with reporters are you?"

"No. But the situation has moved on from preventing the continuing broadcast. The news services are actually reporting on each episode as it's released, operating on the belief that more of the truth is learned in fiction than in the official communications from KOTIS." He sighed. "The hunger for any kind of information about you is immense. We can't deny you are a pivotal part of the world's history, and it is no longer considered acceptable to treat you as something we can keep secret."

"KOTIS decided to turn leak to own advantage?"

"Try to." He gave me a nod for recognising basic media manipulation. "The belief in the leak is useful, and the public battle to suppress the information has added to its value. And the show itself, annoying as this situation is, is unreservedly pro-KOTIS."

"Is going to keep telling them about the things which happen to me?" I asked warily. Evil PR Bitch had run off with my file shortly after I'd gone wandering through Kalasa. "Was kind of glad that stupid dreams weren't going to turn up on gossip forums."

"Perhaps if you hadn't dreamed Kalasa's past so spectacularly that would have been possible." He gave my shoulder a quick squeeze. "That can't be undone, and there's very little chance that we'll succeed in keeping it from leaking for much longer. Rumours are already surfacing. We are very likely to release the scans of that ceremony, and detail the process involved in gaining full access to Kalasa. As for the ongoing relationship with this drama – because so much of it is being taken as truth, we're growing increasingly concerned with controlling the amount of fiction."

"Evil Fourth Squad?"

Maze winced. "One of the things we hope to gain trading information is the ability to correct particularly dangerous errors, and to lessen the damage being done to the squads who are linked to major events. There was a scene in tonight's episode which they've agreed to remove–" He shook his head.

"You see episodes ahead of release?"

"And soon scripts, well before production. Because they're so interested in keeping close to your true story, we don't anticipate needing to demand changes very often." He made a face. "Terrible as it was, the Array massive served to remind more than a few people that Setari are too valuable to this world to purposelessly toy with. And the situation on Kolar was so bad until their Setari tracked down the source of the Ionoth which have been so destructive there."

I wasn't particularly happy, but I could tell the main decisions had already been made. "Can I veto stuff as well?"

Maze agreed to that readily enough, then rubbed his temple. "I've always been more than pleased to ignore these dramas. Having them included in my duties is not a happy development. Fourth is a strong squad, and will weather this, particularly if we can keep dramatic indulgences to a minimum. But there's something I do need to settle there." His mouth had gone all thin, the way it does when he's doing things he doesn't like. "Ruuel recommended the change in instructor for your Sights training, and said that he'd been unnecessarily strict. If Fourth is one of the squads you'd prefer not to work with, I need to know about it."

I could feel my face burn – a mix of anger and embarrassment. "Fourth my favourite squad other than First. Trust Ruuel very much, strict or not. Only thing seriously upset me with Fourth was Sight training with blindfold. Evil Fourth Squad funny at first, but joke get old very quick. Tonight's episode nasty about them again? If following my story close, have reached when I go to Earth near-space? Did they get someone else to save me or something?"

"No." Maze was looking relieved. I expect it would have caused him quite a headache to add Fourth to the nasty squad list. "Everything's a matter of tone and a few extra words. That's partly why this is so difficult."

He gave me the episode, and went to get us something to eat while I watched. It really bugs me that Evil PR Bitch, and who knows how many other people, have watched me wander around Earth's near-space and then talk to my family. The show kept to that pretty well, beyond my home looking distinctly Taren, and that they'd had to make up a translation (subtitles) for my sign conversation. I'd never translated it, and never been asked to – a tiny bit of consideration for which I was grateful. I was surprised how well they'd guessed my family's responses, though they'd made Nick my brother and removed one of my aunts. The girl who plays the sexy kitten version of me is a rather good actress, and you could really see how much she ached to be able to hug her Mum.

Then Lastier showed up, and said almost exactly what Ruuel had said, except he added the things Ruuel had chosen not to say, starting with: "Are you so very selfish?" before explaining the risk I was posing to Earth. Lastier is a very interesting character – all Ruuel's competence, but with portions of Kajal's personality. Not outright evil, but blatantly revelling in his own excellence. The saint-like woman they had playing my Mum looked him up and down and signed: "Cruel eyes. Be careful."

After that it was all very dramatic, with kitten-me being run through a number of near escapes by a superbly competent Setari captain. Who, when I got around to thanking him for rescuing me, told me I was too useful a tool to waste. Kitten-me's face went all crumpled at that one.

I'd wondered how they'd deal with Ruuel falling to his knees after enhancing his Sights, since that vulnerable moment didn't match with Lastier's arrogance at all, but they'd just removed that part altogether. Lastier enhanced after spotting the Ddura, went very still, then practically dragged kitten-me up the platforms – by the wrist not the hand.

A whole heap was made of the Pillar – a lot of the entire series has been about Pillar-chasing. After that, it was almost exact, with Lastier stabilising gates, finally reaching KOTIS. And calling me 'the stray'.

Maze, who had been watching my reactions as the show finished up, was probably a bit surprised when I asked: "Why is everyone weird about Zan being a captain?"

He hesitated before replying, then said: "Combat Sight. Namara is the only captain without it, but is ably demonstrating that the role is not about being the best fighter on a squad."

"Zan linked with main character now – Twelfth likely to come out of this better than Fourth, but don't think she enjoys it. What was scene you had removed?"

Maze grimaced, then showed me a final scene of kitten-me alone in medical, inspecting a circle of dark bruises around her wrist. Ironic, since it looked a lot like the bruises Ruuel *had* given me, when the Ddura was attacking at Pandora.

"They're going to run into trouble if continue to stick to my story," I said. "Ruuel save my life more than once."

"It's an infuriating situation," Maze said. "But controllable since your relationship with Fourth is solid. I do need to ask if your mother truly warned you against Ruuel."

"She just ask if he friend or enemy," I said. My face was hot, but I think I wasn't giving too much away. I've been so careful to keep my opinion of Ruuel to myself – not only because it's so worshipful, but because it's hard to explain. It's not like I think he's perfect. Or even necessarily a generally nice person. Half the reason *The Hidden War* is able to make him into such a grey character is because he's left himself open to being interpreted that way.

Wanting to change the subject I added: "If producers run out of plot ideas, suggest to them on my behalf that they do episode about me being really upset when someone steals my personal file and makes entertainment from it."

After that Maze went with me and Zee to Keszen Point, where we repeated the first tests I did with Zee, to see how they go now I'm manifesting. I had to do each one twice, and the first time not manifest but only visualise, and the second time manifesting. And I'm more or less able to do that. I've got to try and separate out manifesting things in real-space and manifesting things in near-space, which I can't really differentiate between. But it was a good session, tiring, but with less headaches involved.

Maze and Zee were both pleased with the progress I'm making, but had me return to my room before letting me conjure any more Earth images. Which works for me, since I prefer them not to be in the official test logs anyway, and it saves being carted about unconscious. I showed them bits of Sydney, places I miss. Beach, park, the back yard of our house, my bedroom.

I fell asleep after that one, very appropriate. The next episode of *The Hidden War* airs soon, and I'm contemplating trying to be asleep when it does. Maze said Ruuel would be given the episode in advance, so he'll know what's coming. I bet he thinks the energy he has to spend dealing with it a complete waste.

I'm refusing to let myself feel guilty about any of this.

Saturday, July 12

Lastier Fan Club

I hadn't managed to get back to sleep by the time *The Hidden War* aired, and wasn't the least bit surprised when I had a channel request from Mori during the first ad break. Wanting to get it over with, I accepted, and was surprised to find Sonn and Halla in the channel along with the usual *The Hidden War* club.

"My Mum asked if he was friend or enemy," I said, before Mori could even ask. "Maze ask me same thing at lunch."

Glade, after a pause, laughed. "Not often I hear you sounding so impatient, Caszandra."

"Tired of program," I said. "Bad enough steal my life, but would have thought story dramatic enough without messing people about. Is not worth getting angry over, I know, since everyone here seen mission report and know not true, but still very annoying."

"I can't say I'm enjoying watching any more," Mori said. "And yet, not watching and not knowing what's being shown is worse."

"Yes, very much," I said. "Not looking forward to next week, since probably about all the horrid things I said to Maze when I was in medical."

Since I'd already seen the episode, I told them goodnight and dropped out of channel, hoping the last comment would distract them. There was a lot of things I'd thought about saying, but since I'd basically rather not discuss Ruuel with anyone, it had seemed best to keep my reaction brief and very definite.

None of this is enough to bring down my Earth-projections high, but it's irritating.

Merger

Running around the stairs all morning with Mara. Just when I thought I was getting half-way non-pathetic, she shows me how far I have to go. And thinks it's funny.

After lunch both First and Fourth were using the weights room. I do NOT need to see Ruuel working out. Way too distracting, and I'm in this tedious bind where I can't be too obviously seen to be not looking at him, yet really don't want to be caught looking at him.

He had huge circles under his eyes, black and bruised, as if he hadn't slept for days. From the way his squad were keeping an eye on him, they'd reached the point of being really worried, and I had to wonder, from the look Maze gave him, whether a tired Sight talent might be forbidden from going on rotation. He'd hate that.

Toward the end of the session there was a notice to all the Setari about the new paired squad assignments. Twelfth and Fourteenth, both out on Muina. Fifth and Seventh, which I thought highly appropriate. Most relevant to me was First and Fourth, probably because I'd nominated them as my two favourite squads, which I guess was a huge mistake in terms of Ruuel-avoidance.

Fourth put a good face on it, but as I chatted with Glade, Mori and Par afterwards I realised they weren't pleased. We were talking about my legs, and at first I thought it was trying to be delicate about the hideous scars which was making them strange. But it's because the merger makes them the junior squad on all rotations. I think they felt it was a demotion.

Ruuel didn't come near me at all. The last time we spoke was when he dropped a snowball on my face, if you could call that talking. He and Maze said a few short things when the announcement was made, and he was his usual detached self, and I've spent all my time since then worrying about why he wasn't sleeping and what would happen if Fourth were forbidden from going on rotation.

Before the announcement, I'd been thinking of asking at least Mori back to my room to show her some things I'd been trying to explain about Earth, but in the end I just went with Mara, and told her she wasn't allowed to log this projection, and then conjured the video of my last big family holiday. I mainly wanted to see myself, before all this happened. I looked short, weirdly, even though I'm sure I haven't gotten taller.

Mara wisely didn't comment, just gave me a blanket and told me to do some light swimming tomorrow while First and Fourth were off on their first joint mission. I slept very solidly for an hour or so, but then went into this constant nightmare cycle. It's a good sign, really, since they're 'real' nightmares and I recognise them pretty much immediately and can wake myself up. And forcing myself awake isn't giving me as much of a headache any more. But I just want to sleep and not *think*.

Going to go up to the roof. The weather doesn't look great, but not impossible. Maybe the Nuran will show up and distract me.

Sunday, July 13

Speechless

The weather was dreadful. So windy it was hard to stay upright, with occasional drops of rain driven so fast they stung. I was glad of that, though, since gale-force wind makes it hard to think of anything but gale-force wind. I stayed on the roof until it felt like everything had been blown out of my head, then headed back to Setari quarters.

One level down on the final elevator, Ruuel got on as well, still showing little sign of sleep. I hadn't been paying any attention, so when the door opened, I felt my eyes widen at the sight of him, and looked down guiltily. And then felt such an idiot for my reaction that I asked if having two squads together would change the way the rotations worked, or just make them quicker.

"Where the threat is low, we're likely to work in adjoining spaces, with First clearing ahead while we evaluate gates. That will lessen the chance of attracting deep space Ionoth."

He'd sounded unconcerned, but narrowed his eyes, studying me. Then lifted one hand and pressed the back of it to my cheek. Very warm against my wind-chilled skin, and no gloves.

"The goal is to increase your general health," he said, sounding beyond annoyed, suddenly and inexplicably angry. "You're at least capable of judging the kind of weather not to sit outside in."

I couldn't understand what I'd done to make him lose his temper, and though he'd taken his hand away he loomed over me in a way which was almost threatening, making me wish I could back up. And that made me angry in return, so I asked in almost as annoyed a voice as his: "Too valuable be allowed do any living?"

He was very close – so near that I could see the difference between the pupil and iris in his black on black eyes. I'd never seen him less like himself, drawn and tired and glaring at me like I'd done something wrong just by being there. He only had to lower his head to kiss me, bruised my mouth while I stood too shocked to respond, and crowded me into the wall when I started to kiss him back. Every movement shouting anger.

Lifts move inconveniently quickly, and the doors opened on the floor for Third and Fourth's quarters. There was no-one in the corridor, a circumstance for which I am eternally grateful, but Ruuel still stopped kissing me, leaning his forehead against the wall beside my head.

"You've no idea how little I want this," he said, barely audible and not exactly the most encouraging thing he could have said. He sounded furious.

"Actions not match words," was all I could manage, very aware that he hadn't moved away from me, that his heartbeat was as loud to me as my own, that he was so angry.

He let out his breath, more exasperation than amusement, then turned his head just enough to be talking directly into my ear. "You need to be very certain you want this."

The lift doors opened on First and Second's floor, but I was struggling with what he'd said, and resenting the way he'd said it. I'm still not sure if he was doing his best to make me storm off, or was just at the end of his tether. Since he'd never given me any sign that there was a tether in the first place, I was having to adjust a lot of ideas to even begin to answer him.

"What is certain?" I asked, very aware of the way one of his hands had tightened on my arm. "Haven't even ever really talked. Only know that every day, first I know on waking, is that you're not there. I hate it when you're not there."

It was a pathetically scrambled reason, and when he drew back I was sure that I'd chosen exactly the wrong moment to be honest. He wasn't wearing a very promising expression, either, very closed, with that haughtiness which was part temper and part born, I think, out of knowing so much about people. But his hand slid down my arm, and caught mine, and he turned and walked out of the lift, trailing me along behind him into my quarters, into my bedroom.

I was practically having kittens by the time he let go and turned and looked at me, because, seriously, he'd been pushing me away for so long, and now we were jumping straight to sex? Right after he told me he really didn't want to? Not exactly the stuff of romance.

But whatever else, good or bad idea, I wanted him. More than anything. So I followed his lead when he withdrew his nanosuit and took off the uniform harness. Standing in my underwear with Kaoren Ruuel was in a whole different league to Sean J and the two awkward times in the caravan in his parents' backyard. For one thing Sean and I spent a lot of time laughing at our mutual embarrassment, and Sean didn't look one tenth so grim. Nor did he shake just because he touched my hand.

My diligent research with *Super Sight Six* had warned me that sex for a Place Sight talent can be more than a little complicated. Not only is it depressingly clear if your partner isn't really into it, but what they're feeling can ramp everything up until it becomes overwhelming. Ruuel would have had a full serving of my reaction in the lift, and the emotional equivalent of omgwtfomgwtf! had probably reached the point of !!!!!!!!!!!1!!1!! by then. He paused, just standing with our hands linked, down by our sides, and took a few more breaths before lowering his head and kissing me. But at least he'd stopped looking like he was heading for an execution, was intent and concentrated. It calmed me down a few exclamation marks, and we leaned into each other and let it just be kissing for a while.

I let go of his hands first, because I wanted to put my arms around him, and he responded by unhooking my bra. I have no memory of moving to the bed, but we got there soon after. I suppose I should be glad Ruuel doesn't try to be as super-quick and efficient about sex as he is with testing, but he drove me completely insane touching and then pausing to gauge my reaction. We were both breathing like sprinters by the time he stopped being able to be slow and exploratory, and I can actually see the moment on my log because he opened his eyes properly, then shut them altogether for a second. That was around the point I gave up adding exclamation marks, and fuzzed out into white noise.

He held me almost too tightly afterwards, until both of us were breathing a bit more normally, then said, "Shower?"

I nodded, and liked the way he kept hold of my hand. And liked more his reaction to showering together, which started out as a shower, but was mainly being all wet and slippery together in a close, half-lit space with a fortunately solid wall.

We weren't being big on small talk. The only time either of us spoke past that was when we'd switched the dryer on, and were standing tucked against each other just until we were no longer dripping. He was exploring my back – glancing touches on shoulder blade, spine, ribs – and murmured, "I knew if I started touching you I wouldn't be able to stop." Just loud enough for me to hear.

"Not complaining," I said, and if we both weren't by that time beyond exhausted, I would have liked to stay looking up at him. As it was, we curled back into my bed and I fell asleep almost before I lay down. First time I've slept in that room since my dream about the Array massive.

I didn't wake till late into my next shift, nearly lunchtime. Fortunately First and Fourth's rotation wasn't till after lunch. I don't know how many days Ruuel – or Kaoren as I really should call him, even though I haven't yet – hasn't been sleeping properly, but he didn't stir when I slid out of bed to go to the bathroom. Even with him asleep, I suddenly felt awkward about wandering around naked, and pulled on my nightshirt before I slid back into the bed. That did wake him, but only enough to tuck an arm across my waist, sigh, and settle against my back.

My life keeps changing completely. Ruuel – Kaoren – deciding to respond to me is not quite so major as walking to Muina or being rescued from it, but it feels like a close third. I lay wondering if we'd actually have conversations, and what it would be like when we disagreed. I hardly know him. He's a tough but fair captain, super-efficient, serious, and the only thing I know about him outside of that is a couple of glimpses of arrogance, and the possibility that he might have a sense of humour.

And he said he really didn't want to be with me.

I froze there, remembering that first Sights testing session and how he had thought it a bad idea, but had done just what he'd been ordered, and been angry. And Kaoren reacted to my dismay, tightening his arm and shifting in his sleep. I drew back from the brink of the impending wangst storm, though, because I know very well that neither Kaoren nor Tsur Selkie are stupid, and Kaoren faking a romance with me would be idiocy. A metric fuckton of dumb so epically, mind-destroyingly beyond a bad idea that there's not a chance they would go there.

Having decided that, I relaxed and a moment later Kaoren did as well, let out a breath which tickled the back of my neck, and snuggled closer. I really loved that he'd reacted to my feelings, and my brain decided it was full of champagne bubbles, which made Serious Brooding very difficult.

I was enjoying a few highlights of my log when Ghost came to visit, and jumped on the bed beside me. I stroked her under the chin, smiling at the buzz of her purr, but it was only when she poked out her nose, whiskers twitching and quivering, and scented Kaoren's hand that he woke. And jerked so violently backward he impacted with the wall as Ghost, spitting and squalling, rose abruptly into the air above us and hung there – trapped by Telekinesis.

Not how I'd planned to say good morning.

After a few frozen moments he put Ghost down. She immediately ran, and may possibly never visit me again, but that's infinitely better than if he'd killed her. I'm extremely glad not to have to find out how I would have coped with that.

Kaoren's eyes were wide, and he took a long breath, then said: "Give me a moment," and went into the bathroom, leaving me with a total reversal of feeling. No bubbles, just a sinking sense that I'd ruined everything already. I sat on the edge of the bed with my knees drawn up to my chin and wondered how I'd been stupid enough to forget how Kaoren Ruuel had been raised.

But sitting hunched up in a ball playing misery-me wasn't going to help, so I uncurled, rested my hands loosely at my sides, and ran through a couple of the visualisation exercises he'd given me, which are as good for calming yourself down as they are for guiding your dreams. I'm pretty sure Kaoren recognised what I was doing, because he paused a moment at the door when he came back, then sat down beside me and looked down at my hand, just an inch from his leg. He put his own hand in the gap I'd left between my hand and my leg: a very deliberate placement, fingers just short of brushing mine.

"Have you ever touched animal you weren't in process of killing?" I asked, and wasn't at all surprised when he said no. "Sorry," I went on. "Should have thought about that when Ghost arrived."

"Another of the things about this world which barely make sense to you." He shifted his fingers so that one rested against mine. "We both have a lot of learning to do."

This was tremendously encouraging, and I relaxed properly, thinking that of course he would have had to be very very certain about wanting me to have ever come near me in the first place. For all he'd said he didn't.

"Will you tell me why?" I asked, struggling to keep my voice from going small. "Other than second level monitoring, which is – will someone watch this?"

"The beginning." Kaoren didn't sound happy about it either. "To be certain I didn't coerce you."

"Is it against the rules to sleep with me?"

"Not in so many words. Hardly possible to forbid you any form of relationship. But it's been made very clear that you are not an exotic toy." He moved his fingers further, so they curled against my palm. "All that, who you are, oversight committees, the need to even discuss this with anyone – those are annoying, but not by any means enough reason to stay away from you."

I was finding the spare touch of his fingers amazingly distracting – along with the knowledge that Place Sight would make my reaction more than clear – but managed to ask: "Keep nearly dying?"

"That of course is difficult. Even just thinking of you distracts me from the focus I need to be most effective, and I do not want or appreciate that. But, far more than that, you enhance my Sights. I avoid contact with people even when my Sights are at normal levels. And there was a not inconsiderable risk that such extreme sensitivity while sleeping–"

"Worse dreams than me." Another thing which I hadn't even thought about.

"The reverse seems to occur, though." He lifted his hand away from mine, and held it out before him, looking at the outspread fingers. "My ability to control is enhanced, not simply strength."

I felt immensely stupid for seeing how often he had nightmares, how he struggled with all he could see, but never considering what my effect on that part of him might do to his opinion of crawling into bed with me. "But what changed your mind?"

"Four nights of dreams featuring Els Haral."

I didn't understand, despite the twist to his mouth, a kind of disgusted amusement. Then I counted back four days, and realised that when Fourth Squad had arrived back from Muina they'd seen me being so incredibly excited at Els' suggestion that I try projecting memories, and Els being, well, whatever it is Els is with me.

"Jealous." Impossible not to enjoy the idea, for all that nightmares about me and Els had left him dangerously exhausted. I lifted my hand, palm up so it met his from below. "Will have to thank Els for that, some time."

So now I know he does have a sense of humour, because he let out his breath in a tiny snort, and then gave me a "you'll pay for that" look, and then we went back to being immensely non-verbal, up through to a second shower with a lot of steamy kissing, but not enough time for more. Kaoren still came close to being late for a pre-rotation meeting with Maze.

They're all in the spaces at the moment, and I'm not close to having adjusted mentally. I'm not really in the mood for my scheduled swimming, and keep wondering if there's someone somewhere watching me having sex.

Kaoren told me before he left that he'd already reported what we were doing to Selkie, and that Maze would know. That makes me feel more than odd, for all I should be used to my complete lack of privacy. I expect I'll get some very surprised people staring at me by the time the week is done. I have to adjust first, to how quickly and totally things changed.

Rolling around in bed with Kaoren Ruuel isn't going to fix the universe. I'm still this weird thing called a touchstone, who might kill people in my dreams. Monsters and politicians both still want to get their hands on me. And even though Tare and Kolar are taking back Muina, I can't say for sure we're even one step closer to stopping the spaces from tearing apart.

It took all of thirty seconds after First and Fourth went into the Ena for my mood to switch from "unspeakably happy" to "fretting". Every rotation is a chance for something to go wrong. Every day the situation gets worse. I think the biggest thing last night changed is me, my attitude toward being this touchstone. Because if I can figure out what the hell it is I can do, if I can get that under control, maybe I really can do something to fix all this. Maybe I can keep him safe.

Somehow.

Concluded in Part 3: "Caszandra"

TOUCHSTONE GLOSSARY

Agowla	The (fictional) high school Cass attended in Sydney.
Arenrhon	Settlement at site of underground installation of the Lantarens.
Aspro	Aspirin. Headache relief.
Beanie	A close-fitting knitted hat.
Buckley's chance	Buckley was a convict in Australia who escaped and survived by living with Australian Aborigines. The phrase means "nearly impossible".
Carche Landing	The main airport in Unara.
Casszilla	Rawr!
Chapstick	Lip moisturiser.
Cruzatch	A dangerous humanoid Ionoth, shadow burning white.
Ddura	An enormous energy being created by the Lantarens.
Deep-space	The large portion of the Ena which exists between the 'memory spaces'. It is white in appearance, and filled with gates which open directly to real-space worlds.
Deep-space Ionoth	Ionoth which are formed and dwell not in the relatively small Spaces, but instead in Deep-space.
Delar	A Taren measurement unit – roughly 75 centimetres.
Despawn	Disappear, vanish. Taken from computer games where a monster is said to 'spawn' when it appears in the game world, and 'despawn' when it disappears (usually after being killed).
Diodel	One of the ships KOTIS uses to travel between Tare and Muina.
Do Not Go Gentle	"Do Not Go Gentle Into That Good Night", a poem by Dylan Thomas.
Dohl Array	A series of underwater farms on Tare.
Drone	An advanced robot, usually used for scanning and monitoring.
Ena	A dimension connected to the thoughts, memories, dreams and imagination of living beings.
Ena manipulation	A psychic talent which can change the substance of the Ena, particularly in stabilising gates between spaces. It can also be used in a limited way to change 'reality'.
Escort quest	A mission in an online game involving protection of a non-player character while they travel.
Fan service	Revealing or provocative shots of characters in anime/manga.
Fanfic	Fiction based on the stories of others and/or fiction involving a person of whom the writer is a fan.
First level monitoring	Interface monitoring which triggers an alert if certain conditions are reached (eg. loss of consciousness, heart attack). All residents of Tare are on first level monitoring.
Francesca	Francesca is a flowering shrub also known as "Yesterday, Today, Tomorrow" because its flowers fade from purple to violet to near-white as they age.
Gate	A tear or rift between spaces/worlds.
Gate Sight	A psychic talent which can judge the status of gates between spaces.
Gate-lock	An enclosure built around a gate from near-space to real-space to prevent Ionoth from passing through.
Gelzz	A now nearly-extinct cave-dwelling Taren insect noted for its tendency to admit a lingering rotten odour as a defence mechanism.
Goralath	The name originally given to the ruins where Pandora is later established.
Gorra	The first island settled on Tare.
Hasata	A city on Tare.
House Dayen	One of the leading Lantaren groups on pre-destruction Muina, and architects of the Pillars project.

House Zolen	A Lantaren group on pre-destruction Muina believed responsible for the Arenrhon installation.
HSC	Higher School Certificate. Received when graduating from high school in Australia.
Ian Thorpe	A famous Australian swimmer.
In-skin	An immersive interface experience where most of the senses – sight, hearing, touch, smell, taste – are stimulated.
Interface	An in-body nanite installation used by Tarens as personal computers/the Taren internet.
Ionoth	Creatures which form in the Ena, usually remnants of the dreams and nightmares of inhabited planets.
Ista	An honorific for medical doctors.
Isten	Professor.
Joden	The Taren equivalent of a minute, though the unit is longer than an Earth minute. One hundred joden equal a kasse.
Kadara	Naturally-forming massive Ionoth.
Kalane	A medium-sized island city near the Dohl Array.
Kalasa	The training city of the Lantarens.
Kalrani	Trainees not yet qualified as Setari.
Kasse	The Taren equivalent of an hour, spanning approximately two and a half Earth hours.
Keszen Point	An outlying island of Konna used for warehousing.
Kolar	A hot, arid world settled by Muinan refugees, and advanced technologically by the Tarens.
Konna	Both the city and the island where the main KOTIS base is located on Tare.
KOTIS	An acronym for the "Agency for Ionoth Research and Protection".
Kuna	Supplementary memory provided by the interface.
Lahanti	Leaders of the cities of Tare – an equivalent to a 'mayor' of a city-state.
Lantarens	The ruling class of Muina before the disaster. Powerful psychics.
Litara	One of the ships KOTIS uses to travel between Tare and Kolar.
Massives	Ionoth of unusually large dimensions.
Muina	A world abandoned after a disaster brought about by the Lantaren psychics.
Nanites	A machine or robot on a microscopic scale.
Nanna Nap	A short nap in the daytime, for the less active grandmothers.
Near-space	The envelope of Ena immediately surrounding a world, full of reflections of the world as it currently is – and it's most recent nightmares.
Nikko Pen	Permanent marker.
Noob	A new gamer who does not fully understand how to play/someone new.
Not happy, Jan	A popular phrase taken from an Australian television commercial for Yellow Pages.
NPCs	Non-player characters – a gaming term for characters in a game which you are not expected to fight.
Nurioth	One of the largest ruined cities on Muina.
OMGWTF	Oh my god, what the fuck?!
Pandora	First Taren settlement on Muina.
Path Sight	A talent for location.
Pippin	A small animal of excessive cuteness.
Pissed off	Made angry. ['Pissed' can mean 'angry' or 'drunk' in Australia.]
Public Space	Virtual décor visible to all interface users/anything accessible to all interface users.
PVP	Combat in online games where players fight other players rather than computer-controlled opponents.
Rotation	Setari missions in the Ena designed to cover Ionoth respawn near Taren cities.
Rotational space	A space in the Ena which moves so that its gates regularly align and move out of alignment.
Schoolies	Australian highschool graduates celebrating the end of school during "Schoolies Week". Primarily located around the Gold Coast in Queensland.
Second level	A safety/security interface setting causing all sights and sounds

monitoring	experienced by the monitored person to be retained in a secure log which can be accessed under exceptional circumstances.
Setari	Psychic combat 'Specialists' trained since childhood to combat Ionoth.
Sf&f	Science fiction and fantasy.
Shared Space	The interface equivalent of a conference call.
Soylent Green	Is people!
Spaces	A concept used in multiple contexts on Tare, covering 'world', 'dimension', 'area', 'region of the interface', and many others, but most particularly 'a bubble containing a fragment of a world remembered and reproduced by the Ena'.
Stilt	A spindly-legged deep-space Ionoth.
Stray	A person who walked through a wormhole through the Ena to another planet.
Super Sight Six	An old Taren TV series about psychic detectives.
Suyul	A pink flower (also pink/white-skinned).
Swoops	A variety of deep-space Ionoth resembling a pterodactyl.
Tairo	A kick-ass ball sport.
Talent	A psychic ability.
Tanty	Tantrum.
Tanz	Taren air transport.
Tarani	A many-legged deep-space Ionoth reminiscent of a caterPillar.
Tare	A harsh, storm-wracked world settled by Muinan refugees. The highly technologically advanced inhabitants live crammed into massive whitestone cities.
Taren year	One third of an Earth year.
Therouk Island	A food processing island, with a small residential portion.
Third level monitoring	Active observation of everything a subject sees and hears.
Thredbo	An Australian ski resort.
Timesa	A food processing island, with a moderate residential portion.
tl;dr	Too long; didn't read.
Tola	A classification of Ionoth which have little physical substance.
Toolies	Adults preying on teenagers during Schoolies Week/pretending to be a Schoolie.
Touchstone	The subject of the story.
True-space	The world, not the Ena.
Tsa	An honorific which is the equivalent for Mr/Mrs/Ms/Miss.
Tsaile	Commander.
Tsee	Setari Squad Captain.
Tsur	Director.
Twig/twigged	Realise.
Tyu	A zither-like musical instrument.
Unara	The largest city on Tare, located on the island of Wehana.
Unco	Uncoordinated.
Unstable rotation	A rotation where the spaces are more likely to change and bring unexpected situations.
Wangst	Self-indulgent angst.
Wehana	The largest island on Tare, almost entirely covered by the city of Unara.
Whitestone	A building substance formed with nanites.
Wuss	Wimp, coward.
Year 10 Formal	An end-of-year dress up dance held by schools in Australia.
Zelkasse	A quarter of a kasse.

CHARACTER LIST

Squads

First Squad	Second Squad	Third Squad	Fourth Squad
Maze Surion (m)	Grif Regan (m)	Meer Taarel (f)	Kaoren Ruuel (m)
Zee Annan (f)	Jeh Omai (f)	Della Meht (f)	Fiar Sonn (f)
Lohn Kettara (m)	Nils Sayate (m)	Eeli Bata (f)	Par Auron (m)
Mara Senez (f)	Keer Charal (m)	Tol Sefen (m)	Glade Ferus (m)
Alay Gainer (f)	Enma Dolan (f)	Geo Chise (m)	Charan Halla (f)
Ketzaren Spel (f)	Bree Tcho (f)	Rite Orla (f)	Mori Eyse (f)
Fifth Squad	**Sixth Squad**	**Seventh Squad**	**Eighth Squad**
Hast Kajal (m)	Elen Kormin (f)	Atara Forel (f)	Ro Kanato (m)
Dorey Nise (m)	Est Jorion (f)	Pol Tsennen (m)	Pala Hasen (f)
Faver Elwes (f)	Juna Quane (m)	Tez Mema (m)	Seeli Henaz (f)
Kire Palanty (m)	Del Roth (m)	Bodey Residen (m)	Zhou Kade (m)
Tralest Seet (m)	Meleed Aluk (f)	Aheri Dahlen (f)	Kye Trouban (m)
Seyen Rax (m)	Kester Am-roten (m)	Saitel Raph (m)	Zama Bryze (m)
Ninth Squad	**Tenth Squad**	**Eleventh Squad**	**Twelfth Squad**
Desa Kaeline (f)	Els Haral (m)	Seq Endaran (f)	Zan Namara (f)
Zael Toure (f)	Loris Darm (f)	Kire Couran (f)	Roake Lenton (m)
Rebar Dolas (m)	Sell Tens (f)	Yaleran Genera (m)	Dess Charn (f)
Oran Thomasal (m)	Joren Mane (f)	Palest Wen (m)	Sora Nels (m)
Kahl Anya (f)	Fahr Sherun (m)	Zare Seeth (m)	Tenna Drysen (f)
Terel Revv (m)	Netra Kantan (m)	Den Dava (m)	Tahl Kiste (m)
Thirteenth Squad	**Fourteenth Squad**		**Kolar's First Squad**
Teer Alare (m)	Kin Lara (m)		Raiten Shaf (m)
Tekly Roth (f)	Pen Alaz (f)		Arad Nalaz (m)
Elsen Dry (f)	Greve Sanya (f)		Meral Katzyen (f)
Next Urally (m)	Taree Jax (f)		Laram Diav (f)
Rail Sorela (m)	Parally Goff (m)		Dell Taranza (f)
Paza Lagden (m)	Rish Udara (f)		Korali Aerieword (m)

Other

Alyssa Caldwell (f)	Cassandra's best friend.
Cassandra Devlin (f)	An Aussie teenager not enjoying her big adventure.
Clere Ganaran (m)	KOTIS liaison.
Dase Canlan (m)	A junior KOTIS archaeologist.
Deen Tarmian (f)	KOTIS liaison.
Elless Royara (f)	KOTIS technician.
Elizabeth (Bet) Wilson (f)	Cassandra's aunt.
Far Dara (m)	A warehouse keeper.
Hedar Dayn (m)	Kalrani Ena manipulation talent.
Hadla Esem (m)	KOTIS security detail.
Helen Middledell (f)	aka Her Mightiness or HM. A well-off and popular girl who goes to Agowla School.
Helese Surion (f)	Original First Squad captain, killed by a massive.
Intena Jun (f)	Former KOTIS publicity officer.
Islen Lap Dolan (m)	Senior KOTIS botanist.
Islen Lothen Ormeral (m)	KOTIS archaeologist.
Islen Rel Duffen (f)	Senior KOTIS archaeologist.
Islen Rale Tezart (m)	Senior KOTIS 'psychic technology' expert.
Ista Tel Chemie (f)	KOTIS medic assigned to Setari.
Ista Del Temen (f)	KOTIS medic assigned to Pandora.
Ista Kestal Leema (f)	KOTIS medic assigned to Pandora.
Ista Noin Tremmar (f)	KOTIS medic assigned to Setari.
Isten Sel Notra (f)	Pre-eminent scientist researching the Ena.
Jelan Scal (m)	'Psychic technology' scientist.

Jenna Wilson (f)	A friend of Cassandra's in Sydney.
Jorly Kennez (f)	The first Setari to die on duty.
Julian (Jules) Devlin (m)	Cassandra's younger brother.
Katha Rade (f)	A junior KOTIS archaeologist.
Kess Anasi (m)	Kalrani Ena manipulation talent.
Ketta Lents (f)	Wife of Orren Lents – stockbroker.
Kinear Rote (m)	Kalrani Ena manipulation talent, one of twins.
Laura Devlin (f)	Cassandra's mother.
Leam Marda (m)	Unara Transport Department official.
Liane Lents (f)	Daughter of Orren and Ketta Lents.
Michael Devlin (m)	Cassandra's father.
Nenna Lents (f)	Daughter of Orren and Ketta Lents.
Nick Dale (m)	Sue Dale's stepson.
Noriko Yamada (f)	A friend of Cassandra's from Agowla.
Nona Maersk (f)	Aide to the Lahanti of Unara.
Palan Leoda (f)	Wednesday Addams, junior reporter.
Perrin Drake (m)	KOTIS security detail – weapons trainer.
Roke Hetz (m)	KOTIS security detail.
Se-Ahn Surat (f)	An actress who plays Caszandra Devlin on *The Hidden War*.
Sebreth Tanay (f)	Lahanti (mayor) of Unara.
Sue Dale (f)	Cassandra's Aunt.
Tsa Orren Lents (m)	An anthropologist working part-time with KOTIS.
Tsaile Nura Staben (f)	Overarching Commander of Muina settlement forces.
Tsana Dura (f)	A teaching program.
Tsel Onara (f)	Captain of the *Diodel*.
Tsen Neen Helada (f)	KOTIS officer in charge of the Arenrhon site.
Tsen Rote Sloe (m)	KOTIS officer in charge of Kalasa site.
Tsur Gidds Selkie (m)	Senior coordinator and trainer of Setari. Sight Sight talent.
Voiz Euka (m)	A KOTIS technician who created an Earth clock and calendar.

Made in United States
Troutdale, OR
05/16/2025

31396155R00156